POWER DOWN

POWER DOWN

BEN COES

ST. MARTIN'S PRESS ❧ NEW YORK

POWER DOWN. Copyright© 2010 by Ben Coes. All rights reserved. Printed in the United States of America. For information, address St. Martin's Press, 175 Fifth Avenue, New York, NY 10010.

Design by Phil Mazzone

Library of Congress Cataloging-in-Publication Data

Coes, Ben.
  Power down / Ben Coes. — 1st ed.
      p. cm.
  ISBN 978-0-312-58074-2
  1. Special forces (Military science)—Fiction.   2. Terrorism—Fiction.   I. Title.
  PS3603.O2996P69 2010
  813'.6—dc22

                                                                              2010029176

First Edition: October 2010

10 9 8 7 6 5 4 3 2 1

FOR SHANNON

ACKNOWLEDGMENTS

To Aaron Priest, Nicole Kenealy James, Frances Jalet-Miller, Lisa Erbach Vance, Lucy Childs Baker, Arleen Priest, and John Richmond at the Aaron Priest Agency, thank you for believing in me, for helping to improve what I came to you with, for fighting for me. To Sally Richardson, Matthew Shear, George Witte, Matthew Baldacci, John Murphy, Kathleen Conn, and everyone at St. Martin's Press, thank you for your confidence. To Keith Kahla, my brilliant editor at St. Martin's Press, thank you for all you have done. I now understand why so many authors have relied upon your sage advice as they strived to create great thrillers. To Ed Stackler, thank you for your editorial brilliance, your patience, your steadfast belief, your sense of humor, and above all else, for your friendship.

To my military buddies who helped me immeasurably: David Urban, Brian Shortsleeve, Patrick Mastan, Tom Charron, and Darren Moore, thanks, guys. Edith Pepper Goltra, thank you. Sophie Cottrell and Reagan Arthur at Hachette: I am grateful for your guidance and help. To the real Teddy Marks, my godfather, who was a Navy SEAL in Vietnam, thank you. To my brother, Putnam Coes, thank you for helping me nail the hedge fund stuff. To my mom, Susan Coes, who encouraged my writing from the time I could hold a pencil in my hand, thank you.

To my family: Charlie, who lugged steaming cups of coffee up the stairs to me as I pounded away on the keyboard those cold winter mornings. Teddy, who played the piano so beautifully for me as I wrote.

Oscar, who climbed onto my lap wearing his sleepers to snuggle and keep me warm. Esmé, who was born in the middle of it all, a gift from God. I wrote this for you guys. I'm just sorry you won't be allowed to read it until you're at least eighteen.

To Shannon, my beautiful wife, I simply could not have done this without you.

Behold, I have refined thee, but not with silver;
I have chosen thee in the furnace of affliction.

—Isaiah 48:10

POWER DOWN

1

A hundred miles above the equator, a day's trip by boat from the nearest land, in a place where ocean currents collide beneath a vast horizon of black water and starry sky, a 1,500-foot double flame helix smoldered furiously from the cap end of an alloy gas fountain.

It was midnight. The flames could be seen for miles in all directions, interrupting the desolate waters in spectacular orange and black clouds. Though the billowing smoke and fire had the appearance of chaos, they were in fact controlled blazes created by the western hemisphere's largest offshore oil platform, burning off the lighter layer of natural gas that floated like helium above the denser, more valuable petroleum that the $8 billion rig had been built to extract.

This was Capitana Territory, the largest oil strike ever outside of the Arabian Peninsula, a 68 billion barrel reservoir—a "megagiant" in oilman's terms—beneath a section of seabed off the western coast of South America. It was discovered less than a decade before by a medium-sized Texas oil company called Anson Energy, now a juggernaut even among the largest energy companies in America.

A tall bearded man with the name ANDREAS stitched to his denim shirt observed the flame stacks from the steel deck below. His brown hair was long, tousled, and hadn't seen shampoo for days. Startling blue eyes and a sharp, tanned nose pierced out from behind a mess of mustache and overgrown beard. This was a handsome man who didn't care what he looked like, or what his crew thought. He finished a cigarette and flicked it down into the dark ocean below the platform.

If this had been a paper mill in the forests of Maine, Dewey Andreas would have been called plant manager. At a steel mill in Pennsylvania, he'd have been called gang boss. But this was an offshore oil rig, and the four hundred and twenty roughnecks who lived and worked here around the clock, faces and clothing layered in grease, salt, sweat, and oil, called Dewey gang chief. Or simply "Chief."

Most of the roughnecks on Capitana didn't like Dewey Andreas, but they all respected him. On the rig his word was law. Dewey had gotten his oil-drilling education in northern Europe, on the rickety, death-defying derricks off the bitter cold North Sea shelf. He ran Capitana like a U.S. Marine colonel runs a battalion during wartime, with uncompromising discipline, rapid-fire decisiveness, and absolute autonomy. Dewey's eyes told his men that he wasn't about to put up with shit from anyone. He backed up that look with a pair of massive arms, muscled from years of hard platform work, buoyed by a pair of fists that were ready and willing to be put to use in the constant challenge every gang chief on every offshore oil rig in the world faces: keeping the animals at bay.

Dewey didn't tolerate weakness, imperfection, laziness, or insubordination. If you crossed him, you could expect to pay for it with your job, or worse. Rumors circulated among the men about Dewey's capacity for brutality and violence. Still, the pay was extraordinary for the uneducated collection of ruffians who worked Capitana Territory.

The platform Dewey stood on was the central superstructure for all of the territory. The facility itself was a massive industrial city of pipes, metal, ladders, and controlled flame stacks that rose on thick steel stilts out of the dark waters of the Pacific Ocean like a centaur.

In the distance, a series of more than thirty smaller, unmanned tension leg platforms dotted the landscape. These "mini-TLPs" fed into the central Capitana facility and helped create a steady gusher of oil ready for transport to refineries throughout North America. Capitana was the central juncture in a spiderlike network of pipes that lay across more than a hundred and forty square miles of seabed some six hundred feet below the ocean's surface. More than two thousand insertion pipes spread out across the dark and cold seabed below. It was through these pipes that a crude, dense, and immensely valuable mixture of natural gas and oil bubbled up and coursed into the central pumping station beneath Capitana, where it was separated, then pushed upward to the surface.

Capitana's interweaving pipes, flare booms, and steel decking looked like a monstrous erector set. The flames never ceased. Yet Dewey found something peaceful in the dense orange inferno. The flames told Dewey that his rig was performing.

He walked to the marine deck and stared at the flame stacks one last time before heading inside to his office. He was tired but wanted to look at throughput reports before they were sent off to corporate headquarters in Dallas. These monthly reports tracked the volume of oil pulsing out of the Capitana reservoir.

The November throughput report for Capitana Territory showed why the field was so critical. In the thirty-day November cycle, Capitana had produced 54.6 million barrels of oil. This meant annual throughput of approximately 650 million barrels. The average per barrel extraction-to-market expense was $19 for other oil companies. Dewey's men could do it for $11—an $8-per-barrel cost savings. That $8 along with oil prices averaging $55 per barrel meant net profits of more than $7 billion from Capitana Territory this year. That $8 bought Dewey a lot of leeway in the way he was allowed to run his rig.

It was past midnight. Dewey watched as the confirmation ticker from the fax came through, indicating that his reports had made it to Anson headquarters in Dallas, landing on the desk of a man he'd never met named McCormick.

He reached behind him and took a book off the shelf, a thick, hardcover edition of *Moby-Dick* that he kept with him. He'd never actually read it, but he kept it with him because behind it he could hide a bottle of Jack Daniel's. He unscrewed the cap and took a large gulp. *In a minute or two*, he thought, *he would head to his adjoining cabin for the night.*

On the shelf below, a small wooden frame held a grainy black-and-white photograph. He hadn't looked at the photo in a long time. He glanced at it, looked away, then took another large swig from the bottle. Slowly and against his better judgment, he picked up the photograph and put the whiskey down.

Holding the frame in his left hand, he wiped the dust away from the glass with his right elbow. The photo showed a much younger Dewey with a pretty blond-haired woman and a young boy. Behind them, a large, ornate sign read DISNEYLAND. A statue of Mickey Mouse stood to the side. The boy sat on Dewey's lap, a big smile on his freckled face. The edges of his mouth were decorated with the remnants of a chocolate ice-cream cone.

Dewey had a military uniform on, his Ranger tab visible on his shoulder, white thread around its edges, before he'd been asked to try out for Delta. His hair was cut short, his large arm wrapped around his young wife. She looked tiny against him; protected, beautiful, and happy.

Dewey didn't like to think about his past. Most of the time he didn't have to. He went about his work and when thoughts of his old life crept in he simply worked himself and his men harder. More than a decade had passed since it all ended, and he'd spent those years working as hard as he could physically to escape what haunted him mentally. The sight of his old uniform always jolted him, a combination of intense pride and deep hatred, hatred for what they'd done to him, the crimes he'd been falsely accused of, and for the small-minded people who'd driven him from Delta, from the armed forces, from the country he loved. He'd learned to blot it out, to erase the memories, the history, everything, from his mind.

Oil had been his savior; oil and the anonymous, brutal Darwinism that was the life of a platform man.

He took his big, callused right index finger and rubbed it across the small black-and-white face of the boy in the photograph. He held the frame close to his face, a couple of inches from his nose. Robbie was so young then. He was so perfect. He loved Robbie like he'd never loved anything in his life. He thought of how he used to hold his young son, with the boy's head on his arm and his legs in his hands. Dewey closed his eyes. He could almost feel Robbie there with him.

With his other hand, he picked up the bottle and took another swig, then put it down. He walked to the other side of the small office. He placed the bottle on the desk and sat down in the metal chair. In front of him, he held the photo, staring. A gentle smile, the first in a long time, creased the edges of his mouth as he looked at the grainy photo of what was once his family. He closed his eyes one more time and tried to remember. It had been so long; the memories were harder and harder to find.

A sudden noise came from the deck. Shouting. He stood up, walked down the corridor to the deck, and opened the large steel door that led to the outdoors.

On the deck, men were gathering quickly. In the middle of the crowd, two roughnecks were squared off against each other. The fight had already begun. The crowd around the edge of the fight numbered more than twenty and was growing, the yelling getting louder as the roughnecks egged the fighters on. One of the men in the fight was Jim Mackie, a drill team manager who'd worked Capitana for years. Dewey had hired Mackie after working alongside him on a British Petroleum platform in the North Sea. The other man was a young tanker guide from Egypt named Serine.

Mackie and Serine were squared off, Serine's nose and chin flowing blood. Serine was shirtless. His muscles, like most of the workers aboard Capitana, were ripped. A silver knife appeared in Serine's hand and flicked forward, leaving a large gash in Mackie's thigh. Blood coursed down Mackie's leg to the crimson-splattered deck. Around the two combatants, the crowd continued to grow quickly. By the time Dewey reached the outer edge of the scrum, at least fifty men had gathered.

Dewey pushed his way through to the center of the human ring. As he came to the front, he encountered resistance as men fought to hold their prime place at the edge of the fight.

The crowd was excited and tense, hyped by the fight's rising stakes.

As Dewey pushed through, a big man on his left turned quickly in anger. Seeing that it was Dewey, he recoiled and moved aside. The man next to him, an even stockier roughneck, didn't bother to look; he felt Dewey nudge his arm and swung on him. Dewey caught the dirty fist with his right hand. With his left he hammered a fast, crushing blow into the man's rib cage. The man doubled over in pain, but managed to return a blow to Dewey's stomach. Dewey did not even flinch. He delivered another shot with his left as he held the roughneck's fist in his right. This swing landed dead-center on the man's nose, collapsing it and sending him down for good.

The cheering grew louder. Serine had drawn blood again, laying Mackie's cheek open with his blade.

Serine had been hurt as well. His nose looked badly damaged and his left arm was clearly broken, hanging awkwardly at his side. Blood trickled from his left ear, an injury to the head that made him stumble dizzily as he moved.

Dewey had learned long ago to let fights go. It was better to let tensions on the rig settle once and for all than to let them fester, only to explode later on. It was the promise of physical harm, after all, that kept an oil platform stable, not meddling from a supervisor. But this fight would end soon. Mackie was covered in his own blood, the wound on his cheek gaping and wide. Dewey could see the edge of his cheekbone. Serine looked desperate, circling like a maimed animal bent on survival. Dewey stepped forward, toward the two fighters, to break it up. But as he did, Serine's arm flew up wildly at Mackie. Before Mackie could dodge, the knife entered his throat at the larynx. The bigger man stumbled back and away, his chest already soaked in scarlet gushing from the opening in the throat. Mackie attempted in vain to stop the flow and fell to the deck.

As Dewey reached him, Mackie's legs kicked the ground in violent spasms and he began to lose consciousness. Dewey quickly applied pressure to the neck wound, but it was futile, blood gurgled from Mackie's mouth as he struggled to speak.

"A rag, Chief," said one of the men from behind Dewey, handing him a dirty blue cloth.

Dewey stuffed it into the wound and maintained the pressure, but it was no use.

"It's okay," Dewey lied to Mackie. "You're gonna be okay."

Mackie's eyes fluttered and found him. He tried to say something. Dewey leaned closer, his ear inches from the dying man's lips.

"Sally." Mackie coughed. "I love her."

"I know." Dewey's mind flashed on Mackie's wife, back in Cork. "I'll tell her."

Mackie shut his eyes for a moment. He was fading quickly. Then his eyes opened and he moved his lips again.

"Serine," he gurgled. "I found something."

Dewey cradled Mackie's head and stared into the fading gray pools of his eyes. "It's all right, Jim."

Mackie jerked his head back and forth, using the last of his energy. "I found . . ."

"What?" Dewey asked.

"It's them. On the rig . . . they're here." Mackie's voice trailed off and his eyes shut for the last time.

2

SAVAGE ISLAND PROJECT
LOWER NUNAVUT, CANADA
ON THE COAST OF THE LABRADOR SEA

Two continents away, more than four thousand miles to the north, in a remote part of Canadian frontier, the roar of turbines in North America's largest hydroelectric facility joined gale force winds in an overwhelming wall of sound.

A lone man atop the great dam clenched a cigarette and struggled to get his lighter to work. A yellow patch with the word WHITE written on it was sewn into the right chest of a heavy-duty, bright orange Patagonia winter parka. On the left chest of the coat, the letters KKB spread austerely in black thread.

It was past midnight. Jake White stood at the precipice of the three-thousand-foot wall of granite and steel and looked out at the black waters of the Labrador. He took a drag on his cigarette. He smoked too much, he knew, but he'd already lived enough for two men, having survived for so long in this monster of his own creation. Savage Island Project, White's audacious vision, had beaten and bloodied him, not into submission, but into an altogether different state of mind. He'd beaten himself into a place even more desperate and lonely, a place you go not when defeated but after you've accomplished all you've set out to do and there's nothing left.

For two long decades, Savage Island Project had been his singular obsession, the pursuit of which had destroyed his marriage, his relationship with his two sons, and any ties he'd had with life back in Ohio. But here he remained, surrounded by the noise. It penetrated the air with a steady pulse of metallic friction, penetrated it, then surrounded it and pulsated down, then back up; it was everywhere. This was the din that results when you build a wall of cement, granite, and steel more than half a mile high, in a place it's not supposed to be, an awe-inspiring spectacle designed to hold back endless waters meant to flow free. This was the deafening, inhuman sound of man triumphing over nature; of turbines and technology; of all that you must create when you decide to build a wall whose sole purpose is the taking of God's waters for society's use, for a company's profits, for power.

This was the roar of Savage Island Project, the largest hydroelectric facility in North America, a $12.5 billion monolith constructed over a punishing decade in the far northeastern reaches of Canada, in the Nunavut, 575 miles from the last outpost of modern civilization.

Savage Island Project was everything and more than White had dreamed it could be, a massive powerhouse of perpetually renewable electricity. It generated enough energy to power a large section of the eastern United States. Enough energy to make its builder, KKB of New York City, the second-largest energy company in America.

Savage Island had been White's idea, and no one had agreed with him. Not his brother. Not his wife. None of the corporate jackasses at company headquarters. Nobody except for Teddy Marks, at the time a young KKB executive. He had believed. He'd convinced his bosses. Now the dam was complete. Marks was CEO. And the jackasses were gone.

And the noise was everywhere.

As he stood atop the dam, upon an iron stanchion that served as the observation deck, White glanced for a moment behind him, at the outflow area where the water poured in a controlled river after passing

9

through one of the two hundred jet engine–sized turbines of the dam. It was an amazing sight, a full half mile above the man-made dark harbor below. Its edges were lined by a spectrum of small white houses built for the six hundred permanent Savage Island workers and their families.

White turned from the calm waters below back to the unruly sea. It was an astonishing contrast, the ordered valley spread out behind the dam, and the angry Labrador Sea whose whitecap crests pounded at the granite of the dam not more than fifty feet below where he stood. It was this contrast, between man and nature, between unbridled chaos and controlled order, that had come to him some twenty years ago in a waking dream.

He was a manager at KKB's Perry Nuclear Power Plant outside of Cleveland. He'd written his idea down one month after returning from a fishing trip to the Nunavut, near Frobisher Bay, a brutal stretch of rocky coastline at the edge of the Labrador Sea that suddenly notched southward in a unique rivulet more than a mile wide near a stretch of rocks known as the Lower Savage Islands. White had written it down on a napkin as he sat eating lunch in the cafeteria one bland, forgettable day at work.

Now it was real.

White shook his head, took a last drag on the cigarette, and flicked the stub of it into the wind. He walked to the end of the granite walkway that crossed the apex of the dam to the entry door that would take him to the operations center. It was nearly 1:00 A.M. He'd take a last look at turbine performance data before he took the elevator down and then walked to his house in the village below.

As he reached for the door, a solitary figure stepped from the shadows. White looked up, momentarily startled as the dark figure moved swiftly to his left. A hand thrust out, too quickly for him to react or to even begin to understand that he was being attacked.

The assailant grabbed him by his left hand. Twisting with trained, precise force, the killer pulled his arm behind his back and snapped it. The sound of White's scream was loud enough to rise momentarily above the noise of the dam. But it was soon muffled by the killer's gloved hand covering his mouth. Pushing him to the edge of the deck, the killer dropped White's broken left arm and moved his gloved hand to his leg. White tried to fight but it was useless. The man lifted him up. With a grunt, he hoisted him to the railing. His right arm slipped off of White's mouth.

"*No!*" White screamed. He twisted his head around and tried to get a glimpse of the man. He clawed with his one good arm but only scratched air. His struggles were in vain. In the dull light, he saw a face. *Oh, my God*, he thought. Recognition came in the same instant he understood he was about to die.

With a last grunt, the killer brought White to the edge of the deck and forced him over the brink. The ocean pounded violently against the dam, close enough to soak both men with spray. The killer let White fall. Screaming helplessly, the architect of Savage Island dropped into the watery oblivion.

3

CAPITANA TERRITORY

The next morning, they prepared Mackie for burial at sea. Everyone knew the drill. If you were badly injured aboard Capitana, they would bring you to the hospital in Buenaventura, the nearest city to the territory, a day's trip by boat. But if you died, the ocean owned you forever. You signed a document when you became an employee. Religion didn't matter; there were no special ceremonies, no cremations, no special rites if you died aboard Capitana. If you listed family on your sheet, the company would send a letter to them, along with a month's salary, accrued vacation time, and a "memorial bonus" of $10,000. Either way your body belonged to the dark depths and the hungry sharks. That's the way it had to be when you worked 290 miles from civilization.

At six o'clock in the morning, the corpse was brought from the infirmary to the lower deck, wrapped in green tarpaulin, tied tightly then anchored with weights. They placed it atop the launch platform riser, a steel shelf that could be tilted by turning a winch.

Dewey descended the stairwell down to the deck, where sunrise pushed away the gray of night. A strange pinkish haze sat across the humid morning air. Four men attended the body. Three were friends of Mackie's. The other was Chaz Barbo, Capitana's physician. Barbo, by trade, was a welder, but he'd spent six months in medical school in Grenada before being expelled. Aboard Capitana that was enough to make you the authority on all medical issues.

Dewey walked to the body and knelt over the word MACKIE written on the tarp. He had liked Jim Mackie. He thought of Sally, who'd long ago gotten used to not having a husband around. Still, she'd be devastated. Dewey stood up and looked at Mackie's friends.

"You want to say anything?" asked Dewey.

Erin Haig stepped forward. He was a driller, with big, hairy hands, popular like Mackie. Normally he wore an easy smile for his buddies. Today his face looked as sullen as stone.

He knelt next to the corpse of his dead friend. "We'll miss you, Jim. God protect you on your trip. Amen."

"How about you?" Dewey asked the other men.

They shook their heads.

He turned to Barbo and nodded.

Barbo reached up and began turning the winch.

Dewey looked up. On the main deck, the rails were crowded with men, some coming off the night shift and others reporting for day shift. That was good. He wanted it that way. It was important that the men aboard Capitana understand the implications of letting hatreds boil over. It didn't take a veteran gang chief to sense the rise in tensions aboard the rig. An incident like this created rival factions, and Dewey worried that would mean more blood.

Mackie's body began to slide. It careened quickly down and slid smoothly into the sea.

Dewey said nothing and walked back toward the steps. He ascended the stairwell to the main platform. He went to the cafeteria to have some breakfast, a bowl of raisin bran with a banana sliced in it. He ate quickly then drank a glass of orange juice. As he stood to leave, he saw Barbo having coffee at another table. He waved him over to have a word.

"How's Serine?" Dewey asked.

"Getting worse. I thought the rest would help, but something must've happened to his head. We need to get him to a hospital."

"Radio for a chopper. I'll be by to see him in a few minutes."

Dewey left the cafeteria and walked to Capitana's main platform, checking in with his foremen.

At the time of its construction, Capitana was the largest offshore oil platform in the world. The platform spread was as long and wide as a football field. Since completion, Sinopec, the Chinese state oil company, had built an offshore facility nearly three times as big as Capitana in the waters off Shanghai. But Capitana continued to blow away the new Chinese facility in terms of production.

Besides the large living quarters, or "hotel" as it was called, which sat in the middle of the platform, the layout was simple. Every fifty feet, a duct unit sprung up from the ocean. A group of six men managed each of the duct units. Oil came up from the seafloor through the ductwork at the seabed to the pumping station, then up the main pipe that spidered off to ductwork just below the water. The flow had to be managed as it hit the platform and directed into one of the forty different duct units, which was then directed into one of the large barges for storage until it was taken away by tanker. It was simple, boring, hard work.

Dewey made the rounds, walking the outside perimeter of the platform and reviewing production statistics from the night before, displayed on monitors at each station. As he made his way around the platform, he found his crewmen hard at work. This morning, more eyes than usual seemed to glance his way nervously; an uncertain and fragile aftermath in the wake of the fatal fight.

He stopped to talk with Jonas Pierre, one of his foremen, a blond-haired kid from Chico, California. Pierre had served in the Navy, five years aboard the USS *Howard*. He was tall, heavyset, and tough. Dewey trusted Pierre.

"Some night," Pierre said.

"Bad one," said Dewey. "How's your crew?"

"Okay. I had to warn a couple of guys who were mouthing off."

"Mackie's crew?"

"No. Victor and one of the Saudis. Those fucking Arabs, I tell you."

"Watch what you say," said Dewey. "It's talk like that that'll start the next knife fight."

Pierre nodded and looked away.

"Get Lindsay to watch your station. I want you in my office in ten minutes."

"Got it."

Dewey went to the infirmary. Serine lay unconscious on one of the beds. Across the middle of his face, a large bandage had become so saturated that blood flowed from it down Serine's face and onto his pillow.

Dewey pulled the sheet down. The boy's broken arm was set in a temporary cast. Like his pillow, his clothing was drenched in blood. He leaned next to the patient's ear.

"Serine," he said quietly. "Wake up."

There was no response.

Dewey leaned in closer. He pushed the eyelids back on the kid's eyes. There was no movement or reaction. He grabbed the skin on his neck and pinched it, hard.

Serine flinched and groaned, a deep, clotted, guttural noise. His eyes slitted open.

"What was the fight about?" Dewey asked.

Serine stared at him in silence.

"What was the fight about?" he asked again, leaning in closer. The eyes closed again.

Barbo entered the room.

"Did you radio for the chopper?"

"Yes. One and a half hours."

"You should change his bandages, his clothing too. For chrissakes, everything's drenched."

"I changed it an hour ago. I'll do it again."

Dewey walked across the deck to his office.

Pierre waited inside, as requested. Like all men aboard Capitana, Pierre was deeply tanned, and his clothing, face, and hair, by this time in the shift, had a thin layer of silt and grease.

"What do you think?" Dewey asked.

"There's going to be more blood," said Pierre. "I can't remember tension like this."

"Mackie's boys looking for revenge?"

15

"Yeah. And Serine's. They're organized."

"That's why I need your help enforcing the peace out there. We need to keep both factions in line. Get them both cooled off until I can ship a few of them off here. Let me handle Mackie's crew. I know how to handle them. They might do something to retaliate, but I can keep it from spreading. But I need you to come down hard on Serine's crew."

"What's hard?"

Dewey put his coffee down.

"Hard is using your fists when words would do. Force your way into their table at dinner. If you get lip, lock 'em up. That's what I mean by hard."

"Some of these punks have knives. You saw that. He shivved Mackie in the throat."

"If we tried to get rid of all the weapons out here we'd have to shut down production for two days. The guys we'd actually want to disarm would be the ones who succeed in hiding them. Always works that way. Do you have a knife?"

"No."

From a drawer in his desk, Dewey pulled out a large sheath that held an eight-inch Gerber fixed-blade black combat knife, black hockey tape wrapped around the hilt, serrated upper and lower edges, designed to maximize damage after the knife's initial plunge into the body. On one side, the letters D.A. were engraved in script letters. On the other side, the word GAUNTLET was engraved in block letters.

"Here." Dewey handed the knife to Pierre. "I want it back."

"Special Forces issue, right?"

"Yeah," said Dewey. "Use it if you have to. Go after limbs. I don't want any more deaths out here."

"What branch?"

Dewey paused. "Rangers, then Delta. It was a long time ago."

"Delta? I didn't know. What's 'Gauntlet' for?"

Dewey looked down at the old weapon. Probably his most valued weapon, certainly more so than any gun he'd ever owned. More for sentimental reasons than anything else. He couldn't remember all of the times he had used it, but there had been many. In the jungles of Panama, cutting the head off a fer-de-lance, then slicing away the poison sacs and storing the rest for food. Slicing a fresh piece of cheese bought at a roadside market in the south of France during his honeymoon. Killing an Iranian diplomat in the dead of night in a seaside bungalow on the coast of Thailand as the man's wife slept by his side and a small team of guards armed with automatic weapons stood just a room away.

It had been nearly fifteen years since he'd earned the knife.

It was the last week of Delta training. As any Delta knows, the last week was high stakes. It's bragging rights, a fun day for those whose idea of fun is a treetop chute drop followed by a twenty-mile run through the forest with a few hours of hand-to-hand combat mixed in for good measure. They called it "Gauntlet."

They dropped you off with a team, a troop of Deltas, sixteen men in all, in the woods starting forty miles from Fort Bragg, one at a time, by parachute. The goal was to get back to Fort Bragg. Only problem was, they dropped in a brigade of regular army soldiers, nearly three thousand men in all, between the handful of Deltas and Bragg.

Dewey knew it was an exercise in humility. It didn't take a genius to realize that. No Delta had ever made it through Gauntlet. It's supposed to teach you that no matter how smart or how tough you think you are, there's something called overwhelming force. But just because the odds are stacked against you, doesn't mean you can convince a Delta he doesn't have a chance.

That day, Dewey dropped from the low-hover chopper and landed near the top of a big pine, climbing down to the forest floor. He started hiking in the opposite direction of everyone else, over Mount Greeley, through the dense, unpopulated land in the middle of North Carolina nowhere. Bragg was west; he headed due east. Except for a fifteen-minute stop to rest, he hiked all night.

Just after sunrise, he came through a thick stand of pine and was at the edge of a neatly mowed field. He walked up to the farmhouse and asked the gray-haired farmer if he could get a ride to Bragg. The farmer, who barely spoke a word, drove Dewey the hundred or so miles back to Bragg. Dewey arrived to a thoroughly surprised corps. Everyone else had been caught within the first six hours. Some thought Dewey might be dead.

Dewey was the only Delta to ever make it through Gauntlet.

Some of the uptight pricks thought he broke the rules, but that was precisely the point: there aren't any rules when you're at war. The knife was given to him by his fellow class of recruits, a token of their respect for the one who'd made it through.

Dewey ignored Pierre's question. "Let's get out there and put an end to this."

Pierre strapped on the knife and turned to leave.

"Are there any of Serine's friends you trust?" Dewey asked as he reached for the doorknob.

"No," said Pierre. "They're all rats."

"None?"

"Well, maybe one, Esco. He's been around a while."

"Esco, good thought."

"What's going to happen with Serine?" Pierre asked. "Have you seen him?"

"He's in tough shape," said Dewey. "Chopper's coming to take him to the hospital in Buenaventura."

Dewey went back to the deck and talked with each of his other foremen individually. He warned them to keep the men working hard, to drive them today, and to be on the lookout for fighting.

He returned to the infirmary and found Serine unconscious again.

"How long until the chopper gets here?" Dewey asked.

"Soon," said Barbo. "Half hour tops."

"I'll help you carry him to the pad when it gets here."

Dewey went back to his office and sat down at his computer. He leaned forward and put his head in his hands. He considered e-mailing Dallas, but if he reported what happened last night, God knows what they'd do. Bring in the authorities, even shut down Capitana for a few days, a week, a month? Over one death; a fight at that, a worthless fight between two replaceable workers in international waters in the middle of nowhere? No, Dewey had to sit tight for the moment and get this fire under control.

Mackie's words ran through his mind again. Pierre was right. He'd talk to Esco. Esco was an elder statesman as far as the roughnecks went.

Around forty, old for a rig worker. He'd been aboard Capitana nearly five years. He was pleasant, even jovial, got along with everyone. If anyone could, Esco might help keep Serine's buddies in line.

Meanwhile, it would be up to Dewey to pacify Mackie's group. They were pissed off. They would want revenge. *Haig might be able to help keep the peace*, Dewey thought. He'd talk to him and Esco after the chopper removed Serine.

Dewey closed his eyes as the concerns raced in his mind. He leaned back in the big chair, rubbing his temples when the door to his office flew open. It was Pierre.

"You better come," Pierre said. "It's Serine."

Dewey followed him quickly across the steel platform. A few of the crewmen looked up and moved to join them.

"Back to work, boys," barked Dewey. "You heard me."

He walked through the door to the infirmary.

"I didn't touch anything," Barbo said. "That's the way I found him."

Dewey looked down at the bed. Serine's shirt, his face and his pants, the sheets, the bed itself; it was all a riot of blood. In the middle of the mess, the kid's right hand poised above his chest, fingers clenched tightly around the shaft of a knife. The blade had punctured the heart. It was a fresh cut; the blood continued to flow out of the wound.

"Radio the chopper," said Dewey. "We won't be needing it."

4

SAVAGE ISLAND PROJECT

By 7:15 A.M., Jake White's assistant Vida was concerned. She called Arnold Mijailovic, director of security at Savage Island.

"I called his home and his mobile," said Vida.

"Nothing?"

"No answer."

Mijailovic was a squat, bald man with a big forehead. He was born in Yugoslavia, and his face was creased with smile lines around the mouth and eyes. Despite a tough early life, Mijailovic radiated an easy, friendly warmth.

"He's always here by six at the latest. I called the dam. Neither operations or front desk has seen him."

"I'm sure there's an explanation. Let's retrace his steps. We'll look in the dam. I'll send someone over to his home. I'm sure he's somewhere."

He sighed. It wasn't the first time White had gone missing. He was probably asleep somewhere. Or perhaps he'd gotten locked in a room in the dam by accident. If there was something wrong, it was likely that it was a heart attack. White was a heavy drinker, smoker, and eater.

Mijailovic went to the dam, just a short walk from the squat brick building that housed the administration offices. The dam itself straddled the tip of the Frobisher Nunavut and stretched for a half mile across an orphan finger of the Hudson Straits to the northernmost tip of the Lower Savage Islands. At the same latitude as Greenland and Iceland, the temperature here, even in the short summer months, rarely climbed above fifty degrees. In winter, Savage Island remained gray for months. Temperatures during daytime didn't climb above minus forty. When the wind screamed off the Labrador Sea, the wind chill could reach a hundred below zero. Today, in late December, the temperatures hovered around minus fifteen. Mijailovic was bundled in a big red North Face parka as he walked from the office building to the front entrance of the dam.

Inside the gatehouse, he showed his identification card, then placed his right thumb on the black screen. The entrance area was soundproof. You could still hear the din of the turbines, but it wasn't very loud.

"Morning, Arnie," the guard said.

"Steve. You seen Jake?"

"No, I haven't. Not this morning."

"What time did you report?"

"I came on at six."

"Let me see the log."

The security guard punched a few keys on the keyboard in front if him. Mijailovic moved around from in front of the desk and looked over his shoulder.

"There," said Mijailovic. "Nine thirty-eight last night. He signed in. No sign out. Keep an eye out. If he shows up, call me. I'll be in ops. If he's not up there, we'll need to go floor by floor."

Mijailovic walked to the large steel door at the back of the entrance area and opened it. As it opened, the sound of the dam came booming in. He took a pair of orange earplugs from his coat pocket and popped them in his ears.

Mijailovic climbed aboard the elevator. He pulled the yellow latch down and went skyward. After several minutes, the elevator stopped at the top of the dam. Mijailovic got out of the elevator and walked through a door into the operations room.

"You guys seen Jake?"

"No, sir," said one of the engineers. "Not since switch."

21

"Midnight."

"Yup."

"Do you remember who was on last shift?"

"Ned's crew."

Mijailovic picked up a phone from one of the desks and dialed Ned Waters, one of five foremen who managed the engineering crews.

"Hello," a groggy voice answered.

"Ned, it's Arnie."

"Hi. What's up?"

"I'm up here in ops. They said your crew was on through switch."

"That's right."

"We're looking for Jake. He's gone. He signed in last night but didn't sign out."

"Yeah, I saw him. He was in operations until almost midnight. Went out to have a smoke."

"Did you see him come back in?"

"Come to think of it, no. Not unusual, though. He goes out there and smokes, sometimes for hours."

Mijailovic put the phone down and walked quickly through the operations room to the door to the observation area on top of the dam. He climbed the stairs to the platform. As he came to the top of the dam, the wind ripped mercilessly into his face.

"*Fucking A!*" he muttered to no one.

It was a stormy day. To the eastern horizon, the black of the ocean was dotted in whitecaps. The waves slammed into the wall of the dam just below. Mijailovic crossed the observation deck and looked to the outflow area half a mile below. A steady torrent of water cascaded through the turbines below.

In the distance, people were gathered on the shore of the reservoir. His cell phone rang. He started walking quickly back toward the operations room door.

"Mijailovic."

"It's Rand. Better get down here."

Mijailovic closed his eyes. "Be right down. Don't touch anything. You hear me?"

"Yes, sir."

Five minutes later, as he approached the grim gathering of people at the shore's edge, Mijailovic recalled the first time he'd met White. At Perry Nuclear Facility, Mijailovic had been a night security guard. He'd found White passed out one night beneath his desk, dead drunk. Rather than report the incident, he drove White to his home in Shaker Heights. He never said anything to anyone, not even to Jake. They'd been best friends ever since.

A few dozen people had gathered around the corpse. He pushed his way through the crowd.

Face down, the exposed skull of Jake White stared up blankly into the cold December sky. His head had been turned almost completely around on its spine, so that his face stared up while his chest pressed against the cold, wet ground. His neck, Mijailovic saw now, had been nearly severed. His clothing, what was left of it, a pair of green khakis and a white T-shirt, was in tatters. His left arm was gone, torn off at the shoulder. One of his legs had been amputated squarely midthigh.

Mijailovic walked through the stunned crowd to the corpse, pulled off his own parka and covered White's head and upper body with it.

"Get the kids out of here," Mijailovic said without looking up. "Someone go get the stretcher out of the hospital."

"Who is it?" asked a young boy.

Mijailovic looked at the young boy. He didn't answer. He walked quickly through the crowd, back toward the administration building.

"That's Jake White," he heard a woman tell the child as she ushered him away. "The man who built this dam. He's in heaven now."

5

CAPITANA TERRITORY

By evening, Serine was wrapped in tarpaulin and tied with weights. As the sun went down, the ritual at water's edge repeated itself. Barbo brought the corpse to the platform riser. Two of Serine's friends attended the burial. Dewey descended the stairs just as the sun settled on the horizon.

"Want to say anything?" Dewey asked.

Hammoud, an electrician, stepped forward. He knelt next to the corpse. He whispered something in Arabic.

Suddenly, a commotion came from the deck above the platform riser. Dewey heard shouts and looked up. Pierre stood in the middle of a small crowd. He was ordering the group to get back to work.

Barbo turned the metal winch and the riser tilted until the body went sliding down into the sea.

Dewey walked to the stairs and climbed back up to the main deck. Pierre stood in front of the railing at the deck, facing four of Serine's friends.

"What's going on?" he asked.

"These guys were just going back to work," said Pierre.

"Why can't we watch the burial?" asked one of Serine's friends.

"Because I said so, that's why," said Pierre.

A large man with long black hair and a stained, sleeveless Yankees T-shirt stepped forward. "He was my friend."

Dewey moved in front of Pierre, his chest less than a foot from the speaker. The other three men moved forward, toward Dewey.

"What's your name?" Dewey asked calmly.

"Rick."

Dewey stared at the man for several moments. "You work here at my pleasure, Rick. Do you understand that?"

Rick stared back.

"I'm going to ask one more time. Do you understand that you're here to work and that's it?"

"Yes."

Dewey walked forward and bumped him backward, then pushed him aside with his left arm. He was surrounded by the others.

"This thing is over." Dewey stared down each man, daring them to make a move. None of them did.

He moved back to Rick. He looked at him and then turned to walk away.

As he did, Rick spat on the ground.

Dewey whirled and grabbed him around the neck, squeezing hard. Rick made a choking noise as Dewey held him.

Behind, Pierre warned back the other three. One of them said something in Arabic and they all took a step away, then held their ground.

Dewey grasped the man's neck a few more moments. He pressed his thumb into the space next to the man's larynx, which caused severe pain and made it impossible for Rick to move. As the choking sound grew worse and Rick seemed to struggle from a lack of air, Dewey suddenly let go. He fell to his knees.

"Lock this one in the brig," Dewey said. "You, back to work."

Pierre took Rick by the arm and led him toward the brig, a small room attached to the equipment shop.

"It's growing," Pierre said as he walked into Dewey's office a few minutes later and shut the door behind him. "Have you spoken to Haig?"

"No. Or Esco. But I'm about to."

"Serine's people are planning something, I swear it."

"And Mackie's crew?"

"They're pissed," said Pierre. "Gonna be another round of this tonight."

Dewey looked out the window. In the distance, a tiny specter grew, framed by the faded orange of a setting sun: the approaching supertanker *Montana*. Judging from its size on the horizon, it would be there in three or four hours. "Go get Esco and Haig."

Pierre walked out.

Dewey closed the door. He walked through the office to the small chamber that served as a bedroom. He took off his clothing. It had been several days since he'd changed. He quickly showered and got dressed again.

He put a brush through his hair, with some difficulty, then brushed his teeth.

Back in his office he looked out the window. The *Montana* was one of forty supertankers owned by Anson Energy. Two tankers came every week like clockwork, and Dewey knew all of their captains. It took twelve hours to load each tanker with oil. During that time it was customary for Dewey to share a meal aboard the tanker with the captain of the ship in the officer's quarters. Even aboard an oil tanker, the officers enjoyed amenities, and great food was one of them. Each of the tankers had a chef; typically they served steak or fresh seafood caught over the side of the ship.

He wasn't hungry, but he liked the captain of the *Montana*, Pablo Pascoe, a Brazilian. Pablo would no doubt open a decent bottle of wine, an added bonus.

Better yet, Dewey realized, the *Montana* held a potential solution to the rising tensions aboard Capitana.

There was a knock at the door. Esco, followed by Haig and Pierre. All three came in and stood in front of Dewey.

"Close the door," he said to Pierre.

"You wanted to see us, Chief?" asked Haig.

"What are you hearing?" asked Dewey.

Haig and Esco glanced at each other.

"You start," Dewey said to Haig.

"I think there's a lot of hatred of the Arabs right now," Haig said, hesitating. "Jim was popular."

"Are we talking about revenge?"

"I'm not sure. I don't get involved."

Dewey looked at Esco.

"What about you?" he asked.

Esco shrugged. "Two men got into a fight. One died, and his people took their revenge. Now Serine is dead."

Dewey studied the expression on his face. There was nothing, no movement, frown, or anything readable on Esco's face. "Can you help?" Dewey asked.

"I'll try, Chief. I don't know how much influence I have."

"Same here," said Haig. "There's right and wrong on both sides. I'll talk to the guys. Do what I can."

Dewey glanced out the window at the approaching tanker, still far in the distance.

"I know you two aren't causing the trouble. I asked you here because hopefully you can convince others to listen to you. I want you to bring a message to the men. If there are any fights tonight, the men involved will be locked in the *Montana*'s brig. They'll be brought to Buenaventura where I will have the Colombian state police arrest them and charge them with attempted murder, assault, and whatever else I can dream up. Anson Energy will use whatever influence it has to see that these men are put away for a long time."

Dewey paused for a moment to let his words sink in.

"There's a prison called Picalea, in the foothills below the Andes. It's an awful place. In winter, there's no heat. It gets bitterly cold. They don't even have windows in the cells, only holes and bars. The snow comes right in, and all they give you is a crappy little blanket. In summer, well, in summer it gets so goddamn hot you wish winter would get there." Dewey took a step forward and looked at Esco and Haig in turn. "Anything happens tonight, any violence, the fighters'll spend the next decade of their lives in that prison."

27

"Got it," said Haig.

"I'll tell the men," said Esco.

After they left, Dewey sat down to do something he knew he could avoid no longer: draft a memo to the director of security at Anson back in Dallas. After completing the note, though, he decided not to send it. *A couple of deaths*, he thought. *That's all. It's over now.*

He deleted the e-mail as the tanker *Montana* arrived, docking at the derrick's eastern side. It was a massive ship, tall enough to rise darkly above the edge of the platform. Its six-story height would decrease dramatically as the tanker filled with oil.

At nine o'clock, Dewey boarded the *Montana*. At the top of the gangplank waited Captain Pablo Pascoe.

"Hey, buddy," said Pablo. "Hungry?"

"Starved," said Dewey. "Thirsty too."

They walked down the length of the ship to the navigations center, then took the elevator up to the bridge, the top level of the supertanker.

Dewey said hello to the crewmen in the bridge as he walked to the dining room.

"Whiskey, straight up?"

"Be great."

"No ice, as I recall. 'Neat,' yes?"

"You got it."

"How's business?" asked Pablo.

"Steady as she goes. Same old. You know the drill."

Pablo poured two drinks. They took their glasses to the outside deck area. The *Montana* hadn't been to Capitana for several months. Dewey found the temporary relief in its refuge more pleasurable than he'd thought possible. The view from the deck wasn't bad either. The fading sunlight to the west, coloring into a spectacular sunset. To the east, Capitana's massive city of pipes, steel, and flame stacks reflected the retreating light.

"Where you in from?" Dewey asked. "New York?"

"New York, Miami, then London," said Pablo. "My sister lives in

London. We had a good weekend there. Cricket match, picnic, that sort of thing."

"I like London."

They spoke about London, and England, for some time. When they finished their drinks and Pablo went to pour another round, Dewey thought back to the brutal knife fight atop the deck, the deck that from here appeared so quiet and peaceful in the fading evening light. Pablo's tone helped ease him, relax him, and made him forget about the violence of the night before.

But not for long. As they moved into the dining room and the alcohol took effect, Dewey strangely found himself growing more sober, dwelling on the prospect of another bloody night on Capitana.

"Something bothering you?" Pablo asked. "You seem put out."

"Two men were killed last night," Dewey said.

Pablo did a double take.

"What? Are you kidding?"

"No. Knife fight. Bloody as hell."

Pablo shook his head in sympathy. "This is terrible. If there's anything—"

"I may need you to take some men tomorrow. Move a few troublemakers out of here."

"I'm at your service. I'll take anyone you want." Pablo stared at Dewey. "Including you. You look tired, my friend. Maybe you need a break. When was the last time you spent some time in Cali?"

"I can't remember."

"That's what I thought. What do you say? Take a weekend, a week. You really do look like you could use the rest. How about it?"

"I can't. Not with the situation on the rig. Some other time."

They ate dinner and managed to drink two bottles of red wine in the process. They spoke no more of what they'd discussed before. At just after midnight, Dewey returned to the platform and walked back to his office.

The sky, even now, at a quarter past midnight, had a strange paisley glow to it. Part of that no doubt was the burn off from the flare stacks, the orangey, smoke-filled heat waves blurring and lighting their way into dissipation far off, to the east of the rig. But part of it, too, was the horizon. At this time of year, the light never seemed to die.

Dewey watched for a few moments as a crew of men on deck moved some of the duct manifolds to a different part of the tanker. Finally, as they finished and walked away, Dewey looked back to the horizon. He tried to clear his mind. He had to stop thinking about what might or might not be happening, if only for a few minutes.

Slowly, in the big chair, Dewey drifted off to sleep.

Suddenly, he awoke; a knock on the cabin door. He'd been asleep on the chair for hours. The lights were still on. His eyes refocused, looked slowly around the room. His head ached from too much wine. He leaned forward, stood up. He walked quickly across his office to the door.

"What is it?" he asked as he opened the door. It was one of his foremen, Baroni.

"You better come." Baroni's forehead creased sharply with concern.

"What is it?"

"Jonas."

Dewey stood and looked at the clock on his wall. It was four o'clock in the morning.

He put his boots on and followed Baroni. The sound of the sea slapping against the platform combined with the steady hum of the oil coursing into the hold of the *Montana*. It was dark outside, but the deck lay awash in halogen light.

They walked quickly along the side of the big tanker.

"Why isn't anyone watching the loading?"

"I'll show you why."

They passed the hotel and scaled the east stairwell to the sea deck. Ahead, a small group of men was gathered. Red lights from the lower deck cast a muted glow on the scene.

Dewey felt as if he were walking in slow motion.

"I went to hit the head a few minutes ago," said Baroni as they arrived at the scene.

Dewey pushed his way through the circle of men. On the floor of the bathroom, the body of Jonas Pierre lay contorted against the toilet, sideways. His hands were tied behind his back. His big blue eyes stared out blankly, bulging and red. A band of wire dug deeply into his neck, making his face appear almost blue. He'd been strangled to death.

Dewey said nothing as he knelt over Pierre. He was all of thirty years old. He had a family in Florida, a wife named Emily and two daughters.

"Wire cutters," he said quietly. "Someone get me a pair of wire cutters."

A minute later, one of the men handed Dewey a pair of wire cutters. He reached down and cut the band of wire at the nape of the neck. He let Pierre's head fall back into his hands then laid it gently on the steel floor. Leaning forward, he softly pushed Pierre's eyelids closed.

"Wake up Barbo," Dewey said without looking up from the floor. He shut his eyes and rubbed the space between them as he thought. "Tell him to have Jonas prepared for burial. Tell him the men are taking the body down to the riser. Have him meet us there with the weights. Right now."

"Okay."

Dewey stood up.

"Baroni, I want all the foremen at the burial. Go wake 'em up. Other than finishing the loading of the *Montana*, Capitana will cease pumping operations immediately. Everyone is to remain in their quarters, except for the foremen and your crew. Got it?"

"Yes, sir."

Dewey knelt down. He remembered the Gerber combat blade he'd given Pierre. Pierre still wore the sheath, but it was empty. He searched the dead man's body for the knife. It wasn't there.

"Keep an eye out for a black knife, double serrated, six-inch blade, hilt wrapped in tape. It's mine. Jonas had it." He looked at the men standing outside the door. They were silent. He could see fear in their eyes.

"You four carry the body down to the platform riser."

He walked back to the cabin. He went to the bathroom and turned the tap on, splashing cold water on his face. He looked quickly in the mirror. His eyes were bloodred and large purplish bags were under his lids. He looked like shit.

He closed his eyes, leaning forward into the sink. He tried not to think about Pierre. He knew, though, it was his fault. Dewey had gotten him killed the moment he asked him to help out, the moment he gave him the knife. He shook his head in shame and regret. He splashed more water onto his face. He had to stay strong.

They buried Pierre as the dark of night was beginning to ashen into the predawn. All twenty-four foremen stood on the platform riser as Barbo rolled the winch handle and let the young man's body, weighted now and wrapped in tarp, slide with a small splash into the beckoning sea.

Dewey looked up. There were no crewmen watching this time. He walked to the stairs and stood on the second step so that he could see his men.

"Have your night crew stay on until the *Montana*'s done loading," he said to Baroni.

"Got it."

"I want the rest of you to conduct a room-by-room search of the hotel. Every room, every bunk, every drawer of every cabinet, dresser, every bathroom, every man. Work in pairs. Put a piece of tape on the door of a finished room. Any man complains, take them immediately to the brig, on my orders. Any trouble, any fights, violence, whatever, pull the alarm switch next to the door. If anyone attempts to fight, use whatever means necessary to subdue them. One in each pair, you carry something with you, a hammer, wrench, knife, whatever."

"What are we looking for?"

"Signs of struggle. Bloodstains. Pierre had a big gash on his head. He may have head-butted someone. Maybe he got in a swing on his attackers. Look for a black eye, a bloody lip, broken nose, whatever. And find my knife. It's a Gerber, six-inch blade, double serrated. The letters D.A. are engraved on one side. The word GAUNTLET is engraved on the other."

Dewey turned and walked alone up the steps to the central deck then back to his office.

An hour later, Baroni knocked on Dewey's door. "Anything I can do?" he asked.

"I want to speak with Esco. Can you get him?"

"Sure."

In a few minutes, Esco entered Dewey's office.

"Morning," said Esco.

Dewey didn't answer him. He didn't even look at him. He stared out the window at the *Montana* and behind the tanker at the growing orange of sunrise.

"Who killed Jonas Pierre?" Dewey asked.

"What?"

"You heard me."

"Pierre is dead? What happened?"

Dewey turned from the window. He took three steps across the floor of his office and leaned into Esco's face.

"Who killed him?"

"I don't know."

"I told you to put a lid on this, goddamn it. Now I've got no choice. If I don't have a name in one hour, I'll order you and every other roughneck of Arabic descent off the rig for good. You'll all be in the *Montana*'s brig when it leaves this afternoon."

Esco shook his head. "This is unfair, Chief."

Dewey ignored him as he continued to stare at Esco. He reached his hand out slowly and placed it gently around Esco's neck. "If I find out you knew who killed Pierre, I will personally break your neck with my own hands."

Esco remained impassive. "I told you I don't know who killed him. I told Serine's friends what you asked. I'll ask what they know. Why do you blame me? I didn't want Pierre killed. I just want to work."

Dewey removed his hand. "Get out of my office. You have one hour."

Dewey went to the cafeteria. It was empty. He made a pot of coffee, then found some bread, peanut butter, and jelly and made himself a sandwich, even though it was early morning.

After eating, he walked to the *Montana*, climbed the gangplank to the deck, and took the elevator to the bridge.

The *Montana*'s captain, Pablo, stood at the bridge with two other men.

"Morning," Dewey said as he entered.

"Dewey. Morning. How you feeling? My head's a little sore."

33

"Mine too."

"We're almost topping. Should be able to push off by ten, eleven at the latest."

"I need a word," said Dewey.

Two officers walked out of the bridge area to the next room.

"Another man died last night. A good friend."

"Who was it?"

"A foreman, name of Pierre. Kid from California."

Pablo shook his head. "That's terrible. I'm sorry."

"Well," said Dewey, "the situation's different now. I think they were trying to send me a message. Yesterday Pierre helped me keep some of Serine's men in line. This has to stop now, and I'm going to need your help."

Pablo nodded. "Of course. How?"

"It looks like I'm going to need you to take some men to Buenaventura after all. More than I thought."

Pablo rubbed his chin. "How many are we talking?"

"A few dozen."

"That many? Who are we talking about?"

"Serine's crew. All of them."

"Hmm. That could be tough."

Dewey looked at Pablo. "Why?"

"That's a load of guys."

"I don't care if you tie them to the rail or make them swim in the fucking oil. We have a situation that is threatening the livelihood of this rig. That means your livelihood, and mine too. If I need your help in removing that threat, I expect to receive it."

"But why Serine's crew?" Pablo asked. "Why not Mackie's?"

Dewey gave him his trademark glare.

"I'll do whatever you want," said Pablo quickly. "You know that. But I just wonder, why the Arabs?"

"I can't exactly explain it," said Dewey, thinking of Jim Mackie's last words. He softened his tone slightly. "If I'm wrong, I'll be the first to apologize. But Jim Mackie tried to tell me something. Something was going on that I don't understand yet. Mackie was a good man. He wasn't a thug. Serine killed him for some reason. And now Serine's men have killed again. It stops here, Pablo. That's it."

Taking Pablo's nonresponse as a grudging assent, Dewey rode the elevator down to the deck and headed back to his office.

He sat down at his computer. He had to let Dallas know now. For the next fifteen minutes, Dewey drafted a memo that described the events leading to the three deaths aboard the rig. He called the deaths the result of ethnic tensions. But as he wrote, he wondered about Serine's death in the infirmary. At first it had seemed obvious that Mackie's buddies had taken their revenge on him, but now Dewey wasn't sure he believed it. He couldn't explain his suspicion. It was illogical, yet something in his gut told him the Irish didn't do it. Could one of Serine's own crew have done him?

He finished and sent the memo without speculating formally, then tried to put it out of his mind. Next he wrote a pair of letters, one to Mackie's widow and the other to Pierre's. He looked up Serine's emergency contact on his employment sheet; he hadn't listed anyone.

Dewey walked out of his office to check on the progress of the searches. Nothing had turned up yet.

As he went back to his office he looked at his watch. Esco's hour was nearly up. Maybe he'd been too harsh on the engineer. Why should it be Esco's responsibility to find out who killed Pierre? Glancing at the tanker, Dewey also thought about Pablo. He felt bad about that interchange too. He'd have to find some way to make it up to him. When this was over. When the whole mess was behind him.

Suddenly, the deck phone rang. He picked it up. It was Baroni.

"What is it?"

"I thought you should know. Sing saw Esco and a few others arguing with Jonas last night, before he was killed. It was pretty heated."

"Why's he only telling you this now?"

"He's terrified. He was hiding in his bunk."

The anger climbed up Dewey's back as he looked out the window. He stared at the deck outside the hotel. There, on the deck, he saw Esco.

Anger rose like boiling oil in his chest and head. He marched out onto the central deck.

"Esco."

The older man turned.

"Come with me."

"I don't know the answer," Esco called back, shrugging. "I told you. No one knows."

Dewey glared and said nothing. Reluctantly, Esco followed him to the office. Dewey closed the door behind him.

He stepped in close to Esco.

"Why did you lie to me about Jonas?"

"What are you talking about?"

"Don't you dare lie to me twice. You were seen arguing with him just before he was found dead."

"That's not true. I liked Jonas. We argued about the way we're being targeted, that's all."

Dewey took a menacing step toward Esco. He didn't know what to think anymore, but he knew he didn't trust him. He felt the anger boiling over; he wanted to take a swing at the man, to beat the truth out of him.

Footsteps came from the hallway outside the office. Dewey's door swung open.

It was Chuck Walters and another foreman, Victor Wrede, holding something in his hand.

"We found it in Pazur's bed. We've got him in the brig."

Wrede handed it over, black-taped hilt first. He glanced down at the blade and saw the word GAUNTLET.

6

THE PENINSULA HOTEL
FIFTH AVENUE AND FIFTY-FIFTH STREET
NEW YORK CITY

Listen, you son of a bitch, I'm going to say this one more time. We're not for sale. Not at your price. Not at any price. It's that simple."

The speaker, Nicholas Anson, stabbed his right index finger into the air like a dagger, hitting the air dramatically in sync with each syllable. Anson was angry, and it revealed itself in his voice and his eyes; the creases around his eyes furrowed deeply as he delivered his message.

He knew the fundamental importance of leaving absolutely no trace of doubt or wavering in his position. Anson Energy, the fifth-largest energy company in the United States, was, to put it as plainly as possible, not for sale.

It was 6:12 A.M., and Anson was standing on the heated marble floor in the ridiculously oversized bathroom in his suite at the Peninsula Hotel in New York City, in front of the big mirror, alone, talking to himself. He was buttoning his blue shirt, wrapping a tie around his neck, getting dressed for what he knew would be a defining day in his long, difficult, amazing career.

"I don't care how much you're offering," he whispered, leaning up close to the mirror. "This company ain't for sale."

After a quick breakfast, Anson's limousine dropped him off on West Street, in the heart of Wall Street. As he walked into the entrance, Anson couldn't remember how many times he walked Wall Street's corridors in his long career. For good or bad, Wall Street was an incontrovertible fact of life for a CEO of a public company. It was your most hated enemy and it was your best friend, your ally and your adversary. It had financed Anson Energy's rise and it would be there, God forbid, if his company faltered, like a vulture, ready to pick through the scraps of his life's work without apology.

The front entrance to Goldman Sachs was nondescript, elegant, empty. It was an entrance so austere that only the most prestigious financial institution in the world could get away with it. That, of course, was what made it so pretentious. This plain, unadorned space seemed to be saying "Fuck you, buddy, we're so powerful we don't need to impress you or anyone else for that matter."

Anson took the elevator to the fifty-fourth floor and the office of Patrick Perry, a managing director at Goldman, and chief investment banker for Anson Energy.

Anson had known Perry for more than two decades. Perry had handled Anson Energy's first debt placement, a tranche of high-yield bonds totaling $45 million, a laughable amount of money today, but a creative and crucial piece of financing that allowed the small oil exploration company to acquire first six oil leases, all near its Pecos in the Permian Basin of West Texas. All of them were dusters—dry as the desert, containing less oil than your average backyard swimming pool, except for one, a rocky old section of land they called Saranox 66, a piece of land the owner threw in with the other five leases because he thought it was a dog. A piece of land that struck it big less than a year later and turned Anson Energy into a player.

Perry and Anson liked each other. Anson had grown to rely on Perry's sage advice, and Perry, in turn, had risen at Goldman on the back of Anson Energy's astounding growth.

"Morning," Perry said as Anson walked in. They shook hands.

"Howdy," Anson said, smiling. "How are you, Pat?"

"I'm good," said Perry. "You want a cup of coffee?"

"Sure."

"Black?"

"You know it."

Perry's office was large, immaculate. On the walls hung paintings most art history majors would recognize.

"Where is everyone?" Anson asked.

"They're in the conference room. Your boys are in there already. Ralph Fagen from Debevoise is in there as well. The KKB folks should be along around nine thirty."

Anson sat and took a sip from the coffee cup.

"Is Marks coming?" Anson asked.

"Marks will be there. So will Romano, their CFO. Their counsel is coming too."

"So what are they going to say?"

"It should be pretty straightforward. KKB wants to do a deal. They want Capitana and all of that oil you're pumping down there. They'll probably offer some kind of cash-stock mix with a truckload of debt. They want to buy Anson Energy."

"You know, it used to be when one company bought another and the other didn't really want to be bought they called it a 'hostile take-over.'"

"They'll make you vice chairman. At least that's what their bankers are telling us. All your boys'll be protected. This isn't a hostile takeover."

Vice chairman? Anson shook his head in disgust. "I don't want to be vice chairman. Vice chairman is when you turn sixty. Vice chairman is golf three days a week and pretending you know what's going on the other two. I'm forty-six. Alden and I built this thing. I don't want to be vice chairman. I don't want to merge. I just want to run this company like I've always run it."

"Well, you won't be in charge. That's definitely the downside. But instead of being CEO of the fifth-largest energy company in the United States, you'll be vice chairman of the largest. For God's sake, you'll be creating the second-largest energy conglomerate in the world."

"'Conglomerate'? What the fuck's a 'conglomerate'? I'm an oilman. I'd rather pump gas than work for a 'conglomerate.'"

Perry reclined in his leather chair and paused. A small grin spread across his lips as he let Anson continue his rant.

"I'm serious, Pat. You, of all people, should get it. You've been in this whole crazy thing from the very beginning. I had to take a Greyhound bus from Midland to our first meeting. Remember that? I don't need to be vice whatever of the biggest energy company in the United States or the second biggest in the world. I don't want to work for a conglomerate. I'm happy with what we've got, with what we've built."

Perry calmly stood up. He walked to the corner of his office. On a table in the corner, he methodically opened a leather valise and pulled out a piece of paper. Finally, he turned and walked back to his desk.

"Do you know how much you're worth?"

"Ballpark, five hundred million, plus or minus. You thieves would know better than me."

"You're worth seven hundred and twenty-seven million dollars based on the closing price of your stock last night."

"So what's the point? You guys need a loan?"

"The point is, that's a lot of money. But almost all of it—seven hundred million dollars of it—is sitting there in Anson Energy stock. If you tried to sell any of that you'd scare the shit out of the market and your institutional shareholders, analysts on the street, hedgies, everyone."

"You're missing the point: *I don't care.* I'm not looking to sell my stock. Anson Energy's my best investment. Know what I did last week? I called my broker and asked him to *buy* me one hundred thousand shares. I have no desire to sell my stake. I don't need a liquidity event or whatever other fancy term you bankers have for it."

"At least listen to what they're offering."

"I don't want to hear it. I've already made up my mind."

"KKB is willing to pay a forty percent premium on yesterday's closing price. Your Anson Energy equity will be worth about one point two billion dollars at the deal price they're talking. Perhaps more important, nobody will care if you decide to take a bunch of it, all of it for that matter, off the table."

Anson shook his head again, but a small grin emerged on his face, which he quickly tried to hide. He took another sip from his coffee cup, attempting in vain to conceal from Perry his momentary amazement.

"One point two billion dollars?" Anson said. "Great. I guess that means I can finally buy that solid gold beach house I've been eyeing."

"I'm not done. They'll grant you a one percent stake in the merged entity and another half percent you'll be able to personally earmark to your top people. You'll also receive warrants based on gross profit targets over the next four years. That doesn't include salary, bonus, perks, which, as you know, will be substantial."

"What about Alden? What will they do with him? He's the one they should be concerned about. I'm as replaceable as a hubcap. He's not."

"He'll get the same amount as you. I imagine they might try and condition the deal on his coming on board and working for KKB, or at least signing some sort of noncompete."

"Noncompete? Right. Alden would rather give himself a circumcision with a lawn mower."

Anson leaned back and rubbed his eyes with his right hand.

"Why us? Why not Andarko, Marathon, Conoco, or someone else for chrissakes?"

"You know the answer to that: Capitana, plain and simple. This deal is about oil."

"There's plenty of oil out there."

"KKB won't buy oil from the Middle East. Marks won't even consider buying oil from there. They will not acquire a company if it has supply chain within OPEC."

Anson stood and placed his coffee cup on the mahogany desk that separated the two. He walked to the window and looked out. Across the way, in the next skyscraper, he could see a group of men sitting around a large conference table. One of them, a fat, bald man, was gesticulating wildly. Anson wished he could hear what the man was saying.

"I guess it all has to do with how you look at things."

"How so?"

"It's never been about the money. Oh, sure, the first million was nice. But it was something altogether more important. It was about

Alden and me quitting our goddamn jobs and doing something together. It was about never having to eat another bologna sandwich ever again. It was about all those people who wouldn't let us into their world, their business schools, their country clubs." He paused and looked at Perry. "People like you, as a matter of fact."

Perry smiled.

"If I do this deal, I'll be one of them," continued Anson. "I'll lose everything I've worked my whole life for. And I'm not talking about money. I'm talking about achievement."

"You'll be a billionaire. That's a lot of fuck-you money. And if you don't care about the money, think about those people in that conference room or back in Dallas. You give each of your executives a tenth of a point and all of a sudden they're worth fifty, sixty million dollars. You say yes to this and all of a sudden you've made those people wealthy beyond their wildest dreams. Think of your shareholders. This one's simply too good to walk away from."

"All right, I'll listen to them." Anson turned from the window and smiled serenely at his investment banker. "I'll listen long and hard. And I promise I won't even say no until the end of the meeting."

7

Uptown, clouds shrouded Fifth Avenue's skyscrapers in near darkness. The weatherman said the city would soon receive the biggest blizzard in a decade, but it was days away. Its foreboding precursor, the angry clouds, rushed ominously overhead against the metallic skyline.

Above the elegant entrance to the skyscraper at the corner of Fifty-third Street and Fifth Avenue, a small, stark black triangle sat affixed to the crossbeam of a titanium portico. This triangle was no bigger than a dinner plate. That stark black appurtenance was the logo of a company and this was its worldwide headquarters. The company's name was KKB.

Inside the lobby, obsidian marble cast glimmering refractions of light from the immense chandelier that dangled in the middle of the entry space. In the center of the lobby, an abstract spread of a reclining female form in copper and mahogany designed by Henry Moore stood like some piece of modern art. Behind it, a lone security guard stood. Above his head, cut out of the same dark marble, an old railroad clock read the time: nine ten.

Seventy-four stories above, three individuals entered the elevator. One, Albert Romano, KKB's chief financial officer, pressed the button that would send the elevator down toward the lobby. Next to him stood Tara Wheatley, KKB's thirty-six-year-old general counsel. And to her side stood the third occupant of the elevator, Teddy Marks, KKB's CEO.

Marks, a tall brown-haired man, was dressed in a simple, Navy blue Brooks Brothers suit, a slight grin on his face. He was a handsome man, despite a slight limp and a small scar just below his left eye, his hair just a bit too long, healthy, and youthful-looking for his age.

The elevator descended quickly and the three KKB executives walked briskly through the lobby. As they entered the cavernous lobby, Marks looked at the security guard.

"How'd your Rangers do last night, Joe?" Marks asked.

"They won, Mr. Marks," the security guard responded, smiling. "Three zip."

"That right?" said Marks. "I'll be damned. Good for them."

"Your Blackhawks lost, I'm afraid."

"Thanks for reminding me," said Marks, smiling.

Marks continued through the lobby, exiting the door as Romano held it open.

The black Jaguar limousine moved quickly down the FDR Drive. Marks flipped through *The Wall Street Journal* as Romano palmed his BlackBerry and Wheatley read through a thick legal document.

Marks had an easy, laid-back manner. His self-confidence came from a place most of his colleagues had never dreamed of, a place on the other side of the world, Vietnam, where as a twenty-year-old he had started his first of three tours of duty as a member of the Navy's elite warriors, the SEALs. He didn't like to talk about his time in Vietnam, but the knowledge that comes when you've killed with your bare hands on behalf of a cause you believe in, the humility that you earn when you yourself have nearly died for that same cause, that confidence inhabited Marks's every step and moment, and it was an important ally in his climb to power.

Marks would have looked at home in the U.S. Senate or wherever else success has as much to do with looks and communication skills as with intellect. Marks's rise at KKB didn't come from his political skills, however. If anything, the opposite was true.

Marks was a young vice president in charge of business development at KKB. He was hungry and determined to rise. One day over lunch, he listened to a proposal about a hydroelectric facility on the Labrador Sea from a similarly young, hungry, idealistic engineer named Jake White. Marks researched the idea, even flying up to remote Canada on four separate occasions with White. Marks ended up championing the plan of what was now the most important asset in the KKB family of facilities, Savage Island Project.

Marks had fought KKB's CEO at the time, a gruff old man named Emmet Winkler, who opposed the idea. In the annals of KKB history, the development of the Savage Island Project and the bad blood between the two had become legend.

At a board meeting, a member of the board of directors, Boone Pickens, had opened the company's quarterly financial statements and, pointing to a particular line item, demanded to know why KKB had spent more than $80 million on land acquisition in northern Canada. Winkler, caught off guard by the line item and embarrassed by the perception that he hadn't reviewed his own financial statements prior to the board meeting, turned to his then CFO, who informed the board that it had been used "to buy a large piece of desolate tundra in northern Canada in a place called the Nunavut."

Winkler stood up and walked across the room to Marks.

"I told you to drop that fucking dam six months ago!" Winkler had yelled at Marks in front of his board.

"Well, now, this is getting interesting," Pickens interrupted. "Would you care to explain yourself, Teddy?"

It was just the opening Marks needed. Without so much as acknowledging his boss, Marks had stood up and launched into an impromptu forty-five-minute presentation, without notes, on Savage Island Project. Cost, time line, return-on-investment analysis, everything related to the project.

"Do you want KKB to be the biggest energy company in America?" Marks had concluded his presentation. "Or are you content to stay in the backwaters of this industry? I'll tell you right now, I'm not. There are half a dozen companies who would pay ten times what we paid for that land and the rights to this project."

Marks's speech left the entire boardroom silent.

Finally, after a pregnant pause, it was Pickens who spoke. "You got my vote, Teddy."

By the end of the meeting, the $12.5 billion project had been given the green light, and Emmet Winkler had been asked to retire.

Now, two decades later, it was Marks who was CEO. KKB was the second-largest energy company in America. Marks's prediction had come true.

But KKB was vulnerable. Savage Island Project ensured dominant market share for KKB in electricity markets throughout Canada and down the eastern seaboard of the United States. The company's thirteen nuclear facilities were key suppliers to the developing southwest. It was a major owner and distributor of natural gas and coal throughout North America.

But KKB had misfired in its attempts to organically develop petroleum supply. Two projects in Kazakhstan had proven disastrous, costing KKB well over a billion dollars each and coming up dry except for remnant natural gas, which was not worth the cost of trying to transport it to market.

What's more, Marks insisted KKB not buy any of its oil, not a drop, from the Middle East.

Marks was fiercely patriotic and believed Middle East oil was the devil's water. When certain members of the KKB board pressured Marks to rethink his position and keep his political views out of the CEO suite, he threatened to resign. KKB's resulting dependence on electricity made the company vulnerable to a takeover by one of the oil behemoths, BP and ExxonMobil especially.

It was this that had caused Marks to focus on Anson Energy. For while Anson was a smaller player in the U.S. energy business, fifth largest in the country, it had discovered oil—lots of oil. Its strike off the coast of Colombia was the talk of the petroleum world. It was the answer he was looking for.

As the black Jaguar limo made its way toward the offices of Goldman Sachs, Romano's phone rang. As he listened, he looked at Marks, who was staring out the window.

"What's up?" Marks asked after Romano hung up his phone.

"That was Philip," Romano said, referring to Philip Bois, a managing director at Morgan Stanley and KKB's chief investment banker. "Phil spoke to Pat Perry. Apparently Nicholas Anson is adamantly opposed to selling the company to us."

"Does he want to cancel the meeting?"

"No, Phil thinks we should get together anyway. I tend to agree."

"Has Phil previewed the deal to him?"

"He previewed it. You know Anson. He's a dirt farmer, for chrissakes."

"He's not a dirt farmer," said Marks. "He's an entrepreneur who built a great company. He's a classic American."

"He got lucky," persisted Romano.

"Maybe. Who cares? I know we didn't think of looking for oil off the coast of Colombia. Did you have that idea?"

"No, I didn't."

"Well, I didn't either. In fact, not many people did. But Nick Anson and his brother did, didn't they? Our goddamn overpaid E and P team was too busy pissing away two and a half billion dollars in Kazakhstan to think of looking in the friendly waters off Colombia."

Romano sat in silence.

"If we're going to build a great energy company, and if we're going to do it without sourcing oil from the Middle East, Anson is our best option," said Marks. "As for Nick Anson, I know him. Not well, but I know him. He is an honorable, hardworking, humble man. I'd be proud to have him on our team."

"Look, we'll succeed in a takeover of Anson," said Romano. "We've done the analysis. If Nick Anson isn't on board, then we should take our offer directly to the shareholders. We should go hostile."

Marks shook his head. "I don't want to do that. I won't do that. If I can't convince Nick Anson to join us, then we'll find another way to get

47

oil. Either that or KKB will have to find another man to lead the company."

The vast conference room table on the fifty-fourth floor of Goldman Sachs didn't look like the poker table it was. From one end to the other, it measured at least fifty feet long, its deep brown wood matched by dark paneling throughout the room. Wood enveloped you the moment you walked in, making the place feel at once secretive, important, dignified, and the center of the world—a place where important things happened.

Anson and Perry walked into the room. The small talk that occupied the individuals sitting about the table came to a stop. Anson walked to the table and looked up at a handsome, dark-haired man across from him.

"How are you, Ted?" Anson asked as he extended his hand. "What's a nice guy like you doing in a place like this?"

Marks laughed enthusiastically. "I was going to ask you the same thing. Good to see you, Nick."

The two men shook hands, and the serious mood that previously occupied the room broke down in the forced camaraderie of introductions.

"You know our CFO, Al Romano," Marks said. Anson reached out and shook Romano's hand.

"Sure, we've met," said Anson. "How are you?"

"Good, thanks. Nice to see you."

"And this is our general counsel, Tara Wheatley."

"How do you do, Mr. Anson," she said.

"Call me Nick."

"This is Philip Bois," said Romano, "from Morgan Stanley."

"Nice to meet you, Philip," Anson said. "I take it you've met some of the folks I brought with me?"

"That's right," said Marks. "Met Marty," he said, nodding at Martin Ballard, Anson's CFO, "and Ralph." He nodded at Ralph Fagen, Anson Energy's outside counsel from Debevoise & Plimpton. "And of course, we all know Pat. Shall we get started?"

"Sure," said Anson.

"You're a pioneer in this industry," said Marks, speaking directly to Anson, but with a smile on his face, soft-spoken and dignified. "When I was trading oil futures in Chicago, back when I got out of the Navy, I remember reading about you and your brother down in Midland. I was always jealous as hell. I wish I had the guts to do what you did, to go out and start something from scratch, build it up into a great company."

"Well, you're kind," said Anson. "But I'll be perfectly honest. It was a royal pain in the ass."

Marks and the rest of the people in the room erupted in laughter.

"The reason I think back on those days is because it seems to me ironic that we're meeting now to discuss a potential merger," continued Marks.

"How so?" asked Anson.

"Because what I want to propose to you is something very similar to that original gutsy idea you had. I want to propose something just as new, just as entrepreneurial as that original vision you had for Anson Energy. For too long, Americans have been content to get their energy from foreign companies. For too long, the financial terms of our lives have been dictated by a bunch of men in the Middle East who despise us and everything this great country of ours stands for."

Anson nodded.

"I'm talking about a new paradigm here. I'm talking about an American energy company. A company whose very existence is testament to the American spirit. Whose profits stay within our borders. Whose products don't come from the Middle East or any foreign government that is hostile to the U.S. Whose men and women are American men and women or at the very least allies of the United States. This will be an energy company like no one's ever seen before—"

"The biggest energy company in the United States," Romano interrupted, "second biggest in the world."

"I don't care about size," said Marks, glancing at Romano. "I'm talking about something much more important. This will be a company that could help free this country of its addiction to Middle East oil. It's an addiction that not only costs American consumers their hard-earned money, but also lives, the lives of our sons and daughters."

Marks paused and smiled at Anson across the table.

"But I can't do that without you, Nick."

The room looked at Anson, who sat in silence.

Marks stood up and unfurled a large, laminated document. It was a map.

"The red ones are KKB facilities," he said, pointing to the hundreds of red dots that had been affixed to the map, representing KKB hydro-electric, nuclear, and coal facilities, natural gas wells, pipelines. "The blue ones are Anson Energy facilities," he continued. "Imagine the combination of these two companies. With Savage Island Project and its almost endless supply of low-cost electricity, our thirteen nuclear facilities, the western natural gas pipelines, and our multinational distribution network, combined with Capitana Territory and Anson Energy's extensive and growing capacity to produce oil. The thought is just mind-boggling."

Anson looked down at the map. "It would certainly be interesting."

"As president," added Marks, "you'll be an integral part of leadership for as long as you have the desire."

"President?" said Anson, glancing at Pat Perry, who appeared equally surprised. "What happens to you?"

"CEO," said Marks. "We do it together, as partners."

Anson paused and leaned back in his chair.

"If you don't mind, please brief us on the numbers," said Perry.

"The details of the financial package are contained in this draft proxy," said Romano, "twelve copies of which will be dropped off at Goldman by the end of this meeting. But the highlights are relatively straightforward. This is a sixty-five point seven billion–dollar deal. KKB acquires all assets of Anson Energy in a ten-to-six-to-one bond-stock-cash transaction. The bonds total twenty-five billion dollars, high yield; Morgan and Goldman corun the placement. Stock is a straight swap out that takes out Anson Energy's shareholders at a forty percent premium to yesterday's closing price. Cash is for you guys at closing, about three and a half billion dollars. One billion two of that retires your Anson Energy stake. Another one billion is for your brother. The other points can be used for whatever you want, though presumably you'll spread them around to a few of your top managers."

"What about Alden? He's the smart one."

"He can continue working E and P," said Marks, "or he can retire. It's up to him. You tell him I said that."

"I will. My guess is he'd like to keep working."

"We've created a generous incentive bonus plan for Anson management, based on some very achievable EBIT targets. As for salary, office, et cetera, just write your own ticket on that stuff."

Marks stopped talking. He leaned back and smiled at Anson.

"I'm not quite sure what to say," said Anson.

"Say you'll join us," said Marks. "How about it?"

Anson sat back in his chair. The entire meeting had taken less than fifteen minutes. He looked to his right, at Pat Perry, who appeared to be in a mild state of shock. Anson thought of his brother, Alden. He pictured him that day some twenty-odd years ago when they'd hit it, when Saranox 66 struck a triangulated vertical reservoir of light, sweet Permian Basin crude oil, spilling a geyser of thick Texas oil out into the morning sky like a volcano, and how they'd danced beneath it like two children in a summer rainstorm.

Anson looked at Marks and realized for the first time that he hadn't said more than ten words the entire meeting. He'd crumbled like a piece of his wife's coffee cake. All his protestations, in front of the mirror, to Pat, they were all meaningless now. His face, his eyes, his body language—it all gave him away. He'd been taken over, not just the company, but him. He couldn't say no, not to this. This was too fucking good.

He stood up. He extended his hand across the table, toward Marks.

"Let's do it," Anson said.

8

FOSTER-BADENHAUSEN COMMUNICATIONS
EAST SIXTY-FIRST STREET
NEW YORK CITY

As was inevitable in transactions of this nature, where a variety of bankers, lawyers, company executives, public relations consultants, and others become knowledgeable of a pending deal, rumors got out about the KKB–Anson Energy merger. A day after Ted Marks and Nick Anson shook hands, rumors of the deal swirled across Wall Street, sending shares of both companies soaring. By noon the next day, shares of KKB were trading 11 percent higher than the day before, while Anson leaped to a 20 percent premium over the previous day's close.

Janice Gross, director of the Division of Corporate Finance at the Securities and Exchange Commission, phoned Tara Wheatley, KKB's general counsel, to express the agency's deep concerns about the amount of trading activity taking place in the stock of the two companies. Wheatley assured her that an announcement was imminent.

That afternoon, Marks and Anson spent time getting ready for the whirlwind of press interviews that would take place the next morning. Managing the announcement and the attendant press surrounding the process was KKB's public relations firm, Foster-Badenhausen.

Its dapper, polished founder, J. P. Badenhausen, was a former White

House speechwriter and campaign consultant who at some point realized it was far more lucrative to manage the public images of corporate executives than of politicians. Badenhausen wore expensive suits made by a tailor in London and was driven to work in a Mercedes limousine from his mansion in Greenwich to the firm's stucco town house just off Fifth Avenue and Sixty-first Street, around the corner from the Pierre Hotel.

When Anson and Marks arrived, the staff of Foster-Badenhausen was gathered in the lobby. They greeted the two executives with applause, cheers, and glasses of champagne. After a round of toasts, Marks and Anson followed Badenhausen to his office to prepare for the next day's announcement.

"It's an ugly business," Badenhausen said as he led them to the seating area. "You're part sausage maker, part used-car salesman. It will feel uncomfortable. Repeating the same crap over and over will drive you crazy. But it's the only option. Reporters are sneaky bastards. Repetition is the only way to ensure, or at least help influence, the story you want to see written." Badenhausen sat on one of the couches and drained the remaining champagne in his glass. "If the only thing that comes out of your mouth is the positioning statement, they won't be able to report anything else."

"And what is the 'positioning statement'?" asked Marks.

"That's for you to decide. I have a few suggestions."

"Let's hear them."

Badenhausen nodded to one of his assistants, a young brunette with smoldering eyes who sat silently in an Eames chair by the door. She stood and dimmed the lights. Badenhausen pulled a remote control from on top of the coffee table. He hit a button and a set of blinds descended from the ceiling and covered the windows. A screen descended from the ceiling. Bright white lights illuminated the screen.

"This is the sixty-second spot we produced to coincide with the announcement," said Badenhausen. "We had to rush it a little bit, but I think you'll like how it came out. We're suggesting a heavy buy for the next three to four weeks. Evening news, Sunday talk shows, maybe some prime time, *60 Minutes*, the Super Bowl, *American Idol*. Opinion-maker kind of stuff with some fun thrown in. If there's going to be opposition to this deal, we want to destroy it now, preemptively. One hundred million dollars' worth of advertising now will save five hundred million dollars in legal expenses and aggravation later. That's the general idea."

The ad started with a black screen. "Amazing Grace" played softly on bagpipes in the background. The first image cut in: an American flag flying on a white flagpole in front of a sun-dappled, white clapboard rural schoolhouse. The flag's red, white, and blue billowed gently in the wind.

Then, footage from a series of well-known scenes appeared on the screen. The U.S. Olympic hockey team winning the gold medal in 1980 at Lake Placid. Firefighters emerging covered in blood and dust from the burned-out World Trade Center. FDR walking on leg braces across the deck of the USS *Quincy* on the way to the Yalta summit. A marine walking down a dusty street holding hands with a young Iraqi child.

Then, former presidents Bill Clinton and George H. W. Bush, standing next to each other against a black backdrop.

"What does KKB-Anson mean to me?" asks Clinton. "KKB-Anson means gasoline that comes from our allies and not our enemies. KKB-Anson means an American energy company, a company committed to freedom, a company that might, just might, end our reliance on Middle East oil."

"What does KKB-Anson mean to America?" asks Bush. "KKB-Anson means hope. Hope for the future. Hope for our children. Hope for peace in our time."

Then the camera cuts to a young blond-haired girl of ten or eleven. She walks across a field of blond wheat. She holds the hand of her father, a pleasant-looking young man in a flannel shirt and jeans. In the background, the red barn of an Iowa farm looks hazy in the late-summer light. The young girl's pigtails dangle behind her ears. Freckles dot her cheeks.

"My daddy works for KKB-Anson," the girl says proudly as the camera zooms slowly in on her face. "He's my hero."

Then a final image of the flag flying in front of the schoolhouse. The camera moves off the flag and focuses in on one of the windows.

The point of view moves inside the classroom, filled with young boys and girls.

"KKB-Anson," they all yell enthusiastically. *"America's* energy company!"

Badenhausen's assistant flipped the light switch on. Badenhausen hit a button on the remote and the shades lifted back up, revealing the cold December sky. The room was silent.

After a minute of silence, Anson cleared his throat. "Wow."

"That's why we pay this guy so much money," said Marks.

"Actually," Badenhausen said, "this one's on me. That's how much I believe in what you guys are doing."

"That's not necessary."

"Your money's not good here. I mean it. Your check will get ripped up. And by the way, both Presidents Clinton and Bush feel the same way. They each refused an honorarium."

"That was generous of them," said Marks.

"You're a hero for what you're trying to do. This isn't about profits or personal glory. This is about something bigger."

Marks sat back and smiled. He was silent for a few moments. He appeared slightly uncomfortable, even embarrassed.

"No, you're right about that. It's not about profits."

"What *is* it about then?" Badenhausen asked. "You're going to get that question. The harder we pound the patriotic theme, the more it begs the question of why a company cares about anything other than the profits."

Marks sat in silence. "If they ask, I'll be ready."

Badenhausen leaned forward and refilled the empty champagne glasses. He looked to Nick Anson. "So what do you think? *America's energy company.* Keeping America free from Middle East oil. Can you repeat that about a hundred times?" he asked with a smile.

"I think I can handle that," said Anson as he reached for his glass and the three men shared a long laugh.

The next morning, Marks and Anson rang the opening bell at the New York Stock Exchange, the two executives clearly enjoying their time together. Marks even invited Anson and his wife, Annie, to his ski house in Aspen that weekend, an invitation Anson found himself, to his surprise, accepting. The mood on the floor of the stock exchange, and throughout the day, was celebratory.

After opening up trading on Wall Street, the two men held a press conference off the floor of the stock exchange. Present was a room full of reporters from various news outlets; ABC, CBS, NBC, CNN, Fox, Bloomberg, MSNBC, *The Wall Street Journal*, Reuters, *The Financial Times*, *The New York Times*, and a variety of others.

The two executives stayed on theme throughout the press conference.

"Won't this merger create a company that controls a substantial portion of the energy that is produced and consumed in a large section of the U.S.?" Sara Jamison from NBC pressed Marks halfway through the press conference.

"I'm glad you asked that," said Marks. "What this announcement is really about is keeping America free from Middle East oil."

"Isn't it dangerous to give that kind of power to one company?" followed Jamison. "To one man?"

"Dangerous is relying on oil from suppliers who do not have our best interests at heart," said Marks. "Dangerous is depending on others for one of the most critical products used in your daily life. Would you buy a bottle of water from someone who doesn't have your best interest at heart, someone who might in fact be an enemy? A loaf of bread?"

"Do you anticipate any problems getting support from members of Congress, the SEC, or the Federal Trade Commission?" asked Bill Radford from *The Wall Street Journal*.

"When you're creating a company that helps America become independent of Middle East petroleum, I think that's something most citizens will rally around," Anson shot back.

After half an hour of similarly predictable questions, the reporters started to slow down and prepare for the press conference to end. A young female reporter in the back stood up. She had auburn hair, and a yellow cable knit sweater.

"Hi. Astrid Smith, *Baltimore Sun*."

"Good morning, Astrid," said Marks. "What's your question?"

"You say this is all about creating independence from the Middle East, right? But is that really your concern? Shouldn't you be concerned with profits? With financial performance? I mean, my grandparents own KKB stock. They rely on you to create the dividend that allows them to live comfortably in their retirement."

The room was silent. The question Badenhausen had warned of had come. Everyone looked at Marks. He took a few steps to the right, silently, looking down as he walked, deep in thought. He glanced at Badenhausen, who stood against the wall to the side of the room. Marks's limp was visible as he walked. After a moment of silence, he looked at the young woman who'd asked him the question.

"Great question," Marks said after several moments. "Oh, we'll make money. I can assure you of that. Your grandparents can continue to sleep at night. But no, it isn't just about the money. For me, it never was. It never will be. Of course, if I didn't make money for the shareholders of this company, the board of directors would fire me. But so far they haven't needed to. We've done pretty well. You know, I think sometimes it's the guys like Nick and me who don't care so much about the money that end up being pretty good at making it."

Marks paused and smiled. He waited a few moments, looking at the crowd of reporters, then back to the young reporter.

"I fought in Vietnam," Marks said, looking past the wall of cameras and reporters to the young woman. "I almost died there. An Irishman from Boston named Henry O'Brien saved my life. I vowed if I ever had a son, I wouldn't let him die in a meaningless war. I had one child. A son. We named him Henry. I used to call him Hank, God bless his soul."

Marks paused. He walked back to the center of the stage. He turned back toward the reporters, who remained silent, mesmerized by Marks, waiting to see where he would take this clearly unrehearsed moment.

"On August 22, 2006, Hank was killed in Iraq, shot in the chest in a meaningless war, all because the rest of us needed gasoline for our cars. I failed to protect my son. America failed to protect its sons and daughters.

I swore then, if I ever had the ability, I'd do whatever I could to make it so nobody else had to collect their son's remains like I did, picking them up at the airport in a wooden box because the rest of us need our gasoline."

The KKB-Anson merger was the lead story on every network that evening. Badenhausen's positioning worked, and so did Marks's answer. The emphasis on the KKB-Anson deal wasn't about the financial terms of the transaction. The proposed merger wasn't discussed in terms of cost synergies, putting two companies together in order to find duplicative cost centers, like employees, who would then be terminated. The deal had a larger logic to it, a marriage of complementary energy sources, and of supply and demand. But most of all, it was about American energy independence. Several members of Congress, and even the president of the United States, hailed the deal. Marks was celebrated as an American hero.

But in another office high in the Manhattan skyline, the mood was neither patriotic nor happy. In the penthouse floor of a sterile-looking steel and black glass skyscraper at Fifty-first Street and Madison Avenue, the announcement of the KKB-Anson merger was not only expected, it was long overdue.

A young man not more than thirty-six years old sat behind his desk staring at the flat-screen television in front of him.

Alexander Fortuna was handsome, disarmingly so. He looked Mediterranean, with a tan glow to his skin, a perfect nose. His eyes were dark black pools. Their depth had a sinister quality, a dangerous aspect that, when framed against the beauty of the man's face, became somehow disarming. His clothing was impeccable, expensive, custom. A dark blue button-down was tucked into white corduroy pants, formal looking yet casual. He wore his black hair slightly long, down to the top of his shoulders.

Alexander Fortuna had been waiting for this moment. Like a hand on a light switch, the merger announcement caused him to flip on. It was time. The years of careful planning were over. It was his turn to act.

"America's energy company," Fortuna said aloud, to no one in particular, as he watched replays of Marks's press conference on the screen, over and over.

Standing up, he walked to the window and looked to the north. He could see Central Park in the distance, his favorite view.

"America's energy company," he whispered to himself.

9

On the eighty-eighth floor of a skyscraper in the Canary Wharf section of London, a young man sat at a desk of polished steel. It spread out in front of the big window and was at least eight feet long. Four flat screens shone with spreadsheets and colored, fine-print numbers and figures.

Derek Langley was a thirty-two-year-old trader for a hedge fund called Passwood-Regent. One of the two phones on the desk rang.

"Langley," he said as he picked up the phone.

"Hi, Derek. It's me."

"Alexander," said Langley. "Hi."

"How are you?" asked Fortuna.

"Super, thank you, sir."

"Are you ready?"

"I am."

"As we've discussed, I want us to begin aggregating within U.S. energy equities. I want us to buy KKB and Anson, but not a lot, perhaps one hundred and fifty to two hundred million dollars' worth. The rest I want in direct competitors; electricity suppliers, distributors, especially in the eastern part of the U.S. Put at least half and up to two-thirds of Passwood-Regent assets into KKB and Anson Energy competitors."

"Yes, sir. Understood. Southern Company. Duke Power. ConEdison. Entergy."

"Exactly. Start buying oil stocks, too. Use whatever long instruments you feel most appropriate; calls, options, swaps, swaptions, whatever. Nothing that will be too hard to get out of. Lever it up. Press your margin. I trust your judgment. I assume it'll be predominantly straight block trades."

"Yes. I think we can accomplish this without having to do anything overly fancy."

"I want you to make some commodity bets. Allocate at least a quarter billion to oil futures. Currency too. I want us to short the hell out of the Colombian peso. At least two hundred and fifty million."

"Got it."

"Finally, most importantly, I don't need to tell you this, but—"

"Don't aggregate more than five percent of any single company."

"Precisely. We don't want to file a Thirteen D. Don't go anywhere near it."

"Passwood will not own more than five percent of any single company. We won't need to."

"Good. The announcement was a few minutes ago. Did you see it?"

"I did, sir."

"How much do we have in the different Passwood-Regent accounts? I'm including any current long positions, which you'll have to get liquid."

"That's already taken care of. As of last night, we have approximately three point six billion dollars liquid, sitting in cash."

"Invest across the Passwood-Regent entities. Use them all. Spread this around. Don't place too much in any one trade. Self-impose at twenty-five or thirty million dollars per trade. Ideal trade size would be twenty million dollars."

"Got it. How much time do I have?"

"Twenty-four hours."

Langley's receiver went dead. He smiled and took a sip from his coffee cup.

The morning after the announcement of the proposed merger between KKB and Anson Energy, Langley went on a $3.6 billion buying spree. Working feverishly, camped out at his office, he quickly established a series of positions in companies that were direct competitors to KKB and Anson, in oil futures, and in shorts against the Colombian peso. By the end of the trading day, Langley had executed more than 150 trades across fourteen separate Passwood-Regent entities, none of them U.S.-based. About a quarter billion dollars went toward the purchase of KKB and Anson stock.

Fortuna repeated his phone call to Langley twice that same day, once to a young female trader named Orieshe Yang in Hong Kong, at a hedge fund called PBX Fund; the other call to a Wall Street fund called Kallivar, and a trader named Sheldon Karl.

By evening, on three different continents, across three different hedge funds, more than $8 billion had been invested in companies that were direct competitors to KKB and Anson Energy. More than a billion and a half dollars had purchased a smorgasbord of oil contracts. At least half a billion dollars lay in a variety of trades betting the Colombian peso would drop in value.

To make it appear they weren't excluding anyone, half a billion dollars sat in either KKB or Anson Energy stock.

One man controlled Passwood-Regent, PBX Fund, and Kallivar: Alexander Fortuna.

When his three hedge fund managers informed him, in three separate phone calls on the morning after the announcement, that their funds were fully invested as instructed, Fortuna left his office, walked briskly up Madison Avenue for sixteen blocks, then took a left into Central Park. Near the Sixty-fourth Street entrance, he came to the Central Park Zoo. There, he bought a ticket and proceeded straight to the popular polar bear exhibit, where he picked up a pay phone and dialed a number.

"Yes," said the voice.

"It's done. Go ahead as planned."

10

SAVAGE ISLAND PROJECT

Terry Savoy looked out the window of the silver Gulfstream G500. He hadn't been to Savage Island in more than a year. Normally, a death wouldn't be reason enough to make the trip. After all, many men died at Savage Island. But this was different. This was Jake White.

The flight to Savage Island Project was a ballbuster. Windy, with an approach to the landing strip that required a steep drop from 10,000 feet in order to avoid wind shear off the Hudson Strait. At least the Gulfstream was comfortable, and fast, one of four KKB company jets.

Savoy had received the call from Ted Marks's assistant, Ashley, the night before.

"Ted wants you to go up there," Ashley said after telling him about Jake's death. "He said Jake called him last week. He was worried about something. Ted wants you to go see what happened."

"Did he say what he was worried about?"

"No. Ted didn't speak with him. He just left him a voice mail. Nothing specific."

So, Teddy Marks gets a phone call, Jake White dies, and Terry Savoy has to interrupt his vacation to fly to the Labrador Sea in the middle of winter.

"Don't put it down yet!" Savoy said to George Kimball, the pilot-in-command, after getting up from the big leather seat in the cabin and entering the cockpit. "Circle a few times over the dam, as close as you can get."

"It's dark out. We're not going to see much."

"Radio ahead and tell them to turn the lights on, anything they have. Light it up."

Savoy was KKB's security chief. He had oversight of all security at the company's facilities. Investigating White's death fell into a category of responsibility he claimed to dislike, but in reality it was what kept him interested in his job. Most of Savoy's work was numbingly routine: setting up security protocols for each facility, managing people at those facilities according to those protocols, creating screening processes for hiring employees, and establishing facility-perimeter controls. In other words, the job was boring. After a career in the U.S. Army Rangers, the private sector represented easy street, a way finally to make some money and play a lot of golf. But he paid for it, in effect, in boredom. For this reason he welcomed the chance to see and do something more challenging.

"We're coming up on the dam," Kimball said.

Savoy stood behind the young second-in-command and put on a set of Bose headset. The plane flew a few hundred feet above the pines, which formed a carpet of green in every direction. Soon, in the distance, the lights of Savage Island Project came into view.

From the air, the engineering challenge that the company had overcome was evident. The dam stood like a shield, a trapezoid-shaped wall of cement, stone, and steel more than half a mile high, an engineering marvel in the middle of nowhere. It cast its gargantuan height down upon the man-made lake beneath and the workers' village. It was an intimidating sight.

The halogen lights of the dam climbed vertically like a ladder and emblazoned the back wall in yellow light. The lights ran out across the top of the structure horizontally and lit up the observation platform. The plane closed in on the massive wall then screamed over the granite precipice. Suddenly, they were out over the waters of the Labrador Sea.

Savoy shook his head. "Shit," he whispered.

A few minutes later and a couple of more passes over the facility, the jet landed at the airstrip. A white Chevy Suburban was waiting for Savoy.

"Evening, Arnie," Savoy said to Mijailovic as he climbed in.

The facility's security director shook his hand. "How was the flight?"

"Not bad. How's everyone doing up here?"

"Oh, you know, a little shocked."

"I can imagine."

"I've got you at the guesthouse. You want to go there now?"

"No," said Savoy. "I want to see the body."

They passed through two sets of gates and entered the outer perimeter of Savage Island Project. Mijailovic and Savoy showed their IDs at both entrances, despite the fact that the guards worked for them, and despite the fact that Mijailovic had exited through the same gates less than ten minutes before.

Savoy liked the fact they made him take out his badge.

The SUV pulled into a small concrete building next to the dam the size of a convenience store, the hospital.

Savoy found White's corpse laid out on a metal shelf in the hospital's morgue. The room was chilled to near freezing, but it didn't compete with the frigid air outdoors. He walked around the perimeter of the metal table, staring at the corpse. He'd seen plenty of dead men before; this was by far the grisliest.

White was overweight and that was accentuated by the water his body had retained during the drowning. His right leg was gone, ripped off midthigh, a rough and uneven cut, presumably sliced off by one of the big rotors through which he'd been pulled. Half of White's skull was sliced off at the top, exposing brain tissue. White's left arm was also torn off, at the shoulder, a cleaner cut with puffy yellow hunks of fat showing under the skin.

"Have we notified his family?" Savoy asked.

"Not yet. We'll do that today. Not that he really had a family, as such. Wife left him, sons wouldn't speak to him."

"They should know anyway. Unless they object, we should probably bury him somewhere out here, in the woods someplace. I think he would've wanted that. It's your call. You knew him better than anyone."

Savoy walked out of the hospital. Although he didn't show it, he was shaken by sight of White's corpse.

He went to the guesthouse and took a shower then walked to the administration building, a two-story concrete box at the base of the dam. Savoy spent several hours poring through White's office. It turned out to be an interesting expedition, not because he found anything, but because it reminded him why White was able to do all that he did. He was an unbelievably well-organized manager. Every piece of paper was filed, on a yearly basis, by subject, alphabetically, going back five years. Whatever wasn't filed was in one of three neat stacks on his desk. In the middle of the desk was an old IBM computer.

Savoy spent some time on the computer, though it was clear the old machine hadn't been used in a while.

"Box this up and ship it to New York City," he said to Mijailovic. "Send it to a guy named Pillsbury in IT."

"Will do."

"Also, send down the filing cabinets for the last five years. Send them to my office."

"Got it."

The bottom drawer of the desk contained pens, paper clips, tape. The middle drawer had several cartons of Marlboro cigarettes and a few ashtrays, plus some matches. In the top drawer were photographs. Many of the dam in different phases of construction. One photo showed White with Marks, taken at the ribbon-cutting ceremony for the dam. There were three photographs of his sons standing next to White on a fishing trip somewhere.

Another showed his ex-wife, a plain-looking woman with short brown hair, smiling shyly at the camera.

Savoy wasn't a detective. He was a security expert. But he didn't see any signs of desperation here.

As dawn approached, he asked Vida, Jake's assistant, for some Advil.

"Did you see anything funny going on with Jake in the past month or so?" he asked when she brought Advil and a bottle of water.

"Nothing out of the ordinary," she said.

Savoy looked across the room at Mijailovic.

"He called Ted Marks last week," said Savoy. "Were you aware of that?"

"No. But it wouldn't surprise me. They were close. They used to be close."

"Can you run the HR files for me?" Savoy asked Vida. "Go back a year. See if there were any disciplinary cases."

"I'd be aware of them," said Mijailovic.

"I still want it done," said Savoy. Then he softened his tone. "Look, in all likelihood this was an accident. Jake fell off the dam and drowned. Got pulled through one of the turbines and thrown out the other side. Tragic and innocent. But that doesn't mean I'm not going to look at *everything*, including the files."

"I'll run those right now," said Vida.

"I also want to take a walk through the dam," said Savoy.

Savoy and Mijailovic stepped out of the small administration building. It felt even more bitterly cold outside now. The wind howled from the east and came off the Labrador Sea with a vengeance.

"God*damn*, it's cold up here!" Savoy yelled.

"Won't get above zero today. Wind chill makes it feel a lot worse than it is."

Savoy looked to his left at the hundreds of neat, drab gray concrete houses where workers and their families lived.

He looked up at the dam. It stood above the small village visibly from every vantage point, water cascading through its powerful turbines. Even standing at the facility's base, the sound of the turbines was incredibly loud. Though the big river of water shot out less than two hundred feet from where they stood, one could hardly hear the sound of the rushing water over the turbine roar.

Savoy and Mijailovic walked to the dam entrance. They displayed their security badges to the guard and placed their thumbs on a small black screen.

"Take these," Mijailovic said. He handed him a set of headphones. "You'll be deaf in an hour without them."

They climbed onto the steel cage elevator. Mijailovic moved a yellow latch to send it to the top of the structure. They looked out the side as they moved up past floor upon floor of turbine rows. The dam had exactly fifty floors, and each floor was exactly sixty feet high. Each floor was a dim, cavernous pocket that housed four massive turbines.

As the elevator climbed, Savoy stared in disbelief through the grate. He'd seen the turbines before, but his memory didn't do it justice. Caged in polymer steel behind a thick shelf of transparent carbonate plastic, each turbine stood twenty feet high, a massive churning drum of six rotor blades. These churned like jet propellers in speeds directly proportional to the amount of water running through.

Each turbine had at least one man monitoring it at all times, standing at the side of the polymer casing and inspecting the individual rotors for problems. One broken rotor, they knew, if not discovered immediately, could destroy the entire piece of hardware. Each custom-built turbine cost nearly $50 million to replace, not to mention lost revenue from electricity that couldn't be generated.

At full capacity, the blades hummed loudly and were invisible, a whirring rush of metal cranking around as millions of gallons of water pulsated through. The sight of one of these machines was amazing. The sight of four in a row was spectacular. The thought of two hundred of them was hard to contemplate.

They exited the elevator at the top of the dam and walked into the operations center. Theoretically at least, the room was soundproof. Savoy and Mijailovic took off their headphones. You could still hear the tremendous noise of the dam, but at least now you could have a conversation.

This was the main operations center for Savage Island Project, housed in a room that looked like mission control at NASA. Nine technicians per shift kept watch over computer screens under a massive, thirty-foot flat-screen graphic display depicting the real-time operation of all two hundred turbines. In the background, the loud pounding noise of the rushing water was everywhere. None of the technicians seemed to notice.

Savoy and Mijailovic walked past the engineers and Savoy opened the steel door to the outside. They ascended the stairwell in the back of the room and went to the observation deck.

The noise, outside of the soundproof operations center, was again deafening.

Savoy and Mijailovic stared at the violent Labrador Sea. The wind ripped across the great plain of water into their faces. The vast expanse of sea spread east to the horizon. Savoy walked to the other side of the dam, stepped to the edge, and peered over the side. The sky dropped in a curved cement plain to the running river formed by the through water. The line of houses next to the river was visible but tiny, like dollhouses.

"He washed up down there," Mijailovic yelled over the noise, pointing to the shoreline below the town. "This is probably where he fell from."

Or jumped, Savoy thought. *At least that's what I'd do if I had to live in this fucking place.* Savoy zipped his parka and pulled the hood around his head. He stood at the east edge of the deck for a few minutes, staring at the sea.

"You want to go back in?" Mijailovic yelled after a minute.

"I'm going to walk the deck!" yelled Savoy. "You go ahead."

"What are you looking for?"

"How the hell should I know?"

Savoy stepped quickly across the cement, toward the far end of the facility and Mijailovic followed. They walked for several minutes. As they approached the unprotected central part of the dam, the wind picked up in intensity and ripped across the open plain, nearly knocking them over. They saw nothing.

When they got back to the northern entrance to the dam, they descended the stairs and walked back into the operations center. In a conference room at the far corner of the operations center, Savoy sat at the table and removed his parka.

"Just so you know, I had two men walk the roof this morning," said Mijailovic. "I've also done two sweeps of every floor in the facility."

"What about a head count?" Savoy rubbed his hands together, trying to get warm.

"Done that. Every worker is accounted for."

"Were they all here?"

"Here or on leave. As you know, we go four months on, one off. There are always some guys on leave."

"Did you speak with the ones on leave?"

"What would be the purpose of that?" Mijailovic asked, obviously a little perturbed.

"The purpose is following protocol. A man is dead. We don't know what happened. Any time there's even the slightest chance of foul play, the rule book says full staff interviews, even those on leave. According to the protocol, they're all supposed to be reachable."

"Got it."

"I also want to see the full list of workers, ages, nationalities, et cetera."

"Okay."

Savoy looked at Mijailovic as he removed his parka. "Remember, Jake left Marks an odd message. That's the main reason I'm being a hard-ass about this, all right? Besides, what else you got to do?"

"I'll go run a manifest. You want coffee?"

"I can get it. Is there a kitchen up here?"

"Down the hall. Head's down there too."

"Got it."

While Mijailovic found an empty computer, Savoy went to the kitchen. A pot of coffee sat half filled on the warmer. Savoy poured a cup and walked back to the main control room.

As he walked behind the engineers, Savoy took a long look at the big plasma screen in front of the room. He stood behind one of the men at the computer terminal, studying the complex array of lights that monitored turbine activity. He took a sip from his coffee cup. "Jesus, this stuff tastes like shit."

"He's drinking the coffee," one of the engineers said. The others laughed.

"That's probably been sitting there a week," said another man.

"Tastes like it," said Savoy. "No wonder you guys are such a joy to be around."

They laughed again.

Savoy pointed to a row of lights that were flashing orange.

"What's that row of lights?" he asked.

The engineer in front of Savoy turned and looked at him.

"First tier," he said. "Been down almost two months. Problems with three of the four turbines."

"Is there someone there right now?"

"Might be. Don't know."

"It's pretty standard stuff," added one of the engineers. "There hasn't been a time since I've been here that at least one turbine hasn't been off-line."

"What exactly's wrong with them?" Savoy asked.

None of the engineers responded.

He turned to Mijailovic, who'd just come in with a stack of print-outs.

"Does anyone know why the hell these turbines are down?" Savoy pointed again, this time with a hint of anger, at the screen.

"No, sir," said the engineer in front of him.

"It would've been a Jake project," said Mijailovic.

Savoy shook his head in disbelief. "Well, now it's a Terry and Arnie project."

"Here's the FTE manifest. There are six people on leave. I've called all six."

"You made contact?"

"I made contact with all six."

"Okay. Let me glance this over." Savoy pulled a pair of glasses out of his pocket and put them on. "Then we can go look at those first-tier turbines on the way out of here."

After a few minutes, Mijailovic cleared his throat. "Find anything interesting?"

Savoy didn't respond. He was focused on one sheet of paper in particular. He held the paper in one hand as he flipped through the small stack with the other hand.

"Who is Mirin Chaltoum?"

"He's a maintenance guy. Big fellow, strong. Nice kid."

"Hmm. I see Vida ran the manifest against the HR database," said Savoy. "You know, the disciplinary files."

71

"Like I said, I knew about all discipline cases," said Mijailovic. "Even if it wasn't reported, Jake would've mentioned it to me. Especially if he had a serious problem with someone."

"What's a 'blue file'?" asked Savoy.

"A blue file? It means Jake has concerns about someone's behavior, work ethic, attitude, suspicions, that sort of thing. Jake's supposed to send any straight to me, but I haven't had a blue file in more than a year."

"He put a blue file on Mirin Chaltoum two weeks ago."

"It says that in the file?" Mijailovic paled. "Any specific notes?"

"No, nothing. Do you know someone named Amman? He lives with him."

"I know who he is, that's all. Also in maintenance."

"They started work here the same month, three years ago."

"Maybe they're friends."

"It says here he's from Spain. The other's from Saudi Arabia."

"So? You know what it takes to get people willing to come to this place? Jake advertises all over the world."

"You're missing the point. I'm not saying anyone did anything to Jake. I still believe he fell. Or who knows, maybe he killed himself. The point is, no matter what you *think*, you can't just ignore other things. Like two guys starting work the same month, living together, both Middle Eastern, one of them with a new blue file."

"The blue file I get, but these are far from our only Middle Easterners."

"Really? Have you ever counted how many?"

"No."

"Well, while you were taking a crap, I did. You have exactly three. These two, and one other guy, an engineer who's fifty-five years old and has been with KKB for twenty-eight years. I think we can probably trust him."

Savoy stood.

"So what do you want to do?" asked Mijailovic.

"I think one of us should go walk the idle turbines, see what's up. The other should go interview these guys in person. We probably won't find a goddamn thing, Arnie. I'll be the first to admit that. But I have to look. That's my job. And yours."

"I know. You're right. I don't mean to be difficult. It's been a hell of a day."

Together they took the elevator down to the first row of turbines.

"What do you want," asked Savoy, "turbines or Mr. Blue File?"

"I'll look at the turbines," said Mijailovic. "I know my way around in there pretty well."

"Sounds good," said Savoy. "See you back at the ranch."

In a small modular house in the village, two young maintenance workers, Mirin and Amman, put their coats on and walked to the dam. A frozen dirt road led to the front entrance of the dam, where they took turns touching their thumbs to a black screen.

"Hey, guys," the guard said. "First turbine?"

Mirin, the older of the pair, nodded and handed the guard a slip of paper.

Mirin and Amman entered the elevator. At the first floor, they stepped off and removed their bright yellow parkas, leaving them on the ground. They passed the first three turbines, and at the fourth they stopped. Amman placed the large red toolbox on the ground.

The two looked at each other as they pulled the tarp down off the turbine column.

Mirin ran his left hand down the column, looking for the seam. Near the middle of the turbine column, he found a slight ridge in the metal. He turned toward Amman. "I need the drill."

"Yes, yes," Amman said. He reached into the toolbox. "Here."

Mirin took the drill and began removing the bolts that held the steel plate in place. There were more than a hundred of them. For the next twenty minutes, he moved down the hull of the turbine, sweating profusely, nervous sweat. Finally, he finished removing the last of the bolts.

"Knife."

Amman opened the toolbox, pulled out a box cutter, and handed it to Mirin, who gently inserted it in the manifold's seam, cutting away the epoxy liner. He popped the casing open. The two men pushed the heavy casing to the side, then looked at each other. Despite the inactive turbines, the noise of the dam filled the space. The younger of the two men, Amman, wanted to say something, but Mirin shook his head. He walked toward him and hugged him. Then he stepped back and placed his hands on Amman's shoulders. He stared into Amman's eyes.

"It's time, Amman. Mother would be proud."

11

CAPITANA TERRITORY

Capitana was strangely quiet.

Eight hours had passed since Dewey had put every Middle Easterner aboard the *Montana* for transport to Buenaventura. All pumping operations had been shuttered. It would take at least another day to calm the rig down after two days of bloodshed, never mind getting it back to full production.

In his office, Dewey took down the bottle of Jack Daniel's and took a gulp. It was almost three in the morning. He could use a good night's sleep, but it wasn't likely to come tonight. He lay back on the bed with the bottle and a sheaf of faxed pages that had come through several hours before. The moment he began reading, he sat up straight, put aside the bottle, and turned on his bedside lamp. It was a press release:

KKB TO ACQUIRE ANSON ENERGY IN $67 BILLION DEAL; HISTORIC MERGER WILL CREATE WORLD'S SECOND-LARGEST ENERGY COMPANY

(New York, New York)—U.S. energy conglomerate KKB has agreed to acquire Dallas-based oil giant Anson Energy in a $67 billion deal that will create the world's second-largest energy company.

Ted Marks, CEO of KKB, stated: "Through this historic merger, KKB-Anson will be building the largest energy company in America. Most importantly, all of KKB-Anson's products will come from sources outside of the Middle East, ensuring that our customers, employees, and shareholders do not directly or indirectly create financial profits for opponents of American policy. . . ."

Dewey had read about Marks. He'd been in the Navy, fought in Vietnam. Dewey had also read about Marks's crusade to end America's reliance on Middle East oil. Now he was doing it. And in the middle of it all sat Capitana. Dewey shook his head. Talk about awful timing. What would Marks think when he heard about Capitana's sudden shutdown? Dewey was too tired even to contemplate that.

As he lay back, he felt the rig move, enough to make him sit up again. *A wave*, he thought. He reclined once more, taking another sip from the bottle. A noise echoed down the hallway outside his room. He stood and flipped on the main light switch in his cabin. Everything was silent except for the occasional bell or door slamming somewhere on the rig, the ocean patting the tide deck, the wind. Maybe he was getting paranoid from all of the mayhem of the last forty-eight hours. Still, whatever it was, it alarmed him enough to make him walk to the far end of the cabin and look out the window.

What he saw caused him to shudder.

There, against the side of the rig, stood the dark silhouette of a ship, its running lights shut off. He recognized the profile of the vessel. It was the *Montana*.

He walked to the dresser and took his knife from the top drawer. Dressed only in his Carhartts, he walked to the small closet and opened the door. He took out a gray T-shirt and put it on. Then he heard it. The sound of footsteps. Steel-toed boots coming down the corridor to his cabin. He tensed. He felt the warmth of adrenaline in his veins.

The door flew open and Dewey found himself facing four armed gunmen with rifles trained on him. One was Pazur, the murderer of Jonas Pierre; he'd been put aboard the *Montana* with the others, specifically to face charges in Cali.

76

From behind the gunmen stepped Esco. "Drop the knife," he ordered.

Dewey held on to the knife for a moment more, despite the command, and eyed the gunmen. One of the men raised a rifle and aimed it at his head. *Kalashnikov*, Dewey's soldier's brain registered automatically. The gunman fired a round over his shoulder. It ripped a hole in the wall next to the bed.

He tossed the knife to the ground, where it slid beneath the desk. "Where's Pablo?"

Esco walked between the gunmen. He stood in front of Dewey, confident but serious, quietly staring at him.

"Dead," said Esco.

Dewey looked at the gunmen again. He knew he'd regret what he was about to do, but he couldn't help himself. Without warning, he delivered two quick, ferocious punches to Esco's ribs and a right hook to his left eye. Esco collapsed as his gunmen lunged at Dewey, the one to his right striking first, with the butt end of his gun to the side of his head. A gunman to his left kicked Dewey squarely in the groin, folding him in pain. A third man swung at his face and nailed him above his eye, which began to bleed. All four of the men pounded away at him as he descended to the floor in pain from the blows.

"Stop," Esco ordered from behind them after nearly a minute. "We need him alive."

Dewey turned his head slightly and opened his eyes. He was looking straight ahead at Esco's boots.

"Lift him up," Esco said.

Two of the gunmen reached down and picked Dewey up. They placed his arms around their necks and got ready to lead him away.

"You'll pay," Dewey muttered as he stared at Esco.

Esco stepped forward and delivered a last sharp kick to the balls.

They tied his hands behind his back, then stuck a rag in his mouth to gag him. Then the gunmen led Dewey down the corridor to the main deck of Capitana.

Despite the arrival of the armed men, despite the violence of the past days, nothing prepared him for what he saw next. Bodies lay piled at different points on the deck, now dimly illuminated by the sunrise to the east. He counted more than two dozen corpses strewn about. Rage began to replace Dewey's initial shock. As they walked near the edge of the platform, he saw yet more corpses floating in the waters off the platform, then Pablo's corpse lying face-up on the deck.

They led him to the infirmary. Inside, the body of Chaz Barbo lay awkwardly contorted on the ground. His head had been blown off.

The two gunmen threw Dewey to the floor. One of them had a chain and he took it and fastened him to the steel pole at the edge of the room, so that he couldn't get away or even move. They left the room and closed the door.

Dewey sat in a daze. After several minutes, he was able to spit the rag from his mouth. He could taste blood.

Only once in his life had he ever been in a situation worse than this. That was in Panama. He'd been one of the ones in early, sent to kill Manuel Noriega more than a year before Operation Just Cause. They'd gotten trapped in an apartment building down the street from where they knew the dictator was sleeping with one of his mistresses. Some kid in the building tipped off Noriega's men and what was supposed to be a surgical infiltration turned into a shitstorm. Noriega's goons surrounded the apartment building and slowly worked their way concentrically inward, moving in and slowly strangling off Dewey and the four other Deltas on his team. They were saved by the Navy and a pair of F/A-18 Hornets, which came in at four hundred feet and leveled the buildings on either side of the one they were in with AGM-65s. Two Deltas survived, including Dewey.

The Navy wasn't going to save his ass this time.

Dewey closed his eyes and tried to think. Is this what Mackie had tried to tell him? Whatever Esco had been planning had taken years. And for some reason, a living and functioning Dewey Andreas mattered to their plan.

The pumping station. The seabed. The key to Capitana. They needed Dewey to access the main pumping station. This was the most vulnerable part of Capitana, the link to the oil reservoir.

There were two ways to access the pumping station. One was to use a code generated in Dallas upon orders from the CEO of the company. The other was by having Dewey's eyes read by the iris scanner at its entrance at the seafloor.

Something told him they wouldn't be calling Dallas for the code.

Dewey had spent months learning how to be a prisoner, how to survive, how to escape. When you're a prisoner, what's most important is patience and a willingness to seize opportunities when they present themselves. The amount of risk a prisoner should take in trying to fight or escape is directly proportional to the degree of likelihood you'll be killed once you've served your purpose to your captors. If you're being held for political reasons and will likely be released someday, it's best to be patient and wait. If there's no doubt you'll die, then you find a way to act at the first opportunity. If opportunities don't arise, create them.

He reached up and wiped the blood from his eyes. He wasn't dead yet. *I don't want to die—not here, not now.* He thought of his wife and son, both long dead. He had to live. He had to make his son, wherever he was, proud of him.

He leaned back and waited for the gunmen—or rather, the terrorists—to return.

After an hour, three of them came to retrieve him. Two trained their Kalashnikovs on him as the third unchained him from the pole.

They led him out of the infirmary and across the deck. Bodies were strewn everywhere. As they walked past the hotel, he could hear voices. There were still men alive. One of the gunmen opened the hotel door. They let Dewey inside. Hundreds of his men sat in rows on the floor, hands behind their backs. In front of them, half a dozen gunmen stood with rifles and machine guns at the ready.

From the back, a voice called out.

"Chief," a man yelled. "Don't believe a fucking thing they say!"

"They're going to kill us!" another voice yelled out.

From the side of the room, Esco approached. He looked at Dewey. His left eye had a bandage on it now. Dewey's swing had done serious damage.

"If you want these men to live, we need your help," Esco said.

"Fuck yourself," Dewey said.

Esco nodded at one of the gunmen. He pointed his Uzi at one of the workers seated in the front row. He pulled the trigger and blew off the back of the man's head in a violent burst. Behind him, another man screamed. A bullet had pierced the first man's skull and had exited and then entered the second man's chest. He slumped in agony.

"It's all in your hands, Chief," Esco said with a sickeningly serene smile. He turned to the gunman. "Put him out of his misery," nodding to the man who'd been hit in the chest and continued to scream.

The gunman stepped forward and dispatched him with a single shot. More than one crew member began to sob.

"I'll help you," said Dewey. "Let me say something to them."

"Go ahead."

Dewey stepped forward. "There are hundreds of you!" he shouted. He glanced at Esco. "You want to live, storm the gunmen and kill them!"

He got the words out before Esco hammered him on the side of his head with the butt of his rifle. The room full of roughnecks erupted in yelling and screams as the terrorists hauled Dewey away, but volleys of gunfire silenced the outcry and the doors quickly closed.

They pulled Dewey across the deck, the tip of a rifle pressed hard into his back. The sun was high in the sky, scorching hot as they passed downstairs to the freight riser. It was a hub of activity, at least half a dozen of Esco's men running around. Two of the men were already dressed in deep-sea diving suits. At the side of the deck, on the freight platform, a large steel object nearly six feet high reflected the sunlight: a massive bomb.

So he was right. The seafloor was their destination and the pumping station would be their target.

"Put on the suit," Esco ordered.

They unchained him as two gunmen trained their rifles on him. Dewey slowly pulled the heavy suit on as he looked around the platform. He knew most of the conspirators by name, but he didn't recognize the two men already suited up. They looked ex-military. Operatives, perhaps mercenaries. They certainly weren't members of his crew. They must have come with the *Montana*.

It all added up now. A bitter smile spread across Dewey's mouth as he began to see the thread of the conspiracy laid out before him, the sheer scale of it. And he had missed it all.

If he lived, he would find out who was behind the operation and hunt them down. First he'd kill Pazur. Then Esco. Then their bosses, and *their* bosses. For every one of his men they killed he'd kill a hundred; for every drop of blood, he'd spill a gallon; for all of the pain, he would inflict limitless agony on each of them.

But he had to live to do it.

Under a vicious midmorning sun, Dewey and the two guards strapped the steel deepwater helmets on and took the big open-cage freight elevator down. The helmets were very heavy, made of synthetic steel. The body suits were made of triple-redundant Kevlar on steel frames, all designed to withstand the fierce pressure and bitter cold temperatures of the depths below. Each man was connected to the rig by an oxygen tube that extended down as they descended, their lifeline to the surface, fitted with a communications link and a complex air-pressure equalizer that enabled the men to descend and ascend quickly without the usual acclimation periods that a free diver needs.

As the elevator hit waterside, he looked up one last time. He made eye contact with Esco. Then, the platform plunged beneath the surface.

They descended through the murky water. One guard held an old, high-powered APS underwater assault rifle. The APS was a Russian-made armament developed for Russian combat frogmen. It fired long, dagger-sharp steel darts capable of penetrating most material, certainly Dewey's heavy suit. That was how they'd get rid of him after the scanner read his iris, he guessed

The cage dropped straight down, latched between two of the four oil chutes. Halogen lights every ten yards gave off a dull green hue. After more than ten minutes of steady descent, they reached the ten-pole marker, a red and white flash that indicated that they were ten yards above the seafloor.

Dewey remembered now why he didn't take the trip to the seafloor very often. It was a depressing place. It felt like another planet, a dark and silent place, desolate and uninhabited. The cage hit the bottom with a heavy thud. Led by the rifle-wielding diver, he stepped off the grate and onto the seafloor.

Beneath Capitana, the pipes converged at the pumping station, the last part of Capitana that had been installed. Doing so had required six specially rigged oil tankers, each filled on the outer edge with massive weight to act as ballast as the ships hauled the unit between them three hundred miles from Buenaventura on the Colombian coast. The station alone had cost nearly a billion dollars to build and install. Within its six-story housing sat one of the world's most powerful pumping units. Above the intake unit was the processing system that separated raw oil and natural gas then pumped both up to the surface. This, the heart of the rig and its conduit to the Capitana oil field itself, was what the terrorists wanted to destroy.

Dewey heard the radio in his helmet click. The first words were in Arabic, one of the other divers, reporting to the group above. Esco's voice responded in kind. Then Esco addressed Dewey.

"Chief," Esco said. "Can you hear me?"

"Fuck yourself."

"The temptation in the coming minutes will be to not cooperate with us. I want you to listen carefully."

After a minute, someone screamed, then the sound of gunfire ripped through the earphones.

"That was Haig."

Dewey listened as the screaming continued. Then, another gun blast. The screaming stopped.

"In front of me are approximately twenty men," said Esco. "They're what's left of your precious foremen. Every time you disobey me in the coming minutes, one of them dies. Got it?"

"Yes."

Dewey looked around. As always, he was astonished by the sight of the massive structure. He looked at the windowless, six-story cement and steel box that housed the pumping station. Algae and barnacles now encrusted a good deal of the station. Horizontal ductwork spidered out from the station as far as he could see.

"You two, lift it," one of the divers ordered. Dewey and one of the men lumbered forward and lifted the big boxlike bomb. It was very heavy. They walked it a few feet, then put it down. They had to move it in small increments toward the pumping station door. Finally, they made it and set it down.

"Did he do it?" Esco asked through the radio.

"Yes," said the diver now holding the harpoon rifle.

"What explosives are you using?" Dewey asked.

"None of your business," Esco replied.

"HMX?"

"Mmm, so you know a little of explosives? No, not HMX. Old-school, as you say. Wouldn't do what we need down there."

"Cubane?"

"Closer. It's called octanitrocubane. You won't have heard of it."

As Esco talked, Dewey studied the two divers. One stood at Dewey's height, six foot three. The rifle-carrying one was shorter. The tall one would be a challenge. The shorter one would be easier. As long as they had the APS, however, all bets were off.

Once again he recalled the words from training: *If it's a certainty you'll die, then you have to risk it all.*

"Octanitrocubane," Dewey said. "Sounds interesting. Replace the hydrogen in the cubane with nitrogen."

"Thereby removing the need for oxygen, giving us the ability to do what we're about to do."

"So you blow up the pumping station? Someone rebuilds it. What's the point?"

"It's not about the station, Chief; it's about the field."

"All because you didn't get a raise, Esco?"

The radio crackled with laughter.

"Hardly. Although I'll be the first to say you're a stingy mother-fucker."

"If you didn't smell like a goat I would've paid you more."

"Another good one. Very funny. Though I'll be honest, I didn't appreciate that one."

The sound of gunfire echoed through the earphones.

"That was Caldez," Esco said. "He didn't think much of your joke either."

Dewey's stomach tightened. "I've obeyed every order, you son of a bitch!" he yelled. "You said you wouldn't kill any more of my men!"

"Did I say that? My bad. I don't like being compared to farm animals."

Dewey held his tongue.

"We're at the entrance," the tall diver said.

"It's very simple," said Esco. "We know you're the only person who can open the station. So open it."

Dewey stepped into the small enclosure at the entrance to the pump station. His mind raced. If he refused, they'd start killing men on deck. Ultimately, they'd kill everyone, including him. It would deny the terrorists entry to the pumping station, but detonating the bomb outside might do every bit as much damage anyway.

On the other hand, if he let them in the station, he'd have a certain amount of time before the bomb exploded, the men with him, the men atop the derrick, especially Esco, would need time to escape, assuming this was not a suicide attack. In any case, his men would live a little longer and there'd be at least some chance of saving them.

Of course, once he opened the door, he became immediately expendable.

With no good option, Dewey stepped forward into the enclosure and looked through his visor into the small lens. He held his eyes open for several seconds. With a loud noise, the door to the pump station opened, a series of large halogen lights clicked on automatically and illuminated what looked like a massive factory, with literally hundreds of pipes that twisted their way in different formations around a center tunnel that stood vertically and ran upward toward the surface. Four large turbines which were powered by a set of triple-redundant electric cables from above were bolted to the walls and ceiling above the cobweb of piping.

Seize the opportunity, he thought.

Dewey moved. While his captors stared momentarily at the interior of the pumping station, he stepped through the entry alcove, out of the line of sight of the door, toward the tangle of piping. He broke right, stepping along the cement floor of the station, then ducked against the wall, moving toward the back of the room.

He suddenly heard the frantic words of one of the divers in Arabic over the radio.

As long as Dewey was against the wall, he was vulnerable. If he could make it to the far side of the pipes at the center of the room, it would be difficult for the terrorists to get a clean shot. He kept moving along the wall, but looked back, seeing the tip of the rifle emerge from the side of the entrance, now more than twenty feet from where he crouched. The shorter diver was following him, moving in for a shot. More frantic words from the diver echoed on the radio. Suddenly, Esco's voice barked into the radio, also in Arabic, interrupting the diver. Dewey pressed forward, then turned. He watched as the diver turned, stepped back toward the door. Esco had told the diver to stop. *The bomb.* It was the bomb that had brought them down here. Dewey was now expendable.

Dewey watched from the back of the station as the diver slung the rifle over his shoulder and the pair struggled to move the bomb into place. Dewey sidled to the back of the station, where he knew lay his only chance of survival. There he came upon a large black locker. He pulled the door open, revealing an underwater welding unit, a pair of emergency air tanks that could be attached to the valve at the waist belt of the Kevlar suit, and a long combat knife.

He picked up the knife and stuck it in his suit's utility belt, then slipped back into the forest of pipes.

Esco barked more words in Arabic, then cleared his throat and let out a maniacal laugh. "Chief," he said, reverting to English. "In case I don't have the chance to say this in person, I want to thank you for your help. Your mother would be proud of you."

Then Dewey felt it. Imperceptible at first, like a puff of cold wind. He felt the air tug at his lungs. The feeling grew stronger, until he understood what was happening. He was no longer getting air from his tube. He yanked at the air tube that connected to his steel helmet.

"Is that you I hear coughing, Chief?" asked Esco, laughing. "Just swim to the surface. There's plenty of air up here." The sound of his chuckle rattled in the helmet.

They'd left the communications link intact but shut off the oxygen line. The good news was that the diving suit's air valve had a safety catch to prevent pressurized seawater from rushing into his suit and crushing and drowning him simultaneously. The bad news, he had no air. Within a few minutes, he'd pass out. Soon after that he'd suffocate within his mask. He knew he couldn't scale the ladder in time.

Suddenly, Dewey felt himself yanked violently to the side by a sharp tug on his cable. They were trying to reel him in from the deck above, using the mechanical winch. His steel boots suddenly left the ground and he was ripped sideways. Frantically, he drew the knife and cut the cable, air tube, communications wire, and all. He dropped back to the seabed, untethered to the platform above.

Across the pumping station, halogen lights on the helmets of the divers moved out of the alcove, heading for the elevator. Dewey hurried out of the pipe network after them, his chest tightening. But time was passing. He was suffocating.

He came upon the taller of the two men as he opened the door to the elevator. Dewey lunged at him and wrestled him, slow-motion style, to the seabed. Looking up, he saw the shorter terrorist train the APS at him. Then he heard it, like a snapping twig; the click of the rifle's trigger. With all of his strength Dewey swung the big man fully around, letting him fall atop him now, so that his back faced the weapon as it launched. The explosive crack of the APS thundered through the water as the needle-like projectile sliced through water and plunged into the back of the big diver. Dewey looked into the man's helmet, at his eyes, which bulged. He watched as the helmet filled with blood and lethally pressurized ocean water.

The shooter tried to fire again, but the weapon failed. He dropped and lumbered in slow-motion through the freight elevator door.

Struggling to follow, Dewey now knew what it meant to suffocate. He began to feel the pain that oxygen deprivation causes, in the head at first, then pulsing through the body. He tried to breathe one last gulp of air but could not. His helmet was empty. He watched as the second diver entered the cage.

You fucked up, he thought. *You should've gone for the spare oxygen tank.*

Pain consumed him and he felt helpless. The sight of the terrorist climbing into the freight cage intermingled with blackness as his mind began to shut down. At that moment, Dewey remembered his family farm in Maine. He'd always imagined he'd die on the farm. He thought of the fields, wheat-colored and dry.

"Help me, God," he said aloud.

And it was then, from somewhere within himself, where rational thought is secondary and raw, native instinct is the master; where true bravery either flourishes or is altogether absent; where a man's will to survive is either surrendered or burns like an inferno, Dewey found inner strength.

He plunged toward the freight cage. The terrorist, unfamiliar with the lift, worked at the switch to start the elevator's ascent. Dewey flung the door open, grabbed the man's shoulder, and pulled him down. The diver kicked the suffocating, weakened Dewey away, but Dewey grabbed again, this time holding his opponent's leg. Slowly, the diver managed to stand, too strong, too fresh with oxygen.

Desperately, with his free hand Dewey pulled the knife and plunged it into the air valve just above the man's belt, the one place unprotected by the suit's thick Kevlar. Blood shot out into the water like dye. The loss of pressure crushed the terrorist in a swift, excruciating moment as water poured into the suit.

Dewey was delirious. More than three minutes had passed since he'd taken a breath.

Mechanically, he walked back to the pumping station, through the alcove, past the spiderweb network of pipes and cables, to the locker in back, reaching it as his vision blackened. He took the emergency oxygen tank and screwed it to the air valve at his waist. A sharp hiss, then a quieter flowing sound followed. He breathed in. It was the sweetest breath he'd ever taken. For several minutes, he simply breathed, like a starving man at an unending feast.

Finally, he walked out of the pump station. He walked to the bomb;

a padlock held the steel cap in place. He moved back to the dead terrorists and searched each one for the key, finding nothing. He moved from the divers to the ladder and began his ascent. Up top, he knew, Esco and the terrorists would be waiting for the elevator, having lost contact with their men. Waiting for *him*. He began climbing the rungs of the ladder, plotting his response.

12

SAVAGE ISLAND PROJECT

Savoy exited the dam and walked down the hill, past the administration building. After the small grocery store, the houses for Savage Island's workers started, row upon row of squat cement capes.

He walked down the street until he came to number twenty-two. On the side of the small house, a basketball hoop was attached to a makeshift pole made out of the shucked log of a pine tree. Savoy knocked on the front door. No answer. He knocked again. Still no answer. He paused for a moment, looked around, took a step back, then kicked the door in.

After removing the metal plate, Mirin and Amman climbed inside the small opening at the base of the section of dam that housed the turbine. Once inside, they crawled through the rotors toward the end of the cylinder that housed the turbine. The smell grew stronger as they got closer. After a few more feet, the two men climbed into the enclosed chamber at the face of the turbine. This was the cavity through which water would have been coursing, were the turbine open to the sea.

They could stand now. Mirin walked to the end of the turbine. Against the wall stood four large oil drums, connected by a thick white cable.

On the side of the steel drums, in red paint, read the word: OCTANI-TROCUBANE-9.

At the first turbine row, Mijailovic realized he'd forgotten his headlamp. The floor was dimly lit by a halogen light on the side of the elevator. He walked to the wall and felt for the auxiliary light switch. He opened a small steel box and flipped the switch. The floor lit up brightly, revealing a pair of bright yellow parkas piled on the floor near the elevator. He glanced at them, then walked a little more quickly toward the turbine row.

The turbines were all shrouded in bright blue tarps. Beneath each tarp lay a collection of ladders, tools, and equipment. Pulling aside the tarps, he found each turbine in some state of dismemberment and repair.

At the last turbine, the tarp had already been removed. He smelled a faint but pungent smell. It seemed sour, acrid, chemical. It reminded him of something. What?

I know that smell, he thought.

Savoy moved quickly through the small house. Inside the front door, a television flickered. On the screen, a blond female read the news. The room had a small table stacked high with books and magazines. Savoy flipped through them. *Time*, *Newsweek*, *Match*, *Playboy*, and some sort of political magazine in Arabic. Behind the table stood two large reclining yellow Naugahyde chairs.

He walked into the first bedroom and found a neatly made bed. A dresser held a photo of an older, dark-haired Middle Eastern woman.

He walked across the hall. This bedroom was the polar opposite of the first. The sheets were off the bed, piled in the corner of the room. The mattress was pulled off of the bedsprings. He stared for a moment. Then he walked back to the other bedroom and to the neatly made bed. He reached down and pulled the mattress away from the bedspring and threw it onto the floor.

Laid out on top of the boxspring was a set of engineering drawings.

A chill ran down his spine as he studied them. He recognized the arrangement of the turbines. The plans had been hand-drawn but were precise. Arabic script filled the margins. They were schematics of the dam. He searched for the first-tier turbine row. Several large red marks were drawn on one of the turbines.

Savoy ran to the kitchen and pulled the phone from the hook. He dialed Mijailovic's satellite phone and let it ring.

Outside the fourth turbine, Mijailovic shone his flashlight on a slat of metal lying on the ground. Above it was an opening in the turbine. He climbed inside the opening. He moved slowly ahead on his hands and knees, his hands navigating the edges of the dimly lit tunnel. There, inside the turbine column, the smell grew stronger.

He suddenly recognized the smell that was coming from in front of them, down the turbine cylinder. It was the small of the burning wells. The infernos.

The Gulf War. Desert Storm. 1993. The well fires. Kuwait. Long before Mijailovic had joined KKB, he worked for Hulcher Company, one of the private contractors brought in by the Department of Defense to help put the fires out.

The memories raced in Mijailovic's head. Smoldering infernos fueled by chemicals that wouldn't go out. The chemicals were so destructive they contaminated the oil, then devoured the steel of the oil derricks and tubing that ran down into the ground.

"My God," he said to no one. "I missed something."

He heard the sound of metal banging against metal, a door opening or a latch being shut.

Someone was ahead.

Should he leave? Could he get out in time to warn everyone? He felt for his sat phone. He'd left it in his parka.

He started to crawl back toward the opening. The first step was to evacuate the dam. No, not the first. The first was to run like hell until he was on safe ground.

Then Mijailovic heard another sound. Voices. Two of them. He closed his eyes; he knew what he had to do. He turned around and moved toward the noises.

Less than fifty feet away, Mirin continued his furious work. He lifted a small box from the side of the barrels. He pulled the top off.

"I hear something," Amman said, panicked.

Mirin said nothing. He continued his work. Inside the box was a rainbow of wires. Carefully, he pulled the green wire from the bunch.

"Hurry, brother."

"Relax," Mirin replied. "Almost done."

He cut the plastic coating from the end of the wire and peeled it back.

Back at unit twenty-two, Savoy gave up on Arnie and dialed a new number.

"Operations," answered a voice.

"This is Terry Savoy. Who am I speaking to?"

"Al Durant."

"Is Arnie with you?"

"No. He hasn't been back."

"Okay. Listen to me. I want you to order an evacuation of the dam, immediately."

"Are you kidding?"

"No, I'm not kidding. Hit the facility evacuation alarm. Get everyone out of there immediately. Do you hear me? Sound it now. I want to hear it before I hang up this phone."

"Yes, sir."

Savoy listened as Durant dropped the phone on the desk in front of him. He heard some voices mumbling in the background. Suddenly, a new voice came on the line.

"Terry, this is Bob Hauser, foreman in charge over here. Did I hear right? You want an evacuation?"

"You heard right. Sound the alarm."

"I'll need an explanation."

"How's this for an explanation, asshole: there's a bomb in the fucking dam. *Now sound the alarm!*"

Suddenly, above the din of the dam, piercing sirens cut the air. They rang out from every siren and speaker across the small town as red halogens started to flash.

Savoy dropped the phone and went to the street, which had already begun to fill with people. Workers, wives, children.

"Follow me!" Savoy yelled, waving his arms and running toward the administration building. "Everyone, up to the safe zone!"

Inside the dam, the sound of the evacuation alarm roared through the turbine column. Mijailovic winced despite himself. *Terry had found something. Thank God.*

What he saw next caused him to shudder. There, at the end of the turbine column, the two Arabs stood. In front of them, four large oil drums stood in a row, linked by a spiderweb of thick, multicolored wires. Mirin was cutting one of the wires as Amman watched.

"No!" Mijailovic yelled as he climbed into the small enclosure.

Amman turned around and charged at him. Mijailovic ducked and delivered a furious series of punches to the young man's face. He felt the boy's nose shatter under the vicious left hook.

"Hurry!" screamed the boy as he fell to the ground. His cohort reached for the red toolbox next to the oil drums and pulled out a hammer. He missed Mijailovic with the first swing, then hit him squarely in the mouth. Mijailovic's jaw shattered, but he maintained his footing, wrestling the man to the floor. But the terrorist swung the hammer again, this time striking Mijailovic on the ear, and he lost all sense of time and place.

Outside the dam, as sirens blared, a stream of people ascended the cement stairwell to the safe area above the dam.

Savoy stood at the top of the cement stairs and yelled encouragement to the workers, children, and wives as they climbed.

"Come on!" he yelled to the stream of people climbing up the stairs. His eyes moved between the stream of people, climbing the stairs, and the dam to his left.

Mijailovic crawled as if drunk, his only thought the steel drums full of explosives. The blow to his ear had done something to him, and he understood that he would die regardless of what happened next. Still, he crawled on.

"Stop," he slurred.

The man with the hammer kicked him down, then moved to the oil drums. He let the hammer drop and looked Mijailovic squarely in the eye.

"Praise Allah," he said as he moved two wires together until they touched.

The last memory Mijailovic would have would be of heat and white light.

The explosion slashed through the first-floor turbine like a torch through tissue paper. At the dam's outer wall, the cement and steel breached, a section of the dam two hundred and fifty feet high torn away from the main structure.

Savage Island Project had been built to withstand a loss of such a section with a crosshatch of steel layered like madras vertically and horizontally throughout the dam. But it had not been built to withstand the heat that followed the explosive force, an inferno that soon made all metal meaningless.

Outside, Savoy watched in horror as the dam was consumed in fire. Screams penetrated the air from the safe area above the dam.

The heat climbed upward through the infrastructure, ripping out the second, third, fourth, fifth, and sixth-tier turbines. With them came the gale walls of the dam and soon the outtake walls. Within a minute of the explosion, fully six hundred feet of steel, cement, and granite had been decimated, opened once again to the violent sea.

As the heat rose skyward and the pressure from the cold sea violated the breach, an otherworldly marriage of water and fire took out the inner core of the dam, weakening it so that it collapsed inward upon itself.

At this point the destruction went from rapid to sudden. The half-mile-high wall of granite and steel disappeared with a cataclysmic explosion. Frigid, untamed seawater swept away the small town of cinderblock houses. Dark water crashed over the side of the hill and climbed violently up the stairwell. Workers, children, and women who had not made it to the top of the stairs were cleaved from the stairs by the whitecapped deluge. A new round of screams echoed up the hill.

The angry sea reclaimed its own. Savage Island Project was no more.

13

CAPITANA TERRITORY

Dewey climbed the steel ladder, knowing that every minute left him and his surviving crew closer to the detonation of the bomb below. In his attempt to scale more than six hundred rungs, his legs and arms became fatigued quickly. His muscles burned. The weight of the suit, tank, and helmet seemed to grow with every step. He'd been climbing for ten minutes, through the darkness, interrupted only by a dim halogen every ten yards on the nearby elevator shaft. He focused on his secondary goals: learn who was behind it all, then kill Esco.

He watched for signs of decompression in his suit. It would be pressure in his eyes that he would feel first, then pain in his inner ear. If that happened, he would have to stop and let the unit acclimate to the depth, a delay he couldn't afford.

The water grew lighter. He glanced at the depth markings on the ladder. He was within fifty feet of the surface. He kept climbing, breathing hard and coughing. At twenty feet, he could see the geometric outlines of the platform above.

He climbed quickly, energized by the sight of the surface. He could see the letters "AE" on the bottom of the derrick. Seven or eight feet from the surface, Dewey stopped and unclasped the hinges on his steel boots, then pushed them off. They sank like bricks. Now barefoot, he reached to his shoulder and unsealed the suit. The icy water rushed in, soaking his body. He took one last breath of bottled oxygen, then popped the helmet latch. The suit fell away from his body and sank, followed by the helmet.

Still underwater, Dewey unbuttoned his Carhartts and took them off, perched now on the ladder in only his underwear and a T-shirt. He dived away from the ladder and swam as far from the rig as he could, then toward the surface, until he couldn't hold his breath anymore. Even then, he swam farther through the chill Pacific water. Another fifteen seconds, then farther, until he thought he would burst. He aimed for the surface and breached into the warm sunshine. He was at least a hundred feet from the rig.

Looking back, he saw half a dozen men standing on the deck, staring down at the platform riser, training their weapons at the surface near the ladder. Dewey treaded water, fortunate in more ways than one: They were looking at the ladder and little else.

Unfortunately he couldn't return to the rig. Yet what choice had he? His limbs ached. Worse, hypothermia would claim him in minutes, not hours, even here in the ocean near the equator.

Dewey swam back toward the rig in a long, circuitous arc, keeping his head low to the waterline, until he was behind the terrorists. The rig stood on top of six massive steel girders that ran to the seafloor. He swam to the girder farthest away from the gathered terrorists. When he reached it, he grabbed hold of the edge and hoisted himself up. After several minutes of steady climbing, he reached the marine deck. He was now below and to the right of the conspirators. Any noise would alert them to his presence. He peeked through the grating. There he saw six men, still waiting, all with machine guns trained on the surface.

He noticed something to the left. Through the deck grating, fingers dangled down. Blood dripped from the end of the motionless fingertips. It was one of his foremen.

He could hear the faint din of voices. It emanated from the hotel, where his men were still imprisoned.

Then voices, closer, above.

"Where is it?" asked someone.

"Calm down," said Esco. "It'll get here."

"What if he doesn't come?"

"Then we die. But we're heroes. We've done our job."

Dewey spotted Esco and another Arab, Ali, the cook. Esco paced the deck above. He stepped to a spot almost directly over Dewey's head.

"He'll be here in five minutes. Until then, we keep our eyes out for the Chief."

"You think he's alive?" asked Ali.

"No, I don't, you stupid fuck," said Esco. "But if he is, I want to be ready."

Dewey waited motionlessly. He moved his eyes and glanced down the length of the marine deck to the lifeboats. Above the lifeboats, he knew, was his office and adjoining cabin. Esco remained above him for more than a minute, not moving, not looking down. Finally, one of his men called to him and he stepped away. Dewey began crawling beneath the deck. His fingers gripped the steel grate as he crawled, and he pulled himself along as quietly as he could. When he finally reached the edge of the platform, he climbed onto the hull of a lifeboat. Directly above was the window to his cabin. He inched his way to the outer edge of the boat's hull. One slip would plunge him back into the sea. The resulting splash would be followed by gunfire as Esco and his men filled him with lead. He gripped the outer piping. He hoisted himself up by his fingertips to the window of the cabin, and, grabbing the sill beneath the open window, pulled himself into his room.

He walked across his room and stood in front of the mirror. He was a mess, soaking wet, face, chest, and arms bruised. The wound above his eye had opened up. Blood coursed down his cheek.

He dried himself off with a towel. He took a Band-Aid from the first-aid kit and stuck it above his eye to stop the bleeding. He put on a pair of dry underwear, T-shirt, jeans, socks, and a pair of boots.

Dewey removed the mirror from the wall. Behind it was a safe. He turned the dial. He reached inside and removed all of the money he had. Five million Colombian pesos, worth about $2,500, and more than $10,000 in U.S. currency. He grabbed his passport.

Next he went to the dresser, opened the middle drawer, pulled it out, and flipped it over. Taped to the underside of the drawer was undoubtedly the most important possession he owned at that moment: a Colt M1911A1 .45-caliber semiautomatic handgun. He stuffed six extra clips into his pocket, then, from the top drawer, retrieved the leather calf sheath to his Gauntlet knife. The knife was missing; he remembered the confrontation with Esco, before they dragged him away. He got down on his knees and looked beneath his desk. There, against the wall, lay the knife. He picked it up, then stood up, slipped the knife into the sheath, then strapped it around his calf.

Quietly, he cracked the door to his cabin. Just outside the room, Pazur, the scum who'd murdered Jonas Pierre, stood watch, pistol in hand. Dewey gently shut the door. Then he heard a noise. It was barely perceptible at first, but it grew. A distant rhythm patted the air. He looked out the window. As small as a fly on the horizon, a Bell 430 helicopter came into view.

Dewey watched the chopper grow larger in the blue sky, black, high-tech looking. It began its descent toward the platform.

Dewey opened the door. Suddenly bathed in sunlight from the room, Pazur turned to look. For a split second he seemed startled. Then he moved, wheeling his gun at Dewey. But he was too late. Dewey fired one shot into the boy's head, a single tap just above his right eye. The shot cracked loudly, echoed down the hallway. The bullet shattered the terrorist's tanned skull into a dozen pieces and splattered his brains on the metal grating behind him.

Dewey knelt, reached down, and pulled Pazur's pistol from his hand just as the deck door at the end of the hallway opened. In the doorway, a gunman suddenly registered the sight of Pazur on the ground, then Dewey. A moment of shock as he looked at the blood-splattered wall behind Pazur, and Dewey, now moving the Colt toward him. The killer turned to run, screaming in Arabic, just as Dewey aimed and fired. The bullet struck the terrorist in the back of the head, felling him onto the deck just as the door swung shut.

Dewey walked quickly down the hallway. He heard footsteps and frantic words in Arabic, just outside the doorway. At the door, where the terrorists would expect him to emerge, he took a sharp left and shimmied along the piping axis. It was barely wide enough to squeeze through.

Behind him, he heard the sound of automatic weapons being fired at the door. The steel of the door blocked the slugs, but the gunmen continued, trying to shoot a hole in the door.

Dewey stepped more than thirty feet, then angled toward another entrance to the deck, directly across from the door where the men were watching. As he peered out the slat, he saw seven men, weapons drawn. They had stopped firing. They were waiting for him to come out. But waiting at the wrong door.

Overhead, the sound of the chopper grew louder as it descended toward the rig.

Dewey felt a familiar rush, like a drug. All sense of fatigue, all pain from his injuries, simply melted away.

He kicked the door open and walked into the brilliant sunshine of the marine deck, emerging quickly and without hesitation. The loud rhythm, the din of the descending chopper, cloaked the sound of his entrance. He was thirty feet from the doorway where the conspirators thought he would be.

Dewey let his controlled fury, his instinct to survive, and his desire to kill all coalesce in a clarifying moment.

He scanned the scene; seven killers in a loose line outside the far doorway, Kalashnikovs and Uzis out, trained at the door where they thought he would emerge; left, Esco lifting a duffel bag, running to the stairwell that would bring him to the chopper pad. The chopper's wind and din blanketed the platform in chaos.

Dewey stepped forward, arms crossed in front of him, right arm aimed left, left arm aimed right, Glock 39 and Colt .45 cocked to fire.

The closest man, a dark-skinned Colombian named Juarez, saw Dewey, wheeled, started to turn his black Kalashnikov toward him.

Dewey ignited the Colt first, a bull's-eye tap into Juarez's head an inch and a half above his right ear, shattering his skull and arching his large frame in the air for a brief, awkward moment before he tumbled onto the blood-wet grate behind him.

Dewey moved toward the line of terrorists, pulsing the steel triggers of the semiautomatics as fast as his fingers would flex now, sweeping his arms east-west, rotating his torso as lead exploded from the weapons.

One by one, the other killers dropped as slugs pinpointed skull and flesh. The killing arc ended where the last body fell, all seven terrorists down, terminated before they knew what hit them.

Looking up, Dewey saw Esco running for his life up the north stairwell toward the helicopter pad. Dewey dropped Pazur's Glock to the steel deck, unlocked the empty clip in his Colt and let it hit the ground, then pulled a fresh clip from his pocket, clicking it in as Esco ascended. The terrorist had two more deck levels to climb, and he took the stairs frantically, three steps at a time. Suddenly, he dropped the duffel halfway up the flight of stairs, as saving his own life became his sole concern. Dewey remained calm. He stepped coolly into the center frame of the marine deck. Esco glanced down at him as he climbed; their eyes made brief contact, Esco's fear riveted across the space between the men, so desperate was he now to reach the chopper.

Above the scrambling terrorist, the chopper touched down, the rig swayed ever so slightly, and wind ripped from the pad grid down, blowing Dewey's sweat-soaked hair across his face, but it didn't matter now, all he saw was Esco. All he felt was the desire to kill the man who'd killed so many of his men. Dewey stepped slowly across the steel grate of the marine deck. He held the Colt down by his side as he watched Esco climb. He felt the steel of the weapon pressing through his jeans, still hot from the firing sequence. Slowly, he raised his right arm. The Colt found its place in the air, extended at the end of Dewey's arm. He waited, one last moment, as Esco reached the last flight of stairs beneath the chopper pad. He waited, one more moment, then another, and still one more, until the terrorist reached the last step before the helideck.

At the top step, Esco looked down. Dewey made eye contact, then fired, one shot. The Colt's blunt power reflected itself in the thunderclap of the bullet release. Dewey's arm kicked back and he let the weapon bounce up to the sky, for he knew the shot was true. Above the chopper din, he heard the scream, then watched as Esco fell, tumbling down the steel stairwell, tumbling down stair after stair until he came to a contorted rest at the landing a full flight beneath the chopper pad.

Dewey glanced around at the deserted rig. As the chopper's rotors pulsed he could hear the crewmen yelling from the hotel. He ran across the steel deck and unlatched the large steel bolt that held them inside. His crew poured out of the door.

"Thank God, Chief," someone said as he ran out of the mess hall.

"Listen to me!" Dewey yelled. "There's a bomb on the rig. Capitana's going to explode. *Get in the lifeboats!*"

Dewey stood at the door and waved the men toward the lifeboats.

"Each boat takes twenty men. Fill the boats. Paddle as far away from the platform as you can. *Go!*"

As the men began carrying out his orders, Dewey made for the north stairwell. On the third level, he came to Esco's supine body, his eyes staring up at him. Dewey's shot had punctured the terrorist's chest; Esco's chest wound foamed red with each labored breath.

"Chief," he rasped.

Dewey said nothing. He aimed the gun at his head, registered the fear in Esco's eyes.

"Detonator," said Dewey. "Now."

Esco managed a laugh and looked away. Blood coughed from his lips and his teeth became dark with blood.

Dewey shrugged and sent a bullet into his head. He searched the body but found nothing resembling a detonator. There was one last chance.

He climbed over the body onto the last flight of stairs before the helicopter pad. He pushed the door to the landing area open. The wash from the still-whirling rotors caused him to duck as he ran to the open door of the chopper. He climbed inside, weapon drawn.

"What happened?" the pilot shouted over the din. "Where is everybody?"

Dewey studied the pilot, a tanned older man with a shaved head. He aimed the gun at the man's head.

"Esco?" asked the pilot.

"Where's the detonator?" Dewey yelled at the pilot.

"I have no idea. I'm just a pilot."

"Who do you work for?"

The pilot stared at Dewey. He pulled up the collective to get the chopper light on its wheels, in preparation for takeoff.

Dewey raised the pistol, thrust it into the man's ear. *"Where's the fucking detonator?"*

Quicker than Dewey thought possible, the pilot had the chopper lifting into the air; soon it was hovering fifty feet above the derrick.

"Where's the detonator?" Dewey yelled over the engine noise, holding the pistol at the pilot's head. *"Put it down!"*

But it was too late. The helicopter rose above the platform. At this height Dewey had no more leverage over the pilot. To shoot him would be suicide. To jump would be the same. The pilot turned to him and, as if reading his mind, nudged the Colt aside. He pointed to a radio headset. Dewey put it on.

The pilot steadied the chopper and moved the cyclic forward. The chopper began to move away from the rig. Capitana grew smaller as they ascended.

"You killed Esco?"

Beneath them, lifeboats dotted the sea. Dewey counted ten of them, oars chopping furiously at the water as his men paddled away from the rig. He could see more men still on deck, frantically untying, lowering, and loading the rest of the boats.

Dewey nodded. "Where's the detonator?"

The pilot glanced at him and gave a dismissive laugh.

Dewey put the Colt to the pilot's temple. With his other hand he took hold of a finger on the pilot's right hand, the man's pinky. He quickly pulled it backward until it snapped.

The pilot let out a scream, but Dewey held his hand fast.

"The bomb's set, on a timer," gasped the pilot. "There is no detonator."

White-hot anger gave way to an even more corrosive wave of self-reproach. Dewey returned the Colt to the pilot's temple.

"What will you do, cowboy? Shoot me? I don't think so."

The helicopter, which had been steadily climbing, suddenly shuddered.

"The bomb!" yelled the pilot. Dewey swiveled to look behind them.

A groundswell of movement rippled up and out from the water.

Whitecaps suddenly began bursting out in a hundred different places as the seabed detonation reached the ocean's surface. A low, loud sonic boom barreled through the air. The chopper lurched and jerked; the pilot struggled to hold it steady against the shock waves.

The chopper wheeled around violently. In the distance, a mushroom cloud of black smoke burst out from Capitana. The bomb exploded and the rig was now consumed in an inferno of flames. A bright chemical plume of maroon, green, and orange barreled into the sky. Thick smoke swallowed up the horizon. The mini-TLPs, Capitana's satellite platforms, became engulfed in flames and smoke. The picture was chaos.

The boats nearest to the rig were instantly consumed by water and fire. Many seemed far enough away; they might survive. The pilot steadied the chopper and Dewey stared at the rig, the rig he'd helped turn into the most productive platform in the world, the place that for many years had been his home. Now it was a smoldering carapace. A graveyard.

Dewey could only shut his eyes and think about the dozens of roughnecks who were drowning or burning alive. He had never been close to any of them. But they were his men. Some might survive. Most had died. He felt sick to his stomach. He wanted to turn and put a bullet in the pilot's head. But he knew that he needed him to get back to the mainland alive, to find the minds behind this destruction, the architects of this apocalypse.

Patience, he thought to himself. *If you kill this one now you'll die, whoever is behind this will win.*

He tuned the radio to channel 16, the maritime emergency frequency.

"Mayday, Mayday!" yelled Dewey into his headset. "This is Dewey Andreas calling from Capitana Territory. Latitude four degrees north, longitude eighty-two degrees west. We have an explosion at Capitana. Mayday!"

Dewey repeated himself several times, but heard nothing in response.

"I hope you're enjoying yourself," the pilot said, cradling his broken finger. "The radio's on a closed frequency. Nobody hears you."

Dewey sat back, still holding the Colt against the pilot's head. The skyline was a hue of purple as far as the eye could see, the color of a bruise; a perfect symbol of Dewey's own physical state. He was in pain.

His body had suffered damage. Dewey was forty-two years old. Not an old man, but he wasn't young either.

He focused his thoughts. Survival, he knew, had to be his singular objective. Survival. He took a deep breath.

"How far are we from Cali?" asked Dewey.

"Ninety minutes."

A faint, scratchy whisper came over the headset. "Bell eighteen, this is Simon. How was the visit? Over."

The pilot looked over at Dewey. Dewey shook his head.

"Bell eighteen, I repeat. Can you hear me?"

The pilot looked again at Dewey. Dewey pointed at his broken finger. The pilot again said nothing.

"Zaima, I need a signal that you're alive. Over."

Without warning the pilot began talking rapidly in Arabic. Dewey reached out as quickly as he could and ripped the headset from the pilot's head.

"Fuckhead," Dewey said. He took hold of the pilot's injured hand and snapped two more fingers.

The pilot screamed, then panted through gritted teeth. "You will die soon."

They flew for a long time in silence. After a time the horizon took shape, a wisp of arterial green. Then it grew quickly into a shoreline. The cliffs of the Colombian coast arose in dramatic earth tones. Soon, the country rose into sharp mountain peaks, visible past the green rain forest the helicopter now began traversing. After another fifteen minutes the industrial skyline of Cali began to take shape, skyscrapers stacked up in sharp lines at the center of the dusty city. Thick smog hovered like a blanket above the skyline.

Dewey watched the pilot out of the corner of his eye. When their eyes met, he saw fear in the terrorist's eyes. He sensed movement below the man's face, caught the pilot's injured hand settling on the small latch of the compartment between the seats. In a flash the pilot had the console open, his hand inside.

Dewey brought down his left elbow like a hammer, slamming the lid on the pilot's hand. A terrible scream came from the pilot.

"Remove your hand," said Dewey. "Slowly."

"Not long now," the man managed to grunt as he pulled his hand back. "They'll be waiting."

"I'm counting on it." Dewey kept the gun to the pilot's head and reached down with his left hand to open the compartment box. He came up with the black steel of a handgun, a Glock.

"Who do you work for?" asked Dewey.

"You're about to find out."

The city's skyline now dwarfed the chopper. Cali was one of the quickest growing cities of South America, fueled by the tremendous natural resources of the country, and, of course, by drug money and the various industries it spawned and fed, such as banking and shipping. This resulted in a blend of old brick buildings, some of them shabby tenements and squat government-designed industrial buildings, and tall, modern skyscrapers, half of them still under construction.

The chopper headed for the city center, aiming at a blue-tinted glass and steel skyscraper that stood taller than the others. On the roof, around a bright red X, gathered a small group of men, weapons drawn and aimed at the descending chopper.

"You want to meet my friends?" asked the pilot. The roof loomed closer now, no more than a hundred feet away. Half a dozen men, Dewey counted. Too many to manage with his weaponry and their angle of descent.

Dewey pressed the gun into the pilot's neck. "Turn this thing around!"

The pilot ignored him.

The chopper descended into a slow hover above the building, now nearly at eye level with the gunmen. Dewey lowered the Colt and fired a single round into the pilot's right knee. The shot blew his kneecap into bits. Blood spattered like paint drops across the concave windshield of the chopper. Another scream as the pilot cursed in Arabic.

"Take us up," Dewey barked.

Tears of pain streamed from the pilot's eyes, mixed with blood that had spattered from his kneecap being blown off. Dewey aimed the pistol at his other knee.

"Pull up!"

"No!" yelled the pilot.

The chopper suddenly tilted left. The main chopper blade arched to the side, toward a line of armed gunmen, who scattered before the blade ripped the air where they had just stood. Dewey braced himself for what he thought would be the impact of the blade striking the rooftop, but the pilot pulled back, steadying the chopper. Holding his knee with his mangled hand, he managed to continue a wobbly descent. The chopper bounced and weaved in the air just a few feet above the building. The gunmen, who'd just evaded the out-of-control blade, dived for cover again, yelling. The front right skid of the helicopter banged the pad roughly.

Dewey aimed the pistol at the pilot's other knee and fired. The scream was deafening. The chopper lifted momentarily, less than a foot off the ground, arched backward, then started to sweep around out of control counterclockwise.

"Pull up!" yelled Dewey.

The pilot was now covered in his own blood. The helicopter continued to rise in a semicontrolled veer.

"The black building. *Now!*"

As the pilot eased the chopper away from the rooftop, one of the gunmen charged, machine gun aimed squarely at Dewey.

He was a big man, at least six five, and had curly dark hair and sunglasses. He was yelling at the pilot as he aimed.

Dewey kept the Colt in his right hand aimed at the pilot's head. In his left hand he held the pilot's gun. He crossed his left hand beneath his right arm and fired through the door of the chopper. He missed. Fired again. This shot struck the gunman squarely in the forehead. The top of his head came off like a saucer as the man jerked backward from the force of the shot.

"Get us out of here!" yelled Dewey.

As the chopper climbed, the remaining gunmen opened fire. The windshield shattered and bullets ricocheted around the cabin. Slugs hit the chopper's blades, its engines, and its tail. Dewey ducked as low as he could as the pilot pulled the chopper laterally away from the building, then higher into the sky. The chopper was struggling. The engine sputtered.

"We're not going to make it," said the pilot.

The helicopter frame vibrated furiously. The whole machine pitched violently to the left. Smoke enveloped the sky in a cloud of dark black.

"*I can't hold it!*"

The chopper circled uncontrollably downward shrouded in black, as the engine coughed and the main rotor struggled to keep the chopper in the air.

A stray bullet tore into the pilot's head, snapping his skull sideways.

Dewey grabbed the stick, but it was no use. Even if he knew how to fly a helicopter, it wouldn't have mattered. The machine was out of control. It gyrated and dropped uncontrollably downward in a storm of smoke.

As the chopper dropped, it careened toward a smaller, half-constructed building, a skeleton of steel girders tarped in bright orange construction web and debris netting. Its row of girders punctured the air like steel teeth. The chopper continued soaring in a sideways bender, smoke coughing in plumes behind it, toward the corner of the girders. Dewey held on to his seat for dear life as the impact came. The chopper struck down violently into the building. The sound was deafening as steel met steel. The destroyed chopper wedged upside down into a row of girders, one of which stabbed a line through the engine block like a knife through butter. Soon, the smoke was joined by flames, which burst out from a fissure of the main fuel tank.

Dewey quickly scanned the scene. In the aftermath of the crash, the helicopter hung like a Christmas ornament on an extended girder at the edge of the half-constructed building, at least twenty-five stories above the crowded streets of Cali.

The front of the helicopter was aimed skyward. The cabin glass was shattered and for the most part gone.

Dewey looked for his gun and found it beneath the seat. He belted it and felt for his knife. Still sheathed at his calf.

He stood on the back of the seat. The chopper swung precariously back and forth on the steel axis. He lifted himself up. He pulled himself onto the steel girder, out of the helicopter cabin.

The cars directly below him looked like toys.

Dewey knelt atop the steel bar and looked up. A line of gunmen peered down at him from the taller skyscraper, training their weapons. Suddenly, shots rang out. A bullet dinged the girder just in front of his outstretched arm. He had to move. He shimmied away as quickly as he dared and didn't look down.

Then, like a hard kick, a bullet hit him in the left shoulder. It nearly sent him careening off of the steel beam. But he held on. The girder was the only thing separating him from a free fall to his death. The bullet had punctured the top of his left bicep near the shoulder joint. The wound, which seemed to have missed bone, now bled freely. Dewey lay on the girder for a moment, testing the strength left in his arm. With a groan he resumed his shimmying, leaving a trail of blood behind. Finally he climbed down onto a cement floor and found the construction area was deserted. He grabbed a filthy rag from the ground. He tied it around his arm to stem the bleeding.

Dewey looked back one last time. The gunmen were out of sight, but they'd soon be hunting for him in the streets. He turned and walked into the abandoned building, past piles of steel girders and pallets of lumber, toward the stairwell that would deliver him to the anonymous streets of Cali twenty-five stories below.

14

MARKS'S SKI HOUSE
ASPEN, COLORADO

Teddy Marks sat in the leather armchair, staring at the flames burning in the stone fireplace in front of him. In his right hand he held a glass half filled with eighteen-year-old Talisker single malt, a thick Cohiba cigar in his left. Plumes of gray smoke wandered up softly toward the ceiling.

A winter snowstorm blew hard outside, the snow accumulating like a white blanket across the dark Colorado mountains. Marks pulled the leather hassock closer and rearranged his feet on top of it. The song "Jessica" by the Allman Brothers played softly in the background. He took another sip of his scotch, quietly contemplating the perfection of the moment.

On a large, dark red chesterfield in front of the fireplace, Nicholas Anson sat with his wife, Annie. Each held a glass of red wine.

"You sure you don't mind the smoke?" Marks asked.

"Not at all," said Annie Anson. "I kind of like it. Nick used to smoke cigars. I'm glad he quit, but I miss the smell sometimes."

Marks nodded. "This place sits empty ninety-five percent of the time. Drives me crazy. I'm glad you could come this weekend. We deserve some R and R, don't we?"

"Yes, we do," Anson said, smiling. He took a sip from his wineglass.

Marks had bought the place five years before, a sprawling old farm-house in the foothills above Aspen. The place had cost him nearly seven million dollars. Tonight, sipping the peaty-flavored scotch, puffing on a cigar, he could only think it had been worth every penny.

Less than a quarter mile away, a solitary dark figure slipped methodically through the Colorado woods. He'd snowshoed in from a logging road more than ten miles away, tracking across a deserted swath of old growth on the backside of Snowmass. The dark black celluloid of his coat blended against the surrounding pines like camouflage, rendering the man virtually invisible to anyone who might be looking for him there. No one was. Jutting out from his head, ATN PS15-4 night-vision goggles allowed him to see the snow-shrouded landscape as in daytime, but with an apocalyptic green hue behind everything.

The storm had been unexpected, but it made his concealment all the more complete. Otherwise, it was neither a benefit nor a distraction. Simply another factor in a mission he'd been planning for more than three years.

At the edge of the pines, he saw the first sign of the Marks estate, the old barn. Beyond that, he knew, he would find the big stone farmhouse.

The man moved to the corner of the barn and removed the snowshoes, leaving them at the western corner of the barn. Without the snowshoes, the snow now surrounded him up to his waist. But that didn't matter.

As he climbed through the drifts, he ran one last time through the file on Marks.

Marks had spent most of his career at KKB, beginning as an oil futures trader with the company at age twenty-five. He did his undergraduate work at Ohio State in only three years, then got an MBA at night from the University of Chicago. His rise at KKB had been rapid.

The relevant part of Marks's career for the assassin had occurred before Ohio State. In 1969, at the age of eighteen, Marks enlisted in the Navy after reading about how badly America was losing the battle in the jungles of Vietnam and Cambodia. After basic training at Naval Station

Great Lakes, he was asked to join the Navy SEALs, a program of elite fighters who received training in all-terrain warfare: sea, air, and land. After a year of brutal training, Marks and the rest of his team were sent to Vietnam. His team ran infiltration, exfiltration, and search-and-destroy missions deep in the Cambodian jungles.

The assassin removed the night-vision goggles and clipped them to his belt pack. He pulled a pair of wire cutters from a coat pocket and at the side of the red barn opened a small door on the front of a gray metal box. Reaching in, he quickly clipped the phone lines to the house.

The terrorist reached into his coat and removed his weapon, a heavily customized Taurus Cycle 2 semiautomatic handgun with a small, hand-forged custom snubnose black silencer screwed to the end. He moved from the barn through the waist-high snowdrift. At the corner of the home, he inched to the window. Inside, a fire blazed warmly; near it sat his target, Marks, plus a tall man with a receding hairline in a denim shirt and a woman with sandy-colored hair holding a wineglass. They would be collateral damage.

Marks and his guests couldn't have arranged themselves any more conveniently. The intruder took a step back from the window, lifted the gun, and aimed at Marks's head.

It may have been something as insignificant and fleeting as a reflection off the side of his crystal glass. Or perhaps it was the faint whisper of movement in the snow outside the window. Maybe it was just instinct. But in that one instant, as the killer raised his weapon and prepared to fire, Marks felt fear in his heart the likes of which he hadn't felt in years, not since Cambodia; terror he'd known, hated, worked every day since to put behind him and forget about. It was the terror of the hunted.

Marks reeled forward. Like a deer lurching from a hunter, he threw himself out of the leather armchair at the same moment the window behind him shattered. He landed chest first on the hard pine floor, but one slug had found its mark, striking him squarely in the shoulder.

Nicholas and Annie Anson barely had time to react to the gunfire. They watched, stunned, as Marks leapt to the ground. Blood arced from Marks's shoulder and splattered across their laps before they had any notion of what had happened. By that time, the killer had targeted them. Two shots to Nick Anson's head, two more into Annie Anson's chest.

Marks had felt the searing burn of a bullet before. He was hurt, he knew, but he could still move. His premonition had bought him time. He registered the Ansons' deaths peripherally as his instincts raced ahead of his thoughts. He would have to kill this one, he knew, if he wanted to live.

Outside, the assassin moved quickly around the corner of the house. He couldn't tell if he'd killed Marks. He pushed through the snowdrift as fast as he could, inserting another clip into his Taurus.

Marks's shoulder spasmed in agony. As he lay on the hardwood floor, he looked down at his shoulder, concerned by the unabated flow of blood. It spilled onto the ground like water.

He knew that to survive, he couldn't dwell on his injury, and he couldn't stay still. Whoever was out there was a professional. He would not leave until he'd completed his job.

Marks looked up at the fire. His eyes roamed to the wall next to the large stones of the fireplace. There, he saw the big bay window that looked out on the mountain. From behind that window, the killer would have a perfect line of fire. Marks crawled out of the room.

By the time the killer moved through the deep snow around the corner of the house, a minute had passed. When he reached the bay window, the target was gone.

The killer knew the mission bore risk; Marks was not a soft target. Paranoia crowded his mind. He knew the importance now of acting quickly to end this. He couldn't allow Marks the time to react.

He punched his gloved hand through the window. Reaching up, he unlatched the lock and raised the window. Holding the gun in his left hand, the killer placed both arms through the window to pull himself through.

As he pulled his torso over the windowsill, the killer looked suddenly to his right. Marks, covered from neck to waist in blood, was coming at him. Marks's left arm was immobile, bleeding profusely. His right swung the iron poker from the fireplace with brutal force onto the killer's skull. The killer heard himself cry out. As the assassin wriggled the rest of the way in, Marks swung the poker again. Shoulder. The gun fell out of the killer's hand and slid across the hardwood floor and into the fireplace, resting atop the hot coals near the grate.

Marks raised the iron poker again. He stepped forward, anticipating the final blow to his attacker, and swung with fury. But Marks's foot suddenly slipped in the pool of blood on the ground. His balance shifted, the slice of the iron through air came down awkwardly, slower, and the killer anticipated it. He reached up, tore the iron from Marks's hand as it came down.

Marks recovered his balance. He moved forward and sent his right foot squarely into the killer's face. Blood suddenly poured from the killer's nostrils, but he swung the poker's grip up at Marks's hurt shoulder. Marks fell to the ground, blinded by the shock of his pain. The killer stood and raised the poker, only to watch in surprise as Marks rolled swiftly away.

Marks crawled like a crippled dog, pulling himself along the ground with his good arm through a pool of his own blood, inching to the fireplace's edge. Desperately, he reached his hand toward the smoldering fire and stretched for the gun that lay atop the burning coals.

The intruder came from behind him, blood flowing freely from his broken nose and gashed neck. The killer sent the iron shattering down, a crushing blow onto Marks's shoulder. He screamed out in agony.

In front of him, Marks could see the gun resting within the fireplace. He knew that what he was about to do was his only hope of survival. He reached into the hot coals and grabbed the gun.

The metal stuck to his hand like glue, branding itself into the flesh of his palm. Bolts of pain seared through his hand and shot up his arm. The hot metal burned the skin and muscle. But Marks swallowed the pain, wheeled around, and aimed the gun at the killer above him, firing once as the killer struck with the poker again. This time the poker struck squarely across Marks's skull, but he got the shot off. It hit the killer in the neck. It would be Marks's last salvo. The blow from the iron poker was too much, too direct, too damaging.

The killer was bleeding profusely now, but Marks's shot had only grazed him. He raised the poker above his head again, Marks now powerless to defend himself.

Marks struggled to open his eyes. He wanted to see the man who was about to kill him. Mustering the last remnants of his strength, he looked up at the young man.

"Why?" he whispered.

The killer said nothing, only swung the iron poker in a brutal strike at Marks's skull. The killer dropped the poker and stood bloody and exhausted. Only luck had left him alive, not dead alongside Marks, or instead of him. He'd never seen such a will to survive, nor such strength. For a moment, he felt admiration for the man he'd just defeated in battle. But only for a moment.

He reached down with his glove and lifted the still-hot gun from the ground near Marks's hand. He placed it in his pocket. Reaching into his pocket, he took out a small red canister. He sprayed Marks and the Ansons with the canister. He then sprayed a small stream into the fireplace. The flames coursed along the ground to the bodies.

The killer moved to the broken window and climbed back into the cold air. The snow continued to fall in great plumes from the Colorado sky. The blood flowed freely from the assassin's neck, nose, and skull, leaving patterns in the snow. He turned to look inside one last time at the bloody scene. The Ansons' corpses were on fire. The flames engulfed them and soon spread to the carpet. Marks's corpse would be next. Soon, the house would be gone.

The killer plowed through the drifts toward the corner of the barn and the snowshoes that would deliver him back to the waiting sedan, ten miles through the dark Colorado woods.

15

SAVAGE ISLAND PROJECT

Bitter cold wind made the safe area miserable for those who had managed to make it up from the town. The wind off the Labrador Sea crossed the great plain of water that now rushed as it was meant to, as it had for eons before. The pale gray of the horizon grew dark; soon, the arctic night would fall.

Savoy walked among the survivors, searching for Mijailovic. Of the six hundred people who lived at Savage Island, he guessed that less than half stood before him now. The rest had either been caught inside the dam during the explosion, or drowned afterward. Having passed through the crowd several times, he knew Mijailovic was dead.

A strange silence surrounded the survivors, interrupted only by the occasional crying of children. The adults appeared to be in shock.

The cold worsened with each passing minute.

Savoy's mind boiled the situation down to its bare elements. First, the people before him would all freeze to death if help didn't arrive soon. Second, terrorists had struck; they might be targeting other KKB facilities at that very moment.

George Kimball, KKB's pilot-in-command, ran into the crowd, looking frantically around.

"George!" Savoy yelled.

"Terry. What—"

"Did you bring your sat?" interrupted Savoy.

"Here. What happened?"

Savoy looked at Kimball, then stared for a moment at the second-in-command, Aslan.

"Let me talk to you for a second," he said to Kimball. He walked away from the crowd, and from Aslan.

"What is it?"

"The dam was destroyed by a bomb. Terrorists."

Savoy dialed the phone.

"Spinale," the voice on the other end of the phone said.

"Thank God you picked up," said Savoy.

"Terry?"

"I don't have time to talk. I'm at Savage Island. A bomb was set off. The dam's been destroyed."

"What? 'Destroyed'?"

"Yes, you heard me. Destroyed. It's gone. Wiped out. Hundreds were killed."

"For Christ's sake."

"I need you to order a lockdown of all KKB nuclear facilities. Then call Jessica Tanzer at the FBI. Tell her Savage Island was destroyed by terrorists. Tell her we've ordered a lockdown and she should do the same on all U.S. nukes and LNG facilities."

"Terrorists?"

"Yeah. Arnie's dead. Jake White must have suspected something. That's why they killed him first."

"What about—"

"After you talk to Jessica, I need you to get the Canadian authorities up here immediately or the survivors will freeze to death."

"Got it."

"They need to fly something in here. There's a large landing strip. If you have to, have Jessica call someone at DOD and get a military transport up here. It's five degrees out. The wind is ripping off the ocean and night is coming."

"Got it."

117

"Tell Jessica I'm flying to D.C. tonight. I'll call her in a few minutes. But right now, securing the nukes and getting help up here have to be your top priorities."

"Okay. Take care, boss."

Savoy hung up the phone. At the far corner of the safe area, he saw a trailer.

"Follow me," he said to Kimball.

The two went to the trailer. Inside, heavy blankets were stacked in piles against the back wall. On one side of the trailer, more than twenty large kerosene heaters were lined up. Boxes of food were stacked in the corner. The safe area existed for emergencies, for a catastrophe such as the dam failing. But surviving a disaster would be moot if there weren't a way to stay warm for the hours it would take help to arrive.

Savoy walked out of the trailer. "Listen!" he yelled to the crowd. "I need everyone to listen to me." He paused a few moments while people moved in closer.

"My name is Terry Savoy," he said. "I work for KKB. Help is on the way. I need able-bodied men over here immediately. Now. Let's go."

A group of men, shell-shocked from the events of the past half hour, lined up at the trailer.

"Let's get the heaters going first," Savoy ordered. "Line them up every ten feet or so, in a circle. Then we'll pass out blankets."

Soon, the heaters started to flare up and a makeshift assembly line went to work. Men carrying blankets came out and started to pass them out.

Savoy approached one of the men setting up a kerosene heater, a foreman named Ned.

"I have to leave now, Ned," said Savoy. "I want you to take charge. Can you do that?"

He looked at Savoy then looked at the crowd. He closed his eyes for a moment, then said, "I'll do it."

"A plane's en route," said Savoy. "Keep everyone warm. Huddle around the heaters. The heaters will burn for thirty hours or more. They'll be here long before that, I promise you."

Savoy passed through the crowd.

"Are there children who don't know where their parents are?" he asked. A few hands went into the air; a teenage girl with curly brown hair, a small boy no more than five or six years old, a dark-haired girl of three or four who stood alone, in shock. "Let's bring them with us," he said to Kimball. "I'll get the little ones."

Savoy walked back to Ned. "We're taking some of the children. If we missed anyone, if there are children without an adult, assign an adult to them. Don't leave any kids by themselves. Got it?"

Ned nodded.

"Let's go," he said to Kimball. Aslan, the second-in-command, began to follow them back to the airstrip. "You're staying here," Savoy told him.

Aslan stopped and looked at Kimball.

"We need two crew," said Kimball. "You know that."

"I'll take the risk," said Savoy. "Now let's go."

"What, you think *I* had something to do with this?" said Aslan.

"I don't have an opinion and I don't care what you think," Savoy said. "You're not coming. Get over it. Go help get blankets on the women and children."

A few minutes later, as the Gulfstream took off, Savoy looked at the three children. The boy was asleep. The teenage girl had her arm wrapped around the shoulders of the little girl. They looked startled.

He picked up the satellite phone and dialed.

"Spinale."

"It's me."

"Mounties are on the way. Won't be there until sometime after midnight. They scrambled a C-130. Should work on the big airstrip there."

"Good work. Did you lock down the nukes?"

"Done. We established level-two protocols."

"Are you telling me the reactors are still at full capacity? The job up here was done by insiders. Shut the facilities down. Now."

"Got it. Let me put you on hold."

Savoy sat back and shook his head. He closed his eyes and rubbed them.

The phone clicked on again with Spinale's voice.

"Done. Sorry about that."

"No apologies. After we get off I want you to get all employee manifests at the plants. I want all employees of Middle Eastern descent identified."

"What then?"

"Let's ask Jessica. Personally, I'd lock them up and ask questions later. But get her on the phone for me."

A few clicks came over the satellite.

"Jessica Tanzer."

"Jessica, it's Terry Savoy."

"Terry, how are you?" asked Jessica.

Savoy had known Jessica Tanzer, the head of the FBI's office of counterterrorism, for more than a decade. Jessica was Savoy's main point-of-contact within the FBI on all matters concerning KKB security. Because the company owned and operated thirteen nukes, Savoy abided by a complicated set of regulations, security protocols and reporting frameworks that meant nearly constant government interaction. Savoy liked her. She was smart, quick, efficient—and unafraid to make decisions.

"How am I?" asked Savoy. "Let's just say I've been better, Jess. Did Spin bring you up to speed on what happened up here?"

"Yes, he did, but I'm still trying to absorb it. Where are you now? Are you on your way to Washington?"

"Yeah, and I have three kids with me. They'll need care when we land."

"Go to Andrews. We'll have someone there for the children. Are they all right?"

"They just lost their parents. One of them can't be more than four years old."

"We'll take care of them. I'll have a chopper to bring you downtown. Tell me what you know."

"Two maintenance men. Mirin and Amman. I can't remember their last names. Corporate will have them. Been here a while, over three years, embedded. I saw the blueprints. They planted some sort of powerful explosive in one of the turbines."

"Did you keep the blueprints?"

"Yes."

"Did they write anything down on the blueprints?"

"Lots. Arabic, looks like. I saw the letters 'OC' dash nine in a couple of places."

"'*OC nine*'? I'll run that by our munitions people." She paused a moment. "Has Spin told you anything?"

"About what?"

Another second's hesitation. "Capitana's been destroyed."

"What? Colombia? The Anson field?"

"Right. We don't know if there are any survivors. Another massive explosion like yours, this one at the seafloor. The platform was destroyed. That's all I know."

"I was supposed to go down there next week," said Savoy, shocked, trying to catch his breath. "What about the nukes?"

"Nothing. We have them locked down. Not just KKB's. Every nuke in the U.S."

"You need to do more than *lock* down," said Savoy. "These guys were insiders. You need to *shut* down, and look for suspects who fit the profile."

"Can you get us employee manifests?"

"Got them," Spinale chimed in. "You'll have them in a few seconds."

"This was done by embedded employees," said Savoy. "Long-timers. We're not talking about guys hopping on an airplane with a box cutter. These guys worked here nearly five years."

"Got it. Hold on."

The line went silent for half a minute, then Jessica clicked back in.

"Okay, Terry. We're reaching out to the other facilities. We're shutting everything off. We'll talk about how we profile when you get here."

"Now is when they'll run," said Savoy.

"Or maybe it's even past time," said Jessica. "I hear you."

"I don't think you do. We don't have time to *talk* about profiling. You need to do it, take the suspects in, and ask questions later."

"We can't do that. We have a little thing called the Constitution you may have heard about."

"Don't use that crap on me. They attacked us. Don't let them use our laws to protect themselves. What's the first right listed in the Constitution? *Life*."

"We'll work the profile," said Jessica. "We'll discuss what to do with them when you get here. End of discussion."

"Has anyone notified Marks?" asked Savoy.

"We've been trying to reach him," said Spinale. "He's in Aspen. There's something wrong with his phone."

"I can send someone from Denver," offered Jessica.

"I've got Aspen police going up there," said Spinale.

"When you get him on we should reconvene," said Savoy. "We'll need to brief him. The Anson people too. I'm assuming you'll handle the folks in Washington."

"We already have an interagency task force set up: FBI, NSA, Energy, DOD, the White House, CIA, et cetera."

"Okay."

"I have to drop off," said Jessica.

"Let's regroup in thirty minutes," said Savoy. "I'm on Kimball's satellite. You have the number?"

"I have it," said Spinale.

The line went dead. Savoy leaned back in his seat. His head was spinning. He stared at the liquor cabinet on the Gulfstream. He pulled out a bottle of scotch, Talisker, which Marks had made sure every KKB jet had in stock. Savoy poured a small amount into a glass, two fingers, sniffed the scotch, and took a large sip. The warmth rushed through him like a gentle wave. He tossed down the rest of the glass.

Savoy stood up and walked to the cabin.

"What's our ETA?" asked Savoy.

"Two and a half hours away," said Kimball. "Crossing into the U.S. in forty minutes."

"Take it into Andrews. I'm getting a ride into town."

Savoy walked back to the leather sofa in the cabin and sat down. The children were asleep. The satellite phone rang.

"Savoy."

"It's Spin. I've got Jessica. Hold on."

The phone clicked.

"Hi, guys," said Jessica. "How close are you?"

"Two and a half hours. Anything more on Capitana?" asked Savoy.

"We have approximately a hundred survivors. Apparently there was a hostage-taking before the explosion. There may have been some sort of battle before the explosion. It appears the *Montana*, one of Anson's oil tankers, was also destroyed in the blast."

"Christ," breathed Savoy. "How did anyone get away? Did the bombers—"

"Whoa," said Jessica. "That we don't know. We've barely begun rescuing the survivors much less starting to interview them. I have to run, the director's on hold. I'll see you in a few hours. Fly safe."

Jessica's phone clicked out.

"I have something, Terry," said Spinale.

"What?"

"I spoke with the head of security at Anson. The gang chief on the rig, one Dewey Andreas, filed a report yesterday; three men died this week aboard the rig. He blamed it on ethnic tensions. I'm getting a copy of the memo and I'll forward it to you."

"Okay."

Savoy hung up and returned to the cockpit. "I'm going to try and shut my eyes for a moment or two."

"Got it."

He walked back to the cabin and sat down in one of the big leather chairs. He shut his eyes.

The next thing he felt was the wheels of the Gulfstream touching down in Maryland. He walked to the back and went into the bathroom, splashed water on his face, brushed his teeth. The kids had slept through the landing. In the cockpit, he picked up the blueprints.

"Nice job," Savoy told Kimball. "Sorry you had to fly it alone. He's probably perfectly innocent. But we couldn't take any chances. They'll want to debrief you. Make sure the children are taken care of before you leave."

16

J. EDGAR HOOVER FBI BUILDING
WASHINGTON, D.C.

The chopper flight to FBI headquarters took fifteen minutes. Savoy followed the agents across the roof of the building to a doorway held open by a uniformed guard, HK MP7 machine gun at his side. They took an elevator to a floor below ground, then a hallway to another doorway guarded by another uniformed guard with a machine gun.

Savoy entered the room.

In its middle stood a long, rectangular table surrounded by a dozen people. On the walls a series of large flat screens showed a variety of scenes. One Savoy recognized as satellite images of Capitana Territory, the rig now only a red and black plume above dark ocean. Another pair of screens displayed satellite photos of Savage Island Project, first before the explosion, with a thin man-made line across the image that Savoy knew to be the dam, then a live-feed shot of the bombing's aftermath.

A clock on the wall read the time: 4:48 A.M.

"Hi, Terry," said Jessica Tanzer, walking across the room toward him.

Savoy hadn't seen Jessica in at least a year, and the sight of her walking across the conference room gave him the first calm feeling he'd had all night. She was a true pro and projected a sense of self-confidence, despite her young age.

Savoy had always liked her, found her to be smart and honest. It didn't hurt, at least in Savoy's mind, that she was also beautiful. Now, at almost 5:00 A.M., she looked as beautiful as he remembered her, even more so. Long auburn hair, a stern expression on her face, but with a hint of her Irish grin plainly visible beneath the icy demeanor. She took Savoy's hand, shook it, then patted the back of it with her other hand. "Thanks for coming. Let me introduce you to the team assigned to the investigation."

"Before you do that, can you update me on the rescue efforts in Canada?"

"The Mounties are en route. The first plane had mechanical problems and had to land in Nova Scotia. They sent another C-130 up."

"Can DOD send one, just to be sure?" asked Savoy. "It's below zero up there and they have limited kerosene. Can we really rely on the Canadians?"

"I'm with you. In fact, we asked the Mounties to send two planes this time, which they agreed to. They'll be okay."

Savoy nodded and took a seat. He looked around the table at the dozen other people seated around the big mahogany table, ten men and two women.

"You want some coffee?" asked Jessica.

"Sure. Black."

"Introduce yourselves," said Jessica.

"Vic Buck, CIA," said a bald man with a friendly face.

"Antonia Stebbens, Department of Energy," said a tall women with red hair and glasses.

"Louis Conner, FBI," said another bald man with a beard and glasses.

"Reuben McCarthy, FBI," said a tall man with blond hair and a mustache.

"John Scalia, White House," said a young African American.

"Rick Ennis, National Security Agency," said a gray-haired man.

"Jane Epstein, Defense Department," said the other woman, a brunette with short, cropped hair.

"I don't mean to be rude," said Savoy, interrupting and looking around the room. "But I don't need to know who you all are, do I? Just tell me what you need from me."

Everyone looked around the table, their gazes finally setting on the young female head of counterterrorism.

"I guess what I mean," Savoy continued, "is who's in charge? How do you make decisions? For example, I think you should take every single Middle Easterner who works at either KKB or Anson, or at any nuclear power plant in the United States, into custody. Who decides something like that?"

The room sat in silence until John Scalia, from the White House, cleared his throat. "We'll have to work out the proper protocols for decision making. Something like that would, I believe, have to go up through FBI with White House clearance, probably involving the president."

"Time is passing," said Savoy. "Either they're getting ready to strike again or they're not. If not, you will have been safe and you can apologize later. But if you wait, there's a chance they'll do more damage than they've already done."

The room sat in silence again.

"Let's review where we are," said Jessica. She nodded to the blond-haired man, Reuben McCarthy.

"Sure," said McCarthy, standing up. "Savage Island was destroyed by a synthetic explosive called octanitrocubane. This is serious stuff, designed by a professor at the University of Chicago less than a decade ago but never operationalized in any real quantities."

"Until now," said Jessica.

"Until now, that's right," continued McCarthy. "It's almost twice as powerful as octogen, the state-of-the-art compound used by U.S. military."

Savoy nodded, pulling out the blueprints and passing them to Jessica.

"Theoretically, octanitrocubane is the most powerful nonnuclear explosive on earth," added Rick Ennis from the NSA. "But it's hard and expensive to make; even DOD has had a difficult time synthesizing it. NSA was certainly unaware of any rogue able to synthesize it in attack quantities."

"What about Marks and Anson?" asked Scalia.

"We're trying to contact them in Aspen," Jessica replied. "No answer yet."

"Still no answer?" said Savoy.

"Apparently the whole area's in a brutal blizzard. Power out. Roads closed. It's on their to-do list."

Savoy shook his head and bit back a curse. His blueprints were making the circuit around the table.

"These are hand-drawn," said Conner of the FBI. "But they're good. Look at the detail."

"Three years working maintenance," said Savoy. "They knew the place."

"Where were these found?" asked Epstein.

"In the home of the terrorists."

"What were you doing in their home?" asked McCarthy.

"Some time yesterday, the man who ran Savage Island, Jake White, died in what appeared to be an accident. I flew up to investigate. I found a secret file on an employee that White had had a problem with."

"What was the complaint?"

"We call it a blue file. White hadn't put any specific info in it, so all we know is he had a concern with this employee. Unfortunately, White also didn't tell anyone, not even the head of the security at Savage Island."

"So you went over after seeing the blue file?"

"That's right. I had nothing else, so I went to talk with the guy. There was nobody home. I looked around, found these hidden underneath a mattress and ordered an immediate evacuation of the facility. Five minutes later, the dam exploded."

"Why didn't you order the evacuation earlier?" McCarthy asked.

"Like when?"

"Like when you found out White had suspicions. Like when he was killed."

Savoy paused and smiled.

"Go fuck yourself. Why didn't *you* find out about the plot?" Savoy looked around the table. "Why didn't any of you find out? You're the ones who are supposed to be looking for these people. You fucked up 9/11 and now this? And you blame me?" Savoy let his stare settle on the blond-haired FBI man. "When was the last time you ventured out of the comforts of this goddamned building? Finding terrorists is your job, not mine."

"Let's cool off," said Scalia. "We're all on the same team."

"Team?" asked Savoy. "I'm not on your 'team.' I'm a citizen of the United States, looking to you all to protect me and my children. You're the team. Look at what you all missed. This asshole tries to blame me? And now that they've hit us no one's got the guts to use the profile to screen the people who are working at this country's nukes? And why? Because of the Constitution? The men who wrote that document would puke if they saw you hiding behind it like that."

Savoy stood up and walked out. Jessica followed him into the hallway.

"Don't leave," she said as he walked down the hallway. Savoy paused and turned around. "We need you in here."

"You need a scapegoat."

"Come on. Let's do this right. Reuben's an asshole. Come back in."

He looked at Jessica. For a brief moment, she seemed lost.

"I'll do it for you, Jessica," Savoy said.

"Let's keep going," said Jessica as she and Savoy walked back into the room. "What do we have on Capitana?"

"We're still in the middle of a rescue operation," said Epstein from Defense. "The platform is almost three hundred miles from the coast. The ones we've pulled from the water are being interviewed right now. What we know is that there was escalating violence on board the rig, followed by a hostage situation. Then, just before the explosion, there was a gun battle, which nobody saw. The workers were freed by the man who ran Capitana for Anson Energy, somebody named Andreas."

"Dewey Andreas," said Savoy.

Jessica checked her notes and nodded, obviously surprised Savoy would know it. "Andreas fled the rig in a helicopter, for what reason we don't know. We don't know yet if he was involved."

"Whose chopper was it?" asked McCarthy.

"We don't know," said Jessica.

"Where is Andreas now?" he asked.

"We have no idea," Jessica said.

"What do you know about Andreas?" asked Ennis from the NSA, looking at Savoy.

"KKB is acquiring Anson Energy. I was supposed to fly down there next week to look at the facility. Andreas runs the rig."

"We should run a background on him, quickly," said Jessica.

"He filed a report yesterday," added Savoy. "Three men died on the rig earlier this week. I learned about it a few hours ago. He said it was ethnic tensions."

"I want to see the report," said Jessica.

"Me too," said Ennis.

"I'll send it around," said Savoy.

"What does this do to oil supply?" Scalia from the White House asked Antonia Stebbens from Energy.

"I suggest we look at that later," the woman from DOD cut in. "With all due respect, we need to get the investigation rolling before we have time to think about the impact on gas prices."

"With all due respect, it could be directly related to the investigation," said Scalia. "Think about it. Two direct hits to key U.S. supply nodes."

"Are you suggesting this wasn't terrorism?" asked the NSA man.

"I never said it was terrorists," said Scalia. "It is indisputable that this was a coordinated attack on our nation's energy supply. And it was pretty clearly timed to coincide with the merger announcement of KKB and Anson Energy."

Savoy nodded, exactly what he'd been thinking since he'd learned about the Capitana strike.

"We haven't even begun assessing, but it'll be grim," interrupted Antonia Stebbens from Energy. "On the electricity side, Savage Island supplied nearly seven percent of the country's electricity. It was a major eastern seaboard supplier. As for Capitana, last year roughly nine percent of U.S. raw petroleum supply originated at Capitana. Next year that number would have been more than twelve percent. We're talking about the largest strike ever outside of the Arabian Peninsula. This was a major reservoir. Let's put it this way. You could pour Prudhoe Bay,

129

Orinoco Project, Permian Basin, and ANWR into Capitana and barely cover the bottom half."

"I stand corrected," said the NSA staffer. "Who would want to maim our supply points then?"

"Let me finish," said Stebbens. "To maintain supply point, we'll be asking the president to tap the Strategic Petroleum Reserve. We'll have to go back to Venezuela, OPEC, et cetera. I won't even speculate on prices."

"Again," said the NSA man, "who would attack supply?"

"Are you suggesting this was a foreign government of some sort?" asked Savoy.

"We're above your security clearance right now," interrupted McCarthy.

"Blow me," said Savoy. "Either I'm included or I walk out of here and call a press conference telling the world about how you all fucked this whole thing up."

"Please, children," said the bald man from the CIA, Victor Buck. "Answer the question."

"I'm not suggesting anything," said Stebbens. "I assess energy risk and how to prevent it."

Suddenly, a door opened at the side of the room. A tall, brown-haired man walked in and stood. Everyone recognized him. It was the director of the FBI, Louis Chiles.

"Nothing is off the table," said Chiles. "If a foreign government is behind this, we'll find out. But right now we need to focus in on prevention of further attacks. I agree with Terry. Bring in the Arabs, shut down the nukes. Do it all right now. I'll take responsibility for any blowback. Next, we find Dewey Andreas. He knows more about these attackers than anyone alive. He should've made contact by now, and everything could depend on finding him—alive."

Savoy followed Jessica to her office in silence, partly because he was tired, partly because he was disgusted.

It was still dark, but the winter morning's first light was beginning to send shadows into the street. Delivery trucks rumbled down the street in front of her office. It was just past 6:00 A.M.

Savoy entered and stood by the window. "These your kids?" He pointed to a silver frame on the windowsill, two teenage-looking girls holding tennis rackets, dressed in white outfits, smiling.

"Nieces," Jessica said. "Esmé and Katie."

Savoy stared at the photo for a moment. Then he looked at Jessica. "I gotta go."

"What? Where?"

"First I have to make sure everyone from Savage Island made it safely back. Then I need to get an answer from an obviously overtaxed Aspen police force about my missing boss. Oh, yeah, I haven't had a good night's sleep in about a week. I might just take a nap too."

"I hear you, Terry. Look, I'll get my people on the Aspen police. But seriously, we need your help."

"Obviously you don't. That meeting was a joke."

"I know what you're going to say," said Jessica. "I know what you're thinking. That was a formality. We had to have that meeting. McCarthy is from upstairs. He's a lawyer. He's there to make sure we're covering our asses with respect to foreign governments, U.S. law, that the CIA doesn't go where they're not supposed to, that there's process around decisions so that we don't get hauled in front of Congress, et cetera."

Savoy stepped closer to Jessica. "You have a major strike on the United States of America and you have a bunch of paper-pushing bureaucrats trying to figure out how they can waste enough time in the next seventy-two hours to completely miss any chance of catching whoever's behind this. Never mind preventing another strike. The largest single point source of U.S. electricity is gone. The largest oil field outside of the Middle East is destroyed. And all our government can do is sit around some fancy table and see who can ask the most clever questions, who can assign blame, and who can avoid taking risks? Forgive me, but I want no part of that."

Jessica listened to every word patiently. She didn't look away, but nodded at certain points, and smiled at others respectfully. "I agree with you. But does that mean we give up? This is about defending America, Terry. That's why we're in this. That's why you're here. It's why we care. This investigation is going to hinge on four or five people in that room. John Scalia from the White House. Vic Buck from CIA. Antonia Stebbens from Energy, me, and you. That is, if you'll stay. I need you. You're right. This thing is going to be over in a matter of days, not weeks. The cement is drying. We need to act now. And there's one witness who may know more than all the other survivors combined. I need you to help me find him. Dewey Andreas."

Savoy looked around the office and saw the two chairs in front of the desk. He flopped down in one of the chairs. He rubbed his eyes. "I need a cup of coffee."

"You drive a hard bargain," Jessica said, smiling.

"I like you, Jessica," Savoy said. "I'll help you find Andreas, but I want no part of the bureaucracy around here. You have to promise me that."

"I promise. Let's go get a cup of coffee. I need one too."

"I'm too tired to walk."

"I'll go. Sit down. Put your feet up. Be right back."

Jessica took the elevator to the lobby, walked to the Starbucks across the street and bought two large coffees.

When she returned to the office, Savoy was still sitting in the same position. He was asleep.

She placed the coffee cup on the desk in front of her. Savoy stayed in a reclined position in the chair, his eyes still closed.

"I know Andreas," whispered Savoy.

"What?" asked Jessica, leaning forward. "Did you say what I think you just said?"

"Well, I don't know him. My service overlapped with his. When I was a Ranger, he was Delta. He wouldn't have known who I was."

"Why didn't you say something?"

"I don't work for you," Savoy said calmly, opening his eyes. "I don't trust a person in that room. They're already setting him up for a lynching. I'm not going to be a part of that, I'll tell you right now."

"But Dewey Andreas climbed onto a helicopter and fled the scene of the explosion."

"After he freed his men. You have no idea why he got on that helicopter, *if* he got on that helicopter."

"What do you know about Andreas?"

"It's complicated."

"Most things are. We have all day."

Savoy sipped his coffee cup.

"Aw, hell, I hate Starbucks." He took another sip, then winced.

Jessica laughed.

"They run Delta out of Fort Bragg," said Savoy. "I was at Benning, but we all heard the story. Andreas was ex-Ranger. Any Ranger who's recruited into Delta is a point of pride."

"Keep going," said Jessica.

"Like I said, I didn't know him personally. But one day his wife was found dead, murdered in their apartment near Fort Bragg."

"Murdered?"

"It was a big story. The local TV stations got it, the papers, that sort of thing. She was shot to death. Because it happened off base, the case went to the local prosecutor, who had it in for Andreas. Tried like hell to convict him, but a jury found him innocent."

"When was this?"

"Over a decade ago." Savoy stood up. "After they found him innocent, he left. For good. Nobody ever saw him again."

"Was he really innocent?"

"Some people thought so. Others thought those Deltas were strung awful tight."

"What do *you* think?"

Savoy paused and took another sip, wincing again.

"I think he was falsely accused by some podunk D.A. trying to make headlines and get himself elected to the state legislature. No way Dewey Andreas killed his wife."

Jessica sat back. In the distance, the sun was beginning to send bright morning light through the window. In the hallway, the sound of people coming to work could be heard. "And he ends up working for Anson Energy? That's some coincidence."

"Yeah. I read my manifest on the way to Savage Island yesterday. It's the first time I've seen his name in a long time. It might not even be the same guy."

"Name like Dewey Andreas? Come on. It's him."

"Yeah. What they said about a gunfight on the rig? I guess that cinches it. I mean, when I heard that, it really clicked. Deltas are trained to kill terrorists."

"Do you believe the memo? What does 'ethnic tensions' mean?"

"I just don't know, Jess. We need to speak with him."

The intercom on Jessica's desk chimed and a female voice came on. "Director wants you in five minutes."

"Got it," she said.

"Alone."

The intercom clicked off. "I need to head up. I'll have my assistant get you a room at the Willard down the street. It'll be under Tanzer. Go get a few hours' sleep."

"I will," said Savoy. "If you want my help finding Andreas, you got it. But only on one condition: I have access to the same information you do. You get me clearances and all that. If not, forget it. I don't have the time. I'll do my own investigation."

"I think I can do that. Let me talk to the director."

"Also, I want to bring Paul Spinale in here. I need a Sherpa. I need someone who'll manage KKB issues, housekeeping stuff, that sort of thing."

"Makes sense."

"He should get the same clearances I do. He was Navy, intelligence officer."

She nodded. "Okay."

"Spin and I will need an office. Preferably one with a couch."

"Christ, you're demanding. Anything else? Masseuse?"

"If it's a female, yes. I don't want a guy touching my body."

"I was kidding."

"I wasn't." Savoy laughed. They walked toward the door. "One other thing." He took a last sip from his coffee cup and tossed it in the trash. "And I'm serious about this."

"What is it?"

"No more Starbucks. Is there a Dunkin' Donuts around here?"

Jessica entered the director's suite and walked to one of the two large leather couches in front of Louis Chiles's massive mahogany desk. Already seated was Reuben McCarthy. Jessica took a seat next to him. Chiles, who was on the phone, finished his conversation and hung up the phone. He walked around his desk and sat down across from Jessica and McCarthy.

"That was John Scalia," said Chiles. "The president isn't going to tap SPR. They're not going to elevate alert levels."

"I have no comment on the SPR call," said Jessica. "But I disagree on the terror alert. We have no idea where this could go. This could be a general populace threat, or infrastructure. In either case, aren't we better off moving to red?"

"We have no idea what happened here," said Chiles. "If anything we need some time to do some work. The president does, however, want to make sure we have the nukes locked down."

"Already done," said Jessica.

"Scalia did reveal something interesting. They're concerned this is something different, perhaps not a terrorist strike, maybe a sanctioned attack by a foreign government."

"Which one?" asked Jessica.

"He wouldn't say."

"Great. We get to play guessing games with the White House."

"Chill out. All in good time. Let's get back to our work."

"Before we begin, I want Terry Savoy and his deputy Paul Spinale in here on this one," said Jessica. "We need his help finding Andreas."

"I don't like it," said McCarthy. "He's a hothead. We need thinkers."

"Bullshit," said Jessica. "He's not a hothead and he's as smart as anyone else around here. Look, we're talking about a highly decorated former U.S. Army Ranger. Run his background if you want, but I want him with me."

"You got him," said Chiles, looking at Jessica. He turned to Mc-Carthy. "Go."

"First, we have manifests of all employees at nuclear power plants, LNG facilities, and oil refineries in the U.S.," said McCarthy. "We're looking at nationalities, travel patterns, you name it."

"When will we have that list?"

"By noon. I suggest we reconvene interagency then."

"I don't have time for another session like that," said Jessica. "Just give me the list as soon as you have it."

"I'll give you the list as soon as we have it, but I disagree about interagency. We need the meeting."

"I agree," said Chiles. "We don't know anything yet. We need to make sure we're getting access to as much information as we can. We also need to make sure we're sharing whatever we have."

"Understood," said Jessica.

"If I may continue," said McCarthy. "Dewey Andreas. I have information."

"So do I," said Jessica.

"Let me go first," said McCarthy. "It confirms some negative thoughts."

"Go," said Chiles.

"Andreas's American," said McCarthy. "He's from Castine, Maine, on the coast. This was taken the day he enlisted in the army." He pulled out a black-and-white photograph and put it down on the table. It showed a younger Dewey, handsome, with long hair and a tough, smiling face. "He served this country with distinction. Went to Boston College, then joined the army. He became a Ranger, then was asked to try out for Delta. By all measures, he was good, very good. Multiple meritorious achievement medals, two Purple Hearts. Tough as nails. He was in Panama, also on the team that took out Khomeini's brother in Indonesia."

"How the hell did he end up on an oil derrick in the middle of the Pacific Ocean?" asked Chiles.

"That's where it gets interesting. He had a wife who he grew up with. High school sweetheart sort of thing. They had a son who died of leukemia when he was six. One day not too long after that, Andreas came home and found his wife dead. Someone shot her in the head." The room went silent for a few moments. "It happened off base. The local D.A. tried him."

"A jury found him innocent," said Jessica.

"He left the U.S. after that. Nobody saw him again, until now. This was thirteen years ago."

"What do you have?" asked Chiles, looking at Jessica.

"Savoy remembers the case," said Jessica, looking at Chiles, then at McCarthy. "He didn't know Andreas personally, but it was a big story in all the papers, local TV, that sort of thing. The district attorney tried his hardest to convict him and still didn't convince the jury."

"She was killed with a round from a .45-caliber Colt," said McCarthy. "Specifically, Andreas's handgun."

"Are you suggesting you can prove he killed his wife after reading a few articles on Nexis?" said Jessica. "And that this wife-killing ex-Delta's suddenly turned into a terrorist? This is not only not productive, it's ludicrous. We have a larger threat here. Andreas is not our problem. A group of terrorists is our problem. And Andreas may have information critical to solving that problem."

Jessica stood up and left the suite.

"Wait, Jess," said Chiles. "The next interagency—"

"I'll look at the transcripts," she said, and closed the door.

At one thirty, Savoy returned to Jessica's office, and she set him up in a conference room, next door to her office.

"You likey?" she asked.

"Me likey. Where's the couch?"

Jessica rolled her eyes and proceeded to brief him on the latest information from the Capitana survivors about the events during the days leading up to the explosion.

"We need a list of who was on that rig," she said. "You're probably equipped to get it soonest from Anson."

Savoy nodded. "I'll get it."

"How are the Savage Island survivors?" she asked.

"They landed in Halifax a couple of hours ago. They're all at the Marriott. Have your people talk to Spin. He'll arrange access for interviews, that sort of thing."

"Thanks. By the way, I got you and Spin clearance."

A low chime rang out from a cell phone on the conference table, interrupting their conversation. Jessica reached out and flipped it open.

"Tanzer."

Jessica listened in silence, then put the phone down.

"What is it?" asked Savoy.

"That was one of my agents in Denver. Marks's ski house is on fire."

17

Somewhere inside Marks's head, he heard a voice.

"*Get up,*" it whispered. "*This is not how it ends.*"

His own voice, telling him not to give up.

"*Get up,*" the voice said. "*This is not your time to die.*"

He smelled smoke and felt the intense warmth of the inferno around him. How long had he been unconscious? Opening his eyes, he saw chaos. The room was enveloped in smoke and flames.

For the first time, he suddenly registered the intense pain coming from his shoulder, where he'd been shot, and his head. He lifted his right hand and saw nothing but the dark, terrifying color of blood, coursing from his body. As he held his hand up in front of his face, he saw charred flesh from where he'd gripped the pistol from the fireplace.

Marks slowly arched his head around, rotating to see his legs. The flames were almost at his ankles as the oriental rug became overtaken with the spreading fire. He felt a sudden burst of heat as flames leapt to his jeans. He shook the leg and batted the flame out. His legs still worked, a good thing.

"*Start moving,*" the voice urged. "*It will soon get beyond your control.*"

Marks rolled onto his stomach, shouting at the stroke of pain in his shoulder. He looked for a way out. Everywhere, smoke clogged the room. The flames created columns of violent red and orange. The sound was incredibly loud, wood, fabric, and synthetic materials crackling as they burned.

To the left snow blew through a broken window, vaporizing instantly in the heat. The window the assassin had come through was Marks's closest exit point. But to reach it he'd have to cross the heart of the growing house fire.

More flames struck his jeans and he tried to shake them, but the flames clung to the material. Grunting in pain, he managed to put out the flames once again, but they would be back.

Beyond the sofa and the bodies of the Ansons lay another way out, the doorway to the mudroom—and an exit to the backyard. It was his only hope of survival.

He registered the sight and memorized the path to the doorway, then closed his eyes, for he knew he would have one opportunity and that if he was to ever see again he needed to protect his eyes from the searing flames and the smoke. He took one last breath.

Marks placed his blistered right palm against the ground and pushed as hard as he could. He pulled his right knee along the ground beneath him, then the left, so that he was now on his knees. Then, slowly, he moved to his feet and stood.

Above the din of the smoldering house, he heard a penetrating sound, a structural creaking noise, and felt the earth move slightly. He knew that the whole house would soon be destroyed, and the cracking was the sound of the ceiling timbers, weakening as they burned. Another crack, slower and more ominous. He kept his eyes closed, listening, and moved quickly to his right. From above, a roof timber crashed inches from where he now stood, its impact on the floor nearly toppling him.

"*Run!*" the voice yelled. "*Run, goddamnit, run!*"

He ran then, wildly, cutting through the flame wall with eyes still closed, knowing that if he hit a wall or tripped on some other obstruction he would die then and there.

As in a dream, all thoughts were now blurred. Marks felt only the intense pain of the flames against his shirt, his bleeding shoulder, and his scorched palm. The bright light of the fire beckoned him to open his eyes and destroy his sight forever.

And the voice, that was still there too.

"*Run!*" it yelled. "*Run, Teddy, run!*"

He sprinted through the wall of flames and entered the mudroom at the back of the big house. Marks kept his eyes closed, running blindly into yet more heat with a faith and a belief that something cooler, safer, lay beyond the intense heat. Suddenly, he came to the large oak door. He grabbed the searing-hot doorknob. The door swung out and icy air blew past him, jolted him, almost as painful as the flames. He opened his eyes. He saw the back of the house and its yard now covered in snow. The blizzard created a near whiteout. He ran now, his clothing almost completely in flames, and leapt into the snowbank.

A night crewman aboard the Sno-Cat at Snowmass called in the fire. Despite the blizzard conditions, he was able to see the flames from more than a mile away.

The first truck from the Aspen fire department arrived less than six minutes later. It took the first responders the better part of half an hour to notice Marks outside the burning chalet. He looked like a blackened snow angel in a deep drift, his sooty outline already being obscured by rapidly falling snow.

"Do we know who it is?" asked an Aspen police officer as he trailed the EMTs.

The EMTs didn't answer, but put Marks's body on a gurney and moved him to their truck, an oxygen mask to the face. "He's alive," said one of the medics, a woman who held her small hand at the side of the neck. "His pulse is weak, but he's alive."

The other EMT dusted off snow from Marks's body, and inspected the scorched clothing.

"Damage isn't too bad, except the hand," he said. "Christ, the clothing . . . he was on fire; snow probably saved his life."

The Aspen cop suddenly noticed the growing pool of red on Marks's snow-covered shoulder. Violating protocol, he reached down and brushed away the bloody slush. "Look. There's blood pouring out of his shoulder."

The EMT removed the rest of the snow, revealing bare skin and a purplish, raw red wound from which blood poured unabated.

"That's a bullet wound," said the EMT, applying pressure to the shoulder. "He was shot."

"We need to get him to Presbyterian," said his partner.

"We'll stabilize him on the way to Aspen Valley," she told the cop. "Can you make sure they prep the Trauma Hawk?"

"Absolutely. How long until you're there?"

"We'll be there in ten minutes. Make sure it's ready to lift when we get there."

The helicopter ride from Aspen Valley Hospital to Presbyterian/St. Luke's Medical Center in Denver took an hour, and was treacherous. Visibility was horrible due to the blizzard, and wind tossed the Sikorsky S76-C+ about wildly. But it touched down safely almost exactly one hour after the ambulance left the driveway of Marks's ski house.

Two medics greeted the helicopter as it landed and ran the stretcher to the open doors of the roof elevator. Six floors below, they unstrapped Marks's body atop an operating room table, then methodically peeled the burned shreds of clothing from the body.

Across Marks's chest, a jagged purple scar, two inches wide, ran like a ribbon from the left armpit down across his nipple to just above the belly button. On the biceps of his right arm, a small Navy blue tattoo was visible: an eagle clawing a trident, pistol, and an anchor.

Two doctors and four nurses were gathered about the body.

"Navy SEAL," said one of the doctors, pointing at the tattoo.

"How do you know?" asked a nurse.

"That's a SEAL trident on the shoulder," said the doctor as he ran his fingers across the scar. "Look at that stitch work. That's a war scar. MASH work. This guy's seen some serious shit."

As a precaution, they immersed Marks's body in a tub filled with a thick agarlike burn salve called Peroxidol, though his body didn't appear to have suffered any serious burns beyond his palm. He'd gotten out in time. The bullet wound, however, had cost him more than two quarts of blood. They also found several large contusions on his back, neck, and one to the side of the head.

The surgery took several hours. They repaired the shoulder and bandaged Marks's hand. After it was complete, the surgeon turned to one of the nurses.

"I want a brain scan on this guy," said one of the doctors after they had removed the shrapnel and were suturing up the shoulder. "That contusion on his skull looks serious."

"We ought to let the police know about him, too," added the other surgeon. "Someone needs to figure out who he is. There was obviously some kind of struggle here."

"That won't be necessary," came a voice from the doorway. It was Karen Cattran, the FBI's lead agent in Denver. She held open her wallet, showing her badge to the assembled medical team.

"As of one this morning, Presbyterian/St. Luke's Medical Center became a level-one national security site," she said as she walked to Marks's bed. "What that means is that as of an hour ago, access into or out of the building is restricted. Denver police, at the direction of my office, have locked down the facility. There are four armed guards in the hallway outside this room. Other than you all, nobody gets in or out of this room, and I mean *nobody*."

18

RUA BREVA
CALI, COLOMBIA

Dewey emerged from the half-constructed building at street level while the crowd was still gathering. People were pouring into the streets now, most of them staring up more than twenty-five stories above at the helicopter dangling over them, its rear tail rotor sticking out from a girder.

Dewey wasted no time slipping among the gaping civilians, pretending to be as mystified as they, and trying to ignore the growing pain in his shoulder and the plume of dark red flowing from it.

The pain from the bullet antagonized his every move. There was no way to stop the bleeding; a tourniquet wouldn't work. Instead, he held the same filthy rag against the wound.

"Are you all right?" a woman asked as he reached the back of the crowd.

He muttered something in Spanish about falling debris, and kept moving. Any delay right now would cost him his life. The killers would be coming for him.

Where were they? *Who* were they?

He glanced warily around. To his left, at the rear of the crowd, he saw two policemen—one a fat man and the other a tall, gaunt-looking officer—pointing toward him and pushing their way through. Behind them, he saw a well-dressed younger man, dark-skinned, an Afro, leather coat on. He was trying to blend in. But he trailed the policemen too obviously, trying not to be noticed, the only man other than the police not staring at the chopper overhead. Instead he stared at Dewey with cold, determined eyes. It was one of the men from the roof.

Glancing quickly to his right, across more than a hundred people, he quickly made two more gunmen, moving together toward him. It was the way they held their weight as they walked, concealing weapons, and walking just awkwardly enough for Dewey to recognize the altered gait. And the eyes. Those, too, gave them away. He knew the look.

Hunters. Stalking the perimeters of the crowd.

Dewey cut back into the press of people. As he neared the thickest part of the crowd, he suddenly ducked and pushed back to the right. Using his good arm, he surged forward, bent over, at least twenty yards. He moved past several dozen people too busy to look down, the people, now measuring in the hundreds, seemingly more entranced than ever by the chopper hanging above them.

Standing erect suddenly, he saw to his left the back of the killer's head, the one with the Afro, not more than ten feet away. He removed the combat knife from his ankle as he slipped past an old man and a woman standing next to the killer.

The chopper above made a loud creaking noise, and the crowd let out a collective scream as a piece of debris fell from above. As the metal descended, with the noise of the crowd's horror masking what was to come, and their attention on avoiding the falling metal, Dewey came upon the killer, who, unlike the masses around him, continued to cast his eyes desperately across the crowd in search of Dewey. His compact machine gun was now out and in full view, unafraid of even the local police, so important was the termination of his target. Dewey came from behind and wrapped his right arm around the killer's front. He quickly plunged the knife between the man's upper ribs, pulling across in a swift motion that severed all connection the heart had with the rest of the body. Just as quickly, he withdrew the blade and moved on, letting the gunman collapse silently to the ground.

Dewey wiped the blade on his pants and slipped the knife back in the sheath, then stepped backwards. The policemen hadn't heard the strike, but a teenage boy was now leaning over the dead man, and he screamed. Dewey turned and pushed his way back through the fringes of the crowd.

No other gunmen in sight.

Dewey hastened away from the scene and felt a sudden wetness on his hand. Looking down, he saw that his left arm was drenched in blood. It dripped off the end of his fingers, but did not pour. He knew he had time to try to repair it, but not much time, and a hospital was out of the question.

Two blocks away, he ducked into a clean-looking bodega and looked for something to stem the flow of blood. He found a package of cloth dish towels in one aisle. He searched quickly, glancing out the front window, looking for his pursuers. In the last row he found a roll of duct tape. Paying quickly, he ripped open the package of cloth towels and pressed one against the bullet wound in his shoulder. As the young Colombian woman behind the cash register watched, he wrapped the duct tape tightly about the rag and rolled it beneath his armpit, securing the rag tightly against the wound. It was temporary—very temporary—but he had more pressing issues to deal with.

One of the other gunmen passed in front of the window then, and Dewey spied him just before the killer turned to look inside. He ducked behind a red soda refrigerator, and held a bloody finger to his lips, pleading with the woman not to give him away. Frozen with fear, she complied. The man passed, and Dewey moved to the door.

Leaving the killers to the right, he went left, then took another left and went up a busy street. Within a block, the dish towel was drenched and within two blocks he felt his left hand becoming slippery again as blood began to seep out and course down his arm. It would do that as long as the lead remained in his shoulder.

After a third block, he glanced behind him and saw his two pursuers sprinting up the street. They were far in the distance, but they had seen him. He started to take a right, but saw a dead end in front of him. To take a left would enable the killers to cut him off. Dewey regretted not turning at the last street; there was nothing to do now but run like hell straight ahead.

He took the next block at a sprint. Glancing back, he saw a trail of his own blood dripping in his wake. Whatever he did now, he would be easy to follow. He had one other clean towel in his hand, but he knew he would need it. He would have to let the killers follow; he could not simply slip away.

At the next block, he ran right. The humidity was stifling, sweat dripped from his hair, drenched through from his forehead. Cars moved quickly down the narrow street, bumper-to-bumper, the occasional horn blasting. The sidewalks were crowded with street vendors, hawking electronics, watches, artwork, CDs, all laid out on small carpets. Pedestrians crowded in front of the vendors, looking for a bargain. Both sides of the street were lined with shops; a women's boutique, a sporting goods store, a few cafés, a bodega with a bright green sign that said PESSA'S! Dewey sprinted toward the traffic, running between speeding taxis and sedans and the line of parked cars, narrowly dodging cars as he moved, blood coursing down his arm.

"*Sangrando!*" a taxi driver yelled from an open window as Dewey passed, nearly running his dented yellow Toyota into the car in front of him as Dewey kept moving, ahead of his attackers, blood covering his hand as he dashed.

Halfway down the block, he saw a sign to his left: MOTEL EL ROSARIO. It was a shabby-looking place, fourteen stories high, gray cement with small square windows, lines of rust-tinted aging streaking down from the roof line. Dewey cut across a break in the cars, hit the sidewalk, moved past the motel's entrance. At the far corner of the building, the service alley cut between the motel and the next building, and he ran into the opening at a full sprint.

Looking back just as he cornered, he saw the first of the killers at the corner of Omnestra, a block away.

Dewey entered through the service door and ran past a pair of cleaning women on a cigarette break. He took the stairs and climbed, three steps at a time, his heart racing and his lungs burning.

The pain, for Dewey, was just another factor, an element, and long ago he'd been trained to compartmentalize distractions and place them in their respective boxes. Pain had always been one of Dewey's strengths: inflicting it, enduring it. Focusing on that kept him moving. Below, the sound of the killers running upstairs toward him echoed up the well between the stairs.

Each flight of stairs caused the rupture at his shoulder to tear and bleed. His chest burned, while blood loss caused him to feel light-headed. Glancing back from a landing at the top of the eighth flight of stairs, he spied the killers. The first was a younger man, wearing a gray T-shirt with a red Puma logo on it. The short-haired Arab stared forward at his path, moving like an athlete up the steps, no hesitation or fatigue in his pace. A short, shiny black submachine gun he held like a sprinter's baton in front of him, waving it through the air as he moved. But if the first killer was closing in, it was the second who worried Dewey more. Less than half a flight behind the first Arab, the second man suddenly raised his head. His black eyes caught Dewey with a menacing glare, a look of determination, confidence, even enjoyment. The look sent a small, cold tremor through Dewey, an unwelcome sensation that he knew all too well: fear. He quickly tried to push it out of his mind.

The second killer yelled and the first one suddenly raised his machine gun and ripped a quick burst of slugs up the stairwell. Dewey ducked against the wall and continued his ascent, keeping fear as far from his mind as he could by concentrating on, even welcoming, the intense pain that now flowered in his gaping shoulder blade. He could deal with pain, work through it, let it guide him even. But fear had no antidote; it was the enemy of the warrior.

On the ground, blood spatters followed Dewey like the proverbial bread-crumb trail. The blood dripped in a scattered line from his fingertips as he climbed. Soon, he was at the top landing of the motel. A large steel door with the number fourteen on it stood in front of him, leading to the hallway and guest rooms. Dewey stopped, again glanced down, then looked at the doorway. They would follow him, and the blood was their guide. Worse, the blood was now flowing unabated, a steady stream running from his hand, like a leaky spigot. If he did not repair the arm soon, it wouldn't matter if they caught up to him or not; he would bleed out. He could try to take them on the stairs, but he only had two bullets left in the Colt. One false shot and he would die right then and there, outgunned by a pair of fully automatic machine guns with loaded magazines.

Dewey stared at the entrance to the fourteenth floor for several seconds. The sound of the footsteps grew louder from below. He reached for the door, placed his blood-soaked fingers on the steel handle, pulled the door open.

Then he stopped. He let blood course from his fingertips across the cement of the landing to the fourteenth-floor entrance, a rough, crimson line that led onto the dark purple carpet of the floor. He turned, looked down the stairwell in the direction of his pursuers. He pressed his body against the outer wall of the stairwell. Carefully, he began his descent. He hugged the wall as he moved, letting the blood from his hands drip down onto the path of blood already on the ground. He moved down the stairwell, his head light, reeling in pain. The killers were rising quickly he knew, but he kept moving.

With his right hand, Dewey held the Colt in front of him, cocked to fire. He took the first flight, looked at the entrance door to the thirteenth floor, and kept going. At the twelfth floor, he glanced again at the floor entrance, but kept moving.

The scratching sound of shoes on cement came from below, louder, closer and closer now. But still, Dewey moved down the next set of steps. He descended as quickly and as quietly as he could, careful to let the blood from his arm drip onto the same scarlet track he'd left on the way up the stairs.

He could not allow the terrorists to look up and see him, so he kept pressed to the wall. But it meant he would have to guess where they were, and how close they had gotten.

He passed the entrance to the tenth floor, then the ninth, and could, suddenly, hear the fast, labored breathing of the first terrorist, so close now, coming up the steps. And yet, Dewey slipped past the ninth floor, step after step, until he saw the small white number eight affixed to the door of the eighth floor. At the eighth-floor landing, the killers sounded just below him, less than half a flight. A shadow danced ominously on the white wall just below. Pressing his arm and hand against his chest to stop the dripping blood, Dewey slipped through the stair exit into the dim hallway of the eighth floor.

Dewey waited just inside the door frame, his Colt M1911 out, raised and cocked to fire. The men passed the door in a loud sprint, following the trail of blood to the top floor.

Dewey belted the pistol and walked down the hallway. He knocked on the third door, heard footsteps, then said, *"Lo siento, accidente."* He knocked on the next door and heard nothing. He took the knife from the sheath, pushed aside the jamb, and inserted the blade along the door edge, then forced the blade down onto the lock and pushed in. The door popped open. He took the DO NOT DISTURB sign and placed it on the doorknob and shut the door, then chained it.

Inside, a suitcase was open on the floor, a suit laid out on the unmade bed.

He walked into the small bathroom and flipped on the light switch. He reached up and ripped away his sweat-soaked, bloody T-shirt, throwing it to the floor. He stripped away duct tape and pulled the blood-soaked rag away from his shoulder. The blood oozed faster, but he didn't feel much pain. He was going into shock. Feeling dizzy, he reached out and held the side of the sink. He steadied himself but felt faint.

Hold on, he told himself.

It was time. He knew what he had to do. He had rehearsed it several times before in his mind. But now it was time to actually do it.

He reached for the towel on the shelf above the sink. He held a side of it in his mouth then yanked with his right arm, ripping it in half. He took one of the strips and laid it atop his left shoulder. He wrapped it around twice, then pulled as tight as he could.

He took a toothbrush from the side of the sink and lodged it between his teeth, gripping it so that he could bite down and not scream.

He took water from the sink and poured some of it into the wound, then he reached down and took his knife from the sheath.

He leaned close to the mirror and guided the blade to a patch of skin just above the blackened, bruised bullet hole. He bit down on the toothbrush and carefully carved the ruined skin away from his shoulder, widening and deepening the entry wound until the knife tip struck bone. Moaning, he dropped the knife and stuck his fingertips into the open passage. He reached and dug around, searching for the bullet. At first he used one finger, then two. Soon all four of his fingers were exploring the wound. The tissue was soft and warm. His fingers were now immersed in his own shoulder, up to the last knuckle.

The pain encompassed him so completely that he knew he should have fallen into shock. But he did not. He could not. For if he did, he knew, he would bleed to death in a shabby motel bathroom in a poor section of Cali. They'd bury him in a beggar's grave.

He told himself not to look in the mirror, but he had to now in order to have any chance of getting the slug out. He looked for a brief moment at himself, at the eyes of a dead man. He couldn't believe what he was looking at, so bizarre was the scene, so unexpected and random.

And then he kept on digging. Dewey had to survive. For his men, for himself.

At last, he felt a small object. He maneuvered his index and middle fingers around the object and slowly lifted it out. There, in his blood-covered hand, he held a long, misshapen piece of lead, a 7.62 mm cartridge fired from a Kalashnikov. He dropped it in the sink, where it made a dull clank.

He dropped to his knees. For a full minute, he closed his eyes. Then, somewhere above him, he heard the dull staccato of an automatic weapon being fired. They were coming, moving floor-by-floor, looking for him. He stood up. He reached for the small mirror and opened the medicine cabinet. There was a needle and thread, a traveling salesman's sewing kit. He took the needle, which was already threaded with black thread, and slowly pushed the needle down into the ragged wound's rim. With difficulty, he sewed his shoulder back together, then gently washed it.

Down the hallway, he heard a door being kicked in, followed by a woman's scream, soon silenced by automatic weapon fire. Then another door, and a man's voice, yelling something he couldn't understand. Then more gunfire, a short staccato blast that silenced the man's voice. Then more footsteps, closer now.

Quickly, he took the clean, dry washcloth and placed it against the sutured wound. He wrapped duct tape several times around the shoulder, as tightly as possible.

Another door was kicked in. Through the wall, he heard footsteps and words as one of the killers said something to the other. The anger in the man's voice gave him a chill.

Through the window, in the distance, he heard sirens. Dewey moved toward the bedroom. He took the Colt from the back of his pants as he entered the dimly lit room. The sound of a heavy boot struck the wood of the door. The door flew open. The younger killer entered first. His eyes bulged in recognition, excited, surprised he had found his quarry. Before he could swing his machine gun up, Dewey fired a blast into the man's head. The force of the shot pushed the young Arab into the air and backward, momentarily causing him to leave his feet as the back of his skull shattered and blew off behind the force of a single shot from the .45-caliber handgun.

Dewey ducked as the other man blindly opened fire from the hallway, piercing the thin outer wall of the room with bullets as he searched for Dewey with a machine gun. From the floor, Dewey raised the Colt and, searching the wall for an extra moment with his eyes, fired his last bullet, which tore through wall and silenced the other killer.

Outside, the sirens grew louder. Stepping to the window, he glanced as hotel guests ran to the street in terror.

Dewey ransacked the suitcase in the room and found a blue T-shirt, which he put on. He stripped the leather coat from the dead terrorist in the hallway. On the back of the door, he found a bathrobe, which he wrapped around himself. He sprinted to the main stairwell and joined a group of other guests trying to get out of the hotel.

He went through the lobby as a team of SWAT-like police officers entered, helmets on and automatic rifles at the ready. Playing the frightened guest, Dewey moved with the panicked crowd and made it through the lobby.

Two blocks away, he threw the bathrobe in a trash can. In a small electronics store, he bought a cell phone that could make international calls. Down the street, he bought a box of .45-caliber slugs from a pawn shop. Outside the shop, he watched the street carefully until he saw what he was looking for. Half a block away, a businessman closed the door to a shiny black Mercedes, then crossed the street and entered an office building. Dewey quickly picked the door's lock, pulled part of the drive shaft casing back, then spliced the wires together and jump-started the car.

He hit the gas and sped down the city street, which was awash in the sound of sirens and the rush of people. As he drove away from the center of the city, he ripped open the cell phone package and powered up the phone. He dialed a number he knew by heart. After a long pause, the phone rang.

"Anson Energy," a female said. "How may I direct your call?"

"This is Dewey Andreas. I'm the platform chief at Capitana. I need to speak with someone, Nick Anson, McCormick, anyone."

"Please hold, sir."

At a strip mall a few miles from the center of Cali, he parked the sedan and turned it to face the busy street so that he could see approaching cars.

"Dewey, this is Jock McCormick. You're obviously alive. Where are you?"

"Colombia. I need help."

19

Back at Jessica's office, she and Savoy sat in front of a large white board that was covered in writing. In the middle of the white board, the word ANDREAS was written in bold red pen.

Savoy was hoping to get good news about Ted Marks from Presbyterian/St. Luke's Medical Center in Denver. In the meantime, Jessica and he had focused on learning everything they could about Dewey Andreas.

They started by retrieving Dewey's military transcripts, all the way back to his first entrance examination when he enlisted in the army. They also had the results of his entrance test for the Rangers, plus detailed reports of Andreas's activities and progress from his supervisors throughout his brief stint as a Ranger. Jessica was able to get copies of the memo and background reports in which Andreas was flagged as a possible Delta recruit, followed by all reports tracking Andreas's training to become a Delta.

Finally, they had detailed mission reports of top secret operations in which Andreas played a part: a covert attempted assassination of Panamanian dictator Manuel Noriega as well as the later Panama invasion and ultimate capture of Noriega; the assassination of Rhumeini Khomeini, Ayatollah Khomeini's brother; the initial assault on Baghdad during the first Gulf War; a botched assassination attempt on Kaddafi; a successful operation in Odessa to kill four top officers in the Russian Army who were planning a coup against Boris Yeltsin.

The military transcripts added up to nearly six hundred pages. Jessica and Savoy dug in and began studying Andreas's past.

What emerged was a portrait of an ideal warrior, a soldier of extreme fortitude, intelligence, and toughness, with a weakness for alcohol. More than one superior wrote they'd choose Andreas over just about any other soldier in battle.

After poring through Andreas's military records, Savoy and Jessica read the transcripts of his murder trial, along with every bit of coverage it got in the media.

They finished by studying the memo Andreas had sent Anson Energy security detailing the three deaths on board Capitana, as well as transcripts of the exit interviews with the Capitana survivors. After two hours, they put down all the papers and looked at each other.

"So, what do you think?" asked Jessica.

"I think he's Dewey Andreas," said Savoy. "Not some traitor, and not even a murderer who went free. Did you read that the prosecutor was nearly disbarred after the trial for withholding information? Andreas had an ironclad alibi. He loved his wife. Plus, she was mentally imbalanced. He didn't do it."

Jessica nodded and took a sip of coffee. "I agree. So why hasn't he made contact?"

"My guess is, he will. Although it's equally likely he's dead already."

A knock came at the door.

"Come in," said Jessica.

Chiles walked in.

"How's Ted Marks?" Chiles asked, looking at Savoy.

"In ICU," said Savoy. "He has a severe concussion. They cleaned up the bullet wound. He's got a bad burn on his hand, a cut on his head, but he's tough. They said he's going to be okay. They got him heavily medicated at the moment, but I'm hoping to talk to him soon. I'm heading out there later."

"Good. My prayers are with him." Chiles paused. "We're, ah, waiting for you two downstairs."

Jessica looked at her watch. "Sorry. We lost track of time."

"Before we go down, Nathaniel Field spoke with the security chief at Anson Energy," said Chiles.

"And?" asked Savoy.

"There were two ways of accessing the central pumping station at Capitana. Nick Anson and Andreas. We're talking about either a code lifted off a computer in Dallas, or a biometric scan of Andreas's iris. This wasn't a padlock; it was a state-of-the-art security device designed to protect a billion-dollar pump station, not to mention access to the petroleum reservoir itself."

"And they needed Andreas to get inside," said Jessica.

"Right. And apparently they got him to do it. The Anson people never released any code."

"But as Jessica and I have been reading, Andreas's no pushover," said Savoy.

"So you're wondering," said Jessica, "did he help the bombers to spare his crew, then escaped after saving some of them, as the debriefs of the survivors suggest? Or was he in on it from the start?"

Savoy looked away and shook his head.

"Right," said Chiles. "But we need to take this conversation downstairs."

Two floors below, the interagency task force was assembled around the conference table when Chiles, Jessica, and Savoy walked in and joined them.

"Good afternoon," said Chiles. "Sorry we're late. Why don't we start with you, Jessica."

"Sure," she said. "Let's start with prevention. We have lockdown everywhere we want it, where the White House wants it: nukes, LNG, refineries. We've notified allies, et cetera." She turned to McCarthy. "We've analyzed employee manifests at all nukes, LNG, and refineries in the United States for Middle Eastern profile matches. Thanks for the fast turnaround, Reuben. Bottom line is there are only one hundred and fifty-four matching personnel in the universe we're talking about here.

That was a pretty wide arc we threw, too. All one hundred and fifty-four are in protective custody awaiting questioning. They're presumed innocent, but they're not going anywhere.

"Next, Savage Island," she continued. "We have a team trying to trace the octanitrocubane chain. We don't know where it was manufactured. We might never know. We're in the midst of a whole range of analyses on the blueprints, the handwriting, and the two individuals who planned the attack."

"Have we definitively tied Capitana and Savage Island together?"

"Not yet. But it's pretty obvious, since they occurred at the same time, targeted related industries, used embedded Middle Eastern workers, and high explosives. They almost surely planned the attack on Marks and the Ansons, but as of yet, we don't know who 'they' are. That's the key question."

"I can tell you that no one has stepped up to take credit yet," said Myron Kratovil, the national security advisor.

"We have information on the Savage Island subjects," said Vic Buck from the CIA. "But it's not great stuff. Nothing earth-shattering. They're brothers. Real names are Mirin and Amman Kafele. Egyptian. Both were trained in Afghanistan by Al-Qaeda. Mirin was actually one of bin Laden's deputies, but more than a decade ago. He can be seen in a number of period photos. The two men covered up their relationship and backgrounds when they went to work for KKB. That's all we have."

"Al-Qaeda," said Scalia. "So we're likely talking about terrorism after all. What's the status on Andreas, and how does he fit in?"

"Okay," said Jessica. "Andreas ran Capitana. The survivors of the explosion credit him with saving them."

"Have we found him yet? Has he made contact?"

"Not yet," said Jessica, glancing at Savoy, then Chiles. "For all we know he could be dead. We do know, however, that Andreas was present when the bomb was set."

"How do you know that?" asked Scalia from the White House.

"Iris scan. It was the only way to open the pumping station, where they set the bomb."

"Andreas let them in?"

"Yes."

"So Andreas's the main loose strand here," said Kratovil to the room. "Where the fuck is he?"

"You're the national security advisor," Savoy said with heat. "You tell us."

"People . . . ," warned Chiles at the same time Jessica said, "We're looking," and Terry Savoy's cell phone chimed loudly.

Savoy pushed away from the table and answered the phone. After listening for a few seconds, he raised his hand for silence.

"Quiet everyone," Savoy said with a surprised look on his face. "I've got Dewey Andreas on the line."

As Dewey waited to be put through to Terry Savoy, he saw a police car cruise by the mall parking lot. Back in downtown Cali, he'd thought for a moment about going to the police, but he'd quickly dismissed the idea. As he learned during training for covert operations, there are countries whose police forces were rife with corruption, where you couldn't trust their allegiance to the United States. Colombia fell into that category. He ducked as the sedan passed by, then restarted the Mercedes and drove again.

"This is Terry."

"Terry Savoy? This is Dewey Andreas."

As Dewey watched his rear end for cops and gunmen, Savoy told him to hold, then spoke in a muffled voice, apparently to someone else on his end.

"Dewey, I'm going to put you on speakerphone. I'm at FBI headquarters in Washington. So you know, I'm here with Jessica Tanzer from the FBI and an interagency group charged with investigating the events of the past twenty-four hours. We're aware of the explosion at Capitana. Savage Island Project has also been destroyed."

"The dam?"

"Yes."

"Dewey, this is Jessica Tanzer with the FBI. First things first: are you okay?"

"I'm okay," Dewey said. "But there are several hundred men in the water near Capitana. Can you all make sure help is sent out there as soon as possible?"

"We're on it," said Jessica. "We've already got some of them picked up. We're putting everything we can in the water to save the men."

"I've been shot," continued Dewey. "At some point I'll need to get to a doctor. But right now I'm being hunted. I need to relay what I know as quickly as possible here in case they find me and kill me."

"Who's following you?"

"Terrorists. Capitana was struck by a cell of terrorists." Dewey quickly told them everything that had happened since the knife fight between Serine and Mackie, all the while putting distance between himself and the city center.

Jessica Tanzer stopped him when he got to the part about reaching the pumping station. "How exactly did they detonate the platform?"

"They placed a bomb at the seafloor. The explosive was called octanitrocubane."

Jessica nodded to the group. "There's our link." She turned to one of her assistants at a computer terminal at the end of the conference room. "See if we can zoom down onto Cali on the monitors."

Soon, one of the high-res plasma screens on the wall went black as the assistant entered coordinates into her keyboard. A grainy image came into place on the screen, quickly becoming clear, a live, magnified satellite view of Cali. Using Dewey's description of his arrival in Cali, the technician focused the view onto downtown, and then onto a crowd. He brought the view out and over and focused on the helicopter still dangling from the half-constructed skyscraper.

"I'm glad to debrief," crackled Dewey's voice over the speakerphone, "but I am literally running for my life. I killed a bunch of them, but there are more."

"Don't worry," said Jessica. "We're gonna get you out of there."

"Is there an embassy in Cali, a consulate?" asked Dewey.

Jessica looked to Scalia, who looked to an assistant, who worked his computer. "The nearest consulate is Medellín."

"You can't trust the Colombian police, or for that matter the military," said Jane Epstein from Defense.

"What assets do we have in Cali?" Jessica asked the conference room. "Vic, what do you have?"

Vic Buck tapped a few strokes on his laptop.

"We don't have anyone there, not right now anyway."

Epstein picked up a phone and was soon speaking with someone at Defense operations. She placed her hand over the phone handle. "We have a pair of Deltas in the neighborhood," said Epstein. "We can exfiltrate in two hours."

"You were Delta, right, Dewey?" asked Savoy.

"Yeah," said Dewey, traffic sounds and horns blasting in the background. "Bring 'em on."

"Where are you?" asked Jessica.

"Outskirts of the city, to the north. Rua Dista. Looks like a well-off suburb."

"Stay put. We'll have them come and meet you."

"Negative," said Dewey. "Let's set a meeting place. I don't want to sit out in the open for the next two hours while they hunt me. Fact, I can't afford to sit still at all."

"You're right. Throw a street grid up," said Jessica to her technician. On the screen, the photo expanded as he pulled the satellite out. Suddenly, a series of bright yellow street outlines crossed the screen, with names in big letters above them. Jessica crossed the room to the screen. "What's this?" she asked, pointing up.

The image zoomed in on a green field.

"Soccer stadium."

"This?" she said, pointing a few blocks away from the stadium.

"Madradora," said the technician. "A park. There's a church next to it."

"Did you hear that?" asked Jessica.

"Madradora, what section?"

"South part of the city, near the soccer stadium."

"Got it. Two hours."

The conference room speakerphone went dead. The members of interagency looked around the room. Finally, Scalia spoke up. "Well, there's our update on Dewey Andreas."

Jessica gave Kratovil a meaningful look, then caught Savoy staring daggers at Reuben McCarthy.

"I want to hear from Energy next," Scalia said. "Specifically as it applies to motive in these acts of terror. If that's indeed what they were."

All eyes turned to Antonia Stebbens from Energy. "We're analyzing supply and demand activity over the past three years," said Stebbens. "Especially petroleum, but also electricity. Don't ask me what we expect to find, because we don't know yet. But DOE's perspective, for what it's worth, will be focused solely on energy supply, petroleum and kilowatt supply chain. This is the only way we know how to look at it. So we'll do our best to reconstruct inflows, outflows, and map production by modality across the petroleum and electricity supply base and see what we come up with. It's up to you all to place it into a national security context."

The room was silent.

"So we're looking at macro patterns, combined with micro activity," continued Stebbens. "We want to know what has been happening at a global level, then try and understand where these patterns play out by individual companies and or countries. Who's being affected by the growth in importance of Capitana and Savage Island to domestic energy supply consumption—"

"In other words," interrupted Scalia, "who was being harmed most by Capitana and Savage Island?"

"Precisely," said Stebbens. "It might lead us nowhere. But it's all we at Energy can analyze. If there is something there, we should find it. How it relates to the attack on Marks, that's beyond us."

"Isn't that obvious?" asked Scalia. "'America's energy company'? He's a symbol, the godfather of energy independence from the Middle East."

"Again, that's for you to assess, not us. We're quants. We'll tell you what's been happening down to the barrel. We're not going to interpret it."

"How long will DOE's analysis take?" asked Chiles.

"Hours, not days," said Stebbens.

"Good."

"Look, I have to say something here," said Rick Ennis from the National Security Agency. "This is probably relevant."

"What is it?" asked Scalia.

"It's a can of worms."

"Cough it up," said Chiles.

"It's NSA," said Ennis. "This is V-level." He looked at Savoy.

"He's got clearance," said Jessica.

"We had NSA run several tap protocols this morning, referencing Capitana, Savage Island, KKB, Anson," he said. Kratovil, the president's national security adviser, nodded in support. "We went back one year."

"Don't you need a judge's approval to run a tap protocol?" asked McCarthy.

Ennis paused and looked at McCarthy dismissively, then turned to Scalia.

"We gave him the green light," said Scalia. "The president signed an executive order last night."

"Go on," said Chiles.

"There's been growing chatter within OPEC about Capitana. To the point that it's of primary concern. Capitana in particular has been a subject of discussion between high-level government officials."

"What country?" asked Jessica.

Ennis paused and looked around the table. "Saudi Arabia."

"How recent is this chatter?" asked Chiles.

"Last six months."

The room was silent.

"This is a mess," said Scalia. "We need to rethink this. We need to set up some structure here. This could get ugly quickly. This elevates things."

"It isn't elevated already?" asked Chiles.

Scalia looked back at him. "If this was a sanctioned series of attacks or if a government, ally or otherwise, even so much as knew of the existence of the attacks, and didn't let us know, we have, and you'll excuse my French, a serious fucking problem."

20

FORTUNA'S APARTMENT
1040 FIFTH AVENUE
NEW YORK, NEW YORK

Fortuna waved the gray plastic card in front of a sensor next to the elevator buttons. The PH light went on as the elevator began its ascent toward the penthouse apartment.

The key was necessary because the elevators opened up within Fortuna's sprawling residence atop 1040 Fifth Avenue, an exclusive limestone-clad prewar co-op on the Upper East Side, near the Metropolitan Museum of Art. He had the top two floors, more than 14,000 square feet.

The elevator door opened up and he walked in. He stared for a moment at the large Jasper Johns, a huge painting of an American flag that hung dramatically across from the elevator door. On the shining cherry side table beneath the large painting, he placed his cell phone down. He removed his overcoat and threw it on the wing chair to the left of the table.

Footsteps could be heard coming down the hall. Suddenly, a tall man appeared. He was neatly dressed, in a blue button-down and gray flannels. Karim had a face reminiscent of a hawk's, sharp, curving nose, fierce eyes, and hair cropped short.

"So," said Karim, "how was your lunch?"

"Fine," said Fortuna.

As far as everyone at 1040 Fifth Avenue knew, Karim Ajunniliah was one of Fortuna's servants, one of the many domestic employees that helped take care of the personal affairs of the handsome, mysterious billionaire who lived on the top two floors of the building. Like many servants in such buildings across Manhattan, Karim lived in servants' quarters. But Karim was no servant. He'd been sent by Mohammed, Fortuna's adopted father, when Fortuna first moved to Manhattan after Wharton. Karim had lived in Washington and was like a brother to Mohammed. He worked eight years as a sous-chef at the Four Seasons Hotel in Washington, working like any other man while knowing all along that he would one day support the unique destiny of Alexander Fortuna. A destiny that had finally arrived.

Earlier in their association, Fortuna had bridled at the thought of having a caretaker and companion. But soon he saw the advantage of having someone beneath him. For if Fortuna was the architect, Karim was the builder. He ran Fortuna's household. More important, he ran the terrorist network; recruited the men, paid their way, communicated with them, ran them.

Fortuna was as close to Karim as he could be to anyone but his adopted father. But the truth was, the day he'd been torn from his bed in Broumana had seared his soul from any ability to feel emotion, real empathy, or love for another human being. It was Mohammed's brilliance to see this, to understand it, to harvest it, and ultimately to channel it back against itself, and against his adopted country. This would be his contribution to jihad.

"The new Hopper was installed in the bedroom," said Karim. "We had the Wyeth boxed up and delivered to the Wadsworth Atheneum."

Fortuna nodded, moving to a window that overlooked Fifth Avenue. When Fortuna bought the apartment for $37 million, he'd gone through a rigorous application process with the board of the co-op. On the board were descendants of two U.S. presidents, as well as heirs to Andrew Carnegie and William Randolph Hearst, along with a coterie of New York society.

Fortuna lied about his nationality on the application, telling the board he was French, rather than Lebanese. Of course he had false documentation to support this. He also submitted letters, authentic letters, written by no fewer than three U.S. senators, to all of whom he'd contributed a great deal of money to over the years. At the time of his application, he was dating a Hearst heiress, Samantha Biddle Hearst. Her phone call to her great-grandmother, Mia, or "Mummsy" as the grandchildren called her, who was chairwoman of the co-op board, hadn't hurt.

The penthouse contained six bedroom suites in all, nine bathrooms, a gymnasium, a media room, a large dining room with a ballroom attached to it, a massive living room, five working fireplaces, a beautiful kitchen, and a stunning roof deck with a large garden, enclosed tennis court, and a small, kidney-shaped swimming pool and hot tub. The views, especially at the front of the apartment, on Fifth Avenue, were magnificent: Central Park, the Met, and to the left the lights of midtown.

"Your father called," said Karim.

Fortuna turned and looked at Karim for a moment. "I thought he was away."

"Not Mohammed. Aswan. From Broumana. Your *real* father."

"Aswan?" he whispered.

"Yes." He handed Fortuna a piece of paper. "There are two numbers you must dial," said Karim. "Use the London switch. Call from your office. Close the door."

"Yes, yes."

"You can't speak for more than sixty seconds."

Fortuna gave Karim a look. "I know."

He hurried out of the living room and down the hall to his bedroom. Through the bedroom, he stepped through another door. He turned on the lights to his small office. He closed the door behind him, then flipped another switch, which made a low clicking noise. This device scrambled any eavesdropping devices that might be pointed at the room. He sat at the desk and opened a drawer. He picked up the phone on the desk and dialed a number.

The phone rang several times before a strange buzzing tone clicked in. When this happened, Fortuna dialed another set of numbers. In a minute, the phone rang again. This time, a voice picked up.

"Alexander?"

"Father?"

"Yes, son. How are you?"

"Good. You?"

"Old, Alexander."

"We have to talk quickly."

"Yes, yes," said his father. "I called to praise you. You've done excellent work."

"Thank you."

"They tell me it was you who planned it all."

"Yes, it was."

"You've struck a deep blow, son."

"I know."

"Can you send something to our friends? The ones in the tenements?"

"Yes, of course. I'll wire something. It'll be more than they've ever seen."

"Good. We need them making noise. Also, our other friends, in the hills."

"Yes, them too. Are all the accounts the same?"

"I'll ask them to get a message to Karim if anything has changed."

"Right, good."

"We need them making noise, deflecting blame, so that you can stab the knife into the heart of the beast."

"Yes, I know. We're getting closer, Father."

"What's next?"

"The next few days will be severe, truly severe. It will change everything. Watch the news; you'll see, we're only days away."

"When that's done, perhaps you can rejoin me. Before I die."

"I'd like that. How is Mattie?"

"She's married now. She just had a daughter, a girl. Her name is Alexandria, after you. Nebbie is now my right hand. He says hello."

"Good-bye, Father."

Fortuna hung up the phone. He closed his eyes and leaned forward, rubbing them with his right hand. He felt tears well up, but he fought

166

them. He returned to his bedroom and walked into the spacious bathroom. He tried to keep from crying. He walked to the mirror and looked at himself.

"Don't lose your focus," he whispered to himself. "You're so close."

Too close, he often thought.

Fortuna looked around him, at the expansive marble bathroom, the massive stone-tiled shower, the Jacuzzi, the window that framed the broad expanse of Central Park below, its elms and maples dotted with white snow. For as much as he hated America, as much as the acid flowed in his veins, the instinct to harm his adopted country, this venom mingled with regret, a sense of loss; for no matter how much he hated her, America had *made* him, made possible so much of what he had, the vast wealth, the selection of beautiful women, the houses, everything. America had formed him into what he was.

Speaking to his father, then thinking about this . . . it was almost too much. The pressure between the two colliding forces caused him to feel physically ill. He bent over, clutching his chest, knelt on the ground, overwhelmed by an alien surge of anxiety. Uncertainty.

"Stop," he said out loud to no one. "Stand up. It's time."

He went back to the mirror. Slowly, he let his anger transform itself into focus. He reached down and turned the water on, then splashed his face several times. Whatever epiphany had occurred, whatever moment of regret, realization, or loss of will, was gone now. Before him stood once again the hardened animal he'd become; Fortuna, son of Aswan, blade of Allah.

He walked through the bedroom and opened the door.

Karim stood in the hallway. He had a serious expression on his face.

"What is it?"

"Your cell rang. It was Laurent."

"Yes?"

"Something's wrong."

Fortuna walked back into his office. He closed the door behind him. He dialed a number. He knew it by heart.

"Yes," the voice said.

"What happened?"

"Something's wrong, I'm afraid."

"What? Speak."

"It went badly on the rig."

"Badly? The rig is gone, isn't it? *Isn't* it?"

"Yes, sir. But someone fought back. He killed all of our men."

"What do you mean all of our men?

"You heard me. He killed them all."

Fortuna hesitated. "Esco?"

"Yes."

"Who was it?"

"We don't know."

"You don't know?"

"The helicopter came into Cali as planned. But Esco wasn't on board. Only the pilot and a stranger. He shot one of the men on the rooftop of the building."

"What did he look like?"

"They said he was bearded, long hair, Caucasian. American."

"It sounds like the one in charge of the rig—Andreas. Was it him?"

Silence on the other end of the line.

"They were supposed to leave him on the seafloor," said Fortuna.

"Yes."

"Well, then they fucked up. Where is he now?"

"He's in Cali. This only just happened. The chopper crashed into a building. They shot him after the chopper landed. They think they hit him. But—"

"He's gotten *away*?" Fortuna could scarcely believe what he was hearing.

"They're tracking him. He was bleeding badly. But, yes. They're still chasing him. He killed three more men."

"For fuck's sake. Do you realize what Esco *knew*?"

"Yes," Laurent said once again.

"You listen to me. You're to fix this. End it. We have no idea how much Andreas might have learned. Esco knew the targets. Esco knew everything. We trained together. If he got anything out of Esco we—" Fortuna didn't care to finish the sentence. He didn't need to.

168

"I'm nearly out of men, Alexander."

"Do it anyway. Call me when it's done."

Fortuna hung up and dialed a different number.

"Yes," the voice said.

"Where are you?" asked Fortuna. "Can you talk?"

"No, I can't *talk*," said the voice. "What is it? Be quick."

"One of the survivors," said Fortuna. "He could be a problem."

"I know. Andreas. He just made contact."

Fortuna closed his eyes. "How much did he know?"

"He knew the name of the explosive. I don't know what else, specifically."

"He could know more."

"They're extracting him inside the hour."

"That can't happen. You have to take him out, Victor. My men are
all dead."

Vic Buck chuckled humorlessly. "Just take him out, right? You gotta
be kidding. I'm standing in an office two doors down from the head of
counterterrorism. Now I'm supposed to hunt down your problem? Fuck
that."

"He could know enough to find me," Fortuna said evenly. "If he finds
me, he finds you."

Buck's voice turned savage. "Watch it. Don't forget what I do for a living. I won't be threatened. I could just as easily remove *you*."

"If suicide's your taste, you could try," said Fortuna. "But that would
also leave you fifty million dollars poorer."

"Funny."

"If they extract him, you'll be in the gallows within a week," continued Fortuna. "And I'll be dead. We both know the situation. We need
to do something."

Predictably, the promise of more money—obscene money to a government official like Vic Buck—worked.

"I'll do what I can," said Buck. "If your fucking *martyrs* had just
done their job at the rig—"

Fortuna let out a long-held breath as Vic Buck, director of the Central
Intelligence Agency's National Clandestine Service, hung up the phone.

Fortuna stood up and opened the door to his office, walked through his bedroom, along the long hallway, past the kitchen, into the media room, and sat in a big leather chair. He turned on the plasma.

"Can I get you something to eat?" Karim asked.

"Yes. Anything. Pizza."

Fortuna flipped through the channels until he came to Fox News. On the hundred-inch screen, a male reporter stood in front of KKB's headquarters building on Fifty-ninth Street.

. . . the terrible news has sent shock waves through the energy industry. Ted Marks, apparently still clinging to life in a Denver hospital while Nick Anson along with Anson's wife, Annie, just days after announcing the historic merger of the two large energy concerns, burned to death last night in a fire at Marks's ski house in Aspen. . . .

Marks alive was another disappointment in a mission that had started so well. But the CEO's survival did not compare to the threat of a living, breathing Dewey Andreas. Quickly, Fortuna clicked through all of the news channels. Nothing yet, other than the fire in Aspen. Not a word about Capitana or Savage Island.

He walked to the kitchen.

"Have we heard from Mahmoud?" Fortuna asked, urgency in his voice.

"Nothing," said Karim.

"They say Marks is still alive. If they captured Mahmoud—"

"Let's be patient, Alex."

Fortuna went to his bedroom and put on Lycra running shorts, a blue T-shirt and a pair of running shoes. In the gym, he climbed onto the treadmill, set the timer for forty-five minutes, and started running.

His body felt good, strong, no pain. After twenty minutes, he'd run four miles. He was running his usual 5:00 pace. During his junior year at Princeton, he'd run a 4:20 mile. He looked down at the timing split on the treadmill. He pushed in the setting for 4:30. Four and a half miles into his run, he began pacing at a 4:30 mile. He felt the pain in his legs first, then his head. His legs moved furiously and the sweat poured down his forehead. He grimaced as the first minute passed. He worried he might fall off the back of the treadmill but he kept pushing. Soon the second minute passed, then the third. In front of him, in the mirror, he saw his own reflection for a brief moment. He looked slightly crazed, out of control, not exactly the same form he had in college. Still, how many thirty-six-year-old men could run a 4:30 mile? He crossed the four-minute mark. The pain now occupied every fiber in his body. His mind, which had carried him this far, began to abandon him, telling him to hit the red Stop button on the console. Something deeper spurred him on. He counted the final seconds as the distance meter clicked toward the mile mark. At 4:29, he completed the mile. Fortuna reached forward and pressed the down arrow, slowing the treadmill. He reset the meter at a 5:30 pace. He would run another five miles at a more relaxed pace.

But as he ran, he could only think of Esco. As much as he tried to put it out of his mind, he could not. The first time he had met Esco was a decade ago. Esco, thirty years old at the time, had just quit his job as a teacher in Calcutta. They met on the Crimea Peninsula, at the Hezbollah training camps his father had arranged to send him to. They had shared a tent together for more than a year, before he started at Wharton. It was at Crimea they learned how to plan, to build the cell, to fight, to kill. He recalled Esco's hearty laugh, his calm demeanor, and engineer's mind.

Fortuna tried to use the pain of the run—in his head, his lungs, his legs—to blot out the anger he now felt, and the sadness at the loss of his friend. Finally, he found a way to stem the emotion that welled up inside of him for his brother in arms. It was fury, plain and simple, a deep, abiding rage that coursed up into his body as it built. The fury overtook him as he ran, even faster now, sprinting all-out on the machine, the red rage crystallizing into a single word: *Andreas.*

21

Mattie, three and a half years old, climbed slowly to the old, twisted juniper and sat down. She put her thumb in her mouth.

"If you hide there," said Alexander, "Nebbie won't find you. Hide behind the juniper. I'll rescue you. Don't eat the berries."

"Is this okay?" she whispered.

"Perfect."

Down the hillside, Alexander could see the houses at the edge of Ruwaisseh. It was so hot the rooftops appeared to melt in the haze. He smiled. They'd be here soon. It was time to hide.

In Broumana that summer, the day and night blended into an endless hot continuum. On the hillside above the Lazarists Monastery, the juniper berries were mottled with the first patches of red as they ripened. They'd make Mattie hard to see, even in her orange tunic. Nebbie would find her, but it would take time. She was a sacrifice.

Downhill a distance, Alexander found the rock; he'd seen it before and had made a mental note of it. It was an odd formation that spread out horizontally atop the hill, like a reclining woman. This was where he knew Father would lay their belongings: the old wicker lunch basket, a jug of water, and the prayer blankets.

From the village he heard voices, still some five minutes distant. He took off his clothing—all of it. He rolled it up then tucked it in a small hole he'd dug, then covered it with dry soil.

He lay down in the dust. It was scalding hot, but he endured the pain. He rolled slowly down the hill, turning several times. He could taste the dirt in his mouth.

Voices grew louder, followed by the crunching of sandals on the hillside. Alexander crawled back up the hill and nestled beneath a ridge on the side of the big rock. He tucked his head into his lap so that only the smooth surface of his brown, dust-covered back would show. He had become part of the stone.

"Here we are," said Aswan, Alexander's father.

Alexander listened as the sack was placed down on the ground. A tingling sensation filled his heart. He didn't move. They placed the sack on the rock so close to him he could feel a small breeze when the sack was opened.

"I'm so hungry I could eat a horse," said Father. "Don't you have something to do, Nebuchar?"

Alexander hated his older brother. Nebuchar refused to play with Alexander, too old and mature for games with his five-year-old sibling. Except on Sundays, family day. Father made him play. Nebuchar would oblige him grudgingly, though secretly he relished the actual moment of discovery, enjoyed it because with his fist he would rap Alex and even Mattie with a hard knuckle to the skull.

While Nebuchar began to search, Alex could hear his father setting out the plates. He smelled the chicken and garlic, and the figs, he could even smell the rice. His favorite meal. His father cooked only on Sundays and it was the only dish he knew how to prepare, but he did it with elaborate care, in honor of their late mother, he said. The way father did it, the figs cooked for three whole days in the small tandoor oven, heated by the fire, so that they melted in your mouth when you bit in.

"You might as well come out. You know I'll find you." Nebuchar walked to the base of the big cypress. There was a small notch that was just big enough for a coyote or a small child. Empty.

"Mattie!" he yelled. "Alex!"

From the distance, his father laughed. "What? Big man can't find his little brother and sister?" Their father now sat on the rock, not more than a foot from Alexander, drinking a cup of water. "Do I need to come and help you, Nebbie?"

"No! I'll find them."

Nebuchar walked around the cypress toward the juniper, this out of sight from his father. He saw little Mattie, smacked her in the head.

"Got you!" he yelled as Mattie screamed and began to cry. "Where's Alex?" he demanded.

"I'm not telling. I hate you, Nebbie."

"Tell me or I'll hit you again."

"No!" she yelled and she ran to her father.

Nebuchar circled the hillside slowly, eventually reaching the picnic site.

"You hit a three-year-old girl?" their father asked angrily. "That's the sign of a weakling and a coward. You're twelve. No lunch for you today."

Nebuchar was silent. Alex bit his tongue, tempted to laugh.

"I know what goes through that mind of yours," said his father. "I'd suggest you say nothing for one minute. If you raise your voice at me or so much as kick your foot in the sand I'll send you back down to the house and you'll spend the rest of the day washing the tiles on the roof."

Alex shuddered with pleasure, wishing he could see Nebbie's face.

"Where is he? I can't find him."

"What do you mean you can't find him?"

"He's nowhere. I've looked everywhere."

Father removed Mattie from his lap and served her a plate of the chicken. She stopped crying and began to eat.

Father stood and did a slow turn, looking in all directions. "Alexander!" he yelled. "Alexander!" Father took a walk down the hill, then returned. "He's gone, I tell you." Father laughed. "He beat you. And soundly at that."

"Yeah," said Nebuchar, "but when I find him—"

"When you find him you'll congratulate him and leave him alone. Do you understand?"

"Okay."

"Well, anyway, let's eat. I must get back and prepare for tomorrow's lecture."

"But Alex," said Mattie. "Where's Alex?"

"He'll show up," said their father. "I know Alex. Wherever he is, he's okay. Let's eat."

Aswan made himself a plate of chicken, put the cover back on the dish and set it down.

"Jesus Christ, mother of the lamb!" He'd put the dish down on Alex's back. Alex stood up, naked and covered in dirt from head to toe.

"Alex!" Mattie yelled. "Are you all right?"

"I'm fine." Alex crossed his arms proudly. "That's how you hide from the wolf."

"Well?" his father said, laughing, looking at Nebuchar. "Don't you have something to say?"

"Congratulations, dragon," he spat out.

Alex smiled. He walked to the tip of the rock. He knelt down and brushed the layer of dirt from the hole, and pulled out his clothing.

His father chuckled—and continued to do so the rest of the day. "You're brilliant," he said. After Alex dressed, he handed him his plate of chicken. "How did you think of that idea?"

Alex's eyes peered out coldly through the brown dust caked to his face. He stared at his brother. "To hide from the wolf, the only way to survive is to hide in plain sight."

"To hide in plain sight," his father repeated that evening after prayers. "To hide in plain sight."

The wisdom of a five-year-old.

In one brief moment, all of Aswan's unfocused hatred coalesced into a stark course of action.

When the three men arrived that evening, as they had every Sunday evening for two years running, Aswan described a vision that would serve as a blueprint for the terror to come.

"I've had a vision, brothers," he said after the tea was poured. "I know how we'll stab a dagger into the heart of our enemy."

The group of men, four in all, began as a prayer group at the University of Beirut. Aswan, who was chairman of the European Languages Department at the university, had been the last to join. He didn't like to proclaim his religious identity; he thought it was a private matter, for family only.

After his wife Rhianne died, though, Aswan changed. He changed in so many ways even he didn't understand them all. His temper, which before had smoldered like a fire within, calmed. He found that his love for his children, his patience, his joy from being with them, grew. He also began to pray more. Hours at a time. As he did so he became closer with the true meaning.

But if the temper abated and the love of family grew, in some way it was balanced by something else that happened. Aswan began to hate those he saw as responsible for his wife's death. And the hatred became interwoven with prayer.

At his wife's funeral, a colleague from the university named Mohammed invited him to join the small prayer group. At first they devoted the time to prayer, but that soon changed. They started to drink tea and talk, then pray, until finally the prayers ceased altogether and only talk happened.

But the talk . . . oh, the talk. The discussions, they all felt, were nearly as important as the prayer. Because as they talked, they all found a common thread, which became a powerful tether uniting them. They hated America.

Mohammed had earned his Ph.D. at Harvard, as had Palan, the third member of the group. They had shared an apartment on the outskirts of Cambridge. The fourth member of the group, Binda, was a junior professor at the university. Like Aswan, he'd never been to America. But like many who've never been, he hated it with even more intensity than the others.

So they spoke of America's government. How it grew out of bloodshed and recklessly cast its shadow wherever it chose, in Vietnam, in Iran. Of Israel, their most hated enemy, and how America protected her with guns and money.

That fateful Sunday evening, Aswan poured wine into each of the teacups. It was a special occasion.

"It will work this way," Aswan explained. "It can only work this way. . . ."

That next autumn, as planned, Mohammed accepted the teaching post at George Washington University in Washington, D.C. Palan went to America too, taking a job in the maintenance department of a small nuclear power plant in Pennsylvania called Three Mile Island.

And exactly one year after that, young Alexander was ripped from his bedsheets at age six in the middle of the night. He wasn't harmed, but it was sudden and deliberate, like a kidnapping. Unlike a kidnapping, however, it was a plan designed by his own father and carried out by Binda. He took him at three thirty in the morning. Binda muffled his screams with a handkerchief stuffed into his small mouth. When the struggling and screaming stopped hours later, as the dawn approached, he drugged Alexander. It was only Valium, but it stopped the crying.

"It has to be this way," Aswan had said that night with the wine. "It must be this way. Sudden and violent, not gradual." Mohammed and his wife Calla had to become Alex's parents, and not just his guardians. He must be ripped from the womb. "He must be loved like a son by you, Mohammed. Can you love my son? Can you and Calla raise him as Rhianne and I would have?"

"We can. We will."

"I love him the most of all of my children, you see. But I can't tear him from his own home. That must be you. In this way I sacrifice all for our cause, but I'll never recover."

To hide in plain sight, thought Aswan that terrible morning after Alexander vanished, as he shivered in his bedroom, tears flowing down his cheeks, holding Nebuchar, also sobbing, and Mattie, confused and hysterical.

So it began.

In Bethesda, they lived in a sprawling shingle-style home, with Navy blue shutters and a low, white picket fence. In the big backyard, Alexander learned to play football and baseball with the neighborhood children.

He strongly resembled Calla. For whatever reason, despite the fact they weren't related, he possessed her sharp, beautiful nose. His coloring was light, but Mediterranean. By ten he was already six feet tall, and startlingly handsome. At twelve, one of the neighborhood girls, the daughter of a French diplomat stationed in Washington, kissed him on the lips. Also that year, at school, he got into a fight with a child named Kevin, who thought Alexander had shoved him in the hallway. Kevin broke Alexander's nose with his first punch, but it was Alexander who, upon seeing and tasting his own blood, went into a frenzied rage and beat the bully with his fists, not only breaking the boy's nose but also knocking out two front teeth.

Alexander grew quickly to like strawberry ice cream, coffee, girls, and reading, especially Ernest Hemingway. They raised him as an Episcopalian because it was part of the plan that he assimilate. He had many friends, and a best friend, George, the youngest son of a brood of four boys who lived next door. They strung Dixie cups together with a long string between the two big houses so that they could talk to one another, a set of low-tech walkie-talkies. On Sundays, he and George, sometimes with George's older brothers, would walk to the movie theater on Connecticut Avenue and catch a matinee. It was with George that Alex drank his first beer. When George's family moved back to Kansas after his father was transferred by General Electric, it was the most devastating event of Alex's young life.

He couldn't remember the night they'd torn him from his home in Lebanon. Aswan was like a dream father whom, when Alex was alone, he would recall in foggy images, warming him in a way that was just below his ability to articulate in words even to himself. His true mother's face he never forgot, but everything else seemed hazy. Had he *had* another father? Had he even been to that place, or was it a dream? That beautiful city that smelled of ocean and pine and dust?

For Mohammed and Calla, he was a blessing. Who would've known Calla would prove barren? All of her love that she had in her heart, the love she always planned on giving to her own children, went to him. Mohammed was awed by the young boy. In everything he did, Alexander excelled. Like his real father, Alex had a talent for languages. By sixteen he exhausted the Episcopal Academy languages department, and was fluent in French, Spanish, and Italian. His junior year at Episcopal, he scored a perfect 1,600 on his SAT. It was obvious Alexander would go wherever he wanted for college. On the Episcopal lacrosse team, Alex played midfield and was captain of the team his senior year. He loved lacrosse more than anything and was named all-American at the end of the season. When Alex applied to college, it was only to schools that had strong lacrosse programs—Princeton, University of Virginia, Yale, and Harvard. He was accepted by all of the schools and chose Princeton.

All the while, like a cancer, Mohammed slowly, patiently, methodically developed the beast within.

It began innocently enough, in the basement of his house, in a small homemade boxing ring. At nine years of age, he and Alex would go down after dinner and spar, and laugh, and spar some more. By ten, when Alex was already as tall as Mohammed, the sparring became more real. One night, Alex gave Mohammed a bloody nose; the next night, Mohammed returned the favor, then watched as Alexander lost control of his temper and went into a mad and violent frenzy directed at him. Mohammed knew he'd have to harness that anger.

He could never tell Calla what it was all about, though he wanted to. They rarely spoke. Mohammed left for his office at George Washington University by 5:00 A.M. and usually didn't return until after dinner. When he did, he looked at her blankly and would usually go to the basement and read or work on the computer. When Alex returned home from school, he'd join Mohammed there as well.

Calla assumed Mohammed was having an affair. But it wasn't a woman that removed him from the marriage. In truth, he was transformed. The original hatred that had propelled him to the shores of the United States had been forged into the steel framework of Aswan's plan.

Into that scheme he carefully, deliberately, slowly, gradually, but ultimately completely drew Alexander.

As in Beirut, Mohammed formed a small network of like-minded jihadists. There were three in all. Dahim was an academic, an assistant professor at American University. The other, Karim, worked as a sous-chef in the restaurant at the Four Seasons. Mohammed didn't want to risk socializing with any Middle Easterners posted in Washington at one of the embassies. He knew they'd be under surveillance. Both Dahim and Karim were known by Aswan.

In the basement, on Alex's thirteenth birthday, as he opened up the present that Mohammed had given to him, he spoke for the first time about what had to be done.

"Are you old enough to be a man?"

"I'm thirteen, Dad. I'm taller than you."

"I'm not talking physically," Mohammed said. "Are you ready to talk of difficult things?"

Alex was silent. Eventually he nodded. It was then Mohammed told Alex of jihad.

His birthday present consisted of two small volumes, underground books, one a book of poetry by D. W. Myatt entitled *One Exquisite Silence*, the other a novel by Myatt about a future world where America has taken over the world and a young Muslim hero named Basal-el saves civilization.

It was an odd day for Alexander. He didn't like the presents. For the first time, he felt alienated from Mohammed and confused. Mohammed knew that would be the case. It had to begin somewhere.

What began as conversations and confusion between Mohammed and Alex on his thirteenth birthday grew into comprehension and acceptance.

Sometime during that fourteenth year of Alexander's life, Mohammed explained to him that he and Calla were not his parents. Alexander cried. He wouldn't speak to either parent for a week. But it worked. After that week, Alex never cried again.

He lived a schizophrenic life. In the day, he was the president of his senior class at Episcopal Academy. He was captain of the lacrosse team. He was popular. He had a succession of girlfriends.

At night, after his studies, Mohammed would teach him of Allah, and jihad. At night, Alex became a freedom fighter, at least in his mind. At night, Mohammed carefully planted the seeds of a hatred that became the lifeblood of his soul.

On the night before he was to leave for Princeton, Mohammed brought a small television set and VCR out of a closet in the basement.

"What's that for?" Alex asked.

Mohammed was silent. He turned the television set on and pushed a tape in.

"Do you remember Three Mile Island?"

"Yes. The accident at the nuclear power plant."

"You had just arrived."

The black-and-white picture on the small TV became clear. Walter Cronkite came on the set. Mohammed and Alexander watched the tape together, a recording of the *CBS Evening News* the night of Three Mile Island. Mohammed poured two small glasses of red wine from a bottle that was tucked away in a trunk, cabarnet from a small vineyard near Broumana called Chateau Ksara.

"This is being called the worst industrial accident in American history," the voice on the television said. "It's still not known if the cooling mechanism within the containment vessel will be enough to prevent a catastrophic event known as a nuclear meltdown. . . ."

"Why are we watching this?" asked Alexander.

"His name was Palan," said Mohammed. "He was a friend. He and I arrived in America on the same plane from Lebanon. He worked at the plant. This was our first project. He was our first martyr."

Alexander was silent as he stared at Mohammed, then back at the television.

"One man," said Mohammed. "One man maimed America this day in 1979. This was why you were brought to America."

Mohammed reached his arm out then and placed it on Alexander's shoulder.

Alexander shut his eyes for nearly a minute as he realized the implications. Finally, he looked back at Mohammed.

"Thank you, Father," he whispered.

"We'll never triumph if we try and launch missiles from the sky or take hostages like the students in Tehran, or commit suicide on buses," said Mohammed. "Those things only make us feel good. They only make the challenge harder."

"We have to attack anonymously," whispered Alexander.

"Patiently," said Mohammed. "That most of all."

Alexander took a big gulp and finished the wine in his glass. "May I have another glass of wine, Father?"

Mohammed smiled. He picked up the green bottle of cabarnet.

"Yes, you may."

22

U.S. DEPARTMENT OF ENERGY
WASHINGTON, D.C.

Antonia Stebbens walked into the main entrance of the Department of Energy, then took an elevator to the fifth floor. She walked down a long hallway, turned the corner, and walked to the end of another long, windowless corridor. There, she took out a metal pass card and slid it into a small sensor. When she heard a click, she walked through the unmarked door. In front of her was a small elevator. Once inside, Stebbens inserted a different card into the scanner inside the elevator. The door closed and the elevator went down, to a heavily fortified floor eleven stories below her, six stories below ground level.

Entry here began with Stebbens staring into a blue light and trying hard not to blink. She'd stared into the blue light nearly every morning for more than a decade and knew the biometric's foibles and flaws. If you blinked, the machine occasionally registered a false negative, alerting two security guards with weapons drawn. This, of course, was sure to send your coffee flying all over the fingerprint scanner, which came next. She understood why it had to be this way, but if you asked her, it was overkill.

Once the machine determined that the person in front of it was, in fact, Antonia Stebbens, the door on the other side of the metal passage opened. She now stepped inside what was the main U.S. government intelligence-gathering and security control point for all energy-related facilities in the United States: Strategic Operations Center, or SOC.

SOC's primary purpose was oversight of the security of all seven U.S. nuclear weapons manufacturing installations.

While it falls to the president to decide if and when to fire a nuclear weapon, and the Department of Defense does the actual firing, it's DOE's job to build America's nukes, and SOC's to ensure that this process remains secure.

Stebbens's official title was undersecretary of Energy and director of the Strategic Operations Center. She was the boss of a directorate little known even within the U.S. government. It was staffed with two hundred and fifty-eight individuals, all of whom passed rigorous background checks and agreed to allow the government to monitor all of their activities both inside and outside SOC: cellular and wireline phone conversations, e-mail and regular mail, and any other communications inside or outside of work.

Of the two hundred and fifty-eight nonsupport staff professionals within SOC, all had previous government experience. The CIA was SOC's main feeder agency, with the FBI a close second, and NSA just behind. In fact, SOC had more than a hundred and fifty ex-CIA employees, including Stebbens.

Of the two hundred and fifty-eight agents and analysts within SOC, two hundred and ten were detailed to the security of America's nuclear bomb manufacturing infrastructure. The other forty-eight dealt with nonnuclear issues, mainly oil- and gas-related security issues. Refinery security was a main priority, and its subgroup was called SOCOG.

Because the attacks on Capitana and Savage Island occurred during the Christmas holidays, few people were around. But that didn't matter to Stebbens.

Stebbens started today's work by convening her six senior staffers.

"I know you've all been here through the night," said Stebbens. "I appreciate your work. I want to make sure you also express that sentiment to your own people."

There were nods around the table.

"What do we have?" asked Stebbens. She took a sip from her coffee cup. "I have to be back at the FBI in two hours and I need some content." Stebbens nodded to a gray-haired man seated across the table. "Bob?"

"Here's a summary of where we are," said Bob Griffin, who was in charge of the team of analysts looking at petroleum-related activities. He smiled and cleared his throat, pulling a stack of papers from his notebook and passing it around the table. "It's still early. First priority is protecting the remaining sources of petro that impact consumption within the United States. We've set up a protocol within SOC, then live-wired this information across the intelligence protocol. That's now live. It'll be updated hourly. We're actively tracking a month's worth of petro supply, down through individual well hole, tanker, storage depot, et cetera. Our goal is to get that tracking protocol extended out one year, so we have assurance on a secure year's supply of oil."

"Good," said Stebbens.

"Second issue is replacement dynamics," said Griffin. "Are OPEC, Venezuela, et al., prepared to increase production and, more important, give that increase to the United States? This is a more challenging situation. Capitana supplied more than nine percent of America's raw petroleum supply and that number was increasing. We'll need to manage not only the analysis, but will have to participate behind the scenes with State Department and the White House on any implementation. If, for example, Venezuela, Saudi Arabia, or others are unwilling to help, that needs to impact us in real time, again across the intelligence protocol."

"What do we have there?"

"This is really about Saudi Arabia and Venezuela," said Griffin. "Let's start with Venezuela. They could, if they chose, increase deliveries by a million to a million and a half barrels a day by mid-January," said Griffin. "They're stockpiling and the primary barrier there is political. They wouldn't have to increase production, just delivery."

"Got it," said Stebbens, taking notes.

"OPEC, however, doesn't have stockpiles," said Griffin. "China is sucking them dry. In the past six months, Sinopec has been willing to consistently outbid U.S. suppliers by up to ten dollars a barrel. They've taken what was a decent stockpile and monetized it for OPEC, particularly

Iran. That said, they could easily increase production. Saudi Arabia alone could fill most of the existing shortfall created by Capitana's destruction."

"Okay," said Stebbens. "Now what about retroactive activity?"

"We're looking at petro supply and demand activity over the past three years," said Griffin. "If you look at the second sheet, you'll see some interesting preliminary data."

"Go on," said Stebbens.

"The first key finding is that Capitana is harming BP here in the United States. Anson's U.S. market share has quadrupled every year while BP's is falling in almost exact proportion."

"So BP's been the victim of Capitana's growth?" asked Stebbens.

"BP's more than made up for loss in U.S. share by gains in Europe. They've increased their dominance in the European theater. Surprisingly, the decline in U.S. demand hasn't hurt them."

"The plot thickens," said Stebbens, looking at the paper.

"Saudi Arabia, on the other hand, has been hurt on two fronts," said Griffin. "Aramco has been pummeled by BP in Europe. This was their best growth play market and that growth, starting four years ago, halted and has been in steady decline ever since. On one dimension, Aramco's shift to China appears smart. It's their way to recoup losses in Europe. But if you look at chart four, you'll see they've been heavily subsidizing transport costs to China. They're effectively lowering the profit they make per barrel by nearly forty percent. That is dramatic movement by any measure."

"What's worse," said another man, a young brown-haired man with glasses, "is the selling of the stockpiles. Because Ghawar field has such extraordinary baseline cost infrastructure, they have to keep pumping. In our analysis, the Saudis have been selling stockpile to avoid having to shut down certain parts of the field. They're in a challenging, negative production cycle."

The room was silent for a few moments.

"So what you're saying is Saudi Arabia is the primary victim of Capitana's rise?" asked Stebbens.

"It's early," said Griffin. "We have reams of data still to parse." He paused and removed his glasses, placing them down on the table. "But yes. The Saudis couldn't have been pleased with Capitana."

"Meanwhile, they're the only ones who can fill the gap over here?"

"That's right."

"What about kilowatt?" she asked, looking at a young Japanese American woman, Libby Coolidge, who was Griffin's counterpart on the electricity side.

"I'll keep it short," said Coolidge. "One, even before we stepped in, White House, FBI, et al., massively increased security and monitoring of electric infrastructure. We have piggybacked on that and now have the lead on a cross-agency protocol. We're monitoring all existing infrastructure above ten thousand megawatt and reporting across the protocol hourly."

"Excellent."

"Second, replacement dynamics," continued Coolidge. "There are no silver bullets here. We're already seeing rolling blackouts along the East Coast, particularly in the South. Savage Island was not just a growing source of raw electric; it was the leading source on the eastern seaboard. We're talking about a very challenging situation. There's no way to simply tap stockpile here. Luckily we're at the lowest consumption time of the year, especially in New England. We're also increasing output at hundreds of facilities that can fill in the grid loss. They're increasing electric production at Duke, ConEd, Entergy and Exelon, and other civilian nukes, combined with a much more significant input from Canada Power. We should be okay, but it will take time for it to ramp up."

"Got it," said Stebbens.

"Finally, looking back at supply and demand patterns," said Coolidge. "There is an exponentially more distributed population of players on the electric side. Savage Island hasn't necessarily hurt anyone. Sure, we see a decline in a whole gamut of Midwest and Northeast suppliers. I could give you a list. But no one's gotten hammered here. Savage did what they said it would do; it lowered costs. In particular, it knocked the floor out of costs for manufacturers along the East Coast."

"So, in summary, the problem on the electric side is replacement," said Stebbens.

"Exactly. That's where my team needs to spend its time."

"I agree," said Stebbens, standing up. "I leave here in one hour. Pardon the pun, but I want you to drill into the Aramco thing. If that information proves out about depleting stockpiles at below-market financial recovery, that is potentially dramatic information."

"If the Saudis are our only replacement valve, and they had something to do with this, doesn't that put us in somewhat of a bind?" asked another staffer, a middle-aged man sitting to Stebbens's right.

Stebbens paused, looked around the room, and removed her bifocals. "We don't get paid to answer those questions."

Across the Potomac River, in an anonymous-looking, dark glass box of a building in Arlington, Virginia, Rick Ennis walked into a large, windowless room in the bowels of the National Security Agency. The NSA is the U.S. government's cryptologist; the place where electronic information is gathered, synthesized, and analyzed by the government.

The NSA serves as America's electronic eyes and ears throughout the world, using a staggering array of highly sophisticated computers, satellites, and other equipment to eavesdrop on the world's communications, from the most highly sensitive conversations to the most mundane e-mail, text, or phone call. By spying around the clock, on enemies and allies alike, the agency has archived a vast amount of information, most of which the NSA is not permitted by law to look at.

Rick Ennis was the NSA's chief operating officer.

Within two hours of the attack on Capitana, Savage Island, and the attacks on Ted Marks and Nicholas Anson, Ennis sought permission from his boss, the director of the NSA, General Landon Bossidy, to have his team of analysts analyze archived communications going back five years and containing the terms "Capitana," "Savage Island," "KKB," "Anson Energy," and "Marks."

The agency called this protocol of examining old, "accidentally" captured information, trace intelligence amphitheatre, or TIA.

TIA, as everyone at NSA knew, was really just retroactive spying.

General Bossidy in turn asked the White House for authorization. There, the president, who must approve such protocols, took less than ten minutes to authorize the request under executive order.

Now, eight hours after receiving the green light from the White House, Ennis stood in the doorway of the large room and looked at his team of young analysts, fourteen in all, young, highly educated professionals recruited out of the nation's top schools, who sat in a room that took up almost a quarter of a floor at NSA headquarters and looked like a cross between a fraternity house and the National Archives. Paper was strewn about the room, in stacks. Coffee was the lifeblood of the event. Empty cups and the aroma of coffee were everywhere.

"What do we have?" Ennis asked as he walked into the room and sat down.

The group of analysts looked up from their reading.

"I have something," said a young Korean American woman.

"What is it?"

"A ton of talk about Capitana within OPEC. I just read a month's worth of phone calls between a senior executive at Aramco and a senior staffer in Fahd's oil ministry."

"So what?" said Ennis. "Competitive threat. Shouldn't they be studying their competitors?"

The young woman flipped through the papers and started reading aloud.

Chief of Staff: Is it too late to disrupt the project? Does it need to start on time? I thought we had people on the construction team.
Aramco: We tried and succeeded, but only to a certain extent. It's moving ahead. With that much oil we're not going to just stop it.
Chief of Staff: Can't we buy the rights from Anson? What's it worth?
Aramco: Get in line. They've been offered staggering amounts. We missed the window.

"Here's another one," she continued, "between Dubai's oil minister and a woman whose identity we don't have. It's a sanitized phone line."

Oil minister: Sahr-lin—

"The head of Aramco?" asked Ennis.
"Yes, that's right," said the woman, continuing.

Oil minister: Sahr-lin is going to be fired over this project in Colombia.
Woman: Yes, yes, I know. I spoke with him yesterday. He says Fahd
    wants to go to war with the Colombian government. (Laughter.)
Oil minister: I don't see why they're so upset. They have enough oil to
    last until their great-grandchildren are dead and buried.
Woman: They're mad at Sahr-lin. He could've stopped it, as they did
    with Exxon's Mongolia project.
Oil minister: Well, if you ask me, it serves the bastard right.

"That's a smoking gun," Ennis said after pondering. "Follow it. Focus on larger patterns here. Evidence of conspiracy, discussion around operative activities involving Capitana, Savage Island, Marks."

Ennis stood up.

"I leave in an hour for the FBI. If anything nasty pops up, ring me." He smiled at the analysts. "I'll send in some pizzas. You all look hungry."

An hour later, Ennis returned.

"Anything?" he asked as he straightened his tie and sat down in a chair at the table.

"We've got a new line," said a blond-haired woman. "The last two years the Saudis are growing panicked about Capitana, and the Chinese."

"The Chinese?" asked Ennis.

"The Chinese are playing Aramco against BP. Internally, the Saudis are calling the Chinese extortionists. We really need an energy analyst here. They're freaking out about Capitana."

"But is there anything operational?" Ennis asked.

"Would there be?" asked a long-haired, bespectacled analyst. "I mean, are these guys stupid?"

"Good point. I'll be back in an hour."

By noon, the interagency group had reconvened at FBI headquarters.

"Welcome back everyone," said Chiles. "Let's begin with DOD."

"Right," said Scalia, turning to Jane Epstein. "Is Andreas out?"

"The exfiltration takes place in fifteen minutes," said Epstein. "We have the team in place. It's being run directly from Comm Ops at the Pentagon. Should be a piece of cake."

"Good. Then let's hear from DOE," said Scalia.

Antonia Stebbens smiled politely and leaned forward. "First, it's early. I have a dozen analysts who haven't slept in two days in the basement of DOE crunching numbers."

"And?" said Scalia. "Get to the point."

"As I said, it's early," said Stebbens. "This is only preliminary, and I reserve the right to completely alter my findings based upon our continued research and analysis."

"Antonia," said Chiles. "Please."

"Here goes," Stebbens continued. "We have a complicated scenario. In terms of replacement dynamics, we need to approach OPEC, and Saudi Arabia specifically, to fill in the hole that Capitana's loss created. There is no other near-term option as it relates to petro supply."

"Okay," said Scalia.

"At the same time," continued Stebbens, "there is clear evidence that the rise of Capitana most directly impacted Saudi Arabia. To the point that we see evidence that production activity, economics, and decision making within Ghawar field were dramatically affected by Capitana in a very negative way."

"Explain," said Chiles.

"Basically, Capitana pummeled BP's oil business in the U.S.," said Stebbens. "But further analysis shows BP made up market share losses here with gains in Europe. In fact, BP's share gains in Europe more than offset losses in the U.S. BP took share from Aramco. The Saudis lost huge market share across Europe. They're now making it up by selling to the Chinese, specifically Sinopec, at below-market prices. We believe they've sold off their stockpiles of crude to the Chinese at losses."

"Why would they be doing that?" asked Scalia.

"Because they probably feel the need to keep cash coming into Ghawar field operations," answered Stebbens. "They've sold off virtually their entire stockpile."

"So what's the bottom line?"

"The bottom line is the Saudis were hurt very badly by Capitana. Unfortunately, they are also the only ones who can step in and replace Capitana supply. Without immediate effort to fill in the coming drop-off in Capitana petro, there will be oil shock like we've never seen. We need them, and we need them immediately. I'm talking about immediate intercession at the highest levels."

The room was silent for a few moments.

"I should probably pipe in here," said Rick Ennis from NSA. "We're deep into the review of more than a hundred and seventy-five thousand pages of phone conversations, e-mails, and other communications. And what is clear is that there was panic at the highest levels of OPEC, of Aramco, of the Saudi oil ministry and the Saudi government, as it relates to Capitana and Anson Energy. We have yet to find anything operative, that is, any discussion of targeting Capitana. But we wouldn't necessarily see that. They know to have that kind of discussion out of earshot. What we do have is clear discussion of trying to sabotage Capitana: buy off the principals, intervene politically, you name it."

The room was again silent for several moments.

John Scalia from the White House broke the silence. "What will the Saudis want?" he asked.

"For the oil, we're talking hundreds of billions," said Stebbens. "The check that was written to Aramco in 1973 to end the oil embargo was one hundred and seventy-seven billion dollars. They'll want a major down payment. They'll also want guarantees going way out. Ghawar is running down. I can't begin to imagine what they'll ask for in terms of time commitment and pricing, but it's safe to assume it will be expensive and long term."

"They'll also want weapons," said Epstein from DOD. "And not just warplanes."

"So the Saudis had the motive," said Scalia. "The evidence points to them. But even if we wanted to do something about it, we can't. Is that right?"

Nobody answered. Finally, Vic Buck from the CIA cleared his throat. "You have to admit, it's a masterful operation. They fucked us in the ass."

"I have to make a phone call," said Scalia.

23

In the strip mall off Rua Dista, Dewey parked the sedan at the side of the mall, in the middle of employee parking. He unscrewed the license plate on the back of the Mercedes and quickly switched it with the plates on a minivan parked several rows away. At a pharmacy in the mall he bought new bandaging, first-aid tape, and battery-powered clippers. He ducked into a restroom and cut his hair to only an inch long and shaved away his beard and mustache.

An hour and fifty minutes later, he had driven to within walking distance of Madradora in the southern part of the city. It was a hardscrabble section and the Mercedes stood out, so he parked it several blocks away. He walked past an empty soccer stadium, coming at Madradora Square from the south, then changed direction and crossed several streets until he arrived at the back entrance to a church that towered over the square. Entering through a large, red-painted doorway, he stepped into the soaring apse, near the altar. A few old women were at prayer and did not look up as he walked down the side of the church. At the back of the church, he saw a stairwell. He climbed the stairs and was soon in the chancel choir. At the back wall, a transparent pane in the stained glass window gave Dewey a clear look down on the square.

Madradora Square was crowded. Several children played in the middle of the large, grass-covered square, while mothers on benches watched and listened to the laughter as their children ran around. Along the sidewalks at the edge of the square stood several cafés and assorted stores.

Dewey well knew the drill here. After all, he'd performed similar exfiltrations on many occasions. The Deltas were likely in the square right now. If they were good, even he wouldn't recognize them. Perhaps the man stooped over on the front step of the town house to the left, sweeping a broom. Or the coffee drinker at the café, far right.

He looked at his watch and still had five minutes to spare. He was nervous but also excited. He found himself looking forward to seeing how these Deltas did their work—that is, if he still had the skill to spot them.

The time since his service seemed to have passed quickly. He'd lost track along the way, but right now it felt like yesterday—his last hours as a Delta. With each passing minute, with every step closer he got, the feelings rushed back: the sense of steel-bound commitment to the mission, the willingness to kill and die, all of it.

It had been a rainy Friday night at Fort Bragg, a cool evening after a hard run. His team grabbed dinner together after returning from a month-long training jaunt in the Okefenokee swamp in southern Georgia. They'd gone there to learn jungle survival tactics, thrown into the swamp alone, with nothing more than a piece of string and a knife. They were expected to survive, deep in the heart of cottonmouth country. And that was exactly how Dewey had survived, eating cottonmouths and sleeping in the crotch of a tree.

When he finally got home and opened his front door he saw Holly on the floor of the living room. Her head had been blown apart; his service Colt lying beside her. He could still remember the black hockey tape he wrapped around the butt of the old gun, blood pooled around it. Everywhere. Holly's blue eyes staring up at him.

They said it was tough to be a military wife. They didn't have a saying for what it was like to be the wife of a Delta.

Holly had changed after Robbie died. Of course she had. Dewey had too. How were you supposed to respond to the loss of a six-year-old boy? Dewey was asked to try out for Delta the same week of the leukemia diagnosis. He tried to explain it to Holly, that they needed the health insurance, the income. Should he really just quit? She knew as well as Dewey that it wasn't about benefits or money. Delta training offered Dewey an outlet for his anger, the bitterness of watching his only child get sicker and wither. But leaving for Delta training left Holly with nothing, not even her husband. At the very end, in Robbie's final months, Dewey's commanding officer finally granted him compassionate leave, but only after he threatened to quit. He and Holly endured those last days together, watching Robbie die. After Robbie's death, Holly's anger surfaced first, followed by grief, then depression that deepened with each passing day. Finally came the silence.

Dewey realized later that he could never have understood the depth of Holly's despair. Even now he could scarcely imagine what it was like for her to suffer her bottomless sorrow alone.

This was her last statement to him: suicide, with his own service pistol. He understood the message, empathized with it too. She hadn't meant to make it look like he'd killed her, as the police and D.A. claimed. She had only intended to say, "Look at what you left me to do, you and your precious duty. Look at what you've left me to witness alone, so you can be a soldier." That was the significance of his old service gun. It had been a private, desperate gesture, not an attempt to make others believe Dewey would actually kill his wife.

Holly's family had thrown their full support behind the prosecutor, telling them about Dewey's drinking, his temper and tendency toward violence. They refused to admit their only child could kill herself.

And the prosecutor had been only too happy to listen, glory in his eyes for the prosecution of an angry soldier at a time when the military was unpopular. The police had locked Dewey up a week later.

The D.A. tried him in the local newspaper, on the local television stations, long before any trial. Even all that Dewey didn't mind. It was his Delta commander he would never forget. He abandoned him. The U.S. military, who he'd given his life to, abandoned him. They refused to help. After so many years of service, of risking his life for country and force, they'd left him to the wolves.

Still, the jury found him not guilty. It took them only half an hour. For his part, Dewey left the courthouse and never looked back. A month in Nepal and Tibet, hiking. Two months later he applied for a job as a roughneck on a Marathon oil derrick off the coast of Scotland. The rest was history.

Dewey stared through the window in front of him, seeing nothing.

He closed his eyes momentarily and forced himself back to the task at hand.

He made himself scan the square again, more slowly this time. There, on a bench in the middle of the square, a large man with reading glasses sat with a book. *Mark one.* At the back right, the man drinking the cup of coffee turned his head and scoured the scene from behind dark sunglasses. As Dewey watched, he stood up and reached for cash from his pocket to place down on the table. *Mark two.*

Dewey descended the church stairwell and went through the front door of the church out toward the square. Sunlight filtered through a large oak tree in front of the beautiful façade. Across the square, in the middle of where the children played as their mothers watched, the first Delta, the one on the bench, stood. He made Dewey and their eyes met. Dewey began walking down the slate steps of the church toward him.

From the corner of his eye, Dewey became aware of a third man, a tall man with a dark complexion, baseball cap, shorts, and running shoes. He moved quickly from the sidewalk on the right toward the square. Had they sent three soldiers to meet him? Hadn't they said two Deltas would be coming?

The tall man moved quickly. The first Delta, coming at Dewey, hadn't noticed the approaching intruder.

Dewey glanced at mark two, back right, the Delta in sunglasses, who had begun talking with a blond-haired woman. A distraction, Dewey realized, as the long-haired man attempted to brush the woman to the side. A commotion ensued.

Dewey stopped, a cold chill ran through him as he realized it was too late to warn the men who'd come to save him.

A dull, nearly silent thud followed by a pained grunt echoed across the morning air as the blond woman shot the second Delta with a silenced weapon. He crumpled to the ground as the woman darted away from the café down the sidewalk. Dewey looked back to mark one, approaching from the middle of the square. He still didn't see the tall man approaching, now practically on him. Dewey pulled his Colt from the small of his back and began a sprint toward the center of the square. The Delta followed Dewey's eyes and turned to his approaching killer but it was too late. The tall killer's arm shot out and a silenced bullet entered the young Delta's skull just above his eye socket. His head splattered blood as he collapsed in the middle of the square, just feet from where the children played.

The tall man swiveled to face Dewey, the black steel of his silencer aiming quickly and firing. Dewey lunged to the side and felt nothing, but heard a shatter to his left as the bullet met the glass of the church door behind him. He fired the Colt, the crack of unmuted gunfire shocking in the square. Dewey's shot caught the tall man in the chest. A second shot and the side of the killer's head jolted right, blood and skull silhouetting as he fell onto the bright green of the square's freshly cut grass, his corpse following soon after and striking the ground, rolling over just feet from where a young mother held her baby.

The screams of women and children filled the momentary silence following Dewey's gunfire, but Dewey was already turned and running away from the square, looking desperately for the second killer, the blond assassin. But she was already gone. Dewey turned, heading as quickly and calmly as he could for his car. At the side of the church he turned left and sprinted up the brick-paved street. In two blocks he spied the shiny black of the Mercedes halfway down the block.

He had to get away, and quickly. But now he also allowed the obvious question to surface in his mind: *What had just happened?* These were no mere killers. The two who'd just killed the Deltas were not terrorists or mercenaries; they were government-hired, agency-trained *operatives.* What did it mean? Only one group knew of this exfiltration. He shuddered as he realized the implication of it all: *There was a mole.*

He sprinted down the sidewalk, knowing he had to get away. In the distance, sirens suddenly crossed the warm Cali air. Soon the Madradora would be mayhem. He spotted the Mercedes, parked on the street corner a block ahead. But as he came upon the street corner in front of the car, he noticed something, a reflection in the window of the Mercedes, just an instant, a simple swatch of light, then movement: the blond-haired executioner. She stood in a doorway just beyond the street corner, hiding, waiting, arms raised and weapon trained. The reflection in the car window saved Dewey from what would have been, in five feet or so, a warm bullet in the back of the head.

Dewey stopped just before the corner, feet away from where the blond assassin lurked. He looked behind him, down the block he'd just run down, and saw a Laundromat. He dropped back and entered the Laundromat. He ran through the store, pushing his way past piles of laundry and women folding articles, to the back room, where a man sat, smoking a cigarette in front of a pile of papers.

"*Lo siento*," murmured Dewey as he charged through the office toward an alley entrance, gun in hand. The sirens became louder, multiple vehicles joining in the distance.

Out the door and across the alley and through a dented steel door. Inside, stacks of bread loaves, other boxes of food, the smell of meat. He moved through the storage room and entered the back of a bodega. Colt .45 cocked in front of him, he passed a middle-aged woman who fainted as she saw the weapon in his hand. Catching the eye of the man at the cash register, Dewey held a finger to his lips. There, at the side of the entrance, her back to the store, stood the blond assassin.

Suddenly another customer, an elderly woman, screamed as she saw Dewey with gun. The blonde turned abruptly, leveling what he now saw was an HK UMP compact machine gun with a six-inch suppressor on the end. A full auto hail of bullets crashed through the windows as she swept the weapon east-west. The elderly woman's screams ended abruptly as a bullet ripped through her head and killed her. The assassin's bullets shattered the storefront's glass, but Dewey was already down and partially hidden by a chest freezer, which shielded him from the slugs. As soon as the blonde's gun swept past him, Dewey had a clear sight. He fired twice, two quick shots into the assassin's neck and chest, flinging her backward onto the brick sidewalk in a shower of blood and glass.

Dewey ran through the open door and stood over the woman, looking for a moment at the young assassin. She could not have been more than twenty-one or twenty-two years old. The fall to the ground had knocked her backward, a blond wig now lay behind her head. Beneath, brown locks framed a tanned, blood-smattered face. She was a gorgeous woman, her sharp nose framed by high cheekbones, a vaguely Mediterranean cast to her smooth skin. Her eyes looked up at Dewey; brown eyes, deep pools that expressed the pain of the bullets now riddling her body. She clung desperately to life as blood coursed from her mouth, nose, and ears. He looked down at her chest. A stylish white leather jacket was now ruined in crimson, a black hole piercing her right breast.

She stared at Dewey as he stood over her. In the distance, the sound of sirens grew louder. The beautiful girl's lips moved as she tried to say something.

Dewey reached down and grabbed her arms, pulling her up with some effort over his uninjured shoulder. He carried her quickly to the Mercedes as the sirens moved closer to the square. Opening the back door, he laid her down gently on the backseat. She would likely be dead within a minute or two, but maybe in her final moments he could make her say something.

He climbed into the front seat of the Mercedes and started the sedan by again crossing the wires that now dangled below the steering column. He glanced over his shoulder at the critically injured woman clinging to life in the backseat. Dewey didn't care if she lived or died. She had chosen her bloody profession, and like most assassins that had come before her, that decision would soon prove terminal. Still, he couldn't help noticing her age; he couldn't help lamenting the misused youth and beauty that would soon be gone from the earth.

He hit the gas and sent the black sedan speeding down the sun-scorched road. Behind him, a green and yellow police cruiser picked up the Mercedes at the block next to the bodega, marked Dewey, took a right and sped toward him, trying to catch up.

Looking in the rearview mirror, his eyes met the young woman's: still alive. He needed a minute, a quiet place, or she would die before he could try to interrogate her. But the police cruiser was soon joined by another, and he had a situation on his hands.

He flipped the cell phone open and dialed Anson Energy. When the woman answered he asked to be connected again with Terry Savoy. After a brief pause, he heard Savoy's voice.

"Dewey? Where are you?"

"They were waiting for me," said Dewey. "They killed the Deltas. They assassinated American soldiers in cold blood. They knew I was coming. These weren't terrorists. These were professionals. We're talking *operatives*."

"Hold on, I'm going to patch in Jessica."

"*No*, you're fucking not. Someone in that room is involved. Listen to what I'm saying: You have a mole."

"All right, all right. Are you okay? Where are you going?"

"I'm getting out of Colombia before someone puts a bullet in my head. I need the location of the Cali airport."

"Why the airport?"

"Terry, you can help me right now or I can hang up. Your call."

"Are you still near the pickup site?"

"Yeah, heading west on Granada."

"Hold on." The phone clicked as Dewey kept the accelerator pressed to the ground. Dust from the dry Cali road shot up from behind the speeding car, clouding the air between the Mercedes and the first police cruiser, now less than twenty feet behind him.

The phone clicked again.

"You need to head east. Granada will take you away from where you want to go. In a few miles there's a small highway, Route twenty-three, Autopista del Sur. Take it north to Highway Twenty-five. Aragón International is about five miles from there."

"Thanks."

"You must know something. Or at least they think you do."

"Yeah, that occurred to me."

"We need to exfiltrate you."

"*Exfiltrate* me? I'm being hunted in the streets of Cali. I have two police cruisers on my back bumper. I'll be lucky if I'm alive in ten minutes. I called to tell you you have a rat. You got some serious problems to solve on your end before we talk again."

He flipped the phone shut and pushed the sedan's gas pedal to the ground, sending the black car lurching even faster along the crowded city streets. He was a block in front of the first police cruiser, whose siren pierced the air. He ran the Mercedes in and out of traffic, weaving into the oncoming lane as he tried unsuccessfully to build distance between himself and the police cruisers.

At the next street he swerved left. He had a clear lane for a block and he turned and looked at the woman as he kept the car speeding forward. Dewey reached his right hand back and cupped the young assassin's hand. It was a small hand, cold, and he held it in his own. He could see her eyes beginning to flutter as death approached. At this point, force would not elicit the words he needed. Only one thing would: Dewey held her hand, comforting the woman who'd been sent to terminate him.

Looking up at Dewey from the backseat, the woman's eyes found his and she again attempted to move her lips. Blood oozed from the small of her neck as she exerted herself, dark red pouring down over a silver pendant that hung from a necklace at the nape of her tanned neck. She tried desperately to say something, at first softly, then louder, until Dewey could understand.

"*Padre*," she whispered. "*Me perdóne por la vida que he vivido.*"

Prayer. Through clotted throat, now filled with blood, she was praying, asking for forgiveness. But it was not the words she said that sparked something in Dewey's memory, rather the way she said them. He recognized something. It was the stilted, short, harsh imprint of the word *perdóne*. The peculiar accent to her Spanish triggered a recollection from long ago. Noriega. The endless weeks in the sweltering, dirty city, waiting for the order to move in and kill the dictator. He would never forget the way the locals spoke.

Panama.

24

FORTUNA'S APARTMENT

Fortuna kept an eye on the television in the bedroom, set now to Fox News, though the news had broken on every network. Fox showed a split screen, with live images of Capitana Territory on one side of the screen, and an eerie nighttime scene of Ted Marks's ski house in Aspen, still smoldering, on the other side. Fortuna stared for several minutes at the screen, with the volume down. The Aspen footage gave way to the site of the destroyed Savage Island dam.

Across the top of the screen, the banner read: AMERICA UNDER ATTACK.

In his hand, Fortuna held a small green book with Arabic writing embossed into the leather cover. He opened the book up and removed a small photograph. It was a color photo of Esco and him, taken at the Crimea camps.

Fortuna felt the pain of Esco's death more than he ever would have anticipated. When you share a tent with someone for a year, when you learn to plan, to fight, to kill together, when you share so much, you can never remove that bond.

But far worse was Fortuna's fear of what Esco might have told Dewey Andreas. Esco knew *all*. That's what really ate at Fortuna now. They'd both learned to endure interrogation, but Fortuna knew that ultimately the one doing the torturing would always win out. And an ex-Delta could win more quickly than most.

If Esco were tortured, he could have revealed the full breadth of Fortuna's plan, plus laid a trail leading directly back to him.

Fortuna replaced the photo and put the book back on the shelf. He turned the television off.

It was almost 9:00 P.M. Buck should have succeeded in taking out Andreas by now. When Buck would be at liberty to call Fortuna with an update, Fortuna had no idea.

He went into the bathroom and showered, then put on a pair of jeans, loafers, and a plain white button-down. He put a gray sweater on over that. He walked down the hallway toward the elevator.

"Tell Jean to bring the car around," he said to Karim.

"You're going out? What about dinner?"

"I'll be back later. Keep an eye on the news. TiVo anything on the rig or the dam."

Karim handed Fortuna a dark gray overcoat with black velvet lapels.

The car, a Mercedes S600, glided peacefully down Fifth Avenue. At Twenty-first Street, the car turned right and drove for several blocks. It stopped in front of a large brick building, in front of a line of waiting limousines and sports cars.

It was an old warehouse that had once served as a meatpacking plant. For more than a century, the building housed a factory that took large pieces of cow and turned them into steak and hamburger that was packaged up and delivered to restaurants in lower Manhattan. Today, $365 million worth of renovations later, the building housed expensive loft condominiums and on the first floor an exclusive, members-only nightclub called "11."

Fortuna climbed out of the car and walked to the door. A large doorman opened the door for him.

"Good evening, sir."

"Hi, Jack. How are you tonight?"

"Great, Mr. Fortuna."

"How's the crowd?"

"Not bad for a Thursday. I did notice Miss Haviland is here."

Fortuna smiled and handed him a wad of bills, a couple hundred dollars in twenties.

"Thanks, Mr. Fortuna."

"No problem. Stay warm."

Fortuna walked down a hallway, then went through another set of doors, also opened by a large doorman. He handed the doorman his overcoat, along with another wad of bills.

The club looked more like a large, dimly lit living room than a nightclub. Smoke filled the air. To the right, a small alcove housed a wall of liquor bottles. Fortuna walked to the bar. Behind a large block of highly polished wood, a young, pretty brunette stood, smiling.

"Good evening," she said.

"Hi," Fortuna said. "What's special tonight?"

"We're having a Screaming Eagle tasting," she said in an Irish accent. She raised a large wineglass and poured a glass of dark maroon Cabernet into it.

Fortuna took the glass and sipped.

"That's nice," he said, smiling. He took another sip. He stared for a moment at the bartender. She had large green eyes. Her nose was slightly long, sharp. Her brown hair was combed back neatly.

He looked down her body, at her tight black blouse, full breasts pressing underneath. She let him look, unapologetically, appreciatively.

"I'm Alex," he said after another sip. "Are you new?"

"I'm Darien."

"Nice to meet you."

"You too. Have you been a member here for a long time?"

"A couple of years." He took another sip. "This is nice. I think I'll trade it in though. I need something to pep me up. Would you mind pouring me a vodka and Red Bull."

"Sure. What kind of vodka would you like?"

"Jean-Marc, if you have it. Otherwise, Grey Goose."

She mixed him the drink and poured it into a heavy crystal glass. Fortuna sipped it and looked around the room.

"11" was a series of informal rooms, seating areas, large sprawling leather couches surrounding massive low-rising tables. Music filled the room, but it wasn't so loud that you couldn't talk. Groups of people spread throughout the large room, sitting in the different areas, smoking. In a few areas, large plates of cocaine were passed around like hors d'oeuvres. Fortuna saw many people he knew; models, a few hedge fund types, the art community, actors and actresses, but mostly old-line New York City socialites.

He turned back to the bar. "So what's your deal?" he asked. "Actress? Writer?"

She laughed. "Dancer," she said. "Ballet and modern."

"Interesting," he said as he took a sip from the glass.

"Juilliard. I graduate in May."

"Do you have anything lined up?"

"I'll be training in London, under Stephen Greenston."

"I don't really know much about ballet."

She laughed.

"Greenston is kind of the godfather of the modern European ballet, what they call the 'literal' ballet."

"Good for you. Where are you from?"

"Ireland. A small town on the coast, near Kildare. And what do you do?"

"Boring stuff. Kind of like a mutual fund." Fortuna took another sip from his glass. He looked at his watch. It was almost 11:00 P.M. "I'm going to walk around a bit. Thanks for the drink."

"Sure," said Darien.

Fortuna walked through the nightclub, nodding several times at people he knew. At one couch, a group of three men and two women were seated.

"Alex," said one of the men sitting on a couch.

"Hi, Joe," said Fortuna, shaking hands. "Good to see you."

"This is Alex Fortuna," Joe Lombardi said, introducing Fortuna to the group. "Won't you join us?"

"Yes, won't you join us?" asked one of the women, a blond-haired woman in a stunning red dress. She smiled at him. He'd never seen her before.

"Please join us," said another woman, another blonde. This one he did recognize. It was Charlotte Haviland.

"Hi, Charlotte," Fortuna said, smiling. "How are you?"

She didn't answer, instead reclining in the large sofa with her wine-glass, smiling and shaking her head.

In front of the group, on the table, a silver tray sat. On it, several dozen lines of cocaine were neatly cut into lines.

"If you insist," Fortuna said, smiling. He sat down next to the blond woman. She reached forward and lifted the tray, placing it on her lap. She handed him the rolled-up $100 bill on the tray.

Fortuna leaned down and Hoovered up three lines. He took another sip from his glass.

"How do you two know each other?" asked another woman, a brunette who was slightly overweight.

"Alex runs a hedge fund," said Lombardi. "We're in the same line of work."

Fortuna smiled. "Ours is much smaller than Joe's," he said. "He's much more successful. If you want to invest your money, do it with him."

Lombardi laughed. "Yeah, my ass. What are you looking at these days?"

Fortuna picked up the rolled-up bill again and leaned down, doing another line. He smiled but declined to answer.

They talked for a while longer. Every so often, Fortuna turned and glanced at the bar. If she wasn't pouring a drink, Darien returned his look.

After an hour, Fortuna stood up. He walked through the room, elated from the drugs, nicely wired but not out of control; the way he liked it.

He walked back to the bar.

"Good night," he said.

"Leaving?"

"Yes. Early meeting tomorrow."

"I thought you were the boss."

He stood at the bar for a moment longer. They looked at each other, locked eyes. After a moment she averted her eyes.

"I'm done in a few minutes," she whispered without looking back at him, in shyness, just loud enough for him to hear.

They kissed in the Mercedes on the way uptown. When they arrived at Fortuna's apartment, she made him walk her through the entire apartment, room by room. She was astounded by the sheer size of the place, the view, the art, everything.

In his bedroom, they took their clothing off. Fortuna unbuttoned her black blouse. Her body was a hard, sculpted thing of mastery, of beauty, toned from a lifetime of dance.

He took her hand and they walked to the hallway, down to a stairwell that led them up to the rooftop. He opened the door and the cold winter air blew at them ferociously, but they laughed. They ran across the deck to where clouds of steam arose in the lit-up area where the hot tub was. They jumped in, laughing. She moved to him; they kissed. Soon they were making love in the heated water.

At some point, they returned to the bedroom and made love again before falling asleep.

In the morning, it was Sarah, the maid, who woke them up with a tray, on top of which were two cups of espresso, a *New York Times*, *The Wall Street Journal*, and two glasses of freshly squeezed orange juice. It was 7:05 A.M.

"Good morning, Alexander," Sarah said.

"Morning."

They sat and read the papers, drinking espresso.

"I could get used to this," Darien said. She immediately regretted saying it.

Fortuna said nothing. He hadn't heard what she'd said. His eyes were on the *Times* headlines:

KKB-Anson Target of Terror Strike;

Savage Island Project and Capitana Territory Destroyed;

CEOs of Both Companies Targeted for Assassination in Colorado

He picked up the internal phone. He got out of bed and stepped into the bathroom. He dialed Karim.

"Where is Mahmoud?" Fortuna asked, keeping his voice low, his anger nevertheless coming through. "*If he didn't escape—*"

"Mahmoud's back in South Bend. There was a fight. He thought he killed them all."

Fortuna's stomach tightened and he shook his head, trying to control his anger.

" '*Thought*'? Marks might be able to identify him now."

"I know."

Fortuna looked through the bathroom door at Darien, naked on the large bed. He smiled at her. "It's time to tie off the other loose ends," he told Karim as he walked back into the bedroom and climbed next to Darien. He pulled the young Irish beauty closer to him.

"You mean . . ."

"Yes. Today. Right now."

25

BOWEN ROAD
HONG KONG, PEOPLE'S REPUBLIC OF CHINA

Orieshe Yang walked through the ornate lobby forty-four floors below the high-rise condominium she owned near Victoria Peak. It was the Saturday following a successful, though stressful, week. Her schedule hadn't permitted her to go for a run in more than two weeks. Today, she told herself, she would run at least twenty kilometers and let the pain of the long distance cleanse her body and clear her head.

Her employer, PBX Fund, had started the week with just over $3 billion in assets. As of last night, when she left to meet her fiancé for dinner at Cépage in the city's Star Street precinct, PBX's net asset value had tripled.

It had been an astonishing jump, but also a disturbing one. Her boss, a man named Alexander Fortuna whom she'd never met, had directed an investment strategy at the beginning of the week she hadn't fully agreed with, an allocation of all of the fund's assets into one sector, and one specific geography, only to watch as the sector itself was hit by a series of dramatic terrorist attacks.

Almost as if he had known, she thought.

A year ago, she'd left the safety of Wellington Management in Boston, where she had earned upwards of $1 million a year, for the unknown of a secretive hedge fund in the Far East. Her base pay at PBX was more than $10 million. A few years at PBX, she figured, and she could do whatever she wanted. She could teach elementary school, or become a sculptor. After all, she was only thirty-one years old. But now her mind raced. Was she being paranoid? Manifesting some kind of guilt over the money she was making? In addition to her base pay, Yang also earned a bonus based upon the performance of PBX. Last night over dinner, she had calculated what her bonus would be in two weeks, the end of the fiscal year. Net asset value had just soared by $7.1 billion. Her bonus was one-half of 1 percent of the appreciation, after figuring in an 8 percent preferred coupon on the amount of capital in PBX Fund a year ago. In two weeks, if the fund stayed relatively close to where it stood last night, Yang would receive a bonus of $26 million, give or take a few hundred thousand dollars. In her first year with PBX, Yang would take home more than $36 million.

Which only made her feel more unsettled about the week's events.

Yang began her run down Bowen Road. It was crisp out, a perfect day for a run, in the low sixties. She started slowly and soon fell into a groove.

She felt the loosening, calming rhythm of the cadence of her sneakers on pavement. She'd been right: running made her feel much better. For the first time in at least ten days, she began to relax, transported by the solitary challenge of the run.

The vehicle was a short, green delivery truck taking bread to the hotels along the waterfront. As she came to within a hundred yards of the entrance to Bowen Road Park, the truck crossed two lanes of traffic as the driver seemed to lose control of his vehicle. It swerved wildly toward Yang. She didn't have time to scream; she didn't even see the truck until the last second, as she heard a screech of tires just behind her. The truck barreled into her at more than forty-five miles per hour, sending her careening ahead, headfirst onto the hard pavement of the street. The truck kept moving forward, running her over before it crashed into a tree alongside the road. Later, it would be discovered that the truck had lost its brakes. The driver, a Saudi, would cry at the misfortune that his truck, which he'd driven for more than four years, had wrought.

In London, Derek Langley closed the office door at Passwood-Regent at a little after eight o'clock Friday evening, clutching his athletic bag in his hand. It was an old bag, but he carried it with pride. The letters "CU" were emblazoned in red along the side of the Navy blue bag; these were the letters of the Cambridge University swim team, of which he'd been a member nearly a decade before.

Langley liked to go to the Royal Automobile Club, where he was a member, and swim for an hour every night.

He walked the mile and a half to the club. It was cold outside. Except for the young blond attendant at the front desk, the club seemed empty. That's how it always was on Friday nights. He got ready in the locker room, then walked down the marble floored hallway to the swimming pool. Langley dived into the deserted pool and began his swim.

Langley could not help feeling good after the week that had just passed. It had been a glorious week after a somewhat mediocre year. Passwood-Regent began the week with assets of $3.6 billion; it finished the week with $10.4 billion. Before leaving the office, Langley had calculated his bonus. All told, his bonus in two weeks would total nearly $50 million. At twenty-nine, Langley was already worth more than $200 million. Still, this would be his best year ever. He would buy something this year, he thought, as his long, muscular arms slashed through the water. Perhaps a country estate, or a plane. The problem is, he didn't really want either one. The only things he really enjoyed were working and swimming.

Langley's thoughts drifted to Alexander Fortuna. After two years of working for his secretive boss, he was finally going to meet him. Fortuna had told him that afternoon of his plans to be in London in early January. Langley was excited. Fortuna, to the young man, was a hero. Perhaps the best investor he'd ever known, a man who blended a willingness to bet the farm with an almost superhuman ability to wait patiently until opportunities arose. Fortuna, Langley knew, had made his first billion by the time he was thirty-two. Could Derek do that? He didn't see how. Unless he started his own fund, as Fortuna had at a similar age. Something he might just summon the courage to ask Fortuna about.

At some point, a swimmer entered in the lane to the left of him. Langley didn't notice as the dark-haired man entered the pool area. He did, however, notice when the swimmer began working out to his right, a burly man whose back and torso were covered in shaggy hair. He recognized the big man. His name was Malik and he liked to swim Fridays also.

As his hour in the pool drew toward its completion and fatigue began to settle into his arms and legs, he felt hands grabbing at his feet from below. He struggled and yanked his legs but it was no use. He looked beneath him, where Malik and another man were pulling him beneath the water. Each man held a leg. He swung his arms wildly at the men, striking them in the head, in the shoulders. But it was like hitting wooden boards. These men were powerful. The struggle caused whatever breath he still had to be consumed that much quicker. Finally, in desperation, Langley breathed the water in.

Even the best swimmers drown, the papers would later report. He died doing what he loved most, his mother was quoted as saying. At Cambridge, the new pool house, which would be built with money left to the school by Langley, would be called the Derek K. Langley Field House.

In Manhattan, Sheldon Karl stared out over Wall Street from his office window as the week came to a close. From his office on the fifty-fifth floor of the building at 2 Wall Street, he could see the Hudson River and the rest of lower Manhattan. If he looked to his right, he could also see where the World Trade Center had once stood. Karl didn't like to look in that direction, though he'd gotten used to it. Karl's older brother, Fitz, had died on 9/11. He'd worked for Morgan Stanley, a trading firm in the south tower. The plane flew directly into the floor Fitz had worked on.

Christmas was less than a week away, a time during which Karl always thought about his brother. Their parents both died of cancer when he and Fitz were in elementary school. They were both raised by their aunt and uncle in Philadelphia. Until 2001, for ten or eleven years in a row, Karl had spent Christmases with Fitz and his wife, Jenny, at their rambling yellow colonial house near the ocean in Westport, Connecticut. The day after Christmas, they'd pack their bags and drive to Stowe for a week of skiing. Now Jenny was remarried to a writer for *The New York Times*, a bearded intellectual who seemed to like talking about himself, politics, and little else. The last time Karl saw them was at a dinner more than a year ago, on the Upper West Side, at which Jenny's new husband, after a considerable amount of red wine, said that the terrorists who'd flown the plane into the World Trade Center were misunderstood, that the only way we would ever stop more 9/11s from happening would be to understand them and their motivations, and to help educate them about making "better choices." Karl had walked out of the dinner and never looked back. He didn't particularly like politics, either side of it, but he knew an asshole when he saw one.

The hedge fund he worked at was small compared to many of the funds on Wall Street. Below $10 billion in assets, a fund is considered subscale. Below a billion, a fund is considered a hobby. But Karl knew that no firm could match Kallivar's performance that past week. *My God*, he thought as he shut down his two computers. *The numbers are real. They're actually going to hold.*

In one week, the assets of the firm had more than tripled. Kallivar's $3.2 billion now totaled more than $10 billion. His boss, Alexander Fortuna, had called him that afternoon to congratulate him on a good week. Fortuna had recruited him from his old firm, Sowbridge Capital. They'd worked together at Sowbridge before Fortuna left, "retired" as he told Karl and the other investors at the firm. When Fortuna decided to start investing his own money in a new fund, and asked Karl to oversee it, he'd been flattered. Fortuna, everyone at Sowbridge knew, was not only a billionaire, but was the best investor at the firm.

In three years at Kallivar, Karl had made more money than he knew what to do with. Instead of buying a house up at Stowe, he bought part of the resort itself, from AIG. He owned an entire floor of the Stanhope, where he lived, across from the Metropolitan Museum of Art. He collected art, wild modernist art, including a sculpture of a mutilated cow encased in glass, which he'd kept for a year in his living room before donating it to the Whitney.

In two weeks, Karl knew that the year's check would be the biggest yet. As he stood looking out the window, at the darkened skyline, at the city he'd once been so intimidated by, then enthralled with, a city that he now understood and had mastered, he realized he'd give it all just to get his brother back, even if it was only for a minute. The only thing that diminished his sense of achievement was his solitary status. Sheldon Karl was lonely.

He shook his head. He always felt this way around Christmas. Time to go grab a drink. Friends from Wharton were gathering that night at a restaurant on the Upper East Side. Then he'd go home and do some lines of cocaine and call Tina. At $5,000 a night, not exactly his girlfriend, but less expensive than a wife. And easily the most beautiful woman he'd ever met.

Karl called his car service. He took the elevator down to the ground floor and buttoned his Burberry overcoat. He walked outside and climbed into the dark Lincoln sedan.

"Evening, Mr. Karl," the driver said.

"Hi, Bobby."

"Straight home, sir?"

"No. I'm meeting some people for dinner. Sistina's."

"Second Avenue?"

Karl nodded.

As the sedan glided quietly onto Water Street, he took *The Wall Street Journal* from the pocket on the back of the seat in front of him and glanced quickly through the headlines. An article caught his eye, analyzing the effects of the destruction of KKB's hydroelectric facility in Canada, and the explosion off the coast of Colombia, at Capitana, Anson Energy's big petro strike. A dot portrait of CEO Ted Marks's smiling, handsome face stared from the paper just above the fold. For the first time, Karl learned that Marks had nearly died in what seemed to be an assassination attempt linked to the explosions.

A strange feeling came over Karl as the sedan went uptown and he read the article. Kallivar had lost more than $400 million in KKB and Anson Energy over the past two days alone. But Kallivar's climb, he now realized, was sparked by KKB and Anson.

He thought back to the conversation with Fortuna. The entire strategy had been his.

He swallowed as he pictured Fortuna, walking out the door that last day at Sowbridge. Only thirty-two years old, and already a billionaire. His long, dark hair combed back, down to the tops of his shoulders, slightly unkempt. Lusted after by so many of the young, single women at the firm, even the married ones. His long nose and big, brown eyes. Fortuna, he now realized as the sedan climbed onto the on ramp of the FDR Drive, is a terrorist.

Fortuna is a terrorist.

"Jesus Christ," he whispered to himself.

The Lincoln climbed into the passing lane along the FDR and quickly gained speed.

"Why the FDR?" Karl asked.

"Fundraiser tonight at the Waldorf. The mayor. Traffic's all knotted up midtown."

The car went fast. Faster than usual. At some point, the car lurched right, swerving to pass a car, then swerved back. The tires made a slight screeching sound.

"Slow down, Bobby," Karl said. "There's no hurry."

But the luxurious sedan didn't slow down. It tore north on the FDR, the sound of squealing tires growing more frantic as Bobby weaved between drivers. Karl tried to lean forward, but the movement of the car was so sudden and violent, it was difficult. He was able to read the speedometer; it read 105 miles per hour.

"For fuck's sake, Bobby, slow down!"

But it was no use. His driver wasn't listening. Karl then understood what was happening. He reached for the lock on the door. He had to get out of the car. Even at this speed, he had to jump and try and save himself.

He grabbed the lock and tried to move it. But it wouldn't move. He pushed and pulled it with all of the strength he had, but it was useless.

He reached forward and grabbed Bobby by the neck. He grabbed his chin and tried to move his head around and force him to look away from the road, so that he would perhaps crash into a guardrail. But he held his head firm; he was stronger than Karl had imagined. The driver reached up and grabbed Karl's hand with his right hand while he kept his left on the steering wheel. With a swift downward motion, he snapped Karl's wrist, breaking it in an instant.

Karl screamed. Another violent swerve sent him flying backward into the backseat.

Then he saw it ahead as they flew beneath the Fifty-ninth Street Bridge, a cement barrier. The sedan was now moving at more than 110 miles per hour. A large cement barrier separated the exit ramp from the FDR. Nothing stood between the sedan and the approaching cement barrier.

In a fiery moment, it was all gone. The impact of the Lincoln sedan pulverized Sheldon Karl, erasing with him Alexander Fortuna's last loose end.

26

THE WHITE HOUSE
WASHINGTON, D.C.

In the West Wing of the White House, four individuals were seated in the office of Jane London, chief of staff to the president: London; Myron Kratovil, national security advisor to the president; Bill Holmgren, head of the CIA; and Roger Putnam, U.S. secretary of state.

The West Wing of the White House had a busy but surprisingly cozy atmosphere. The ceilings were low, the walls adorned with large, historic paintings and photographs. Staffers walked the hallways with energy and, usually, a smile. The carpets were lush, vibrant reds with beautiful patterns. The general feeling was one of luxury, preppiness, and history, like an old home in a wealthy town in New England.

John Scalia, deputy national security advisor, walked hurriedly into the office to join them, settling in a chair at the edge of London's desk. "Evening, everyone."

"Let's hear it," said Putnam, the secretary of state. "As it is, I'm already late for my flight to South Korea."

"You might want to consider postponing, sir," said Scalia.

"And why is that?"

"The president authorized a special NSA protocol thirty-six hours ago," said Scalia. "We went back almost a decade and opened up electronic and audio vaults within NSA. The bottom line is the intercepts show clearly that there have been discussions for some time about sabotaging Capitana."

"And who was doing the discussing?" asked London.

"The evidence," said Scalia, "points to Saudi Arabia. We have multiple NSA intercepts in which high-ranking Aramco executives and government officials discuss the harm Capitana could cause, before it was built, during construction, and currently. We have the foreign minister discussing it. We have planning discussions about embedding people at the rig. It's messy. It's why I called this meeting."

The room was silent for several moments.

"Saudi Arabia?" asked London. "A sanctioned attack? By the government? There's just no way."

"It would explain the bombers' access to such cutting-edge munitions," said Kratovil.

"Do they actually talk about blowing up the facility?" asked Putnam.

"No, they don't," said Scalia. "But they come damn close."

"They wouldn't," said Holmgren. "If something was being planned it wouldn't be on the phone, e-mail, whatever NSA is using these days, unless they were complete idiots, which Fahd, Bandar, and Aramco are not."

"They have the motive," said Scalia. "Capitana has killed the Saudis, taking market share, and adding to a host of production woes in their biggest reservoir, Ghawar field."

"Look, the Saudis aren't starving," said Kratovil. "They have more than a third of the remaining oil and natural gas still in the ground. That's worldwide."

"I'm not saying what they did, may have done, was rational, Myron. They've badly mismanaged Ghawar field. They need to plow hundreds of billions into Ghawar to complete it as well as harvest other fields. The combination of Ghawar's decline in productivity, and Capitana's rise and appropriation of market share, has harmed them severely."

"So the idea is they hired some ex Al-Qaeda types to do this?" asked London.

"It wouldn't be hard," said Holmgren. "They're all over the place. Like rats."

"Even if you're right," said Putnam, "the Saudis would never do this. The ramifications would be too big. They wouldn't piss us off like this."

"Well, that's interesting," said Scalia. "Because now the question becomes replacement dynamics. Savage Island is relatively straightforward. Electricity supply settles into the grid. Within the week, Savage Island wholesale megawatt will be largely replaced by other generators of megawatt, mostly domestic, natural gas plants, nukes, some Canadian hydro, coal. Straightforward, simple, no problems. The problem is oil. Where do we get the oil to replace Capitana? Do you realize that Capitana supplied more than nine percent of U.S. oil last year? This year it would've been nearly twelve percent. It's still climbing."

"Where do we replace that oil?" asked London. "The president doesn't want to tap SPR."

"The reality is SPR will not suffice even if we did," said Scalia. "Energy has analyzed the replacement dynamics. The loss of Capitana has created a dramatic hole in the U.S. petroleum supply chain that has really only one viable solution."

"Saudi Arabia," said Putnam.

"Exactly," said Scalia. "There's only one place we can go. Saudi Arabia has us in a box."

"They've built what Kissinger referred to as an Anonymous Circle," said Kratovil. "They've entrapped us, they possess the only way out, and no one knows except us and them. To go outside the circle would be suicidal."

"Call it whatever the fuck you want, Myron," said Putnam, standing, his face turning beet red. "This is war! If this is true we should vaporize the entire fucking Arabian Peninsula!"

"This is just bloody Machiavellian," said Holmgren. "Couldn't they simply pick up the goddamn phone and tell us they have a problem?"

The room was silent again.

"All right, I'm canceling Seoul," said Putnam. "I want you with me," he told Scalia. "We'll need some of the intercepts. We need hard evidence. Get your energy person. I want to be airborne within an hour."

"Energy believes there'll be a hefty price, perhaps in the hundreds of billions," said Scalia.

"We'll need to brief the president," said London. "He's due back from California within the hour."

"The Saudis will deny everything," said Holmgren. "I'm not a diplomat, but my suggestion is you go straight to the bargaining table. Avoid even *talking* about the attacks. Just get the oil pumping again. Nothing good will come of a confrontation over the destruction of Capitana and Savage Island. Let my people deal with that side of the equation."

"If your people had dealt with that side of the equation we wouldn't be in this mess," said Putnam. "Teddy Marks is a friend of mine. I served with him in Nam. I'll be goddamned if I'm not gonna say something. I'll get the oil flowing again, don't you worry. But those fuckhead Saudis will know goddamn well that we know what they did."

In Jessica's office, Savoy told her about the failed extraction at Madradora.

"How the hell could they have known?" she asked.

"Andreas didn't have much doubt."

"What did he say?"

"That someone in your interagency group is bad."

Jessica paused to think of the implications. She placed her right hand on her forehead and rubbed it for several seconds.

"Where is he now?"

"Don't know. He hung up on me. He was running from the local police and God knows who else."

She shook her head and looked at her watch. "What about Ted Marks? When do you leave for Colorado?"

"I leave in an hour," said Savoy.

Jessica stared down at her desk for a moment, then walked to the window and looked out at Pennsylvania Avenue.

"What is it?" asked Savoy. "Andreas?"

"Yeah, that. But it's this Saudi angle too," she said. "The group's taking it seriously, and I know we have to. But I don't see it. I . . ."

"Want my opinion?"

"Sure."

"Forget the fucking Saudis," Savoy said. "Someone in that room"—he pointed his finger toward the ground, indicating the interagency conference room several floors beneath them—"is involved in this. For blood or money, they're bent, and they're scared, and they'd like nothing more than to have the government chasing its tail in Saudi Arabia. You need to start looking at the people who knew about Madradora immediately. And you'd better be extremely careful. Watch what you say and who you say it to. That's how they found Andreas."

Jessica nodded, still uncertain.

"But even more important, don't let on that you suspect a goddamn thing. Trust me, if there's a mole—and they think you're onto them—then you've just put yourself in grave danger."

By 1:00 A.M., the secretary of state's Boeing 777 was airborne out of Andrews Air Force Base.

On board were Putnam, Scalia, Stebbens, and a smattering of specialists from State, NSA, and the Department of Energy. The flight would take six hours.

The plane had three sections: the secretary's section, which consisted of a large stateroom and private office; a staff section, which housed two conference rooms, a couple of private offices, and several rows of seats; and the back of the plane, which looked like the first-class section of an airplane, and was used when media traveled with the secretary of state. No reporters had been invited on this trip. Except for a couple of translators, the aft compartment was empty.

Putnam was a legend in the diplomatic corps. He was serving his second stint as secretary of state. He served his first tenure under President George H. W. Bush, during which time he helped broker the end of the Gulf War. Now, at sixty-eight, Putnam was older, and it showed. He immediately retired to the large plane's stateroom for a nap when he got on board.

Scalia sat across from Stebbens in the staff area. He hadn't slept in more than twenty-four hours. He closed his eyes and fell asleep as soon as the plane reached cruising altitude.

After an hour, he was awakened by one of Putnam's staffers. "Jane London's office just called," said the young woman. "There'll be a call in twenty minutes with the president."

Scalia went into one of the bathrooms and washed his face. He went to the conference room.

In the stateroom, Putnam was on a conference call with the president. Putnam's booming voice, which could be heard through the door, indicated he and his boss were arguing.

"I don't want this devolving, Roger," the president said to Putnam. "We need to calmly and quickly get the Saudis to alter their production cycle and get Capitana's oil replaced. I don't want this becoming a diplomatic battle or a personal one."

"They just attacked us, sir," said Putnam.

"Someone did."

"They nearly killed a friend of mine, someone who fought for me in Vietnam."

"*Someone* did, Roger."

"And our response is to fly over and hand them a check? Forgive me, but I'm not sure I agree with that stance. This was an unprovoked attack. They murdered hundreds of people."

"Spare me the lecture," said the president. "I'm as angry as you are. If they did it, I'll be the one screaming 'kill the bastards.' But we don't know who did this. And we need the Saudis' oil right now. I would not accuse anybody of anything, especially an ally, until we have proof. When we have proof, get out of my way because I'll be the one who turns Saudi Arabia into a glass fucking parking lot."

Putnam paused.

"Get the rest of the group," said the president after a few moments. "I have a Homeland Security briefing I need to get to."

Putnam waved at the window to the conference room. Scalia and the others filed in and took seats around the conference table.

223

"Who's there with you, Roger?" the president asked, his disembodied voice coming from a speaker at the center of the table.

"Mr. President, you have me, along with John Scalia, Antonia Stebbens from Energy, and two of my deputies from State, Garen Adams, who oversees our Middle East desk, and Hank Bishop, who as you know is the undersecretary for operations."

"The purpose of this call," said London pointedly, "is to review any further developments as they relate to either Capitana or Savage Island, and to discuss the agenda for tonight's meeting between the secretary of state and King Fahd."

"From FBI, there have been no major developments as it relates to either attack site, other than more direct links between Arabs who were on board Capitana and Al-Qaeda," said Louis Chiles, piped into the conference call from a remote location. "We've identified some of the men from Capitana, going from Anson's records and our debriefings. A number of the men aboard the rig trace back to the early days of the organization and received training at various camps. Additionally, the apparent leader of the cell, a man called Esco, was a student with Hezbollah's number two, Sheikh Muhammad Hussein Fadlallah, more than two decades ago at Cairo University."

"So there's a clear Al-Qaeda connection?" asked the president.

"Lots of them, but distant in virtually every case, and all dated. These were no leaders here. We seem to be talking about midlevel operatives who subsequently disappeared and resurfaced."

"What does it mean?"

"We don't know."

"It could mean a lot of things," said Holmgren, also from Washington. "But we're getting nothing from our informants within the two groups. Nobody knew about this. You don't see the two groups collaborating on anything. Hezbollah despises Al-Qaeda. It doesn't make sense that they'd be working together. Also, both groups love headlines. They would've taken credit, if you ask me, if either were involved."

"Unless someone paid them a great deal of money," said Putnam.

"Let's get to Saudi Arabia," said the president. "Antonia, we know

Saudi Arabia had it in for Capitana, how it hurt them. But there was no direct motive for hitting Savage Island, right?"

"Right," said Stebbens. "In an energy context, Savage Island had little material impact."

"Yet the attacks are clearly linked by a couple of things," said Chiles. "Same explosive type, highly sophisticated stuff that is new, not yet black market available, and exceedingly difficult and expensive to manufacture. Now links between the individuals involved, via Al-Qaeda and Hezbollah training camps. And timing, of course."

Putnam cleared his throat. "What if Savage Island was a decoy, a way for the Saudis to say, 'Why would we do this?'"

"There's no logic to it other than the inexplicability of it," said Holmgren. "As you say. But it seems a stretch. Especially when you add in the murder of Anson and attempt on Marks. That seems like a purely symbolic act."

"Right," said the president. "The 'decoy' theory is circular reasoning. I don't mean to sound like a skeptic but it doesn't add up."

"Nor can we rule it out," said Chiles. "At least not yet."

"We don't know either way," said the president, "yet you land in Saudi Arabia in hours. We need a game plan."

"To get back to the energy issue, Mr. President," said Stebbens, "Saudi Arabia is our only option. They have the oil and can ramp up quickly, but at a cost. Their reserves have largely been sold off to China. We have approximately three weeks to run through whatever Capitana throughput was either en route or in refineries, so time is not on our side. We need to start filling the pipeline in a matter of days to avoid shock."

"What'll they ask for?" asked London.

"Whatever it is, we need to understand that the cost to our economy in not having adequate supply is staggering," said Stebbens. "EIA rough estimates were just sent to my BlackBerry—I'll forward them around. They say once the supply chain thins, the cost of gasoline could spike to seven or eight dollars a gallon. Our models show that every dollar over four dollars a gallon costs this country roughly twenty billion dollars a day in GDP. Those numbers are rough, but they could actually be low."

"Even if the Saudis didn't have anything to do with this, they have us by the balls," said Holmgren.

"It cost the United States one hundred and seventy-seven billion dollars to end the oil embargo in 1973," said Stebbens.

"In 1973 dollars? My God, the sky's the limit now," said London.

"This is shooting from the hip, but based on our experience in '73, and given the urgency this time around, I wouldn't be surprised if they ask for four, five, six hundred billion dollars," said Stebbens. "Nothing would surprise me."

"Are you hearing this, Roger?" asked the president.

"I hear you," said Putnam. "And here's how I'd approach it: remind King Fahd which military superpower enables him to continue to live as royalty, the one country that helps him stop the natives from busting down the front gates and throwing them out on their keisters." The secretary of state paused. "They need us as much as we need them. I'd tell them we know that they just attacked us, we have evidence linking government officials and Aramco brass to the attacks, and we don't intend to pay a dime. In fact, I'd demand some heads on a platter along with the oil."

The conference line went silent for a few moments, until the president cleared his throat. "That approach, Mr. Secretary, could leave us with no oil at all. That's an intolerable risk."

"This country was built on intolerable risks," said Putnam.

"Tonight is not about building," said the president. "Tonight is about defending the country and preserving economic stability. The Saudis, if it was indeed the Saudis, which I am still dubious about, won this round. Period, end of statement. We need to find out why we didn't know about this plot, where in our intelligence infrastructure we could have and should have caught this. If nonterrorist states are in fact co-opting Al-Qaeda we need to get to the bottom of that. We need to do a lot of things. But tonight, there's one job: get the oil flowing. That is our mission. That is your mission. Nothing else. Spend as little money as possible, but bring home the oil. The risk created by any kind of confrontation is unacceptable."

The phone in the conference room on the secretary of state's jet went dead. Putnam didn't even look around the room. He walked back to his stateroom and slammed the door.

Four and a half hours later, Putnam climbed into the back of a waiting black Mercedes stretch limousine at the U.S. Air Force Base in Riyadh, Saudi Arabia. The limousine and its six-car motorcade cruised through the late evening across Riyadh to the massive complex that served as King Fahd's central palace.

Putnam stepped out of the limousine and walked up the steps of the palace, where Roland Que-Marosali, Saudi Arabia's foreign minster, met him.

"Good morning, Mr. Secretary," Que-Marosali said. "How was your flight?"

"Nice to see you, Roland," said Putnam, shaking Que-Marosali's hand. "The flight was excellent, thank you."

They walked through the elaborate entrance atrium in the palace and down a long hallway, lit by a series of massive chandeliers. They walked through a large set of French doors. Inside was a spacious living room, decorated with tapestries on the walls, chandeliers, dozens of large couches and chairs.

Seated on a couch in the middle of the room was King Fahd. Next to Fahd was one of his sons, Prince Bandar. At the side of the room, several well-dressed staff members stood at attention. Fahd and his son stood up as Putnam entered the room. They walked slowly toward Putnam.

"Welcome, Roger," said Fahd.

Putnam took Fahd's extended hand.

"King Fahd," he said. "Thank you for seeing me on such short notice. My sincerest apologies."

Putnam shook Bandar's hand as well.

"Come, come, Roger," said Fahd warmly. "You're always welcome in this house."

"Yes, Mr. Secretary," said Bandar. "We look forward to hearing how we might be of service."

"Thank you, Prince Bandar."

King Fahd returned to his seat on the sofa, accompanied by Prince Bandar. Que-Marosali, the foreign minister, sat in a chair across from them.

A servant came forward. He placed a tray down on the table. On it was a silver service full of coffee, as well as tea and some cookies.

"Please, help yourself," said Prince Bandar.

"A cup of coffee," said Putnam. "Black."

The servant handed the secretary of state a cup of steaming coffee. He took a sip and looked across the table at King Fahd. "I'll be brief."

"We assume this has to do with Capitana," said Fahd. "We're so very sorry your country has suffered these tragedies."

"Thank you. It's been a difficult week. The reason I'm here now, sir, is to ask for Saudi Arabia's help. The loss of Capitana creates a challenging situation for the United States."

"Yes, I would imagine," said Bandar. "By our own estimates, Capitana was on pace to produce twelve percent of U.S. oil next year, scaling to nearly a fifth of your supply sometime in the next five years. Its production seemed to have no limits. It was an impressive field."

"What I'm here to seek your help on is Saudi Arabia's willingness and ability to step into the breach that's been created. To put it bluntly, America needs to quickly create an alternative to Capitana."

"Go on," said Fahd.

"You're the only country capable of filling the void. I'm prepared to negotiate long-term supply commitments, and to compensate you for your flexibility in this matter."

The room was silent. Prince Bandar leaned forward and prepared a cup of tea, which he handed to his father.

King Fahd took a small sip, then looked up at Putnam.

"Saudi Arabia is America's friend," said Fahd. "As long as the Fahd family rules Saudi Arabia, we will always be America's greatest ally. We'll help you, Roger. But getting our production up to the levels required to fill this sudden loss of petroleum, this is indeed a challenge. It's no secret Ghawar field is in decline. It costs us more and more to bring declining volumes of oil up from the ground. Every barrel becomes more expensive as it becomes harder to locate, find, and produce. To now add what would be hundreds of billions of barrels of incremental demand would pose a major financial drain on our resources. The oil is there, but getting to it is very expensive."

"I understand. We would never ask you to be the sole bearer of that up-front cost."

Fahd looked at his son, Prince Bandar. "Salim," asked Fahd, "what would it cost to finish completion of Ghawar, including the southern territories?"

Bandar looked at Putnam. "It would cost seven hundred billion dollars."

Putnam calmly took another sip from his cup.

"Roger, we would never ask the United States to pay that entire amount," said Fahd. "After all, we will ultimately be the beneficiaries of America's increased consumption."

"Understood," said Putnam. "You wouldn't want to appear greedy."

"My proposal to you would be we share in the cost," said Fahd, stroking his beard. "America invests five hundred billion dollars in jump-starting Saudi Arabia's infrastructure and locking up increased output. In return, I would begin diverting what we can to your shores immediately—what reserves are in storage in Ghawar and in other fields. That can begin as soon as this evening."

"Where do those reserves now stand?" asked Putnam. "How much is actually there? I understand that much of Saudi reserve has been taken by the Chinese over the last year."

Fahd looked at Putnam, then at his son.

"The Chinese have a big appetite, you're right," said Bandar. "They're buying everything they can from whomever will sell it to them."

"Why then has Saudi Arabia not invested in production at the new fields?" asked Putnam. "Why is there such an investment required to complete Ghawar? If you have a customer such as Sinopec, if you're serving the fastest-growing economy in the world, why don't you have the resources to reinvest? Why not charge them now? Must America pay for what will ultimately benefit the Chinese?"

The room was silent. Fahd stood and walked to the window, which overlooked the lights of Riyadh. "We haven't planned well. Imagine, if you will, a restaurant somewhere. A small, family-owned restaurant. In this restaurant, there are only two chairs. Behind the counter, a hundred different people wait for the money that comes in. They must split it up, dollar by dollar, as it arrives. Then one day, into the restaurant walks a very fat man. He sits on a chair, but he practically crowds out the other chair. He slobbers. He orders everything on the menu. He pays. The hundred family members are happy. It's more money that evening than they've made in years. The next day the fat man returns. He orders even more. He's gotten bigger too. No customer can even fit now on the other chair, he needs both, he's so fat! But today, when the bill comes, he pays half of what he paid the day before. He leaves no tip."

"The Chinese are ruthless," said Bandar.

"They're customers, and we value them," said Fahd. "But they use their size to place themselves in a unique and powerful position. They exploit. It's their nature."

"I understand the situation, Your Majesty," said Putnam, leaning back in the big couch. "But five hundred billion dollars is outrageous. You know it and I know it. America will not pay that much money for your help."

"In 1973, you invested nearly a hundred and eighty billion to end the oil embargo," said Bandar. "In today's dollars, with inflation, that would be nearly nine hundred billion dollars."

"Unlike you, Prince Bandar, I was alive in 1973," said Putnam. "I remember what happened. The oil embargo was a mess that was brought on by American policy makers. We paid to correct the sins of our own mismanagement. This situation is completely different. America has been attacked. Not one but two major strategic assets have been destroyed. We didn't bring this attack on. It was brought to our facilities and our shores and our citizens. And now we reach out to you as allies." Putnam looked at Bandar coldly. "What if we had asked for an 'investment,' to use your term, before we stepped in and saved you from Hussein in 1993, when he was at your doorstep like a hungry jackal? What if we had our hand out then as you do tonight? What would we have asked for? What was it worth to the Fahds to save all that they have?

Two trillion dollars? Five trillion? But no, we asked for nothing. We risked American lives to stop the enemy and beat them back."

"Let's be honest," said Bandar. "That was an act of self-preservation by the Americans. In 1993, the fields of Saudi Arabia and Kuwait produced nearly forty percent of U.S. petroleum. You saved yourselves that night."

Fahd walked from the window to the couch and sat next to Putnam. "What we offer you is reasonable. What I said about the hundred family members at the restaurant. Imagine a number one thousand times as large. There are princes across the country and their spending only grows. I have my own pressures. Someday, you will not be seated in this comfortable sofa, nor will I. Someday it might not be someone who is willing, at whatever the price, to step into the breach, as you say. You're lucky. The Americans are lucky. Lucky to have friends like the Fahds, like the Saudis."

Putnam could feel the redness beginning, first at his neck, then rising through his cheeks and nose, up through his forehead, anger, hatred, beginning to boil. He held the cup of coffee and took a sip. Then, staring at Fahd, he took the small cup and hurled it at the window where Fahd had just stood. The cup smashed against the thick glass, sending coffee all over the window before the shards of white and blue china dropped to the floor.

King Fahd and Prince Bandar remained motionless, in shock.

"Friends?" asked Putnam. "Your own foreign minster plotting with senior Aramco officials to sabotage Capitana as far back as 1998."

Across the room, Que-Marosali, the Saudi foreign minister, who'd been silent until now, rose from his seat.

Putnam continued. "We have evidence, piles of it, linking members of this government with what happened at Capitana."

"This is outrageous!" yelled Que-Marosali. "Why would we do this?"

"You know why. You saw what Capitana had the potential to be. You tried to buy it. You offered to pay obscene amounts of money for it. You recognized before it was even built the significance of the strike."

"There are many elephants out there," said Que-Marosali.

"Bullshit," said Putnam. "None that hurt you so severely."

"This is outrageous," Fahd whispered, shaking his head. "In all my years, I've never been so deeply offended."

"You're offended, sir?" asked Putnam. "How do you think we feel?"

"Where is this 'evidence' you claim to have?" asked Bandar angrily. "So we were upset at what Capitana has done to us. So what. There's a giant leap from being upset to committing acts of terror."

"Do you deny it?"

"Of course we deny it!" yelled Que-Marasoli. "How dare you accuse us of such acts!"

Fahd looked ashen and stunned as he sat in silence and watched his foreign minister and his oldest son scream at the U.S. secretary of state. He held a hand up to silence them. Finally, he looked up at Putnam.

"We'll continue to honor our military alliance with the United States," said Fahd. "I've known you more than thirty years, Roger. I have to believe there's something the matter with you. We would never do anything to harm the United States, not intentionally. I want you out of my house. The offer I made earlier is gone. You can find your oil elsewhere."

It was 6:00 P.M. Saudi time when Putnam climbed back on the airplane.

"How'd it go?" asked Scalia.

Putnam stopped and looked at Scalia and Stebbens. His face was ashen. "We have a problem," said Putnam. "I need to call the president."

He walked past Scalia and Stebbens, shut the door to the stateroom, and dialed the three-digit code that would ring White House Control, which would then find the president.

"How did the meeting go?" asked the president when he came to the phone a few seconds later.

Putnam paused. "Not well. I failed. Went off script. I made the accusation."

There was a long silence.

"I thought we discussed this."

"We did."

"I was crystal fucking clear, Roger."

"You were. You were crystal clear."

"God*damn* it!" yelled the president. "Do you understand the situation we're already in? Do you understand what happens in three weeks, a month, when the tanks start running dry? You arrogant son of a bitch!"

Putnam was silent.

"How clear did I make it to you? What the fuck have you done?"

"I'm sorry. I'll have my resignation on your desk by the time the plane lands."

The president was silent.

"I held back," said Putnam. "We had a deal ready to cut. They wanted five hundred billion dollars."

"Five hundred billion," said the president. "Holy shit."

"I negotiated. Then, at some point, Fahd said something that triggered something in me. I lost it."

"What exactly do you mean you 'lost it'?"

"I accused them of being involved with the attacks. I threw a teacup against the wall."

"My God, what were you thinking?"

"I was thinking about Ted Marks. I was thinking about how angry I am. I lost control."

"Now we have to rescue this," said the president. "I can't accept your resignation. We can't give the Saudis, or anyone for that matter, the power. I might have to do it later, in case five hundred billion dollars and your scalp gets the oil flowing again. You deserve to be fired, you stupid son of a bitch. What you did tonight wasn't just a disavowal of my direct orders. You hurt the country. But right now we need to go into salvage mode. In fifteen minutes I want to talk about what we're going to do."

Over the next two hours, as the secretary of state's plane returned to the United States, the president and his senior staff attempted to mitigate the damage caused by Putnam's accusations against the Saudis. But it was no use. King Fahd had gone to sleep. Prince Bandar was unwilling to speak with anyone. The highest-ranking official reached was Saudi Arabia's ambassador to the U.S., who was awakened at the Saudi Embassy near the Watergate in Washington and asked to come to the White House. By the time he arrived at the White House, he'd been briefed, and instead of discussing the situation used the occasion to lodge a formal diplomatic protest and demand Putnam's ouster.

By midafternoon, King Fahd called an emergency meeting of OPEC to discuss the incident. At the meeting, held by teleconference, Que-Marosali described the meeting with the U.S. secretary of state. He expressed King Fahd's indignation at the United States. The governing body of OPEC, the foreign ministers from the seven oil-producing states in the region, expressed their unanimous support for Saudi Arabia and demanded Putnam's firing. More important, the group agreed to hold production level and not help the United States with its oil problem. A broken teacup was turning into a shattered alliance.

By late afternoon in the United States, someone within the Saudi government leaked the story to *The New York Times*. They ran an online article about the disastrous Fahd-Putnam meeting. As expected, the price of oil futures, already more than $50 a barrel higher in the wake of the attack on Capitana, leaped on the word that a deal to resupply U.S. oil supply had not been reached with the Saudis. By noon, the price of a barrel of West Texas Intermediate, or WTI, the kind of light, sweet crude oil produced in Texas and the Gulf of Mexico, and a good indication of where oil prices would go, crossed the $200 mark for the first time ever.

27

Ted Marks awoke and tried to register where he was, to remember something, anything, that would give him a clue as to where he was, why he was here, but he was at a loss.

Slowly, he opened his eyes and looked to the left. He sensed a dull pain on that side of his head and felt a gauzy stupor from what must have been powerful painkillers running through his veins. His nostrils were irritated and he suddenly became aware of tubes up into his nose. The room was a hospital room. Sunlight came in through a large window to the right of his bed and he saw skyscrapers in the air near the building. How long had he been there?

Looking down, he lifted his arm and saw the bandage around his hand. He suddenly remembered the battle; reaching desperately into the fireplace for the handgun. He winced in anger and it all came back. The killer. The fire. The murder of Nick and Annie Anson. He winced again and closed his eyes.

Several hours later he awoke again. Nighttime. Pain from his shoulder intense. The painkillers didn't feel as strong in him, but he felt much more lucid. The room was dim. A single light shone to his left, a reading light. In the chair, a man sat, reading a book.

Marks swallowed, then spoke. "Anson," he said.

"I know," said Savoy. "They came for you. There were tracks through the woods. Blood. You injured him."

"What day is it?"

"It happened last night. You've been out twenty-four hours. You were airlifted here. You're in Denver. They removed a bullet from your shoulder. You have some bleeding in your skull. He struck you pretty hard with something."

"Poker, from the fireplace."

"Ouch."

"Was it the merger?"

"It's bigger." Savoy stood and walked to the side of the bed. "Savage Island is gone; so is Capitana."

"No," he whispered. "Tell me you're . . ."

The look in Savoy's eyes said it all.

After a few moments of silent shock, Marks asked, "Were there survivors?"

"Yeah. Half of the people at Savage Island survived, far fewer at the rig. We were lucky any survived."

"Terrorists?"

"Probably. Or mercenaries hired by a foreign government. They don't know. They're working on it."

Savoy brought Marks up to speed on everything he knew; the events at the dam, the reports on Capitana, Dewey Andreas.

"It's all gone," said Marks after several minutes of silence. He closed his eyes. "Everything we worked so hard for."

"We can rebuild it," said Savoy.

After a long pause, Marks opened his eyes and looked at Savoy.

"You can rebuild it, Terry," he said. "I'm going to find the motherfuckers who did this."

28

Jessica entered Chiles's office alone.

He turned from the window, looked up at her. "What is it?"

"Madradora," she said.

"What about it?"

"It failed. The two Deltas are dead. Killed, gunned down in broad daylight."

Chiles paused, stared at Jessica. "What about Andreas?"

"He called it in. He killed the shooters. He's running."

"Killed who? Who does he say did the shooting?"

"He was unequivocal," she said. "He says they were operatives."

"Operatives? You mean terrorists?"

"No," said Jessica. "Professionals, hired guns, most likely. Which, if true, would mean that the planned exfiltration was leaked. It means someone in the room at the time the plan was made—"

"There's a mole," interrupted Chiles.

"That's what Dewey thinks."

Chiles leaned back in the big maroon leather chair. He closed his eyes, rubbed the stubble that had aggregated on his chin.

"So what do you want?" he asked.

"Authorization," she said. "We need to start a track protocol. Financials, e-mail, phone records, everything. Mole hunt."

Chiles looked skeptical.

"I'm not convinced," he said. "One call from Andreas? Maybe *he* killed them."

"I'm not convinced either. But if there's even a chance, we need to start looking."

Chiles nodded.

"I agree," he said. "Do it. Run it out of here. But keep it quiet."

29

By the time Dewey made it to Highway 25 the woman in the backseat had died.

He took the highway after several miles of breakneck driving down narrow Cali streets ahead of two green and yellow police cruisers.

Dewey could have pulled over and left himself at the mercy of the Cali police, the local government, and ultimately the Colombian government. But the existence of a mole in the interagency group changed everything. If the traitor could arrange to take out two Deltas, he could easily get to him elsewhere. A jail cell in the country's corrupt western drug capital would be an easy place to manufacture the accidental death of a prisoner. No, surrendering was not an option.

He took the highway entrance at seventy miles per hour, swerving right and hitting the sharp curve of the entrance ramp with the screech of tires beneath him, barely keeping the sedan under control. The first police cruiser, just yards behind him, temporarily lost its traction in the sharp turn. Its rear end bounced against the guardrail, sending the cruiser in an uncontrolled spin in the middle of the entrance ramp. The other cruiser passed it and tried to move closer to Dewey but the dustup with the first sedan provided Dewey with several hundred feet of new freedom, and he didn't let up.

Highway 25 was crowded but moving quickly. Dewey pushed the accelerator to the ground and kept it there. Soon the Mercedes sped down the two-lane highway at nearly 115 miles per hour, pushing the envelope of recklessness.

After several minutes of driving, a blue traffic sign above the highway showed an airplane. Aragón International Airport, five miles away.

With the relative comfort of the distance gained from the police car, plus a clear lane of traffic as far as he could see, Dewey took the cell phone from his lap. He pressed the camera icon and the display screen changed. Looking for a moment behind him, he held the phone above the dead assassin's face and snapped a photo. He shut the phone and turned back to the road.

Driving skills were a core competency in Delta, and Dewey now thanked God for all of the endless hours he spent behind the wheel that one summer so long ago. There were two keys to evasion tactics when driving. The first was obvious: speed. They taught you how to handle the effects of high speed, what it will do to a vehicle, how to plan for upcoming turns, different terrains, even catching air. As Dewey checked the speedometer, which now showed 122 miles per hour, he felt the training rejoining him.

The second key was the element of surprise. That was always a harder one, especially at high speed, but he began to work out a plan.

Within a few minutes the signs for Aragón International became multiple as he approached the facility. Planes overhead seemed barely to clear the mountains that ringed Cali's airport.

The police cruiser would expect him to be running for the airport. Dewey kept the Mercedes in the left lane as the exit to the airport came within view on the right. At the exit ramp, he swerved right. In the rearview mirror, he watched as the police cruiser followed suit, moving rapidly up the highway's breakdown lane, trying to cut Dewey off. In response, Dewey settled back into the left lane. Cars filled the center lane between the approaching police cruiser and the Mercedes. At the last possible moment, Dewey feinted right, as if to cut across to the airport exit, then swung abruptly left, back onto the highway, racing past the airport entrance. The policeman was trapped behind a line of cars and soon Dewey was out of sight.

Less than a mile past the airport Dewey saw a crossover gap in the guardrail between the east- and westbound lanes of traffic. He slowed the Mercedes and swerved into the small gap, then hit the accelerator and lurched forward into traffic. To his right, Dewey saw a young Colombian man in a decrepit, rust-covered Volkswagen Rabbit. Dewey cut off his car, bringing him to a halt. Dewey climbed out of the Mercedes amid slowing traffic and the blare of horns around him. He moved to the Volkswagen, revolver out, and signaled for the man to get out of the car. The driver complied quickly, arms raised.

The traffic on Highway 25 began to resume its normal speed around the incident. It clearly wasn't the first time the local population had witnessed a carjacking in broad daylight.

Dewey squeezed into the Volkswagen, backed up, and maneuvered around the Mercedes, hitting the gas. Soon, he was back at the eastbound entrance to the airport. He moved into the entrance lane and settled into line. He had lost the tail, but they would be waiting at the airport.

Sure enough, at the entrance to the parking garage, one of the police cruisers was already in position, no doubt looking for the black Mercedes.

Dewey passed the cruiser and parked the Volkswagen in short-term parking, then walked to the airport entrance.

Aragón International was a four-story yellow cement building that spread out in a rectangle beneath the scorching Cali sun, the surrounding peaks forming a stunning backdrop in the distance. Dewey entered the building and went quickly to a restroom. There, he waited until he was alone, then unzipped his leather jacket. He looked in the mirror. The bandaging on his wound had seeped through and dark red now saturated the gauze and his blue T-shirt. He went to the last stall and shut the door. He quickly removed the old bandage. The wound had formed a small outer ridge of scab, but the center of the gash remained raw. A trickle of blood leaked out. It was healing, but the trauma at Madradora had not helped. Still, the homemade suture seemed to be holding. And there were no

241

signs of infection. He replaced the bandage with a new one from his pocket, wrapping another piece of duct tape tightly about the shoulder.

Back in the main arrival and departure area of Aragón International, Dewey glanced around him, looking for signs of trouble.

Beyond airport security, he spied a small gathering of policemen. On one side of the large main room of the facility, four uniformed officers stood beneath the arrival portico. One of the officers gesticulated emphatically, commanding the others, Dewey guessed, as to the importance of capturing the one who'd left him trapped in the breakdown lane at the first airport entrance.

The evasion had served its purpose to lose the initial tail, but they knew he was here. They weren't idiots.

Dewey moved into the crowd at the center of the chamber and walked beneath the large arrival and departure screen. Reading down the screen, he found two flights leaving within the hour: to Medellín and Havana.

Dewey walked to the ticket counter, where a young Colombian woman in a Navy blue uniform smiled at him.

Behind her, just feet away, one of the uniformed police officers walked quickly by. He inspected the line as he did so, staring for a moment at Dewey. Dewey kept his eyes focused in front of him, not down, staring at the woman behind the counter. The policeman paused just beyond the woman's shoulder, then moved on.

"*Adónde, señor?*" she asked.

"*Habana,*" said Dewey. "*Unidireccional.*"

After purchasing the one-way ticket, Dewey entered a souvenir shop and bought a baseball cap. Then he went to a small café and ordered a steak sandwich, glancing around the airport as he waited for his order to come.

The four policemen had been joined by others and soon he could count a dozen officers in total.

By now, they no doubt had found the Mercedes on the highway, the owner, and perhaps even had a description of him. At least the hat provided some cover.

The officers searched among the crowd at the airport, scanning the main arrival and departure area with serious, intense looks on their faces. Dewey knew time was now working increasingly against him. He watched as the minutes on the overhead screen moved ahead.

An officer was posted at each entrance to the large chamber, while several officers patrolled through the atrium.

The flight to Cuba boarded in ten minutes.

As he waited for the sandwich to arrive, a young officer in a brown uniform walked through the small café, staring at each table. At his table, the officer paused for several seconds and stared at him.

"*Hola*," Dewey said politely.

The officer nodded, saying nothing.

He was onto him. Dewey knew that, and the next minute would determine his fate.

The officer had no radio, and Dewey knew the young man was looking for a backup to help him.

Dewey moved.

Standing, he walked toward the rear of the café, aiming now for the restaurant restroom. Its entrance stood out of sight from the main airport concourse and it represented Dewey's only hope of escape.

As Dewey expected, the officer followed. He was now confused, his inexperience showing as he began to panic.

"*Parada*," the officer said as Dewey crossed the café. Then louder, "*Stop!*"

Dewey continued to walk through the small, nearly empty café, pretending not to hear.

He made it to the restroom door and pushed it in, entering quickly. It was a large, well-lit space. He went to the urinal and stood, as if about to urinate. The door opened and the young officer entered, gun out now and aimed at Dewey.

"*Estate quieto!*" yelled the officer. "Don't move!"

Dewey let his mouth gape, pretending to be shocked.

"What have I done?" Dewey asked, feigning fear.

With his empty hand, the policeman signaled for Dewey to move toward the wall.

"Spread your arms," he said. "*Now*. Against the wall. Feet too."

Dewey walked to the wall, spreading his arms and legs. He heard a jingle as the officer pulled handcuffs from his waist belt. Looking over his shoulder, Dewey watched. As the policeman began to place the steel cuff on Dewey's right wrist, Dewey swung the arm back and sent a vicious elbow to the side of the officer's head. The policeman stumbled backward, trying to maintain the aim of his handgun. A fraction of a second later, Dewey followed the elbow by turning and unleashing a sideways kick with his left foot that flung the pistol from the policeman's hand. Dewey stood over the young man, who cowered beneath him. Dewey finished with a well-calculated right hand to the temple, knocking the policeman unconscious but sparing his life.

He exited the restroom and walked inconspicuously through the café. As he passed his table, he grabbed half the sandwich, now sitting on a plate, and dropped a few Colombian bills on the table.

At the Avianca gate, boarding had begun. A dark-skinned female customs agent stood, inspecting passports, swiping them under an infrared scanner.

Anger suddenly filled Dewey's head as he realized the implications of the coming moment. After the customs agent swiped his passport, his name and location would immediately pop up on the Interpol grid. Most likely, whoever was behind the attempted take-out at Madradora would already have him flagged. And while Cuba would be a difficult place for legitimate American government agencies to reach him, the mole wouldn't have that problem.

He swallowed, less nervous than embarrassed at the thought of his grave miscalculation. He should have fled in another manner; by road, by boat. He should have holed up somewhere and waited for Savoy to extract him properly.

Behind him, he glanced back and saw a commotion of police officers, likely now aware of the café restroom incident.

He was trapped, and he knew it. He thought back to his training, but came up empty. There was nothing he could do. As an elderly woman in front of him handed her passport to the customs agent, he pulled his U.S. passport from the pocket of his jacket.

Then, suddenly, another memory came to him. Fenway Park. An afternoon so long ago. With his father, they'd bought bleacher seats to a game. They could barely see the game, but it didn't matter to Dewey, so amazing was the experience of his first visit to the ballpark. In the seventh inning, he'd held his father's hand as he led him toward home plate. He remembered being excited, scared even, as they came closer to home plate and the prized seats behind it. Then, at the entrance to the row that led down to the Red Sox dugout, he watched as his father handed the usher a $20 bill, asking the man to let Dewey watch the rest of the game at the end of the aisle next to the field. He'd watched three innings that day, standing there, his father smiling in the September sun from an exit ramp thirty rows away.

Dewey reached down into his leather coat and pulled the large wad of cash from the pocket. There was still more than $10,000 there, at least a year's wage for the customs agent. It was all Dewey had. He kept $1,000 in his pocket, then folded the remaining wad of cash into the passport and handed it to the stone-faced agent. She opened the small passport, eyeing the money. She looked up at Dewey, their eyes meeting for the briefest of moments. He stared back blankly, knowing his fate was now beyond his control, that his life now lay in the hands of the severe-looking government employee in front of him. He followed her eyes as she glanced behind him. No fewer than six officers now hovered in the atrium behind the line, searching methodically from gate to gate.

She looked back at Dewey. His eyes moved toward the passport scanner. Hers followed his, then looked back at him. Their eyes met again. Ever so subtly, he shook his head quickly, letting the woman know what he needed. *Don't swipe it*, he thought. The agent paused. Then, she moved the passport toward the screen. He felt his stomach suddenly drop. But her arm kept moving, past the screen, swinging the passport down to her side, where she removed the money. She handed the passport back to him.

"Enjoy Havana, *señor*," she whispered.

30

INTERMODAL FACILITY AND BREAK-BULK WAREHOUSE
PORT OF LONG BEACH, CALIFORNIA

In the bathroom off the warehouse floor, Neqq leaned in closer to the mirror and examined his eyes. Bloodshot. He hadn't gotten much sleep last night. They were closing in. He felt it. They knew something.

Neqq felt alone, and for good reason. He'd been isolated for nearly five years now, living in a six-story apartment building on the outskirts of Long Beach. He missed Jamrud. Mama and Papa, Vishna al-Katar, his teacher at the madrasah, the food, bhindi gosht with green chili sauce . . .

And now, at risk of being discovered, who could he talk to? The answer was no one. He was utterly alone. The question wasn't would they catch him. The question was when. Should he set the bomb off now, himself, as he was instructed to do if they got close? Should he hang himself so that he became just another anonymous suicide, an immigrant, dangling from a beam in the ceiling? This was what they were taught: Don't run. Commit suicide. You will still be a martyr. To run is to get caught, to admit guilt. There cannot be suspicion.

Neqq knew he was part of an elite group. He knew the name of its leader. He was a legend, a hero. He wasn't supposed to know his name. But he did: Alexander.

Neqq didn't know how many others there were in total who had come out of the madrasah, but in his class alone there were six men. They didn't know why Imam had chosen them. He certainly wasn't the smartest, or the most faithful. But he never complained. He never questioned. He'd thought about it a lot all these years; why him? Why Barush, his best friend, why was he left behind? The others who were selected with him? They were the quiet ones. The ones who didn't argue, didn't complain when one night dinner wasn't there because Imam didn't have the money to pay for food. They were not even allowed to say good-bye to their parents. That was probably what hurt the most.

From the madrasah, they had driven in a convoy to Karachi, then took the plane with Russian writing on the side to Kenya. It was Neqq's first time on a plane. From the remote airstrip in Kenya, they drove on a yellow bus for five hours into the desert. The camp was plain, large, spreading out in all directions as far as you could see. Tents. Obstacle course. The rat-a-tat of the firing range on the hill. It was called Al Nar, *the Fire*. There was a long, sloping rock against which they had strung tents for shelter. Every day, there were courses for learning how to shoot, how to fight. They learned explosives. This is what they learned: the material is like clay. You can throw it against the wall, even run it over. You can even eat it in small amounts; your body will pass it without harm. But if you charge it with two negative ions at the same time—a special detonator called a T7.4—that soft material will make the world come down around you.

They showed it once. They set off an amount the size of a baseball. They set it off nearly a mile in the distance. The explosion rocked the ground, even from so far away. The next day they climbed into the crater and it was still warm. The crater was more than four hundred feet across.

That was why he was there. They all knew that the day they set off the explosion.

They spent five months in Kenya, sweating like dogs, starving, learning how to kill, learning how to set the explosives, understanding what it meant to be a *cell*. One day, someone smarter than he decided they were ready. They went back to Kenya, then sailed to Marbella, in southern Spain, aboard a dilapidated schooner. They flew from Gibraltar to

Canada, to different cities in Canada. He was sent to Montreal. There, he stayed in an apartment near McGill University for more than six months, waiting. He was forbidden from going to a mosque, forbidden from communicating with any of the others, even if he ran into them in the street. The letter came one day in May. In it was a Canadian passport, a bus ticket, a key to a locker in the Des Moines, Iowa, train station. He remembered laughing because he was so happy to be finally going somewhere, doing something. Laughing because he didn't know where Des Moines, or Iowa for that matter, even was. Two days on the bus to Iowa. In the train station, the locker contained eight cashier's checks, each for $10,000. In the locker, a glossy brochure showed the Port of Long Beach, California: "America's Gateway to the East." The biggest port in the United States. The busiest port in the United States. He knew then what was next. Finally, there was a phone number on a piece of paper. He knew he was to call when he arrived and had a place to stay. In one respect, he remembered thinking, it was by far the most important item in the locker. If he lost that number, he would lose his connection, his purpose, forever. He remembered thinking it would have been easy to simply walk away. To take the money and walk away. Perhaps that was how they tested them? Perhaps they knew that some would walk, and those that did, they wanted no part of, for they would not last, would not have the fortitude to do what was next. He committed the number to memory. Even this day, he awoke repeating the number as if in a reverie, repeating it like a song that will not leave your head.

He called the number and gave his new address. After that, every month or so, a box with a check in it arrived, and a care package with cookies, toothpaste, other things. But the only thing that mattered was the toothpaste. That was what everything was all about. And every month, when the package came, Neqq cashed the check. He ate the cookies if they weren't stale yet. Most important, the reason for the care package, the reason for it all, was the toothpaste. He opened the toothpaste and sniffed; the smell was mild, like a faint whiff of gasoline. Octanitrocubane.

He looked one last time at himself in the mirror of the restroom. *They'll torture it out of me*, he thought. *I'm not strong enough.*

248

Neqq leaned back and turned the water off. He reached out and grabbed a paper towel and dried his hands. He left the bathroom and walked back to the warehouse floor. His shift would begin in fifteen minutes. He smelled the smell he'd grown to love, a combination of sea salt from the ocean water just beyond the warehouse doors, and the smell of oil, spilling now and then from the big container ships.

Perhaps they aren't closing in, he thought as he walked across the warehouse floor, past pallet upon pallet of stacked cargo—rolls of paper, lumber, anything you can imagine could be made in China—looking up at the ceilings more than six stories in the sky. *I'm driving myself crazy. Imagining everything.*

Still, Mr. Sargent kept staring at him. Mr. Sargent was the general manager of the intermodal facility, Union Pacific's massive warehouse, loading dock, and container storage area. Here, America's largest railroad took inbound freight, mostly containers coming out of the Far East, and removed them from the big container ships. They stacked them somewhere in the 3,200-acre outdoor storage area. The gigantic container ships would arrive weighted down like they were about to sink, stacked high with thousands of the forty-foot containers. Overhead gantry cranes on the docks lifted the containers up one by one and moved them from the ship like an assembly line, efficiently and quickly, to the dock staging area. There they were placed on chassis attached to trucks. The drivers shuttled the containers to the large storage area, where the drivers were directed about the mazelike network of sections, organized methodically by type of cargo, the date they were to be shipped, and end destination. Neqq drove a reach stacker. He was there to grab the heavy containers off the truck chassis and place them down on the ground or on top of other containers.

The warehouse was at the edge of the container area, right along the docks. They needed a warehouse for the break-bulk shipments—cargo that wasn't in containers, but rather was on pallets and needed to be sheltered from the elements. The warehouse was also where the workers' lockers were, the bathroom, cafeteria. They even had a gym there.

It was hard to believe the hunk of material in the bottom of Neqq's locker could destroy the building, a large section of the container field, and most of the docks at the port. But it could. It would. Soon, it would.

He checked that morning, first thing. Every Tuesday. It was all in place now: the octanitrocubane, the detonator. He'd wedged the last pieces into place a few months ago. The detonator had arrived more than three years ago. It was in a box, disguised as a children's toy, part of an erector set. The toy had even been wrapped so that it looked new. But Neqq knew exactly how to tell the detonator parts from the pieces of the toy. It took him almost an entire weekend to assemble the complicated thing. But when he tied off the last wire and soldered it to the cellular antenna, he knew it was perfect. That next week, he'd brought it to work. He set it in the explosive material beneath the foot joist in his locker just after lunch that Tuesday. There it had sat for nearly two years now. It had long since been buried by more octanitrocubane, sent in the toothpaste tubes. There it all waited. Waited for someone, somewhere, to set off the detonation. Neqq knew how to detonate the bomb, if he had to. But he was supposed to wait for the detonation. Wait, unless he knew they were getting close. *Should I set it off?* he asked himself.

Neqq knew the odds were one in three he would be there when it was set off. He worked an eight-hour shift. One in three. He always thought about that. Did he want to be there? If he wasn't, would they come looking for him? Would he stay in Long Beach? In California? America? He had always thought he wanted to be there. It would be easier in so many ways. No one would look for him then. But recently, he'd begun to think about his family. They didn't even know he was alive. Imagine walking into the little home, just outside the town center. "Mama," he would say to his mother. He knew she would cry when she saw him at the door. The thought nearly brought tears to his eyes as he imagined it.

He stood at the edge of the building and stared. In front of him, he could see eleven reach stackers just rumbling to life as he and the other drivers got ready for their shift. To the left, the warehouse was filled for as far as you could see.

To his right, through the six-story warehouse doors, he saw a big container ship coming in. He could see a couple of crew members at the front of the ship. He stepped to the end of the dock and stood next to one of the big yellow steel ballast ties. One of the men, an Asian man, waved to him. Neqq waved back. Sometimes, he would dream about climbing aboard one of the container ships, going on an adventure, getting away from the inevitability of it all. But then he would remember his place. His duty. *Jihad.*

Beyond the ship was the ocean, just now beginning to shimmer in the morning light. How much longer would he stare at the ocean? When would Alexander press the button and make it all go away?

"What are you looking at?" Mr. Sargent said.

"The boat, sir," said Neqq. "I'm always amazed."

"What country are you from?" asked Mr. Sargent.

"I think we've talked about this before, sir. Canada. I'm from Montreal. You asked me this before."

"Canada," said Mr. Sargent as he stared at Neqq. Neqq became uncomfortable. He felt cool sweat come into his armpits. "O Canada," sang Mr. Sargent, eyeing Neqq severely. "We stand on guard for thee."

Neqq grinned nervously.

"Get back to work. There's containers to off-load."

Neqq walked quickly back to the number six reach stacker and climbed up into the cab. He found his safety helmet. He took the silver key from the overhead visor and placed it in the ignition, then pressed the small red button to the left of the transmission and felt the massive million-dollar piece of machinery come to life.

It must come soon, he thought. If Mr. Sargent searched his locker, if he truly ripped it up, he would be lost. They would lock him up, interrogate him. Could he survive the torture? Should he commit suicide tonight?

His mind raced as he moved the gear into drive. It had been so long now. It was time. He did what he always did at moments like these, repeating the Sharia. He drifted into the focus of his work, driving the big machine out through the warehouse portal to the container field.

31

FORTUNA'S ESTATE
FURTHER LANE
EAST HAMPTON, NEW YORK

Fortuna gunned the engine of the black Aston Martin Vanquish S as he made his way out Route 27 through Long Island. He had left Manhattan late and thus avoided much of the traffic to the Hamptons. It was nearly nine o'clock at night. He could've gone to Chelsea Piers and taken a helicopter out to his estate, but he wanted to drive instead. The two-hour drive would give him the chance to clear his mind.

Dewey Andreas ate away at Fortuna like a cancer. Try as he might, the thought of the survivor, the man who'd killed and likely interrogated Esco, grew like an abscess with each passing hour. Buck still hadn't called, which couldn't be a good sign. In frustration, Fortuna had called Buck, several times now, and still he hadn't responded. Fortuna slammed his fist down on the dark wood of the steering wheel.

The road was black in darkness as he finished the final miles before getting to his estate. A fresh snowstorm left a white parchment on either side of the roadway. He probably was going too fast for the conditions. A patch of black ice would have sent the $280,000 vehicle flying into a snowbank or a tree. At north of eighty miles per hour, and with no seat belt on, it would be fatal. But Fortuna found it hard to care. He liked the speed. He cruised through Southampton, Water Mill, and Bridgehampton. The streets of the towns were decorated for the holidays. Couples walked along the sidewalks, bundled up in bright-colored ski parkas and long overcoats, coming from one of the town's restaurants.

A week before Christmas, the village of East Hampton was festooned with lights and decorations. The shops in town alternated between the family-owned institutions, meat markets, candy stores, and coffeehouses that had been there for decades, and the newer entrants to the area, like J.Crew, Burberry, Tiffany's, and Starbucks, that came with the ubiquitous wealth. Less than a mile beyond the small village, he took a right onto Egypt Lane, then a left on Further Lane. A mile ahead were the stone pillars to his estate. He took a right at the big elm tree, through the unmarked stone pillars. He'd removed the small sign that said EAGLE ROCK, the name given to the estate when it was built in 1908 by one of Henry Clay Frick's sons. He'd found it pretentious.

At the push of a button on the dashboard, the black steel of the large gate swung inward and he pulled the Aston Martin down the long driveway that led to his seaside mansion. Fortuna had bought the house a week before his twenty-eighth birthday. At the time, it had cost him $18 million. He knew he'd make a lot more money in his career; the cost hadn't even raised his eyebrows.

The driveway bent left, then straightened and dipped along a sleek and thin path of pebble stone, bordered on each side by the monotony of white slat horse fence. The driveway went for nearly a quarter mile, descending toward the water past tennis courts, the pool house, and pool, now covered. The house itself was a stunning shingle-style mansion that rambled along Long Island Sound's blue-watered edge, surrounded by wide manicured lawns, sculpted boxwoods, and beech trees, all now blanketed in snow.

Fortuna climbed out of the car and walked to the front door. As he stepped onto the slate steps, the door opened.

"Good evening, Alex," a woman said. Celia Rosemont, Fortuna's caretaker at the estate, was a plain-looking woman, in her fifties, neatly attired in a gray sweater. "How was your trip?"

"Good," he lied, presenting his usual calm and confident exterior. "How are you?"

"Great. Can I get you something?"

"Yes. A glass of wine. Open a bottle of Silver Oak, please. I don't care what year."

"Are you hungry? Can I have Jessica make you something?"

"Yes. Surprise me. No seafood though. Maybe a steak, pasta, whatever. I'll be in my office."

Fortuna walked through the entrance hall, through the living room, into a small door in the back of the room. Inside, a fireplace in the center of the back wall glowed with orange flames. Above the white marble mantel hung a Picasso oil of two boys playing with a ball. To the left, a large tan, custom-made sofa and two chairs surrounded a table with magazines laid neatly out on top of it. To the right, a large mahogany table sat to the side. On top of the table, a large flat computer screen stood, the only object, other than a keyboard, atop the big table.

Fortuna walked to the desk and sat down. He opened the cabinet behind the chair and turned on the computer.

Entering a series of passwords in a succession of screens gained him entry into a highly secure network.

He spent the next half hour looking at the performance of the three hedge funds, Kallivar, PBX, and Passwood-Regent. All showed similar growth in net asset value, as he expected they would. Each suffered losses in the investments in KKB and Anson Energy. Those losses, in total, amounted to approximately $660 million. But those were the only losses in a two-day period of unbelievable financial performance.

All told, in two days, at least on paper, Fortuna's three hedge funds had created more than $17 billion in new wealth. Fortuna now controlled nearly $27 billion in assets. And values would likely climb higher as the smoke cleared and tensions dissipated.

Of course the government would ultimately come to question the suspicious trades and accumulation of wealth, but for the moment, they had their hands full, investigating the attacks. Soon, they'd have much more to worry about. And by the time they focused on Fortuna, he'd be gone.

Next, Fortuna skimmed media coverage of the funeral of Nicholas Anson, then coverage of the destruction of Savage Island Project and Capitana. According to the pundits, Al-Qaeda took top honors as suspect of choice.

Celia entered the office and placed a wineglass down in front of him. "Jessica is whipping up steak au poivre."

"Great." Fortuna took a sip from the wineglass.

"Would you like a salad?"

"Please." He didn't look up from the screen.

Celia walked to the door to leave. "You received a phone call," she said, turning around.

Fortuna's back stiffened. "Oh?"

"He said it was urgent. Wouldn't leave his name. He was a bit abrupt, actually. Said you would know who it was."

"Got it."

As soon as Celia left, Alex picked up his phone. There were two phone lines to the estate; the main phone line, which was used throughout the house, and a single phone with a separate line and an expensive array of tap detection and encrypting technology, which was the one he now used. He dialed the same number he'd tried five times in the past four hours.

"Yeah," the voice said.

"Where have you been?" said Fortuna. "Is it done?"

"No. He got away."

"For fuck's sake," Fortuna said angrily. "So now the government has him?"

"No. Andreas killed the people I sent, then he ran. Cali police gave chase but lost him near the airport, and they couldn't find him there. No one knows where he is. He's disappeared."

"Tell me, then," said Fortuna between clenched teeth, "how do you propose to find him now?"

"I don't know."

"You don't *know*?"

"We have problems on two fronts now. We have this fucking guy, who may or may not know something which could trace back to us. And now we have the very real possibility that interagency will start looking for its leak. Someone will know immediately that the group is compromised. There is no other explanation. We were the only ones who knew about the rendezvous in Cali."

"How many people are we talking about?'

"I don't know. Ten, twelve maybe."

"Bloody fuck, Vic. Who'd you send in there, a bunch of retards?"

"I had an hour to put the operation together. They were from a group I've used before, no problems. I'm hanging way the hell out on a limb. I'm cutting it very close to the bone here. This is just the kind of thing that'll get me caught. That will get *us* caught."

"Meaning?"

"I used people connected with my group, guys we've hired on jobs before. Do you realize how easily this could come back to bite me?"

"I assume you covered your tracks."

"If they run a textbook mole hunt, looking at finances, phone docs, that sort of thing, I'm fine. I've run more mole hunts than I care to remember. But this is serious shit. After 9/11, Capitana's got people fired up. I mean, where are you going next with this, Alex? What's the next target? If this gets any more dangerous, I would not be at all surprised if every member of interagency is interrogated. I'd recommend it if I saw this happen the way it went down. A shot of one of these new synthetics our pharma squad has developed and I'd be telling them everything."

"Who would run it?"

"FBI. It's their lead. Our best hope is that they're distracted right now. But that's wishful thinking."

"So what the fuck do you suggest we do?"

"Me? I'm going to run. I need to get out of here."

"You can't run," Fortuna said. "You know that. I need someone inside there telling me how close they're getting to me. I was clear from day one. That's why you're getting so much goddamn money. You're the canary in my coal mine."

"Well, that's all well and good, Alex. But *think*. If they catch me, they catch you. Pay me the rest of my money and I'll disappear for good, guaranteed. You can keep doing whatever you have planned. They're not close to finding you at this point, not within a hundred miles. Hell, they think Saudi Arabia's behind it."

"You are not running, Vic. That's not our deal. You get paid on completion. You want the other forty million, you protect me while I finish the job. And if you do run, I will still complete the job, and then I will find you. When I do, you will learn what real torture is all about. None of that pussy-shit CIA crap. I'll have you flown to Crimea. I'm talking Stone Age, prebiblical kind of shit; chains, fire. You get my point?"

Fortuna was standing now, the anger coursing through him. He turned toward the large stone fireplace and hurled his wineglass into the fire, where it shattered against the back of the hearth.

Buck was silent.

"I'll call you in a few hours," said Fortuna. "And you better answer this time."

"I want more money, Alex."

"What?"

"You heard me."

"That wasn't our deal."

"I'm changing the deal. You were supposed to kill this guy out at sea. Things have changed. I'm at *great* risk here. You want me to hang around, be your eyes and ears, the price just doubled."

"Doubled?"

"You heard me. A hundred million. That means ninety million more you owe me."

"Fine," said Fortuna. "But only upon completion."

"No. I want more. Twenty-five million, immediately."

"You greedy fuck. I'll wire you five million dollars tomorrow morning. That's it. Get back to your precious little interagency. If someone starts talking about a mole, deny, deny, deny. Then kill whoever it is that suspects something."

"Brilliant, Alex."

Fortuna hung up. As he ended the conversation, a knock came at the door. In Celia's hands was a dinner tray, which she set down on top of the mahogany table.

"I'll ring you when I'm done. Smells delicious."

He cut into the steak. It was red and slightly warm in the center, but charred on the outside, just as he liked it. He took a few bites. Not surprisingly, he found his appetite had dissipated.

Fortuna went upstairs to the master suite. On the walls hung a stunning series of paintings by Ellsworth Kelly, large canvases with geometric squares of color, paintings he loved dearly, the first serious art he'd ever purchased. Now he barely noticed them.

"Andreas." He said the name out loud. It left a bitter taste in his mouth. He opened the top drawer of his dresser and removed a silver box. Inside, he pulled a small silver spoon and scooped a gumdrop-size pile of cocaine and sniffed it into his right nostril. He did it again, this time in his left nostril. The burn calmed him, channeled the anger back into confidence.

He changed his shirt, putting on a striped button-down and a dark blue sweater. He brushed his teeth, then walked back downstairs. He took his overcoat out of the front closet and put it on.

Celia stepped out of the kitchen.

"I'm going out. No need to stay up."

"Have a good night," she said.

He drove through East Hampton and back out to Route 27. In Southampton, he took a turn onto Gin Lane and drove until he came to a set of large granite pillars that were illuminated with red and green lights. He turned into the driveway. The pebble lane stretched for as far as he could see, down into the distance toward the water. As he came closer to the big house, each side of the driveway was lined with cars.

The annual Christmas party thrown by the Manhattan art dealer Johnny Caravelle was in full swing. Fortuna drove down to the large circle in front of the house. The house itself was a sweeping stone mansion that perched at the edge of the ocean, built in the 1890s by Conrad Seipp, the founder of the Seipp Brewing Company. In the middle of the circle, a large fountain streamed with water. Atop the fountain, a small conifer stood outside the arc of cascading water, decorated in white lights and colored Christmas bulbs.

Fortuna opened the door and left the car running for the valet.

"Evening, Mr. Fortuna."

"Hi. Merry Christmas," said Fortuna.

"Merry Christmas to you, sir."

Fortuna walked in through the big front doors. Inside, the large center hallway was brightly lit. A Christmas tree stood more than twenty feet high, decorated with lights, flowers, bulbs, and figurines. Beneath, box after box of presents filled the space at the base of the tree. To the side of the great entrance hall, a fireplace five feet tall roared with flames. The room itself was crowded with people, most of whom Fortuna recognized: prominent financiers, members of the media establishment, CEOs from the corporate world, a few celebrities from TV, internationally celebrated artists, a movie star or two, several well-known athletes, heavily decorated wives, and a smorgasbord of young beauties, models galore.

Fortuna handed his overcoat to the maid and walked into the party. He circled through the rooms glancing at the guests, saying hello to those he knew. Music played from a Steinway in the corner; a woman in a long black dress played Christmas songs. As always, women turned their heads as he walked by. Fortuna liked to meet their gazes with blank stares; he'd gotten so used to the sensation of being looked at by members of the opposite sex it didn't even cause him to think twice when a beautiful woman stared at him, or came up to talk to him, gave him her phone number, or even openly propositioned him.

He walked through a large room filled with couches, chairs, and fireplaces on either end.

"Hey, Alex," a man yelled from across the room. He had an Australian accent. It was Caravelle. He crossed quickly from across the room. "Merry Christmas."

Fortuna walked up to Caravelle and shook hands warmly.

"You've outdone yourself. Great party."

"You're late," said Caravelle. "Several of the prize Sheilas have already been taken."

"I'm here for the eggnog."

Caravelle laughed. "Yeah, right. I know why you come to my parties."

"I like to see you too, in all sincerity. You know that."

"Of course I know that. By the way, what was the name of that girl you shagged July Fourth?"

"She was your guest. How the hell should I know? She was good-looking, wasn't she?"

"Wars have been started over uglier girls," said Caravelle. "She was someone's guest, as I recall."

"Any equals tonight?"

"Leona Lewis is here."

"I'm not into celebrities," said Fortuna. "Although, she is a stunner. What about models? Did you do your usual cattle call over to DNA?"

"You know it. You'll find something you like, I'm sure. Thanks for coming, Alex."

"I wouldn't miss it. By the way, is that a personal O'Keeffe? It's stunning." Fortuna nodded to the wall above the fireplace. A massive Georgia O'Keeffe painting sat above the black marble mantel. A simple yellow adobe home sat beneath the sun, the dark brown hills behind it capped with snow.

"Not for sale. Unless you really wanted it. Funny money sort of thing."

"How much funny money?"

"Five million."

Fortuna paused and stared at the painting. "Done."

"Can I at least keep it through the end of the party?" Caravelle laughed.

"Yes. Just don't sell it to someone else."

Fortuna went to the bar and ordered a mojito. He circulated through the party. He spoke with several people he knew; the CEO of ABC, a partner at Blackstone he went to Princeton with, others. He had another mojito, then another.

He went and sat next to a blond model from Russia, Olga. She had stunning eyes, and a longish, sharp nose. She was with a friend, another Russian, with long brown hair. Fortuna preferred the blonde. They sat on a big red leather couch, speaking to each other in Russian.

"Hello," he said as he sat down next to them.

"Hi. Merry Christmas," the brunette said. Her Russian accent was heavy.

"Hi," said the blonde, smiling at Fortuna.

Then, in Russian, the blonde said to the brown-haired beauty, "He's cute. Should we take him upstairs and fuck his brains out?"

Fortuna smiled. "That would be nice," he responded in perfect Russian.

Their momentary surprise was followed by laughter.

On the way through the entrance foyer, he stopped at the bar and grabbed two bottles of Cristal and three glasses.

He led the girls upstairs to a suite of rooms at the western end of the house, overlooking the swimming pool.

They started by climbing into a warm bubble bath in the big marble tub. Fortuna watched as the two girls kissed each other. One of the models moved down and went down on the other as he watched for several minutes. Then they moved over next to Fortuna, and he wrapped his arms around both of them. The brown-haired girl went beneath the water and went down on him while he kissed the blonde. When she reemerged, to catch a breath, they all laughed. The two models took turns.

After the bath, they went to the bedroom. They each wore big terry cloth bathrobes. The blonde went to her small clutch and pulled out a small silver box. Fortuna pulled a large, walnut-framed mirror off the wall. The blonde laid out several lines. Fortuna grabbed a crisp bill out of his pocket and rolled it up. They took turns snorting the lines of cocaine. Soon, the robes fell off and they started to have sex.

Hours later, they fell asleep as the sounds of partiers below died off and the sound of the ocean slapping at the shore created a soothing rhythm.

Much later, Fortuna awoke, his arm still wrapped around the sleeping blonde. The brown-haired girl's feet were next to his head. He looked at his watch; it was five forty-five in the morning.

Fortuna quietly got up and put his clothing back on. He left the room and went downstairs.

He circled back through the big living room to take another look at the O'Keeffe. Beneath the painting, on top of the mantel, an envelope with the word "Alex" sat.

He opened it.

> *AF,*
> *If you feel like a game of squash, call me. Hope you enjoyed Team Russia. I'll have the O'Keeffe delivered to Manhattan.*
>
> *—Caravelle*

Fortuna walked to the closet and looked for his overcoat. It wasn't there. He walked to the door. Outside, bitter cold greeted him. It was refreshing. He saw the Aston Martin at the far edge of the circle. He walked to it, and climbed in. The keys were in the ignition. He turned on the car and ripped up the long pebble driveway.

Back home at his East Hampton estate, he went straight to his office and called Karim in Manhattan.

"Good morning," said Karim. "No call yet from Buck."

"I talked to him last night," said Alex. "Where's the remote?"

Karim didn't answer for a second. He cleared his throat. "The one in the East Hampton house is in the bottom drawer of the desk. The one here in Manhattan is in the ivory box below the Caravaggio."

Fortuna opened the bottom desk drawer and removed a silver object, slightly larger than a television remote. The remote detonator had two keyboards, one with letters and the other numbers. A thick black antenna folded against the side.

"Give me the codes."

"The codes? Why?"

"Just do what I *fucking* say, will you?"

"They're programmed into the speed dial."

"All forty-one?"

"Yes—but the cells are not all ready. You can't just—"

"Then give me the code for one that's ready. A big target. *Now.*"

"Okay, okay. Press twelve."

32

INTERMODAL FACILITY AND BREAK-BULK WAREHOUSE
PORT OF LONG BEACH, CALIFORNIA

Neqq felt the first tremor as he sat in the cab of the reach stacker, and he knew.

As the tremor moved the ground, in that first moment, he did not even have the time to move his hands from the gears of the big machine, but he did have time to register the feeling of soft material on his neck, chamois from the sweatshirt he'd purchased from the Target store in Long Beach, soft down against his skin, the last memory he would have on this earth.

The tremor occurred less than four seconds after the detonator that rested in Neqq's locker received an electronic signal sent via cellular transmission, a signal telling it to pulse on. The tremor occurred less than three seconds after the detonator pulsed on and sent two identical negative ion sparks into the suitcase-sized glob of octanitrocubane mashed into the space below the foot joist in the locker. Less than two seconds after the charges turned, there occurred a reaction in the chemical makeup of the material, causing its cubane atoms to suddenly, atomically, turn upon themselves and flee the once-stable assembly of like atoms and seek oxygen and carbon, to seek it with such hunger and force that the air became like food before a ravenous, starving wolf; the air became consumed outward from the locker in white fire and heat so intense that, could it be measured, it would have resembled the air less than a quarter mile from the bomb that fell on Nagasaki.

By one second before the tremor in Neqq's cab, the massive explosion catapulted outward and leveled the large warehouse and tore across the great plain of decking at water's edge, striking wood, steel, container ships moored at deck edge, gantry cranes on the docks, and, of course, people. It liquefied anyone and everyone in the warehouse, Mr. Sargent, the men and women who worked in the cafeteria. There was no pain, no recognition, nothing; no time.

The crater grew as the air fed the explosion to life. And when it reached Neqq's cab halfway across the container field, nearly a half mile from the locker, it was moving at more than a thousand miles per hour. The containers were flung like cards in a windstorm. What terminated Neqq in point of fact was a steel beam from a container blown across the sky. It sailed across the sky like so many others and separated Neqq's torso from his waist like a knife through butter, though it was soon joined by a wall of destroyed steel and metal; he was soon but a smattering of small parts, the largest the size of a Tootsie Roll, most just wet molecules within the slowing, but still growing, crater of destruction.

Soon the Port of Long Beach was a ball of fire, destroyed by one man, a boy really, who just five years before had, in his wildest imagination, dreamed only of saving enough money to purchase his own cow and join his father farming in the dry plains near Jamrud, growing enough wheat to make bread to feed himself, his mama and papa, and perhaps even a family of his own.

33

WASHINGTON SPORTS CLUB
M STREET, N.W.
WASHINGTON, D.C.

Jessica's cell phone rang as she was getting off the treadmill at the Washington Sports Club, practically deserted at such an early hour. The ring tone—three quick beeps that chimed repeatedly without stopping—meant the call was from CENCOM. Despite her already-elevated pulse, Jessica's heart jumped.

"Tanzer," she said.

"Hold for CENCOM Commander Fowler," said a voice, then two quick clicks.

"Jessica, it's Bo. We have a level red."

Suddenly, across the television screens that filled the walls in front of the dozens of treadmills and StairMasters, rowing machines and other pieces of exercise equipment at the tony sports club, the images all became one; a live shot from a distance of several massive mushroom clouds— orange and black explosions spread out over the horizon—flames ballooning out at several points. She ran to the nearest screen and read the ticker at the bottom of the screen.

"Long Beach?" she asked.

"Affirmative," said Fowler, the agent in charge of FBI Counterterrorism Central Command. "The port's been wiped out."

"Chiles?"

"Already en route to the White House. You're to meet him there. A car should be out front as we speak."

"Stay on the line," she said.

Jessica ran through the exercise room to the woman's locker room and grabbed her clothing from the locker then ran from the club. She walked quickly down M Street toward a black sedan that was parked in front, steam coming from the exhaust pipe.

"What have we got?" she said into her phone as she climbed in the backseat.

"It's a fucking mess, Jess. We have a massive explosion of indeterminate cause that occurred less than ten minutes ago at the Port of Long Beach. The detonation happened on shore, based on what the satellite images are telling."

"So it wasn't shipborne."

"No. There are forty or so piers at Long Beach. Most were destroyed, along with several ships, one of which was an Exxon supertanker. According to someone at the company, they had not begun off-loading product yet, which means almost two million barrels of petrol is helping fuel the fire."

"How many dead?"

"No estimates yet. There are thousands of port employees. It was the four to noon shift, which is the busiest time. Rough estimate: a thousand to two thousand."

Jessica finished changing her clothing in the back of the sedan as it sped toward the White House.

"Let's prepare an elevation memo for the president. We need to move to severe, clamp down at the ports immediately, airports, the usual. I want that on my BlackBerry in three minutes."

"It's already there."

"You're good, Bo."

"I had a good teacher."

She closed the phone as the sedan entered the White House grounds

266

through the back gate, between the Old Executive Office Building and the West Wing of the White House. Her phone rang—again CENCOM.

"Tanzer."

"CENCOM, hold please for Terry Savoy."

Two clicks on the phone, then Savoy came on the line.

"Hi, Jessica, it's Terry."

"Hi, Terry." She hesitated, thinking what to say, wondering whether Savoy knew yet. "How's Teddy Marks?"

"I'd call him 'spry,' but he'd probably kick my ass for it."

"Good. Look, I can't talk for long. I'm heading into the White House. Long Beach has been struck by a bomb."

"I know. That's why I'm calling."

"I'm going into the Situation Room. I need to call you back."

"Wait, Jess."

"What is it?"

"Remember what we talked about? Have you started looking at interagency?"

"Yes. I spoke with Chiles. I have a team in place. We're looking at everyone who was in the meeting where Dewey's exfiltration was discussed."

"Are you walking into interagency?"

"Yes."

"This is just my opinion, but I don't think you can tip your hand. That means not letting interagency know Dewey called after Madradora. You can't even let on that you know about Madradora."

"You're saying lie to the president of the—"

"You have a spy inside interagency. They're working with the terrorists. They could *be* the terrorist. If he or she is in the room, you mention the attempt on Dewey and the mole will cease all activities. We can't let them shut down. Right now he, or she, is the *only* link we have to this terrorist network. Long Beach shows where this is going. It's unpredictable—and it's escalating. If they think you're looking for them, they will run. If they have the capability to get two killers to Cali in less than two hours, trust me, they'll be able to disappear. We don't want that. They could lead us to the terrorist."

"I have resources on it," said Jessica. "But I have to tell you, I'm still not convinced. You're guessing there's a mole based on one phone call from Dewey Andreas."

"No, I'm basing it on the fact someone sent in a team to kill him before we could exfiltrate him. There was a very limited number of individuals who knew of the exfiltration and where it would take place. *All* of them were in that room. Dewey knows something and they're trying to take him out."

"DOD is going to know they have two dead Deltas."

"Of course. But let DOD announce it. And let them, and everyone else, assume the terrorists in-country followed Dewey. You need to sell that to whoever the mole is. But while you do that, remember what Dewey said: They were *operatives*. Not a band of Al-Qaeda thugs. Hired professionals."

"I know. Look, I'll do the best I can."

"Good. And good luck. We'll call you in a few hours."

"Who's 'we'?'"

"Ted and I. We're leaving Denver this morning. We're going to Manhattan. We're going to do a little research, make some calls."

Jessica stopped in her tracks. "You're serious."

"Dead serious. Think about it. Ted and I can do some work without interagency oversight."

Jessica smiled despite herself. "I thought Marks was barely conscious in ICU."

"Oh, he's conscious all right. Don't forget, Jess, he's an ex-SEAL. Frankly, he's the toughest son of a bitch I've ever met. Someone just leveled the company he spent half his life building. Let's just say he's motivated."

One story below the ground floor of the White House, the Situation Room was filled with military officers and top national security and law enforcement aides. The Situation Room was bright with lights, all surrounding a large conference table. On the walls, screens displayed various live feeds from the disaster at the Port of Long Beach. To the right, an odd-looking contraption on the wall above a desk was a two-way air chute, similar to a drive-through bank deposit system, a relic from the White House's past built by FDR, that enabled notes to be sent securely from other parts of the White House and Old Executive Office Building.

The mood was electric—with anxiety, a certain quietness that comes with shock, and fear.

Jessica entered the room and took a seat next to Louis Chiles. She quickly counted fourteen people, including the chairman of the Joint Chiefs of Staff, national security advisor, the secretaries of Defense, State, Energy, and Homeland Security, and many others, including most of the interagency group, including John Scalia, Vic Buck, Jane Epstein, and others.

"Jess."

"Hi, Lou."

"Tough morning."

"I've got an elevation memo ready to go. Obviously we're recommending that we elevate to 'severe'—code red—clamp down on infrastructure—ports, airports, et cetera."

On one wall, a large screen showed the same live shot from Long Beach, a CNN feed from a helicopter a long distance away from the fires. Because the chopper had to stay at a distance to avoid the intense heat, the view was a wide panorama of the coastal area of Southern California surrounding the port, the dark of the night interrupted by the lights of Long Beach and its buildings and roads, surrounding neighborhoods leading down to the water. In the middle of the screen, four large fiery clouds of smoke and flames reached into the sky: the inferno that was now the port.

The president entered the room, followed by his chief of staff, Jane London. The president was dressed in a blue checked button-down without a tie, and he carried a cup of coffee.

"Morning, everybody," the president said as he sat down. The president looked pointedly at Secretary of State Putnam. "I think we can now assume Saudi fucking Arabia wasn't behind the attacks."

Putnam nodded. "Yes, sir. No question. Long Beach changes everything."

269

"Before we get a briefing on what just happened, what are we recommending so we can get some direction out to law enforcement?" asked the president.

He looked to his left at Myron Kratovil, the national security advisor.

"I haven't had time to poll, Mr. President," Kratovil said. "However, I think we're all going to be of the same mind here. Let me ask it this way: is there anyone who does not think we should elevate to red?"

Around the room, silence. The government's top echelon of law enforcement, military leadership, and national security all agreed to recommend to the president that he formally raise America's terror alert to its highest level, code red, indicating to the public a severe and imminent risk of terrorist attacks on the country.

"There's your recommendation, Mr. President."

"Accepted," said the president.

A young military attaché placed a document in front of the president, which he signed. The officer walked quickly from the room and began a process which would result in the modern equivalent of a telephone tree; from the White House, the order would quickly be disseminated first to branches of the military, then to states' governors and attorney generals, who would then inform county and municipal law enforcement, that the nation's terror alert had been elevated. Practically speaking, however, most people who would need to know would have already assumed this to be the case. Already this morning, several commentators on TV had asked the question as to when the president would raise the alert level. At the same time law enforcement was notified, so too were various parts of the country's economic and manufacturing infrastructure: ports, nuclear power plants, and other generators of electricity, refineries.

"All right, Jess," said the president, "let's hear it."

"At four fifteen A.M. Pacific, a bomb detonated at the Port of Long Beach," said Jessica. "Casualty estimates between one and two thousand. Fires are nowhere near being under control. That should take at least another twenty-four hours. From the nature of the blast, our munitions experts say it's likely that it contained octanitrocubane."

"I'm guessing that'll only be the first of many other connections linking this to the prior attacks," said the president.

"I believe there's a larger implication," said Jessica.

"Go on."

"We're looking at a new terror network here," said Jessica. "Anonymous, unpredictable, embedded. Different from what we've ever seen before. As with Capitana and Savage Island, no one's taking credit."

"That's what worries me most," said the president. "It's arbitrary."

"We can infer that they're focused on infrastructure," continued Jessica. "With this explosive in hand, if they wanted to, they could easily be killing many more people. But they're not. Which only adds to the unpredictability. I don't see how we can begin to anticipate where they're going next."

"That's not very encouraging, coming from the head of counterterrorism," said the chairman of the Joint Chiefs of Staff.

"One of the more illuminating aspects of octanitrocubane, we've learned, is the high cost of synthesizing and producing it," said Jane Epstein from DOD. "Our own munitions labs have been unable to produce it in any scalable quantities. The group behind this has a lot of money and is highly, highly sophisticated. This is not meth lab sort of stuff and you can't make it in the back of a cave. This is like manufacturing a three-stage pharmaceutical."

"We're working with CIA and Interpol to run the POI database against chemical, weapons, and pharma manufacturers," said Jessica. "It's a wide net, but it's all we have at this point. We'll develop a list of possible places this compound is being made and go one-by-one with local law enforcement to do inspections."

"That's it?" asked Kratovil.

"FBI munitions is en route to Long Beach," said Jessica. "We'll try to develop a signature from the debris at Long Beach. An identifying odor, hopefully, that we can train dogs on. If we can do that, we could, in theory develop protocols at U.S. Postal, FedEx, UPS; try and get lucky if they're still sending this stuff around."

"Sounds like we're grasping at straws," said the president. "What are we doing beyond playing defense here?" He looked around the table at his top law enforcement and national security advisors.

"The answer, Mr. President, is running hard at the few leads we have," said Jessica. "We have survivors at Long Beach and teams debriefing to see if we can piece together any links or information. We now know the individuals who spearheaded both Capitana and Savage Island—we have CIA, NSA, and CT teams running hard at their pasts, trying to assemble connections."

"What about Ted Marks?" asked the president.

"Marks survived and we've already done a sketch of his assailant and have it out on the wires, down through law enforcement," Jessica said, handing out copies of the artist's rendition created by the FBI just a few hours before at Marks's hospital bedside. "It should be in the world's newspapers and on television starting this morning."

Jane Epstein from DOD raised her hand to say something, but the president waved her off and picked up the black-and-white sketch. He stared at it, then stood up from his chair. "This narrows it down to Arab males between the ages of eighteen and forty," he said, shaking his head. He looked around the room, then stood up. "So basically, we don't have shit. Call me when we do."

The president turned and walked out of the Situation Room.

Back at FBI headquarters, Jessica went directly to Chiles's office, along with Jane Epstein from DOD, John Scalia from the White House, Rick Ennis from NSA, and Vic Buck from the CIA.

Chiles turned on the television on the wall of his office, displaying the same scene of the port, still burning in the distance. Firefighting helicopters could be seen spraying the flames from above with orange chemicals.

"You were going to say," said Chiles, looking at Epstein, "before the president left the room?"

"Thanks for extending the meeting, everyone," said Epstein. She looked around the group. "Madradora went badly. The two Deltas we sent in to exfiltrate Dewey Andreas were murdered. Terminated in broad day-light."

"What?" said Jessica. "Killed by who?"

"We don't know. We had no one else on the ground, and the Cali police don't have much of a clue, to be frank."

"Has anyone spoken with Andreas?" Buck asked.

Everyone shook their heads, including Jessica.

Chiles looked at Jessica, then turned to the group and said nothing.

"All right, then," said Buck. "Do we have his cell number?"

"No," she said. "When he called in earlier, it was through the Anson switchboard."

"Do we even know if he's alive?" asked Ennis.

Epstein shrugged.

"Could Andreas have misidentified our men?" Buck asked.

"You mean misidentified, as in killed American soldiers?" said Jessica sharply. "He was a Delta himself. I can't imagine him making that kind of mistake. Can you?"

"All we know is two Deltas were sent to exfiltrate him and now they're dead," said Buck.

"That's not all we know," said Epstein. "There was a gun battle, according to witnesses. There's one dead gunman in addition to our Deltas. He doesn't appear to be of Arabic descent. He looks Latino. The Cali police are doing their best, but I'm out of resources in the immediate area."

"I'll get a team in there ASAP," said Buck. "But it seems pretty obvious they followed him. He's been out of active duty now for over a decade. Add to that the fact that he's hurt, tired, rattled. He made a mistake and they found him."

"I agree," said Jessica, lying. She stared at Chiles, trying not to look too obvious. "I need to get back to Long Beach."

Jessica shut the door to her office and sat on the leather couch next to the window. She shut her eyes for a few moments and tried to clear her head. Opening her eyes again, she looked out the window to Pennsylvania Avenue. It was Sunday morning and the street was largely deserted. In front of the FBI building, she saw a dozen soldiers with weapons out. *Threat level red.* Citizens would already be feeling the impact of the heightened security advisory. Not only at federal and state buildings, train stations, ports. Major airports already looked like armed camps, and the levels of scrutiny given passengers had risen exponentially. In the coming days, random searches would be replaced by searches of *all* passengers. No more carry-on baggage. Profiling was becoming a thing of the past because all citizens were being put under the microscope. They had to.

Jessica, whose job it was to stop terrorism on America's shores, tried to imagine the face of the person behind it all. Was he Arab? In a cave on the border between Pakistan and Afghanistan? In a sweaty, crowded apartment in Islamabad or Karachi? Or maybe Munich or Paris? This wasn't like searching for a needle in a haystack. It was searching for a grain of sand on a beach. If only she knew *which* beach.

One person might have the answer to that question, whether he knew it or not. Unfortunately, he was either running for his life in South America, or already dead.

She walked back to her desk and dialed her phone.

"Yes," answered Savoy.

"It's Jessica. Has Dewey contacted you again?"

"No," said Savoy. "How'd interagency go? Did Defense break the news?"

"Yes. Thanks for the call earlier, you were right. Let me know if Dewey calls."

"Absolutely."

"Where are you?"

"We just landed. Ted has a TV interview to do."

That night, *60 Minutes* did a special two-hour episode, featuring coverage of what they dramatically titled "America's Hiroshima." Live on-scene reports from Long Beach and a special aerial camera dropped from the sky close into the wreckage showed the incredible destruction wrought by the bomb.

But the segment that was promoted the heaviest—and which attracted the highest Sunday night audience in CBS history—was the interview that ran in the last half hour.

From the living room in Ted Marks's Manhattan apartment, Steve Kroft sat across from Marks and interviewed KKB's nearly murdered CEO.

A jagged cut across the top of his right cheek held stitches, and his right eye was slightly black. Still, Marks looked good. If anything, he looked like a warrior, a cross between a presidential candidate and a soldier fresh from battle.

Kroft, and the nation, sat mesmerized as Marks told the minute-by-minute details of the attack on the house in Aspen, the murder of Nicholas and Annie Anson, the brutal fight with the killer who had invaded his home.

"One last question," Kroft asked as the interview came to a close. "What's your opinion of what happened at Long Beach? Is it connected?"

Marks's thick brown hair was parted and still neat-looking. His handsome face nodded in silence at Kroft.

"Of course they're connected," said Marks. "Long Beach. Capitana. Savage Island. What happened in Aspen; they are all connected. America is being attacked. And make no mistake, the terrorists are winning."

Marks sat up in his chair. He stared fiercely into Kroft's eyes.

"But what we've seen is not the end of this story. It's the beginning. There are terrorists on our shores, in our midst. And what they want right now is for us to panic. They want us to suspend our laws and turn neighbor into enemy. But we can't do that. Because then it will be the end. Then they'll win.

"There'll be people who, in the hours and days to come, will say that Long Beach was somehow our fault. That Capitana was caused by our appetite for gasoline, Savage Island by our never-ending need for electricity and power. Well, sorry, but that's not America's fault. I'll be damned if we're going to apologize for our success, for our way of life. Give the terrorists credit; they're attacking us at our most critical sources of economic activity. But the way to stop the attacks is not to apologize, to cower in the corner, or to change our ways. The way to stop the terrorists is plain and simple. We must hunt them down. We must capture them. Then, with God on our side, we must kill them."

34

PARQUE CENTRAL HOTEL
HAVANA, CUBA

The Parque Central was a massive, majestic granite hotel built in the 1880s. Dewey checked in, feeling more exhausted than he could ever remember. His room, the clerk said, overlooked the Grand Theater. Dewey nodded, caring only about two things: calling Terry Savoy, and getting an hour or two of sleep.

"Savoy."

"It's Dewey."

"Dewey, man, are we glad to hear you're alive."

"Me too."

"Where are you?"

"I'd rather not say, Terry," said Dewey.

"What do you mean?"

"I mean I'm done. This wasn't my battle to begin with. I've told you everything I know. I'm going to take a few days' rest, then disappear."

"Have you seen the news?"

"No."

"The terrorists struck the Port of Long Beach. Wiped it out. Same explosive, but more than two thousand dead this time. It's absolute chaos up here. Government's clueless. They need a lead, big-time. You may be our best hope. We believe—Jessica believes—what you said about there being a mole. The head of the FBI authorized an investigation into the interagency group. We're going to find him. But we need you too."

Dewey listened, staring out the window.

Savoy paused to regroup. "Let me ask you something about the attack at Madradora. You said the Deltas were hit by operatives—not Middle Eastern–looking terrorists or anything like that. Right? Can you tell us *anything* more?"

"I can show you something. I'm sending a photo to your phone." He brought up the photo of the dead woman and texted it to Savoy.

"Got it," Savoy said after a few moments. "It's grainy. Who is she?"

"One of the assassins. She's Panamanian."

"Let me show this to Jessica and I'll call you right back."

"Why? You got the photo. That's all I've got. I'm done."

"What's your number? I'll call back in five."

"I'll call you," said Dewey.

He hung up, dropped the phone on the bed, took a shower, and then called room service for a meal of eggs and bacon. He went to the mirror and looked at his shoulder wound. It was raw and painful but not septic. He cleaned the wound with a moist washcloth then redressed it. He would need some new bandages and antibiotics.

Finally, Dewey picked up the hotel phone and dialed.

"Savoy."

"It's me."

"Hold on." The phone clicked. "Dewey, you've got me, Jessica, and Ted Marks."

"We're glad you're alive," said Jessica. "Where are you?"

"I'd rather not say," he said.

"Okay," Jessica continued. "Good job getting the picture. She may be traceable. I'll run it through Interpol."

"You do what you want," said Dewey. "But I wouldn't run it through Interpol, CIA, or any other government database. You run that photo through and they will know, before you do, how to erase that lead. By the time you get there, the lead will be gone. There's someone high up, in your town, your building even, watching out for signs that we're onto them. Don't take this personally, but for all I know it could be you."

"Yeah, you're right," said Jessica. "But it's not me. Right now, we're running a tracking protocol on all twelve participants in this morning's interagency where the Madradora meet up was discussed. I have a team of agents scouring financials, e-mails, phone records, travel patterns, you name it, on everyone who knew about your exfiltration. Including me, by the way. We're going to find whoever it is who betrayed the United States and got those soldiers killed."

"What about the photo? How are you going to run that?"

Savoy broke in and said, "Ted and I will follow up on it ourselves."

"Dewey? This is Ted Marks. Any idea why they want to kill you so badly?"

"I'm not sure. I already told you everything I know about the Capitana attack, but obviously they can't know that. Maybe they're afraid I know more than I really do."

"Maybe there *is* something else," said Jessica. "Something you know, but aren't thinking of. A small detail that will help us. We still need to make arrangements to bring you in."

Dewey stood and looked in the mirror. The feeling of turmoil, inner conflict, felt like it was going to paralyze him. Something old and long dormant stirred in him, a feeling of duty. A familiar sensation that he associated with being briefed on a mission for the first time. The sense of anticipation that a Delta felt when the hunt was about to begin. When he believes in the mission with every ounce of his being. A feeling Dewey realized he'd almost forgotten.

He stepped from the mirror and walked to the window, looking down on the crowded street in front of the Parque Centrale. He closed his eyes and let the feeling subside. For as much as he felt the desire to return to the United States, he also remembered how he'd left; accused of crimes he didn't commit, left to defend himself all alone. He'd lost his family, then his reputation, his calling, everything. Yes, he wanted to help find the terrorists—for his men who died aboard the rig, for himself. But he fought the instinct, pushed it back and away, steeled himself.

"I've told you all I know," said Dewey. "I'm out."

" '*Out*'?" asked Jessica. "Done? Just like that? We *need* you. Don't you care about the fact that thousands of people are dead, that terrorists are attacking your country?"

"Of course I care. But it's not my battle. Not now."

Dewey glanced at his knife and handgun, both lying on the bed. He listened to the silence coming from the phone.

"Good luck," Jessica said, a trace of bitterness in her voice. "Please call if you think of anything else."

Dewey hung up the phone and lay back on the bed.

But all need for sleep seemed to have vanished. In fact, suddenly, he couldn't imagine sitting in the room for a moment longer. An intense feeling of guilt, shame even, came over him. His country had asked for his help, and he refused. He fought to shut the feeling out of his mind. He would go for a walk. Tomorrow, he would fly somewhere else. He would escape again, disappear. He'd done it once, after all. He owed no man. Tomorrow he would run again.

Dewey tucked the handgun into his pants, knife into his ankle sheath, then left his room. He walked out through the entrance to the Parque Central. For the next hour, he walked the streets of Havana. He was surprised at how happy people seemed, how kind. They said hello to him as he passed them. The sun beat down and it felt good on his shoulders and face. He stopped at a *farmacia* and bought new bandages for his shoulder and a bottle of antibiotics.

Dewey went back to the hotel. He walked to the newsstand in the lobby and bought a copy of *The International Herald Tribune*. He paid and walked through the lobby and sat to have a cup of coffee at the hotel's restaurant.

"What would you like, *señor?*" the waitress asked. She was young, with long black hair, and pretty.

"Espresso," he said.

He sat back to read the paper. The words quickly became a meaning-less blur, though, as his mind roamed. He replayed the events in Cali, at Capitana. He felt confused, anxious, a pit in his stomach. When the check came, he reached into his jacket. In the pocket, he felt his passport and the small wad of cash he hadn't handed over to the customs agent in Cali. He pulled out the photo of Holly and Robbie. Would his son be proud of him today? He couldn't bear to imagine the answer.

He went for a walk. Near the piers in south Havana, he stopped to buy cigarettes, and he took one out and lit it. It tasted good. He hadn't smoked in a couple of days.

"We *need* you." Jessica's words ate at him. The guilt came back again, a bitter feeling that he tried to push out of his mind. He wanted a drink. He finished the cigarette and flicked it into the ocean off the end of an old wooden pier.

"It's not your battle," he said aloud, to no one, as the darkness settled over the western horizon. "Leave it behind."

35

KKB WORLDWIDE HEADQUARTERS
FIFTH AVENUE
NEW YORK CITY

Ted Marks limped out of the elevator. It was Christmas Eve. The seventy-fourth floor was dead quiet. He walked down the hallway, entered the outer office where his assistant Natalie normally sat. He crossed through the room and walked into his office, past the two large leather sofas at the center of the massive room, then past his desk. At the window, he stood and stared out at the Manhattan skyline. Snow was falling in thick, heavy lines across the black sky. Suddenly, he felt sharp, stabbing pain emanating from his hand. He turned, walked to his desk, pulled a bottle of Advil from the top drawer of his desk. He opened the bottle and tossed down four pills.

Looking down at his desk, he noticed the stack of clippings, articles Natalie had collected about the announcement of the KKB merger with Anson Energy. It seemed so long ago now, even though it had been only four days. He felt disconnected from the events of the past few days, as if they'd happened to somebody else. Then the pain struck again, this time from his shoulder. Marks had been trying to deal with the pain without the Percocet, a bottle of which he carried in his pocket. But he knew he would need some soon. He would wait until after the meeting. He needed to be sharp before the others.

He returned to the window, feeling nothing but frustration as he stared into the monotony of the blizzard, the quiet of his palatial office suite offering little calm to a man and a mind so used to action, so deeply angry about the events of the last week, about the destruction of his life's work. It was the unknown that ate away at him like a cancer. Even with the help of the Percocet, he had barely slept for two nights in a row. He would barely sleep this night. He had to do something.

Suddenly, he heard a dull knock on the door to Natalie's office.

"Come in," he said loudly.

"Hi, Ted," said the voice. A short, wiry man with curly black hair and thick glasses peeked his head in the door. Joshua Essinger ran KKB's proprietary trading desk, overseeing eight traders who collectively managed a portfolio of more than $25 billion. Essinger's desk invested money off the KKB balance sheet, buying securities across the energy complex, though mainly oil, natural gas, and electricity futures, a financial tool by which KKB was able to smooth out the peaks and valleys that were typical of an energy company whose value was, to a certain extent, dictated by not only the success or failure of exploration projects, but also by the whims of fluctuating commodity prices. Essinger was hired by KKB after a highly successful career as a commodities trader at Morgan Stanley.

"Josh, come in, sit down," said Marks.

Essinger crossed the office and sat, somewhat delicately, on one of the leather couches.

"I have a question for you," said Marks.

"Yes, sir. Name it."

"If you knew about Savage Island ahead of time, about Capitana, how would you go about profiting from it?"

Essinger sat up, shocked for a brief moment. "Well, that's an awkward sort of question—"

"I'm not saying you did it, Josh. I'm asking how you *would* do it."

"Do you think someone actually did this? Profited from it? Wasn't this an act of terrorism?"

"I don't know what I think," said Marks. He stepped from behind his desk, limped to the sofa across from Essinger, sat down.

"Okay, okay. No, I understand. Well, the obvious answer is I'd own a bunch of shorts against us, KKB and Anson."

"Yeah, that's what I figured."

"But that's not actually the best way. Problem is, you can only buy so many shorts. It's just not a big pool. Sure, I could make some money, but the truth is, it's capped. I'm thinking, depending on collars, limits, that sort of thing, you might have been able to make high nine figures, maybe a billion or two."

"That's a lot of money."

"Sounds like a lot, but not in context. Depends, of course, on how much I'm running, but let's just assume it's the billion we have in cash on the desk. With the kind of quantum devaluation that just occurred with both companies, if I knew about it ahead of time I should have been able to make, I'm thinking, north of ten billion. Ten-x just feels right. Maybe higher."

"Right. But still, it's the quickest—"

"Shorts are also too obvious, Ted. They're not going to risk being on the money side of these shorts."

"So how would you—"

"Simple. I buy the shit out of competitors. Name it, I'm buying it. Electricity stocks—ConEd, Entergy, Southern, Duke, et cetera—oil and gas stocks, BP, Exxon, Valero, Andarko, et cetera. I can run a regression on it, but I don't need to. All those guys popped pretty hard in the past few days, since Savage and Capitana got leveled."

"So, next question," said Marks. "Can we look and see if someone did this? A company, a government, hedge fund?"

"Well, sure, we can try. It'll be tough. There are myriad ways to cloak a trade. If I did what you said, I'm doing everything I can to hide my trades. Offshore funds named after similar legal entities, pass-throughs buying ADRs, then flipping them out. That said, there are ways. I'd look at patterns and I'd look at dollar volume relative to overall balance sheet. I mean, Fidelity probably bought a billion worth of each of those stocks I mentioned in the days leading up to the attacks, but they're running trillions and it's being managed across dozens of energy-related entities, know what I mean?"

"I think so."

"Under any circumstance, the longer you wait, the harder it is to look back. You need to look right now."

"And that's because?"

"These guys are criminals, right? They're smart. They understand they need to break away from the money. So right now they're probably selling out of their positions. It won't be easy to find them. Then they'll wind down the legal entities that wired the money, cleared the trades. They'll be gone soon."

Marks sat back, nodded. He felt another sharp tear of pain in his palm. This one would not go away. He leaned forward, his eyes watering.

"I want you to look into it, Josh."

"I will. How soon?"

"Now."

"Now meaning today?"

"Now meaning thirty seconds after you walk out of this office. I need you to hit it hard, immediately."

Essinger stood. "I'll get on it right now."

"I'll call you from the road," said Marks, standing up. "In the meantime, you find anything, you call me, Terry, or, if you don't get us, Jessica Tanzer at the FBI. Here's her number." Marks handed Essinger a slip of paper.

"Where you going?"

"Panama."

36

Buck arrived at his desk at CIA headquarters in Langley, shut the door, took off his jacket, and threw it on one of the chairs in front of his desk. At his desk he keyed up one of the three computer screens.

Quickly, he keyed in a series of passwords and was suddenly at a screen that read:

AMPHITHEATRE ARCHIVAL SET 117

He clicked on the hyperlink next to the word *video* then entered another password. Then, he entered that day's date. He waited for the prompt, then entered a period of time: 7:00 A.M. to 7:20 A.M.

After a few seconds, a live shot video suddenly appeared in color showing the front of his house in Alexandria. He sat back, sipped his coffee cup, and watched. There was no activity until 7:11 A.M. Then, he watched as the image of himself on the screen suddenly appeared from just over an hour ago, leaving his home, first walking out the door, then, a minute later, his car backing out of the driveway.

Exactly twenty-four seconds after his sedan sped away, an image appeared. A Ford Taurus station wagon, which slowed at his driveway, stopped for ten seconds, then sped off.

"Fuck," he said to himself. He knew it was coming, but the confirmation stung. They had started the hunt.

Buck exited the system, then turned to the second computer screen. He again entered a series of passwords, moving through a succession of screens that were blank, save for the password entry boxes. Finally, at the fourth such screen, he paused.

Buck was now preparing to connect to the Internet through a system that had been put in place more than a decade ago, a "safe circuit" system designed by CIA technologists during the early phases of wireless encryption. These circuits enabled secure side routes through dial-up access points throughout the world, a low-tech but secure way to gain access to the Internet without the fear of signal and thus content theft. With the improvement in encryption methods, the CIA safe circuit system had long ago been shut down, except for one circuit that Buck himself had, as Kiev station chief, kept active, against orders. The actual circuit was the size of a penny, and was housed on a small telephone switch at the Hotel Budapest in downtown Kiev. No one at the hotel knew about it.

Buck entered the digits of a local Kiev phone number which he had long ago committed to memory. Suddenly, unbeknownst to any other human being in the world, he was online.

A black screen appeared with a small yellow dot, which Buck clicked twice. Russian words appeared.

PROMINVESTBANK

He went to the customer log-in page, typed an account name and password, hit Enter. After a few moments, an account page appeared. It was the bank account of a man named Petr Dmitrov.

For more than fifteen years, Vic Buck had also been Petr Dmitrov. And Petr Dmitrov was very, very rich.

A smile crept across Buck's lips as he read just how rich Petr Dmitrov in fact was.

The wire from Fortuna had already hit: $15,100,008.77.

Not bad for a kid from Fresno.

Buck had long ago learned to put aside any kind of guilt or moral quandary caused by his actions. He knew he was harming his country, that the blood of innocent Americans was on his hands. But it didn't bother him. Unlike other turncoats and traitors whose stories he'd studied or knew so well, Victor Buck's treason had no epic moment, no single event that pushed him to decide to betray his country. No, he knew his decision had been all about greed. He'd grown up poor, without a father, raised by a mother who worked so hard as a cleaning woman that she was dead before little Vic was even out of elementary school. His poverty was the fuel behind it all, the chip on his shoulder that had led him down this miserable path.

Now, as he looked at the account balance on the screen, Buck again asked himself whether he should leave the United States now and forgo the remaining payment. Fifteen million was a lot of money. But was it enough? Buck hoped to live a long life, lavishly, and protecting himself from the combined might of Alex Fortuna and the U.S. government would be costly.

He closed his eyes and rubbed his temples. *Don't fuck this up,* he thought. *You're so close.*

It had become exponentially more dangerous since the failure at Madradora. If they had just terminated Andreas, everyone would have assumed it was the terrorists, following him. But now, the failure demonstrated just the opposite; the ineluctable, indisputable fact that someone within U.S. interagency betrayed the exfiltration plan and set up Andreas for termination.

Buck felt his world quickly closing in. Yes, he could run, but he needed the money. He wouldn't see it if he left now. But the longer he stayed, the more likely it was he would be found out. He felt his heart racing. *Calm the hell down.*

Buck exited the screen and reached into the middle drawer of his desk, taking out a Valium, which he broke between his fingers. He popped half into his mouth. He dabbed at his forehead with a shirtsleeve. Despite the bitterly cold temperatures outside, he was sweating like a pig.

They were now in the part of the game where everything could go wrong with one false move, one bad decision.

And he knew they knew.

He'd been around enough mole hunts to know they had narrowed it down. Tanzer was the one. She knew. He saw it in her eyes. It had hit him the moment Jane Epstein told the group the Deltas were dead. Jessica hadn't looked at him, and that was it. It was the way she'd willed herself to precisely not look at him, at that moment. A quick glance, then to Scalia. Assiduously avoiding his eye. Then the way she acted oh-so-casually, as if she didn't know Andreas had narrowly escaped. As if he hadn't called in. Yes, Jessica Tanzer knew. And unfortunately, she would also be the one running the hunt.

Buck thought quickly now. First things first. It wasn't only Jessica Tanzer that he had to deal with. He also had to handle Dewey Andreas. He went to his third computer screen, clicked the interagency sheet. He scanned the names, contact numbers of everyone on the sheet. What he was looking for wasn't there. He got up, walked to the sofa at the far side of his office, unbuckled his briefcase. He picked up a sheaf of papers. He found a sheet, the same interagency contact sheet, but a printout of it. At the bottom, in his own neat handwriting, he saw the name: Terry Savoy. His cell phone number. Savoy would have been the one who'd gotten the call from Andreas.

Buck went back to the first screen. He went into a simple CIA cell-trace database, entering his password. He came to a light blue screen, no writing. At the center of the screen, a rectangular box. He entered Savoy's cell phone number. After a full minute, a long list of phone numbers appeared. He scanned the list quickly, finding mostly domestic numbers. Then, he saw a number that stood out. A phone call Savoy had received the day before, an international number, the exchange 537 in front of it.

Buck knew the exchange by heart. After all, he'd visited the country at least two dozen times during his long career. *Havana*. Clever choice, Cuba. Andreas couldn't have chosen a better place to escape the influence of a U.S. government mole.

Next, Buck used a reverse directory to pinpoint the location of the call. The Parque Central. Buck sighed. He had stayed there himself.

Suddenly, his cell phone buzzed.

"Yeah," he said.

"How was that?" asked Fortuna.

"Long Beach?" responded Buck. "Last count, there are more than two thousand people dead. I thought this was about infrastructure."

"Does it hurt your tender conscience?" asked Fortuna. "You already sold your soul. You didn't complain about hundreds dead when you cashed the first ten million. You won't be saying anything when you're lying on a beach somewhere. I'm striking economic targets. If I wanted to kill people there would be many, many more dead. But right now, there's only one person you and I both *need* dead."

"I know I'll be in hell after all is said and done. But I'll be several floors above where they put you."

"Blah, blah, blah. You're boring me."

"You're the devil," said Buck.

"Then who is the guy who helped the devil?" asked Fortuna. "Is he better or worse?"

Buck rubbed his right temple, staring in front of him. A photo of his father and mother sat in a wooden frame.

"Well?" said Fortuna. "You get the next five?"

"Yes."

"And how close are they getting?"

"Close enough. The mole hunt's official now. I'm being watched. There's only one move that makes sense, for both of us. Alex, let me run. Be smart about this. If they capture me, I will trade you for my life. It's that simple."

"What ever happened to loyalty?"

"*Loyalty?* Have you ever been waterboarded, Alex? Loyalty is the first thing to go."

"Listen to me well," said Fortuna. "I am not telling you this again: you will not get another penny until this is over. And if you run, I will find you. And I will kill you. And then I will kill your wife. You stay until we finish the job, starting with the death of Dewey Andreas. Are we clear?"

Buck struggled to control his temper, reminding himself that—

money aside—Fortuna posed as much of a danger to him as he did to Fortuna. They were at a standoff, at least for the moment. And he needed the rest of the money.

"I know where he is," he said at last.

A predatory silence inhabited the other end of the line.

"Where?"

"He's in Cuba. Havana."

"Can you take him out?"

"In Cuba? No. Anywhere else, maybe. But I'm limited there. At least on this kind of time frame. Besides, I have someone else to take care of."

"Who?"

"The person who suspects I'm the mole. She also happens to be running the mole hunt."

Fortuna remained silent for a moment. "Havana," he said, thinking aloud. "Do you have a location?"

"The Parque Central Hotel. That's where he made the call from."

"All right. I'll clean up your mess."

"*My* mess?" asked Buck. But before he could continue, the line had gone dead.

Fortuna left his office and took a cab uptown.

At home he went to the kitchen. Karim poured him a cup of coffee as Fortuna told him what he'd learned.

"Call the airport," said Fortuna. "I'm going to do this myself."

"I don't think that's a good idea," said Karim.

"I don't care what you think," said Fortuna. "Who else can we send?"

"Mahmoud."

"And jeopardize Notre Dame?"

"Notre Dame is ready," said Karim. "The detonator is set."

"The sketch of Mahmoud that the police made with Marks is everywhere. Plus Mahmoud's injured. We can't send him."

"Actually, sending him out of the U.S. may be the best for all of us," said Karim. "And he's our toughest."

Fortuna gave him a look.

Karim shook his head. "No, Alex. It can't be you. You're too important here. Besides . . ." Karim paused.

"Speak," Fortuna said. "What's on your mind?"

"It doesn't matter."

"Goddamn it, say it!"

"We hunt Andreas as if he's the devil himself," said Karim, shaking his head. "I ask myself, why? If he poses such a threat, then we should set off the rest of the bombs—the ones that are ready—and be done with it. Not risk all on the pursuit of one individual. We're losing sight of the big picture."

Fortuna grabbed a mug and pulled the carafe from the coffeemaker, pouring himself a cup.

"We've made billions," said Karim. "We have the resources to go on forever. Long Beach was a fantastic success. We have more than twenty cells ready to be set off. Let's set them off, then get the hell out of here."

Fortuna laughed heartily, but his eyes showed no humor. "With no trading positions established? I've just begun reallocating money from the energy project. What do you know about this? Nothing! Do you realize how difficult it is to move a billion dollars, much less ten, twenty? We've worked for more than five years now; I've worked my whole life for this. To attack now without the trading positions in place would be pointless."

"I thought the point was to harm American economic infrastructure. That's why we were sent here. It's why you were brought up here. 'Silence, anonymity'; isn't that what your father wrote? We've done our harm, and we can do more, right now. Fifteen or twenty more bombs will *devastate* America. Why do we need to make money from it? You'll be in a league with Bin Laden after this."

Fortuna drank the last sip from his coffee cup, then suddenly hurled it in Karim's face, striking him squarely above the right eye, shattering the cup into pieces and causing Karim to fall back, holding his head as blood began to trickle from the gash.

"You compare me to Bin Laden? That mouse who hides in the mountains and fucks goats because he's too scared to stand up and fight? You compare me to a dirty Saudi whose only goal is the taking of innocent lives when I've stabbed a blade into the heart of the guilty, into the soul of the infidel? Do you even understand what it is we do, what we've done, what we're going to do, you stupid fuck?"

Fortuna stepped toward Karim, who held his hand over his badly bleeding right eye. Fortuna struck him hard across the skull, sending him flying to the floor.

"You think we've won because we blew up a fucking dock? An oil rig? A dam? Because we made money? You quote my father? The man who abandoned me when I was five years old? Oh, yes, he had so many ideas, didn't he? They all had their ideas, didn't they?"

Fortuna kicked him hard in the ribs, two, three, four times, each kick more vicious than the last. He finally stopped and stood over him.

"I was the one who was torn from his bed as a child. I was the one who lost his family because of these great ideas and words you now quote. Now you want to walk away because it's too dangerous? Because we might get caught? We might *die*?"

Fortuna walked to the counter and lifted the carafe. He poured himself another cup of coffee, then walked to Karim. He stood over him and began pouring hot coffee on the unconscious man's head and back. After a few seconds, Karim moved and screamed as hot coffee burned his neck and back.

"Get up," said Fortuna. "Before I kill you."

Slowly, he turned over onto his side and looked up at Fortuna.

"*Get up*," said Fortuna. "Go to South Bend. Get Mahmoud. But he can't go alone. You need to send in two men."

Karim nodded from the floor, tried to stanch the blood flowing from above his eye.

"You'll need to bring weapons. Mahmoud will not have time to prepare."

"I know. I'll make all the arrangements."

Mahmoud pushed the wheeled bucket down the empty hallway. He used the mop, which was stuck into the top, to push the yellow bucket past the bank of elevators. He opened a large green door and went inside. Inside

293

the large maintenance facility, a line of lockers was empty except for a lone black man, who was buttoning his dark green uniform.

"Hey, Mahmoud."

"C. J."

"How's it going?"

"You know. Not bad."

Mahmoud stood at six feet four inches, broad-shouldered, muscled, and tan. He limped slightly as he walked, though his physical strength still emanated from his powerful frame as he walked. His arms were thick with muscles. A red and green tattoo of a snake covered his right biceps. Mahmoud's neck was wrapped in a bandage. He had told his coworkers, those who asked, that he'd fallen off his mountain bike on a gravel road, hence the neck wound, his limp, and the broken nose.

In truth, he felt lucky to be alive. His battered body now showed the side effects of his vicious battle with Marks, a battle he'd barely won. The fact that Marks had somehow survived the battle, after he'd left him for dead, made Mahmoud more ornery than usual.

Mahmoud wheeled the bucket to a large utility sink in the corner, lifted it up and emptied the bucket, then wrung out the mop. Above the sink, a clock on the wall read two forty-five.

He finished putting the mop and bucket away. He walked to a small, windowless office behind the line of lockers. He knocked on the office door.

"Yeah, Mahmoud," said the man who was seated at a desk, Mahmoud's boss, John Garvey, the head of maintenance for Notre Dame's Stadium.

"Thank you for seeing me, Mr. Garvey."

"For the thousandth time, call me John."

"Sorry, yes, John. I need to ask a favor."

"What is it?"

"My uncle died," said Mahmoud.

"I'm sorry to hear that."

"I'd like to ask if I can leave early today. I need to take a day or two off."

"How early?"

"Right now."

"Now?" asked Garvey, pausing. "I don't see why not. How much time off do you need?"

"I don't know. Perhaps tomorrow. Perhaps I return day after to-morrow."

Garvey typed a few strokes into his computer. "You haven't taken vacation in more than a year."

"I know."

"You lose vacation time if you don't use it."

"I know. It's just—"

"Go be with your family. See you Thursday. If you need to stay longer, go ahead."

"Thank you."

Forty-five minutes later, Mahmoud stood to the side of the Atlantic Aviation tarmac at South Bend Regional Airport. Next to him stood a wiry, tall man named Ebrahim, like Mahmoud a maintenance worker at Notre Dame Stadium.

Mahmoud stared at the dark black tar of the landing strip, waiting. It was a cold day out, but sunny, in the forties.

To the north, he saw the outlines of the jet. By the time it hit the end of the landing strip, he knew it was his flight. The Gulfstream 450 had a distinctive look, completely black. It glided down the tarmac. The sound of the jet's thrusters being reversed was loud, but smooth. The door fell open to the ground and the two men walked across the tarmac and climbed aboard.

Mahmoud was first up the steps. He looked around the cabin. Karim sat on a leather seat in the back of the jet.

"Hello," said Mahmoud as he took his place in the seat diagonally across from Karim. Ebrahim took the other seat. He remained silent.

"What happened to you?" asked Mahmoud, staring at the cut above Karim's eye.

"Shut the fuck up," said Karim. He stared out the window. After a minute, he turned and looked at Mahmoud, taking in his bruised nose, still swollen from its break, and the bandage wrapped like a handkerchief around his neck.

"Are you strong enough to do what we must do?"

"I'm alive." Mahmoud stared down at Karim. "That's all that matters."

The Gulfstream took off and headed southeast toward Havana. Karim, Mahmoud, and Ebrahim stood up from their seats and sat on the ground, on their knees, facing the left side of the fuselage. They prayed for the next twenty minutes.

After they prayed, they sat in their seats.

"He's in Havana," said Karim when they had finished. "We know where he's staying. You follow him, find him, kill him tonight. No mistakes."

"Who is this American?"

"That you don't need to know. He's a threat. Like Marks, only much more so."

"What do you want me to do with him?"

"He's a tall, middle-aged American. He'll stand out like a sore thumb. You find him, you kill him. Then back to South Bend."

"That's all? Just kill the American?"

"That's all."

"What does he look like?"

Karim placed a black-and-white photo of Dewey on the seat in front of Karim. "It's from many years ago. He was in the military."

"Branch?"

"Army. His name is Andreas. Dewey Andreas."

Mahmoud held the photo in front of his face for more than a minute, studying Dewey's face. "He doesn't look very pleasant."

"We understand he had a beard and long hair as recently as two days ago," said Karim. "That may have changed. He doesn't look as good as the photo. He's older."

Mahmoud continued to study the photo. He looked up at Karim and handed it back to him. "You told me Marks had a military background. That he was a U.S. Navy SEAL, that he might be difficult. You also said he was as old as a grandfather and limped around like a woman. Do you remember?"

"Yes."

"Marks nearly killed me. And now that's all you can tell me about this one?"

"We're trying to find out more," said Karim. "He was in the army, like I said."

"Then you're a fool, or a liar."

"Don't you speak—" Karim began.

"If I don't," Mahmoud cut in, "we may fail. If I'd been more respectful of Marks, I would've carried my UMP in with me. If this matters, you have to tell me everything you know. What branch of the Army?"

"Rangers. Then Delta."

"Fuck," said Mahmoud. He sat in silence. "I know Delta," he said. "We studied them at Jaffna Camps. They're a nasty bunch."

"So are you."

"How old is he?"

"Forty-two."

"What happened in Colombia?"

"Nothing. That's outside your cell."

"Then put it *in* my cell."

Karim shook his head, exasperated. The plane suddenly tipped its nose downward as a bell went off in the cabin, indicating that they were in an approach pattern to Jose Marti International Airport outside of Havana.

"Andreas was in charge of the Capitana rig. He ran it. We had a group of men there. We needed his help to get into the target, the pumping station at the seabed. Something happened. We don't know what. The cell should've been picked up by helicopter just before the detonation of the facility and flown back to Cali. But when the helicopter arrived, only Andreas was aboard. He must have taken over the rig."

"CNN said a hundred men survived."

"Yes. But we succeeded despite that. The problem is, the man who ran the cell knew a lot. He knew everything. Andreas may have gotten information out of him."

Mahmoud nodded and closed his eyes as the Gulfstream swooped down and made its landing on the private terminal airstrip at Jose Marti

Airport. The jet taxied to a stop near the entrance to a small brown brick building that served as the private air terminal.

"There's a white van in the parking area just behind the building."

Mahmoud and Ebrahim climbed out of the jet. From the bottom of the plane's steps, Mahmoud turned.

"I will wait for you here, in the plane. If anything happens, text me immediately."

Mahmoud took a last look at Karim. He shook his head, then turned to walk away.

"He's dangerous," said Karim from the top step of the jet. "If you see him, shoot to kill. Even if in public. If you must martyr yourself . . ."

Mahmoud registered the words without turning to acknowledge them. He and Ebrahim walked quickly toward the brick building, passing it on the left, then saw an old white Ford van awaiting them in the gravel parking lot. Mahmoud's limp lessened, his mind began to sharpen as the mission took over.

Ebrahim drove from Jose Marti to downtown Havana, toward the port. When they arrived at the port, Ebrahim found a remote street near the fishing piers on the western side of the port. It was an older section of the port, with dilapidated corrugated steel warehouses perched atop crowded docks, lined with small fishing boats.

Ebrahim drove the van as Mahmoud remained in the rear of the van, preparing. He changed out of his clothing and put on the outfit Karim had packed, jeans and a gray T-shirt; anonymous, unnoticeable. Mahmoud inspected the weapons that were in the duffel. Karim had packed two HK MP7A1s, three silenced Taurus Cycle 2 9mm handguns, and a pair of long, serrated SOG combat knives.

"After we kill Andreas, perhaps we can invade France," Ebrahim joked from the front of the van as he looked at the arsenal in the rear-view mirror.

Mahmoud remained stone still; his face registered nothing.

37

Within one hour of his meeting with Marks, Joshua Essinger had gathered seven of the eight traders who worked for him. The eighth trader was already on his Christmas vacation, fly-fishing in Bali.

The trading floor looked not dissimilar to the control room on a nuclear submarine. The room was windowless, but bright and immaculate. Each trader had his own rectangular table atop which sat, depending on the trader, between four and a dozen flat plasma computer screens. The tables circled around a large, round cherry table that Essinger had had custom-made in upstate New York. On the table, a series of flat screens created a dodecagon, a twelve-sided circle of flat plasmas, each of which mirrored the trading activity of the individual traders, allowing Essinger to monitor their trades. Four screens were tied to Essinger's own portfolio.

All told, "the desk," as Essinger's operation was referred to, ran between $25 and $35 billion depending on the day of the week, invested across the energy complex.

Four massive, custom-built plasma screens, ten feet high and sixteen feet wide, covered the four walls of the trading floor. On one screen, a map of the world spread out in light blue, green, and black. On the screen, every oil and LNG tanker in the world currently in transit was displayed in real time. Another screen displayed all electricity generation activity in the United States, also in real time, ported directly from the grid. Both screens enabled Essinger and his traders to analyze and predict commodity flows, spikes, gluts, and patterns, and construct trades around them whose goal was twofold: to hedge specific KKB production, and to make KKB money. The two were not necessarily always compatible, which was why Joshua Essinger and his young traders made so much money.

On the next plasma screen, a detailed list of all positions the floor was in at that moment. This one looked like Chinese algebra to everyone except Essinger and his team.

Finally, a last plasma played Bloomberg, sometimes Fox, volume down.

"Thanks for coming in, guys," said Essinger, pacing around the center island. "I need your help on something."

"You still haven't found a date for New Year's?" quipped one of the traders, a Wharton-educated math whiz named Tino Santangelo. The rest of the traders started laughing. Essinger remained stone-faced.

"Yeah, well, unfortunately, Tino, your mother couldn't fit on the plane so, yes, it looks like I do need a date," said Essinger. More laughter, even from Santangelo. Then Essinger turned, held a remote aimed at one of the large plasma screens, clicked it. Suddenly a video feed of Capitana, smoldering in smoke and flames, played. He aimed the remote at another plasma screen. A live shot video of the Labrador Sea where KKB's Savage Island facility had once stood, now just dark blue ocean framed by snow-covered coastline, void of any trace of human activity.

"No, I need your help doing something serious," said Essinger. "We're going to find the motherfuckers who did this."

The room went silent.

"So you're probably asking yourselves, how the fuck are we, a bunch of overpaid, highly educated, some would say brilliant, nerds with smallish biceps and little to no training in weapons, self-defense, or any other black art, how are we going to find the badasses who did this?"

"I own a BB gun," said one of the traders.

"We're going to make the assumption that whoever was behind this was trying to make money from it. If you knew these two events were coming, what would you do? Well, the answer to that's easy."

"Buy comp."

"Correct," said Essinger. "So if I'm buying comp, what do I have to do?"

"Well, obviously, place the order, make the trade, wire the money, clear."

"And who do I do that through, that is, if I'm a really smart son of a bitch like the people behind this thing?" Essinger pointed to the Capitana video. "Where do I clear my trades?"

"I go outside the broker-dealer, right, boss?" asked Santangelo.

"Some other, smaller broker-dealer. Foreign?" asked another.

Essinger paused. Then, he shook his head.

"I create my own broker-dealer," said another trader.

Essinger grinned. "Wrong. All of you. There is no other on-ramp to the trade. I have to take my trade to one of the four horsemen to clear it. Morgan, Goldman, JPMorgan, Credit Suisse. That's the bottom line. This group is relying upon the fact that there will be literally millions of transactions on or around this time period, even in a segmented industry complex, like energy. They're counting on it. They're also counting on the secrecy of the broker-dealers. Confidentiality, that sort of thing. But what are they not counting on?"

Essinger looked around the room.

"They're not counting on the SEC, right?" asked Santangelo. "They're not counting on us pointing this out to the SEC."

"Two for two, Tino," said Essinger. "Wrong again. Christ, I've got pets smarter than you. We go to the SEC and we can kiss the data good-bye. They'll block it off, lock it up, and we'll see neither hide nor hair of it for six months while some bureaucrat fiddlefucks their way through the data. By the time they figure out who did it, the terrorists will be long gone, and more important, God knows how much more damage they'll do to our country." Essinger paused. "No, what they're not counting on is the fact that KKB is about to use its massive leverage to strong-arm the crap out of these guys to get at this data. And, they're not counting on Igor."

Igor was the trading floor's "IT guy." He had three Ph.D.s, one from Carnegie-Mellon, two from MIT, all in math or computer-related fields. Igor was twenty-nine years old.

"So here's what I want," continued Essinger. "Get on the phone, now. Call the head of broker-dealer at each house: Morgan Stanley, Goldman, JPMorgan, Credit Suisse. Get them at home, in the Hamptons, Gstaad, Aspen, wherever the fuck they are. If you have to, run it all the way to the CEO suite. From me, and from Ted Marks. Got it? Ask nicely, then threaten. Threaten to remove all of our trading business—and we *will* do it. I want all energy complex–related trading activity in the month leading up to the attacks. I want subsidiary-level activity: U.S., England, Switzerland, Hong Kong, Taiwan, Europe. Have them omit any plain vanilla trades: Fidelity, Vanguard, et cetera, if they can."

"I'll take Goldman," said one trader.

"JPMorgan," said another.

"I got Morgan Stanley," said another.

"Credit Suisse here."

"Now the rest of you, divide up the banks. Call their compliance people. Same thing. Get all trading activity for the month leading up to the attacks."

"Josh, that's going to be more data than we can process," said one of the traders. "I mean we're talking—"

"Good point," interrupted Essinger. "Someone call Igor and tell him to get his Russian ass in here. He's going to be eating about fourteen terabytes for dinner tonight."

38

Marks and Savoy took one of KKB's shining silver Gulfstream 500s from New York City to Panama City. On the way, they dropped into Reagan National Airport and picked up Paul Spinale, Savoy's deputy.

They also brought along Dr. Harvey Getschman from Presbyterian/St. Luke's, the surgeon who had performed surgery on Marks's shoulder. A former army doctor who spent two tours in Iraq, Getschman needed little inducement to take some time off and accompany the two men, though he sat in the aft compartment and was not privy to the trip's purpose.

The doctor was there to help administer Marks the drugs he still needed to control the pain from his hand and shoulder as well as rebandage both injuries every few hours. The potential for bleeding was still a problem in both wounds and the risk of infection remained severe. In medical protocol, and in the opinion of Getschman, Marks had climbed out of his hospital bed at least a week prematurely. But when the explosion at Long Beach occurred, and the doctor realized Marks and Savoy were somehow involved—on the side of the good guys—Getschman devised a traveling pack that would enable Marks to leave the hospital in comfort.

Besides clothing and weapons, a large duffel in the leather captain's chair across from Savoy held the most powerful weapon Marks possessed: $10 million in cash. It was his own personal cash, not all of his savings, but as much as Savoy could carry. Truth is, Marks was worth more than $100 million and he would have brought it all if necessary. The money was there because Marks felt they didn't have time to fuck around. They had hours, not days, and the stakes were escalating. The money to him was meaningless anyway. He had no family anymore. The only allegiance that burned within Marks now was to the country he loved. Through the sharp pain that stabbed at his hand and shot up his arm, a more powerful feeling coursed in his veins; the feeling of intense hatred for the traitor who somehow, somewhere was helping America's enemies destroy her. He would spend every nickel he had and then, if necessary, tear the shirt off his back for just one moment with the treacherous bastard.

In Panama City, a private car met them at the airstrip and took Marks, Savoy, and Spinale to a meeting with the deputy minister for Panama Economic Development, a young, overweight Panamanian named Orvela Marcados-Sariga. PED would have been the department KKB would work with on development-related projects in the country, such as the acquisition of mineral and drilling rights. The meeting had been hastily set up by an executive at the foreign desk at KKB headquarters in New York.

They met at a private table at Yuca, the opulent restaurant in the ground floor of the Hotel Grand Prix.

"We've heard about the attacks on your company," said Marcados-Sariga. "And on you personally. I hope you will accept our condolences."

"Thank you," said Marks.

"Coming so soon after the attacks, I assume this is related?" asked Marcados-Sariga.

"Your assumption is correct," said Marks. "I'll get right to the point. The time for KKB to pursue new foreign investment has come—sooner than we could have anticipated. We're looking at two significant development projects within your country: the Heley tar sands project and the development of an offshore gas territory near Miraflores. Either one of these projects, if developed, would mean billions of dollars to Panama."

"Yes, I have worked on both of these projects," said Marcados-Sariga. "It is very exciting news, Mr. Marks. We have tried to be helpful in any way possible to the executives of your company."

"Which my people and I appreciate, *señor*."

"How can I be of help to you today?"

"We want to speak with someone within the Panamanian security forces," said Savoy. "Someone high up, and preferably someone who is knowledgeable on internal Panamanian security issues. Someone at PPF."

Marcados-Sariga set down his glass and looked from Savoy to Marks. "What does it have to do with the projects?"

"Nothing," said Marks. "Other than we expect cooperation and discretion. Otherwise, you can kiss the projects good-bye. We'll take our business elsewhere."

"I understand," said Marcados-Sariga. "This can certainly be arranged."

"How quickly?"

"Certainly within the week," said Marcados-Sariga. "Sooner if possible."

Marks opened his briefcase. He pulled out several bricks of $100 bills and placed them down on the table.

"That's a hundred thousand," said Marks. "For you. We want a meeting this afternoon."

The Panamanian's eyes bulged as he stared at the money.

"Let me make a call."

Two and a half hours later, with a slightly lighter duffel bag in the trunk of the sedan, Marks, Savoy, and Spinale pulled into a gated compound an hour's drive from downtown Panama City.

The location served as the headquarters of Panama's special forces commander, General Sarijo Qital. It was one of more than a dozen such compounds spread out through the Panama countryside. Qital, a Western-educated man of fifty, had been brought in by Panama's president to help clean up the country and attempt to rid Panama of its legacy drug industry and private militias. Consequently, the outlaw groups who still controlled the large drug trade in Panama despised Qital. He had been targeted many times and needed to rotate on a nightly basis between the "camps," as he referred to them.

"He will meet with you," Marcados-Sariga had said after arranging the meeting. "The president himself is forcing him to do it. Qital is a difficult man, I must tell you. He has a short temper. Good luck."

After driving from the city into the hills, they followed the directions that had been given them, taking a left-hand turn up a small, nondescript dirt road. After a mile, they came to the gates. Two men dressed in plainclothes bearing automatic machine guns met the sedan at the gates. They asked Marks, Savoy, and Spinale to step from the vehicle and patted them down. Searching the car, they looked at the duffel bag, opening it up, then zipped it back up. It wasn't the first bag full of money the men had seen. They signaled Marks, Savoy, and Spinale up the long gravel road through lush, yellow Guayacan trees. At the end of a winding slope, a massive brick building sat in the midst of a clearing.

Spinale parked the sedan in front of the building as six men emerged and surrounded the car. All of the man were soldiers and wore khaki military fatigues except for one man, a tall figure who wore a Navy blue suit with a yellow and green striped button-down shirt, no tie. The man walked in the middle of the soldiers and approached Marks as he walked up the paved pathway toward the building.

"*Señor* Marks," said the man. "I am General Sarijo Qital."

Marks, Savoy, and Spinale followed Qital to the brick building, Marks carrying a slim steel briefcase, Savoy and Spinale the duffel bag. They walked down a long, windowless hallway and followed him through a door that led to a veranda overlooking miles of jungle.

General Qital sat first in one of the wicker chairs that occupied the deck.

"Thank you for meeting with us, sir," said Savoy as they sat down.

A soldier brought four bottles of water and placed them on a table in front of them, then left.

"I was *ordered* to meet with you," said Qital. "I know of the attacks of the past week, and I understand the extent of your losses, Mr. Marks, and please accept my regrets, but you'll have to forgive my bluntness: I am a busy man with problems of my own. I don't appreciate being pressured by my own president to meet with some wealthy American who needs a favor."

"Our country is at war, General Qital," said Marks. "And when we're at war, so are you. Forgive *my* bluntness, but we need your help to win that war."

Without looking chastened, Qital subtly softened his voice. "What do you want?"

"Information," said Marks. "And your discretion. And we need it immediately."

"Information?" Qital said, leaning back. "Let me give you some information." He laced his fingers together, as if in prayer, and placed them before his mouth, speaking in audibly restrained tones. "Two days ago, a group of four men entered a schoolhouse an hour from here and opened fire, killing eleven children. Why? Because one of the children is the daughter of a Panamanian who is responsible for buying farmland in Panama on behalf of the Starbucks Corporation, land they can grow coffee on. They killed the man's daughter, and all of this little girl's classmates, because the cocaine lords need the land for their own use. *Eleven children!* Can you imagine? They don't kill the father himself, no. They kill his daughter, her friends, *children*. If you think you're the only one at war, you're gravely mistaken."

Marks stared at Qital in silence, nodded. "I understand, General. We will find our information from another source. Thank you for your time." Marks stood up to leave.

"One second," said Savoy, still in his seat, now leaning forward and staring Qital in the eye. "What you don't know is there's a traitor inside the U.S. government, *actively* working with the terrorists. That person hired one, maybe two, Panamanian assassins to kill American soldiers and attempt to assassinate a material witness. A photo of the assassin is our only hope of finding the mole, and maybe stopping the terrorists."

Qital looked intrigued, despite himself. "Obviously I didn't know

307

that. Please sit down, Mr. Marks." He whistled. When a soldier came he held up three fingers. The soldier returned carrying four bottles of Heineken. "I'm sorry for my insensitive words."

Marks and Savoy shared a look, then Marks returned to his wicker chair. In a hostlike gesture, Qital toasted them and took a big sip from his beer. "I know what happened in Colorado, Mr. Marks. I know the feeling to be hunted in your own home."

Marks nodded and took a drink while Savoy opened the briefcase and removed a manila folder. Savoy pulled a grainy, somewhat blurry photograph from the folder. Despite its low quality, the photo's subject came through: the startling face of a dead woman, eyes open, staring blankly up into the sky, blood lining her lips, her stunning beauty acting as a disturbing counterpoint to the stark violence the photo implied.

"We need to know who she is, and who she worked for. That's it. We'll pay handsomely for the information."

Qital held the photo for several moments, staring at it. Finally, he shut his eyes and, with his other hand, reached up and rubbed the bridge of his nose in thought.

"Can you help us?" asked Savoy.

"I trained her," said Qital finally, opening his eyes and looking at Marks. "Her name was Sassa Cortez. We . . . well, we had a very close relationship, one time."

"Did she work for PPF?" asked Savoy.

"She left a year ago," said Qital. "I don't know where she went."

"Can you find out?"

"Yes," said Qital. "I will help you. But I have to ask. Why isn't the CIA digging into this?"

Marks gestured to Spinale, who pulled the duffel bag from behind the chair.

"Earlier I mentioned discretion," Marks said. "There's almost ten million dollars in that bag. If you can find out who hired Sassa Cortez and keep it between us, it's worth that much to me personally to not have to answer that question."

39

J. EDGAR HOOVER FBI BUILDING

Two doors down the hallway from her office, Jessica walked into the windowless conference room. The table was large enough to accommodate more than twenty people, and it was packed.

"Okay, everyone," Jessica said as she moved to a seat in the middle of the table. "I apologize for being late. Let's get moving."

"Where should we start?" asked a middle-aged man sitting directly across from her, Jessica's chief of staff Tony Fogler.

"Long Beach," responded Jessica. "Then interdepartmental, closing with the explosive chain. We need to make it quick."

"Got it," said Fogler.

"I'll start," said T. J. Chatterjee. "We're at level red across—"

"No, start with ports," interrupted Jessica. "Long Beach specifically."

"Yeah, good point," said Chatterjee. "Oliver's running that."

"Ports are shut down everywhere," said Oliver Smith. "No boats out, no boats in. We're scouring employee manifests—"

"Long Beach?" asked Fogler. "Come on."

"Yeah. We're looking at every employee who worked at Long Beach in the past two years. There were more than four thousand. It's taking time. But the new Homeland database is working extremely well. It's grabbing flags from a bunch of places we would have had a tough time locating, Customs, Interpol, DEA, local police, et cetera."

"I assume you're not just running a criminal profile—"

"That's right. We're running a criminal profile as well as three ancillary modules. The database is extremely extensible. We have a traveler profile running, looking at any employees who visited the Middle East in the last decade. With few exceptions, it pulls from an Interpol data set, so they would not have had to fly a U.S. carrier nor travel directly to or from the U.S. It's very powerful stuff. Let me tell you, you travel to someplace in the Middle East and unless you got there on a bike or a camel, you'll be in the database basically until you're dead. We're also pushing employee data against purchase criteria, seeing what, if anything, the credit card companies have."

"What would that surface?" asked Jessica.

"Weapons, bomb components, certain subscriptions. We're even running what the credit data people call a 'cuisine' profile, flagging anyone who ate at certain types of places in Orange County, falafel joints, that sort of thing, cross-referencing all of it. We're going to be thorough here."

"I like it," said Jessica.

"Same with wireless and wireline data from the telcos," added Smith. "If any Long Beach employee had Middle East ties, made phone calls over there, we should find it, though, of course, the disposable calling cards don't get tracked. That said, if they bought disposable calling cards with credit that will get flagged."

"Make sure you're hitting service providers," said Jessica. "Food crews, railroads, trucking companies that do business at the port."

"Absolutely," agreed Smith.

"You mentioned the other ports—"

"We've shut down all ports in the U.S., including LNG facilities. No boats in or out until Coast Guard does a level-seven screen, then we'll let them move. Should be tomorrow sometime."

"Airports?" asked Fogler.

"Every airport has elevated threat level clearance, according to TSA. Things are starting to slow down dramatically, especially in the East, compounded by the snowstorm, which is moving up the coast. You know, when they go from random bag checks to serial the impact is just dramatic, really slows things. We've asked the carriers to consider rationalizing schedules in the coming week. But they're all pushing back. This is a very critical time for them, lots of travelers, profits, you know the drill. That said, cancellations by travelers are spiking since the explosion, as you might imagine."

"Is Customs working the profile?" asked Jessica.

"Yes," said Chatterjee. "It's all we have at the moment. So far, there have been several dozen flags, three of which are being detained for further questioning."

"What are we doing with them?"

"Two were East Coast. Boston, Baltimore. They're both at Quantico. But there's nothing there."

"The third?"

"Customs flagged someone at LAX last night. Iranian on a student visa, coming in from Puerto Rico. We have him at FBI regional. We have a team that began an interrogation sequence last night. So far, it's been unproductive; we may need Lou's authorization for a pharmaceutical package."

"Get the paper," said Fogler. "Run it through me."

"Borders?" asked Jessica.

"Lock down," said Sarah Wells. "The Canadians have been somewhat helpful. If anything, we're seeing lines building up getting out of the U.S. We have a book profile going and so far nothing relevant has popped."

Jessica reached forward, grabbed a glass, poured herself some water, and took a sip.

"Barry, what about the explosive?" she asked. "Anything?"

"Yes," said Barry Urquhart. "We have two tracks going and we might have gotten lucky in, of all places, Canada. The team we sent up to Savage Island was unable to take any kind of water or soil samples. It's basically open ocean now. There's just too much current and the throughput is too cold to spend a great deal of time in. Whatever was there is gone. What we were able to pull out was a bolt, part of some steel rebar. It was a monumental effort. One of our divers almost drowned. But we have the piece. It has trace factors of the octanitrocubane on it. By tonight, we should have a quick test on the material."

"Meaning we'll have the sniff test that soon?"

"Yes, and we'll FedEx it immediately to TSA, Customs and Border Patrol, DEA, and any other government entity that has canine capability set. By around 9:00 P.M. tonight, keep your fingers crossed, we'll be sniffing for octanitrocubane at every travel or shipment nexus in the United States. East Coast will have it by supper time."

"Get it overseas."

"Absolutely, done. FedEx is preparing literally thirty-seven thousand envelopes as we speak. They've agreed to put more than a thousand workers against this. We owe them a thank-you. This stuff will move out of Memphis as soon as we get it there."

"Good work. Give that diver a raise."

"I will."

"What about the source?" asked Fogler.

"I'll take that," said Katherine Fawcett. "We'll ask local law enforcement—here and overseas—to spearhead that. We're waiting for the data run from Commerce. Once we have that, we should have a large but addressable universe of possible places this stuff was manufactured. We'll just have to go one by one, knocking down the list. That's the plan."

"Okay, that's a wrap," said Jessica. "Anything else?"

"Yes," said Fogler. "Before you came in, we were talking about resources, Jess. To summarize the mood generally, coming from all departments: we don't have enough people. Down through the ranks, nobody minds working 24/7. But there just isn't enough manpower."

"I hear you," said Jessica. "Unfortunately, we would normally turn to the National Guard around now. But they're at full deployment in Iraq and Afghanistan. All I can tell you is lean on your interdepartments. Especially local police forces. T. J., get Homeland to use their fire department affiliates to do some of the port work. I know it's tough right now. The key is putting in place the foundation that will hopefully produce a lead, a link. Make sure everyone knows what they're looking for and what to do if they think they found it. That's the key. It won't be a tidal wave that washes up on the beach and brings a bunch of guilty people with it. It will be one boat, one skiff, one dinghy in the ocean. We need to find that dinghy."

"Got it," said Fogler.

"I want to reconvene tonight," said Jessica. "Don't worry about dinner; I'll order Chinese. One thing I want to say: you know what I would do. Like you all, I'm stretched thin right now. Take a ready, aim, fire approach. When in doubt, act. I have your back. Just try and be smart about it."

Jessica stood, turned, and walked out.

Back in her office, Jessica's phone buzzed. She hit the red speaker button.

"Tanzer," she said.

"You want to see me, Jess."

"Yes."

In a minute, Jessica's door opened. A tall Hispanic man with graying hair entered the room. He was slightly overweight, and had a somewhat disheveled look; his tie was askew, one of the front flaps of his button-down shirt hung down over his wrinkled khakis.

"What do we have on the mole, Hector?"

Hector Calibrisi was, like Jessica, one of nine FBI deputy directors, in charge of international affairs. Calibrisi was a former CIA agent and Jessica's closest friend inside the FBI. It was he whom Jessica had asked to run the mole hunt.

"We're twenty-four hours into it, Jess," said Calibrisi. "What can I tell you? We have twelve people who were in that meeting where the Madradora exfiltration was discussed. In addition, there were four other individuals who were made privy to Madradora. All of them were at DOD."

"And what have we found?"

"Let's start with what we're looking at, okay? I want to make sure I'm not missing anything. I've never run a mole hunt before."

"You're an ex-agent," said Jessica. "You know where to look."

"Ah, so in other words, you think I was, or could have been, a double agent and therefore could use the extensive knowledge I already have of hiding funds, communicating with the enemy, that sort of thing, to find our mole?"

"Exactly," said Jessica, smiling. "I mean, look at your wardrobe, Hector." She glanced at his wide, cheap polyester tie and old shirt. "Hermès tie. Armani suits. Was that shirt custom-made?"

"Actually, no. Only the food stains are custom. This one's from a burrito I had for dinner last night."

Jessica laughed. "Thanks," she said. "I needed that more than you know."

Calibrisi sat down in one of the two chairs in front of her desk.

"So, all kidding aside, here's what we're doing," said Calibrisi. "I have about a dozen agents on this—"

"You have authority to go up to thirty if you want."

"Yeah, I know, but I don't need to. A lot of this is just data mining. We're looking at everything about the people in that meeting, including you, by the way, Jessica. Cell records, e-mail, Web use, travel, purchases, relationships, professional background. We've also got surveillance across the group. Of course, most of our time is being spent on finances."

"And do we have anything so far?"

"No. Nothing yet. But I do have suspicions about one person in particular. Maybe it's just because I spent so many years over there."

"Vic Buck?"

"Yes. The guy has just done a lot. Traveled a lot. He lived in Beirut for six years. Beijing, Hong Kong, Kiev, St. Petersburg, Cape Town. He's been to every city in the Middle East at least half a dozen times."

"So how close are you to turning something up?"

"It's going to be hard to prove anything, to pick the wheat from the chaff. He will have an argument for any suspicious activity we front. Alibis, reasons he was in a certain place, with a certain person, at a certain time. Even if we thought we had him on something, if we develop a connection, it's going to be really hard to prove it. The second thing, we're probably not going to be able to get at the places and modalities Buck would use if he was working with whatever group is behind all this. I mean, there is a lot of dark activity we are just not even aware exists. For example, do you remember that cell phone that was found on the corpse of al-Libi, the guy who ran Al-Qaeda's main training camp in Afghanistan? It had its own frequency and satellite. Think about that; he had his own satellite. If Buck's doing something, he's going to do it using things like that, and it's going to be nearly impossible to get access to them. He runs National Clandestine Service for the Central Intelligence Agency. He knows what the hell he's doing. Look, I reported to the guy for a decade. He's arguably the best operative in the U.S."

"What about other members of the group?"

Calibrisi shook his head. "Nothing. A bunch of Cub Scouts. Jane Epstein has more than a million bucks in her savings account, but she inherited it. Look, we'll keep digging, but the bottom line is, it's Buck. It has to be him. Just by the process of elimination."

"So what do we do?" asked Jessica. "Bring him in? Interrogate him?"

"I . . . don't know. That's for you, Lou, maybe even the president, to decide. That's a tough one."

"Tell me about his financials."

"Nothing unusual. He has a few hundred thousand in a 401(k). His wife has a little bit of money. Nothing weird. No other financial ties. Sometimes we would see agents take money and buy equity in a company somewhere, usually the country they intended to run to. You find that by a travel pattern correlated to alias and in-country incorporation or legal activity. That's what I have most of the team focused on right now. If we find something interesting, we dig in. Unlikely, but that's where I'd go if I was trying to hide some money."

"Sounds like a—"

"Needle in a haystack," said Calibrisi, nodding his head. "Exactly."

"But is there anything else about Buck that makes you suspect him?" asked Jessica. "I mean, of all people. He does not seem like someone who would betray his country."

"We looked at that, too," said Calibrisi. "Biography. Education. Employment history. Psychographic. Demotions that might lead to bitterness, et cetera. I agree with you, there is nothing there to suggest a grievance or motivating event. The guy has done a lot for this country. He's come damn close to dying several times. High-risk sort of mission work. Do you realize that in 1983, after the Beirut suicide bomb that killed so many marines, Buck went in, alone, at night, and killed Arafat's head of security, one of the guys who helped design the bombing in the first place, El-terhassa? I mean, that was a legendary hit. So no, it doesn't fit. I suspect him only because I just see eliminating every one else in that room really quickly."

"And because of his background, we might never eliminate him or prove anything."

"Or find anything," added Calibrisi.

"Ambiguous. I hate it."

"I'm sure my background has some ambiguity in it too," said Calibrisi. "It's the nature of being an ex-spook."

"So what do we do?"

"Well, you do what we're doing. You excavate anything and everything in this guy's background. You watch him like a hawk. And you try to develop something from one of these events that ties back to him, gives you good reason to bring him in."

"I think we should bring him in now."

"And do what? Board him? Run a pharma package on him? I mean, it's a slippery slope, Jess. You have nothing solid to go on at this point. If you start to do things like that, you're stepping over the line. Just my opinion."

"I don't like waiting. Two thousand people died today at Long Beach."

"That doesn't give you the right to torture Vic Buck," said Calibrisi. "Look, that's one man's opinion. It ain't my decision though. It's Lou's, the president's. Take it to them if you want."

Jessica leaned back, thinking about how to proceed.

"In the meantime, I'll keep going. We might find something. I know what I'm doing. We're tightly focused. If he slipped up at some point, we will find it. What's going on with the investigation down in Cali? Have the dead operatives given us anything to go on?"

"Not yet," said Jessica.

"What about the guy we were exfiltrating?"

"I wish I knew the answer to that," said Jessica.

40

PARQUE CENTRAL HOTEL
HAVANA, CUBA

Dewey walked from the hotel to a travel agency two blocks away. He purchased a one-way ticket to Melbourne, Australia, leaving the next afternoon. He didn't have a plan beyond landing in Australia. Just get out of Cuba. Tonight he would drink, maybe stumble back to the hotel. He wanted to push aside the events of the past few days.

He had dinner at a small restaurant near the port. After he ordered, he went back to his hotel room. He went to the bathroom and removed the Colt from the back of his pants.

He looked in the mirror. He threw water across his face, washing his short hair with soap in the sink. He put a fresh bandage on his shoulder.

He tucked his handgun back between his belt and the back of his pants, then walked out of the Parque Central and into the crowded streets of the city. The temperature stayed in the mid-sixties at night, and the sidewalks pulsed with energy as people poured out for the evening.

He walked through the east side of the city, toward where the Parque Central concierge told him the nightclubs were. At Paradiso, he took a right. The streets were densely packed with people. Many turned and stared at the big American. He was taller than most of the Cubans. A few said hello to him as he passed, or nodded. But for the most part they just stared at him, a six foot three Americano walking among them.

He walked into the neighborhood at the end of Paradiso, the Julio. The rapid, deep sound of Caribbean music filled the street air. Loud, booming drums mixed with a fast beat. Groups of young women stood on the sidewalks, beautiful Cuban women, waiting to get into one of the nightclubs that were crowded into the end of the small street. Everyone smoked.

He walked to the front door of the closest club, a place called Zanzibar. It was packed with people and the music grew louder as he walked inside. He went to the bar and ordered a whiskey.

He stood at the bar and turned, looking at the crowd. He sipped his drink as slowly as he could, but it was hard not to down it quick. He ordered another one and paid. He talked briefly with a young Cuban woman who had long, black hair, a pretty dark woman with large, warm brown eyes. She introduced herself—Sanibel. He spoke with her for a few minutes. Then he circled the perimeter of the dance floor. He finished his drink and left.

He went to three more clubs. He had a drink at each of the clubs. He was starting to feel the effects of the alcohol by the third nightclub. It was past midnight. With no better notion in mind, he returned to Zanzibar, looking for the young woman, Sanibel. He ordered a beer at the bar.

Sanibel returned from the dance floor. She was sweating and even sexier than he remembered. Her white short-sleeve shirt barely covered her chest; he noticed for the first time how large her breasts were. She approached the bar and stood. She was with a man now, a young, scraggly-looking guy with a beard. She glanced from the end of the bar at Dewey and smiled. He signaled to the bartender, and had him bring her a glass of champagne.

She said something to her dance partner and left him for Dewey.

"Thank you," she said in English, toasting him with the glass.

"You're welcome."

"What's your name again?" she asked. "I'm sorry."

"Dewey."

"Hello, Dewey," she said, extending her hand. "Journalist?"

"No."

"Military?"

"No. Tourist. You?"

"Teacher," she said. "From Havana. I teach math."

"Do you like to dance?"

"Sure."

They put their drinks down on the bar and went to the dance floor. They danced for several songs. Sanibel was a natural dancer and she moved around Dewey in time with the music, smiling at him. She rubbed against him. He was loose from the alcohol and he let it course through him, and tried to keep up with her. At some point, she took his hand as they danced and they held hands through several songs, dancing closer to each other. He leaned forward and kissed her. She tasted sweet, and her lips were soft. He wanted to take her back to the Parque Central. He would, if she would let him. Perhaps one more dance, another drink, then back to his suite. He liked her.

Then, over her shoulder, across fifty feet of dimly-lit room and hundreds of people, Dewey saw the man who had come to kill him.

He was Arab, dark-skinned. He stared at Dewey from across the room. He held no drink. He was dressed in a gray T-shirt, muscled. His eyes were dark and serious; they traced Dewey as he moved.

Dewey continued to dance with Sanibel. He stayed close to her, but kept a subtle eye on the stranger. He didn't want to let him know he knew he was there. He looked for others but saw no one. Sanibel moved in closer again and put her hands around him. First on his back, then lower, as she kissed him. Her tongue entered his mouth this time. It tasted sweet, of champagne. He kissed her back. The man kept his eyes on him from afar. Then, suddenly, almost imperceptibly, he glanced behind Dewey, toward the bar. Dewey swung Sanibel around.

At the bar stood another killer, this one shorter, with a mop of hair, younger than the thug in back. He too looked dangerous, and he did nothing but stare. They'd surely seen him before then. Had the alcohol dulled him? It was too late to worry about that. He had a situation on his hands. He would need to kill them.

The thug in back moved first.

He stepped quickly through the crowd, pushing aside people. Dewey turned. His partner at the bar moved forward at the same time. Dewey spun around again. The man at the back reached for his waist. Through the crowded dance floor, he could see the man raising his gun.

Dewey's first concern was Sanibel, whose arms were wrapped around his neck. As the first man approached, he attempted to throw her to the ground, out of the firing line, but she resisted, a look of fear crossed her face, fear of Dewey, who she thought was trying to harm her. She pulled out of his grip. The man in back fired.

Suddenly, a silenced slug missed Dewey and ripped through Sanibel's neck, and she was knocked backward, screaming, but still upright. Blood coated her neck, her hand reflexively reached for the wound. Another bullet, this one through her chest, and Sanibel tumbled over backward as the dancers in the immediate vicinity spread apart amid screams and pandemonium. She collapsed in Dewey's arms, rapidly bleeding out. Screams echoed above the loud music and soon the dance floor was chaos as people ran for the door.

Dewey ran with the crowd as the two men chased him. He ran to the left of the crowd and kicked open a door near the bar, away from the entrance. He sprinted down Paradiso, then took a left on a side street. Halfway down the small, darkened street, he saw a woman reach into her handbag to get a set of keys. She stopped at an old Mercedes sedan.

At the end of the street, he saw the two killers running quickly through the crowd.

"Give me the keys," he said. He held the Colt against her side. "Scream and you die."

He took the keys from the woman, pulled the car out, and sped down the narrow street, leaving the woman standing in the middle of the street. He turned left to go back toward the Parque Central.

As he drove up Paradiso, he saw a set of lights go on in the small rearview mirror. The terrorists were a quarter mile back. They had marked him. The lights of a white van came into view behind him, several blocks to the south. He sped past the Parque Central.

Dewey drove up the central hill that ran through the middle of

Havana, past the Capitol. He sped through the city's business district, a handful of tall cement office buildings. Behind him, the lights of the van twinkled in the rearview mirror, getting closer.

The business district transitioned into suburbs, tidy streets lined with small, squat brick and cement houses. Dewey kept the pedal to the floor, pushing the sedan as fast as it could go. But the killers closed in. Dewey kept the pedal down, but it wasn't good enough, and by the time the suburbs started to turn into farmland they were at his back bumper.

In the rearview mirror, he saw one of the killers lean out, a black machine gun in his hand. Bullets flew at the Mercedes, the sound of lead striking metal, then the rear glass shattered. The small roadway tightened into a dilapidated one-lane road, and Dewey swerved at a telephone pole, down another road, creating a temporary gap between himself and the killers.

In the distance, twenty yards ahead, he saw a rusty shack at the edge of the road, next to a break in the fields of tobacco. The van's lights came into view again behind him, then more bullets, and he ducked as a spray of lead shattered the windshield of the Mercedes. Suddenly, Dewey swerved the Mercedes toward the rusty shack, aiming straight for it before skirting it at its edge and barreling the old car down through the break in the field. He was on a dirt road that went through the fields. The tall green tobacco stalks cascaded over the dirt roadway and brushed across the broken windshield of the Mercedes, pushing shards of glass down onto Dewey's lap. He pressed the accelerator down to the floor and sent the old car lurching forward as fast as it would go down the dirt path.

In the mirror, he saw the lights behind him as the sedan entered the field road.

He drove for a hundred yards. Clouds of dust shot out as the tires of the car tore down the small path. He reached forward and cut the headlights of the old car. He now drove in blackness, trying to stay straight, not letting up on the accelerator, letting the sound of the stalks of tobacco rattling against the roof guide him through the field.

In a sudden motion, he swerved the car to the left, pulled back on the emergency brake, down into a row of tobacco stalks, swerving wildly in a 180-degree turn that left the car facing back toward the dirt path from the edge of the stalks, then jumped out of the vehicle, taking the Colt with him, lunging behind the Mercedes as the lights from the terrorists' van shot down the path. He felt it then, the adrenaline, coursing down through his legs and arms. A smile spread across his lips as their vehicle plunged through the thick dust and tobacco. He moved back, behind the Mercedes, and braced himself. The lights grew brighter and the engine revved as the van closed in. Without warning, the killers' van barreled into the darkened Mercedes, crashing into the steel front of the parked car. The noise was horrendous, the unnatural sound of metal meeting metal, glass breaking, and screams from inside the van as the terrorists were caught by surprise by the parked car. The van flipped on its edge, slid, then flipped completely over onto its roof, which crushed the van in upon itself.

Dewey stood up and stepped into the pathway behind the wrecked van. The engine whirred as one of the tires continued to gyrate in the night air. Moans of pain came from inside the destroyed van. Dewey reached inside the Mercedes, turned the headlights on. Only one worked, and it illuminated the overturned, destroyed van that lay smoking in front of the Mercedes.

He moved quickly toward the van with his Colt in front of him. He walked to the driver's side and looked in. It was the short one from the bar with the mop of hair. He lay on the ground, what had been the ceiling of the van, crumpled up. His face and head were covered in blood. He was young, early twenties. Dewey reached in and felt for a pulse; still alive. He felt for a weapon as the man looked up at him. He found a silenced handgun next to the man's left leg. He picked it up and tossed it into the tobacco field.

He walked around to the passenger side and pulled the dented door open. It fell off its hinges to the ground. The tall killer was wedged against the dashboard, his head turned helplessly toward him as he kept his handgun aimed at him. He was covered in blood; it was the terrorist from the back of the club, the one who shot at him, who killed Sanibel. He reached in and grabbed his thick, muscled arm, pulling it behind his back and yanking it up until the humerus bone snapped. He then put both of his hands on the man's head and pulled him from the van, placing him on the ground in front of the Mercedes' shining headlight. He checked him for weapons, pulled a knife from a sheath at his left ankle and a handgun tucked into his pants below his back. He threw both weapons into the field.

He went back and dragged the driver from the van and set him next to the other man. Dewey pulled a knife from a sheath at the man's calf, finding him equally badly injured. The driver's legs were broken, the right badly contorted in the middle of his thigh. The taller man was in slightly better shape, though dazed and bloody.

Dewey propped them up. The bright headlight shone in their eyes. He leaned against the dented front of the old Mercedes, next to the light, and kept the Colt trained on them.

"Welcome to Cuba."

41

Joshua Essinger stuck his head inside the office door.

"Got anything yet?" he asked.

Igor Karlove sat at his computer, back to the door. He said nothing. In fact, he didn't even turn around. His long, blond hair was combed back and it covered his ears. From earbuds his iPod blasted *Exile on Main Street* so loudly that the vocals were audible from the doorway.

On the computer screen in front of him, lines of letters and numbers were scrolling down quickly. Every once in a while, Karlove would hit the keyboard, type something, then sit back and watch as script rolled across the screen.

Essinger walked up behind Karlove. He reached down, pulled the buds from his ears. The Russian looked up nonchalantly.

"Hey, Josh."

"How's it going?" asked Essinger.

"It's going."

"How long's it going to take?"

"There's a lot of data here. It's going to take a while. I had to take down the KKB network and tap capacity. Any CPU not logged in is helping out. I also asked a buddy over at EMC to let me use one of their stack farms. It's just a lotta fucking lines."

Karlove reached out, hit the enter key, typed something furiously, then sat back.

Eight hours after Essinger's meeting the evening before, most of the data was in: a list of all energy complex–related trading activity in the month leading up to the attacks that had cleared through Morgan Stanley, Goldman Sachs, JPMorgan, and Credit Suisse, the four major broker-dealers in the world. The information was held in secure, heavily encrypted databases within each financial institution. With approval had come not a big file or set of files, but rather, a temporary entry provision, essentially a password, that enabled Karlove to access the data and extract it from the four databases within each firm. Karlove had had to write a program that accomplished three objectives; extract the data, format it in a common framework, and purge any trades that were made by one of the big "vanilla" mutual funds. The data involved was massive—more than seven billion lines of code. But the program that Karlove wrote was elegant, brilliant, and stunning in its simplicity and efficiency, and less than five thousand lines of code. It would have taken one of the big consulting firms weeks to develop a program to accomplish what was needed by Essinger. It had taken Karlove less than four hours.

The problem was, once written, the execution of what was in essence a toll system—weeding out good data from irrelevant data—required an almost unbelievable amount of computing capacity.

"So how much time are we talking?"

"Hours, not days," said Karlove.

"How many hours?"

"I don't know. But once we have the blocks of data sets, that's when the real art comes in. We need to build a force-rank algorithm. That's what I'm going to do while I'm waiting. So once we get the data into buckets, we can whittle it down to the specific institutional events."

"Okay. I have no fucking idea what you just said, but obviously keep me posted."

"I'm assuming you want me to omit any firm that was long in KKB or Anson? I'm assuming any firm buying KKB and or Anson wouldn't be behind the attacks, right?"

"Yeah, weed those guys out too." Essinger patted Karlove on the back, then turned to walk out. At the door, he suddenly stopped.

"Actually, Igor, don't remove those guys. I'm assuming whoever did this is as smart as you or me. If it was me, I would've bought some KKB and Anson for appearances' sake."

"Ten four."

As Essinger left Igor's office, the renewed blast of the Rolling Stones faded quickly behind him.

42

It took Qital less than an hour to call Savoy with the information he needed. Marks, Savoy, and Spinale had been waiting in the KKB jet back at the airport, where Dr. Getschman had time to rebandage Marks's shoulder.

"She was working for an outfit out of Guatemala City," Qital told Savoy over the phone. "A security company called Centrix. They do corporate work, guarding development projects, senior executives, that sort of thing. I don't have an address for the outfit, but if you ask the right people, you'll find it."

"Great information," said Savoy, making notes. He nodded to Spinale and made a motion with his index finger, indicating the need to get ready to take off. "Thank you, General."

"Mr. Savoy?"

"Terry."

"Terry, finding Centrix is the least of your problems. These are, how shall we say, *black hats*."

"Meaning?" asked Savoy.

"Real mercenary types. Not typical ex-military. Not just security contractors. I'm talking about a rougher crew. I am told many of them came out of Nicaragua. Sandinistas. Death-squad type of stuff. Wet work."

Savoy nodded. The Gulfstream's engines were roaring. "Got it."

On the plane, Savoy told Spinale to track down a firm called Centrix using an old contact from the military. He cautioned him to do it quietly, under the radar.

It took less than an hour to fly from Panama to Guatemala City. The KKB jet landed at La Aurora Airport on the outskirts of Guatemala City as the late afternoon sky was turning orange and the sun was low on the western sky.

When they landed, Savoy walked to the main terminal and rented a tan Chevy Tahoe from the Hertz desk. By the time he'd driven the SUV to the private terminal, next to the Gulfstream 500, Spinale had something.

"I got it," said Spinale. "The outfit's called Centrix-Lassa Security. Where are we?"

"We're at La Aurora."

"We're close. They're nearby. They have an office downtown, but they also work out of a building near La Aurora; looks like a warehouse with a landing pad for helicopters."

"Makes sense," said Savoy.

"The address is 1244 Bolivar. We take a right out the airport exit and drive on the access road less than a mile, then make a left. My guess is they won't have a sign posted."

"I'll man the phones back here," said Marks as his doctor redressed his burned hand. Despite having come this far, Marks couldn't hide his obvious fatigue and an ashen complexion. "I want to talk with Essinger and see how his analysis is going. You two are going to have to do this one without me."

"Me?" asked Spinale. "You want me to go into this place? I mean, I was in naval intelligence. I don't know what the hell—"

"You'll be fine, Spin," said Marks. "Piece of cake. Just try not to shoot Terry, okay?"

The building that housed Centrix-Lassa Security was a large green warehouse—with no sign on the front. Bolivar was lined on both sides with such warehouses. Most of them offered some sort of shipping and logistics services. The Centrix-Lassa parking lot held a few dozen cars, with a couple of motorcycles mixed in.

Savoy and Spinale drove by the building twice. Across Bolivar, down the street a few hundred feet, they parked in an empty parking lot. Night was coming. They waited, watching from across Bolivar as the Centrix-Lassa parking lot gradually thinned out. When only one car remained, Savoy turned on the Tahoe and drove back up Bolivar. He came to the end of Bolivar and took a left, then another left, coming down a street called Via Rio behind the Centrix-Lassa building.

Savoy turned into an empty parking lot. He drove to the back of the lot and they came to a parking area across from the rear entrance to Centrix-Lassa. Three helicopters sat on the pavement behind the building. One looked relatively new, a white Bell 412. The other two were older, a Russian Mi-8 Hip, black with orange trim, missing its tail rotor, and a green SA 330 Puma.

Savoy parked the Tahoe. The sun had set and the sky was now dark. A lone lamppost between the two buildings illuminated the parking lot. Savoy opened the duffel bag in the back seat and took out the Smith & Wesson 1911 Koenig semiautomatic. From a side pocket, he screwed an HTG silencer onto the weapon. He reached in and handed Spinale another handgun, a Wilson Combat CQB semiautomatic, also with an HTG silencer screwed onto the end. He grabbed a set of wire cutters.

They climbed out of the SUV. Looking up, Savoy took aim at the lamppost and shot quickly, the tinkle of shattered glass hitting pavement as darkness descended.

At the fence that separated the two parking lots, Savoy cut an opening in the metal fence and they climbed through. Spinale followed Savoy as they walked quickly across the Centrix-Lassa facility. Past the helicopters, they came to the back of the windowless building. A back door was locked. Savoy looked up.

"No security cameras," he said quietly.

"Are you surprised?" asked Spinale. "We're in Guatemala."

"I'm going to the roof," said Savoy, looking up. "Hopefully there's a skylight."

"You gonna fly?" Spinale asked, looking around. There was no ladder, just the back wall of the steel building.

"You forget," said Savoy. "I was a fucking Ranger for five years."

He holstered his weapon. At the corner of the building, he found the metal ridge that ran vertically up the building's edge. He gripped the seam in his hands and lifted himself up, leaning back so that his feet could press hard against the building. He moved quickly up the building, breathing heavily as he went, shimmying with his hands and feet. He was soon at the roof, where he pulled himself up onto the roof. He sat for a few moments to catch his breath, then leaned over the edge. He could barely see Spinale through the darkness. He nodded, then gave him a sign indicating he was going to move down the roof.

Spinale moved to the side of the building and walked slowly toward the front of the warehouse, hugging the side of the building and remaining in the shadows.

Savoy stepped gingerly down the roof until he came to a skylight. Light emanated. Looking down into the skylight, he could see most of the building. It was partitioned into training cells. In one area, ropes dangled down from the ceiling; in another, a climbing wall; several rooms from what looked like a house, an old bus, the cockpit from an airplane; all designed to enable training in commando scenarios. A dojo stood off to the side. The building was deserted for the night. In front, behind another partition, several offices sat empty.

Savoy slowly raised the skylight. Next to the skylight, one of the climbing ropes was attached to the roof inside the building. Savoy reached out and placed his hands on the rope. He quietly climbed inside the skylight and eased his way into the space, shimmying silently down the rope, as he had been trained to do so long ago as a Ranger. He felt the familiar pressure on his fingers, the burning in his muscles that he'd initially hated, then grown used to. He descended in a whisper. At the cement floor, he stepped onto the hard ground softly. He pulled the Smith & Wesson from his holster and walked to the back of the warehouse, where he opened a door and let Spinale in.

"Let's make it quick," Savoy said as they walked to the front offices. "We may have tripped an alarm."

In the front office, they searched for any information they could find. Savoy ransacked one office while Spinale went to the computer of one of the offices he'd seen from above. He performed a simple desktop search, starting with Andreas, then Colombia, listing his search results with the most recent first. A series of recent e-mails came up. Spinale saw the word Madradora in one of the subject lines—an incoming message to Centrix, setting up the hit on Andreas and the Deltas in Cali. He then took the DNS source from the HTML and wrote it down on a piece of paper. Then, typing furiously, Spinale opened up the internal KKB security server, which he was able to access from anywhere in the world with Internet connectivity. He opened an application called Sarajevo, developed by the National Security Agency more than a decade ago, which enabled users to decode encrypted DNS addresses. He fed the encrypted address from the piece of paper into the Sarajevo entry line and hit return.

Savoy entered the office.

"In about ten seconds," said Spinale, "I will tell you the name and address of our precious mole."

"You're kidding."

They stared at the computer screen until finally the words appeared on the screen.

BUCK, VICTOR A., 17 OLD DOMINION, ALEXANDRIA, VA

"Ever heard of him?" asked Spinale.

"Oh, yeah," said Savoy, staring at the screen, nodding. "He's the NCS chief at Langley. We'll need to move quick."

43

ES CADA FARM
OUTSIDE OF HAVANA, CUBA

The terrorists were slumped over against the side of the turned-over van. Their faces were covered in blood. The shorter man's eyes had closed. He was unconscious, badly injured in the crash.

The larger man stared up at Dewey.

"What's your name?" Dewey asked.

He said nothing.

"I'll ask one more time. What's your name?"

The man didn't respond. Dewey aimed the Colt at the man. He sent a shot between the man's legs, into the ground just inches from his crotch.

"Mahmoud," said the larger man with the broken arm.

"Why are you trying to kill me?" asked Dewey.

Mahmoud coughed and blood trickled from the side of his mouth. He didn't respond. He stared back at him contemptuously.

"Are you Al-Qaeda?"

Mahmoud continued to stare. Dewey walked forward. He took the toe of his right boot and stuck it under the head of the unconscious one. He flipped the man's head backward with his foot. It bobbed limply backward. He leaned over and felt the pulse at the man's neck. He kept the Colt trained on Mahmoud as he leaned over.

"What was your friend's name?"

"Ebrahim," said Mahmoud.

Dewey reached down and searched through his pockets. He pulled out some cash and a few coins. He reached to the man's neck at a leather necklace that was wrapped around it. A small silver circle was attached to it. Dewey ripped it from the man's neck. Other than the money, that was all he found. He stared at the silver decoration on the necklace, looking for some sort of clue. After a moment, he tossed it to the ground.

Suddenly, without provocation, Dewey pulled the trigger of the Colt and sent a bullet into Mahmoud's ankle. Mahmoud let out a scream and leaned forward to grab at the wound.

"Where were you trained?" asked Dewey. "Crimea Camps? Jaffna Peninsula? Northwest Territories? Kabul? Kenya?"

Mahmoud looked up as he clutched his ankle. "Jaffna," he breathed.

"Did they teach you about torture?" asked Dewey.

Mahmoud's shrug said it all.

"What's the most effective torture?"

Mahmoud looked up at him, desperation in his eyes as blood continued to pour down his face. "Electricity," he whispered.

Dewey leaned down, next to Mahmoud, who closed his eyes. "Who's behind it?" asked Dewey, leaning forward. "What's next?"

"I can't tell you that."

"You destroyed Capitana, Savage Island. Why?"

"Why? Because we hate you, that's why."

"It doesn't make sense. These were terrible targets if you want to kill people."

"It's not about body count. It's your greed. Your way of life. The way to destroy you is by hitting the greedy Americans where they feel the most pain; in your wallet. People are casualties, that is all."

"What about the World Trade Center?"

"Al-Qaeda. I applaud them. They're my brothers. I trained with them at Jaffna. I worked for Bin Laden. But they have different goals."

"Like what?"

"You don't see us," said Mahmoud. "We're everywhere now. Already we've hit you so hard and you don't even know it."

Mahmoud leaned back, smiling. He sweated profusely, breathing hard as he tried to control the pain.

"We're everywhere. This energy project, Capitana, the dam in Canada? These were appetizers. Long Beach. Where are we going? Who knows. I don't even know. Three Mile Island; do you still think that was an accident? It wasn't. It was our first operation."

Dewey stood up and walked to the car. He leaned back against the Mercedes, next to the headlight.

He aimed the Colt at Mahmoud. He let another shot fly through the air, this time striking him in the groin. Mahmoud screamed and reached down to stem the tide of blood.

"The forty virgins won't be very happy about that one," said Dewey.

He strode forward and sent a kick into Mahmoud's stomach. Then he began the beating in earnest.

Dewey had been trained in administering torture. All special forces are; how to give it, how to receive it. Every man was different. This one took it gracefully, swallowed the pain. He was a tough one. Dewey would have to beat him hard. He'd have to break a few more bones. The problem was, he didn't have a lot of time; Mahmoud would be dead soon. He needed something, anything.

He didn't like to cause pain. Few men did. All things being equal, Dewey would've preferred to be on a beach, or reading a book, or drinking. But as he stared at Mahmoud, he knew that he had the enemy in front of him, his enemy, America's enemy. He held in his hands a piece of an extremely vital puzzle. And a cold killer to boot.

He kicked him again, this time in the chest, heard ribs crack.

"Who tried to kill Marks? Was it you?"

Mahmoud spat blood on the ground and looked up at Dewey, silent.

"A pussy like you couldn't have been the one to take down Marks. Was it him?" Dewey looked toward the dead body.

"It was me," groaned Mahmoud.

Dewey leaned back against the Mercedes.

"He was tough," whispered Mahmoud after a few moments. "Fought hard."

"But why Marks?" asked Dewey. "I can understand Capitana and Savage Island."

"He's a symbol." Mahmoud struggled to remain upright against the side of the car. Blood covered him everywhere.

"For who?"

"I can't tell you," said Mahmoud. "Even if I wanted to. Can't. Cells."

Dewey moved forward and knelt so that he was in the terrorist's face. An image of the burning oil derrick at Capitana came into his mind. He stared down at Mahmoud, thought of the World Trade Center, the images of the men and women jumping from the top of the building as the flames engulfed the upper floors, jumping rather than waiting for the heat to consume them alive.

He hadn't asked to join this war. It had found him. The enemy had accidentally pulled him in. Their shitty luck, and his, that he knew how to survive. To fight.

"You know Marks lived. You failed."

"I know."

"When I put the last bullet into your thick head it will be for him."

He grabbed Mahmoud's left hand. He took the index finger and slowly bent it back, at the knuckle in the middle of the finger until it snapped. The man screamed.

"Give me a name, a place."

Dewey snapped another finger, then another. Mahmoud screamed with each pop.

"Who is it?" yelled Dewey. He snapped Mahmoud's thumb back. Mahmoud's eyes rolled around in their sockets. He was in agony. He stared at Dewey at last.

"Notre Dame," Mahmoud blurted out. "My cell. That's all I know."

"Why?"

Mahmoud remained silent.

Dewey stared at Mahmoud. "Why Notre Dame?"

"The football stadium."

336

"Your buddy, was he there too?"

"Yes."

"How? Octanitrocubane?"

"Yes, yes. Detonator. My job is to set it. That's what we all do. Someone else has the detonators. We don't know where."

"Who?"

"Karim," he whispered. "The only one I know."

"Where is he?"

"New York City."

"Last name. What is it?"

"I don't know."

"Who's your contact?" Dewey screamed. "What's his last name?"

"Karim. That's all I know." Mahmoud remained silent. Dewey reached for his right hand. He began by snapping the middle finger. Mahmoud let out a loud yelp, then began a long, low keening, punctuated by labored gasps for air.

"What does Karim do?"

"I don't know."

Dewey grabbed the man's index finger.

"They never tell me," Mahmoud said, sobbing now.

"How do they pay you?" Dewey repeated. "How do you know he's in New York?"

Mahmoud's eyes began to fade. He was in shock.

"How do you know he's in New York?"

"He said something once, by accident. About Central Park."

Mahmoud stared at Dewey. He remained silent.

"What's the next target?" he screamed. He snapped Mahmoud's index finger.

"Soon," Mahmoud whispered. "It will happen soon. That's all I can tell you."

"What is soon?"

Tears rolled down his cheeks. "Kill me," he whispered. "Please."

"How did you get here?"

Suddenly, Mahmoud looked up, alert. His eyes looked to Dewey's right, at the ground. The cell phone.

"How did you get here?" Dewey repeated.

"Plane."

"Where is it? Is it still here?"

Despite his extensive injuries, despite the blood that now covered him, Mahmoud suddenly lunged for the phone. It was a weak move, though, which Dewey easily stopped with a hard kick to the chin, sending him backward against the car bumper.

"The plane's waiting, isn't it?" Dewey asked. "You don't need to answer. You fucking idiot."

Dewey walked back to the Mercedes. He grabbed the Colt and returned. He aimed the gun down at his head as Mahmoud's eyes followed. It was over. There would be no more revelations, not from this one. He aimed the Colt at the terrorist's chest. He pulled the trigger and sent a bullet through his heart.

He searched his pockets for anything that could help, evidence of any sort, found nothing.

He walked quickly to the Mercedes and turned the key in the ignition. He inched out and took a last look at the bloody scene. Tomorrow, some poor tobacco farmer would get the shock of his life.

He drove down the field road and beyond, back toward Havana. He drove as fast as the car would take him. He was tired, but his mind raced as he plotted his next steps.

He opened his cell phone, but had no coverage. The Mercedes had one headlight now, no windshield, was badly dented and riddled with bullets. Still, it moved. It was difficult to see as he negotiated the dark countryside. After a few minutes, he began to see ramshackle cement homes. He was getting close. He tried the cell phone again.

"Tanzer," said Jessica.

"It's Dewey."

"I thought you were out."

"They found me. Two of them. I trapped them. They're dead. I got a little info."

"What? Where are you?"

"Cuba. Get a team to Notre Dame. The football stadium."

"The stadium?"

"Yeah."

"My God—" He heard her clacking away at a keyboard. "Okay. I'll get a team out there to rip the place up. Octanitrocubane?"

"Yes, remote detonator."

"Remote detonator? All right, let me get that to my team. Hold on."

The phone clicked and Dewey drove for several seconds, waiting. Finally, Jessica returned.

"We're scrambling bomb logistics out of Indiana State Police, Quantico. Did he give any other targets?"

"No. He would have if he knew. He called himself Mahmoud. He only knew about his own cell. He mentioned a person—name of Karim—from New York City. He mentioned Three Mile Island."

"Three Mile Island?" Jessica asked incredulously.

"Yeah. Said it was their first target."

"I'm running the name Karim. Looks like there are more than three hundred in New York City alone."

Dewey kept driving. Small cement shacks turned into larger ones, clusters of homes, then shops, followed by strip malls. He was close to Havana now, on the outskirts.

"I need your help," said Dewey. "Can you tell me where the private terminal is at Jose Marti?"

"Hold on."

Dewey saw a green sign with an outline of a plane.

"Got it. That would be Terminal Two. Where are you?"

"Calzada de Bejucal, heading north."

"Okay, hold on. Got it. You want to take a left onto Vantroi. The terminal will be on your right."

"Thanks."

"What's your plan, Dewey? Why the private terminal?"

"I'm not sure. I might have something. I'll call you."

"The Cuban authorities are going to find the bodies. Am I right? Let us bring you back in. You do not want to be stuck in a Cuban prison. There won't be anything we can do."

Dewey saw the sign for Avenue Vantroi. He swung left, under the streetlight.

"I have to go." He flipped the cell phone shut.

He hung up and drove along Vantroi for half a mile, slowly now. He passed the main entrance for Terminal Two. He parked the Mercedes on a side street, next to a dark warehouse, climbed out, looked around. Vantroi was empty. To the right, down the street a few hundred yards, he could see the terminal, a long, plain cement building. Lit, but no activity. He checked the clip on his Colt, then tucked the gun into his shoulder holster. He reached down, felt for his Gerber blade tucked into his ankle sheath. He moved down the empty street toward the chain-link fence that ran around the airport.

He quickly scaled the fence. At the barbed wire strands that ran in a taut line atop the fence, he placed his hands between two wires, then leaped up, cartwheeling over the fence and falling to the ground inside the airport, rolling. He felt pain jab at his shoulder. Looking at his arm, he noticed a small trickle of blood. He reached down to his ankle and removed the knife, held it in his left hand, tucked the blade up flush against his wrist and forearm. He walked through a parking lot half filled with maintenance vehicles, security vans, fuel trucks, and food service trucks. Past a small, empty maintenance building, two stories high. He stalked in the darkness, through the lot, came around the corner of the building.

In front of him, the private terminal. The building itself was a two-story cement structure. Most of the lights were off. The planes were spread out in orderly rows in front of the building, at least thirty in all. Most were small, single-engine turboprops. In the far corner, off to the side, one plane stood out; a long, sleek black jet that Dewey recognized immediately; a Gulfstream 450.

Dewey checked his watch: 4:17 A.M.

In the distance, a large cargo plane was taking off from in front of the main terminal at the other side of the airport.

The black Gulfstream glinted under distant lamplight. Dewey moved from the corner of the darkened maintenance building to the last row of small planes in front of the Gulfstream. He moved to the far left of the line of planes, away from the terminal. He moved in a crouch down the line of small aircraft, hidden by the shadows. At the last wing set, he stopped. The Gulfstream faced the private terminal, and was set apart from the smaller, single-engine aircraft, which were parked in rows in front of the nose of the plane. The jet's door was shut. If somebody was inside the plane, they had a bird's-eye view of everything in front of them. It would be impossible to approach the plane without being seen. It would also be impossible to get inside the shut plane.

Staring for several seconds from a crouching position beneath the wing of a Cessna, Dewey could see a dim light on in the main cabin.

Turning, Dewey moved quickly back down the line of planes, then doubled back to the maintenance building. He resheathed the knife at his ankle, moved along the wall of the building. He saw a door and moved to it. He stepped back, then took three running steps, kicking the door just to the right of the knob. It crashed open, the lock block tearing out of the wooden wall and splintering the jamb to the ground. He flipped on the light, looked around. Lockers, a lunchroom. He moved to the line of lockers, opened them until he found a green uniform hanging inside one of the lockers. On the chest, in yellow letters: SEGURIDAD. He put the green button-down shirt on, then the hat that hung on another hook inside the locker. He moved to the door, turned the lights off.

He smashed a window on the driver's side of a white security van, pushed the glass out of the way, reached in and opened the door, then climbed in, ripped the plastic casing off the steering column, spliced two wires together, and started the van. He drove out of the parking lot with the van's lights off, away from the private terminal along the dark tarmac. After several hundred feet, he turned the van around, flipped a switch on the console that turned on the van's headlights. He noticed a yellow siren light on the dashboard. He flipped the switch beneath it and the light went on, flashing a bright orange light. Dewey drove quickly down the tarmac toward the Gulfstream. He swung the van in front of the Gulfstream and parked to the left, directly in front of the jet's door. He pulled the hat as far down over his forehead as he could, climbed out of the van. He started waving his arms as he walked to the door, trying to get the attention of whoever was inside. In his right hand, Dewey held up his cell phone.

Another light went on, and the face of a man appeared at the window.

"*Emergencia!*" Dewey yelled. "*Telefonazo!*"

Dewey repeated himself several times.

"*Emergencia*," Dewey repeated, waving the open phone in front of the window. He acted slightly frantic.

Finally, he heard a loud bolt click, then watched as the door popped open and slowly started to move down. It swung slowly down, coming to rest just above the black tar. In the door frame stood a middle-aged man, Arabic in appearance, semiformally dressed. His nose was badly cut.

"What is it?" asked the man.

"*Es una emergencia*," said Dewey. He stepped forward to hand him the phone. "*Un hombre está en la línea. Quiere hablar con el Señor Karim.*"

At the name Karim, the Arab dropped his arms and gestured for the phone, taking one, then two steps down the stairwell.

"Give me the phone," he demanded.

Karim took the third step, his hand extended to meet Dewey's. As he hit the third stair, Dewey lurched, grabbed his arm tight at the wrist, then yanked a vicious pull, tearing him down the stairs, but holding on. He whipped the terrorist down to the tarmac, face first, slamming him into the ground. Then he moved forcefully toward his back, no hesitation. He popped the Arab's right arm behind his back, yanked up. The bone snapped. The man screamed out in agony.

Dewey suddenly sensed movement inside the aircraft. Glancing up at the doorway, he saw the black leather boot of another man slip from the cabin into the cockpit, the pilot, he guessed. Dewey ripped the Colt from his shoulder holster, moved toward the bottom of the stairs. As the muzzle of a machine gun suddenly appeared in the door, Dewey quickly analyzed the pace of the barrel's movement, waited another half second, timed it, then crept quickly up the stairs and fired as the shooter's head appeared. Dewey's bullet ripped the left side of his skull clean off, his face a bloody wash against the walnut of the jet's minibar.

A sharp kick suddenly struck Dewey in the left knee from behind, and he fell down the stairs, rolling to the hard tarmac. It was Karim on him. The Arab, broken arm to his side, followed with another hard kick to Dewey's bad shoulder, then another kick to the right arm, which sent the .45 spiraling out of Dewey's hands to the ground. Despite sharp pain in his shoulder, Dewey stood up, only to be met with a knee in his groin, then a furious left arm strike, this time at Dewey's chin, which took a glancing blow.

Dewey struggled to gain his balance. Karim's martial skills were impressive. He had to act quickly, he knew, or the Arab would take him down.

Dewey watched as the Arab's torso started to turn, anticipating the next kick as it swung roundhouse through the air; Dewey pulled back just in time, ducking, the boot passing his head within an inch. Dewey reached to his ankle, pulled the Gerber from the sheath, and by the time the terrorist's leg was back on the ground, Dewey thrust forward, stabbing the knife blade an inch above Karim's left knee as deeply as he could thrust it, more than four inches deep, then ripped it sideways, severing all ligaments and cartilage. Karim screamed and fell to the ground, clutching the maimed knee.

Dewey pulled the Gerber from Karim's leg, took a step back, pulled the hat from his head, and picked up the Colt from the ground. The blood had started to flow in earnest from the shoulder wound, and he glanced at the fresh stream running to his elbow. He wiped the bloody knife blade on his pants.

As he lay on the ground, the Arab's left hand suddenly shot up to his mouth. Dewey lurched down at him, stomping his boot onto the arm, keeping it from the terrorist's mouth. He knelt atop the Arab's chest, his knee pressed hard against his neck. He took the Gerber blade, inserted it into the terrorist's mouth, vertically, so that the sharp part of the blade was pressed to the man's tongue, the serrated razor teeth of the upper blade against the roof of his mouth, then pushed in. The terrorist groaned. Blood suddenly streamed from the fresh cut lip, from the tongue, but the Arab's mouth was now propped open by the knife and he could not close it if he tried. Dewey reached his hand inside the open mouth, felt the molars. The top left one popped loose and Dewey removed it. Looking down, in the faint light from the cabin of the plane, Dewey saw a small white pill: cyanide.

"Don't worry, you'll die soon, Karim," said Dewey, standing back up. "Just not yet."

Dewey holstered the weapon, then dragged Karim up the stairs of the jet. He pulled him to the back of the thin aisle between the big leather seats on each side of the plane's tight cabin. Dewey flipped him over, took his left arm, the good one, and pulled it upward until it too snapped at the elbow. Karim screamed out again in pain. Dewey ripped his uniform shirt off, then tore it into strips. The first he used to tie around the Arab's mouth, drawing it tight, tying it off. The second strip he wrapped around the man's thigh, making a tourniquet to stop the blood flow from the deep gash above the knee. He then tied a third strip around Karim's good leg, at the knee, and tied it off to a piece of steel beneath the frame of a seat. He tied another around Karim's forehead, creating a tight clamp which he tied off to another piece of steel, so that he could not move. The last strip Dewey tied around his own shoulder, about the bandage, trying to stem the flow of blood from the homemade yarn suture, now ruptured. He ignored the pain. He stared for a moment longer at Karim, then turned. He dragged the dead pilot down the stairwell, pulled him to the back of the security van, then lifted him inside.

He climbed back inside the Gulfstream, waiting. He looked at his watch: 4:40 A.M. The private terminal remained lifeless. He walked back to check on Karim. Still alive, not moving. He returned to the cockpit and waited. At 4:55, he saw movement. A man exited the terminal building and walked down through the rows of aircrafts. He walked to a small, old model, white citation jet. The entrance steps to the jet suddenly came down, the man climbed the steps, entered the plane. Dewey moved. He quickly descended the Gulfstream's stairs, then sprinted toward the citation, more than a hundred yards away, its back to him as he ran. When he got to the plane, the steps were down. Dewey climbed the steps, pulling the Colt from his shoulder holster. He looked right. The cabin was empty. He ducked into the cockpit, Colt cocked to fire. A gray-haired man with a white polo shirt was sitting in the captain's chair.

"Are you the pilot?" Dewey asked as he entered the cockpit.

The man looked up, startled. "Yes," he said with a thick Spanish accent. "Who are you?"

"Come with me," said Dewey.

"Yeah, right." The pilot laughed. "Get out of here before I call airport security."

Dewey raised the Colt and aimed it at the man's head. "Stand up, do what I ask, and I won't kill you."

The pilot raised his hands. "What do you want?"

"Right now? You to shut the hell up," said Dewey. "You're flying to the United States. Once we land, I promise you'll be safe."

The man sat in the captain's chair. He was silent, and looked at Dewey with disgust.

"Let's get going," said Dewey.

"I need my first officer."

"You'll do a fine job without him," said Dewey. "Let's go. Up. *Now*."

Dewey pressed the weapon into the pilot's head as he stood. He moved it to his back, then followed him down the stairs as he descended.

"Straight ahead," said Dewey. "And before you think of screaming or running, don't. I *will* kill you."

They walked down the dark row of planes. They boarded the Gulfstream.

"I've never flown a Gulfstream," said the pilot.

"Now's your chance," said Dewey.

The man looked back down the cabin aisle, noticed Karim, tied up and bleeding; he gasped in shock.

Dewey pointed the Colt at the cockpit, encouraging him to enter. The pilot sat down in the leather captain's chair. After acclimating himself to the cabin, he turned the plane's controls on and prepared for takeoff. After a few minutes of checks, he inched the plane forward and moved across the tarmac toward the runway. He put the headset on. Dewey reached out, yanked them off.

"I need to get clearance—"

"Take off," said Dewey. "Stop fucking around."

The jet moved slowly to the end of the runway. The sky was beginning to ashen as morning approached. A faint, dark outline of ocean was visible behind hills above the airport. At the end of the runway, the pilot pushed the throttle forward and sped down the runway, blasting into the sky.

Dewey waited until they were several minutes out of Cuban airspace, then tried to call Jessica, but had no coverage. He put the headset on and turned on the radio set.

"This is an emergency," said Dewey. "I am an American flying out of Cuba and I need to speak with the FBI."

"Aircraft transmitting on guard," came the voice. "This is Miami Center. State your request."

"Can you switch me to a secure frequency?"

"Move to 132.2."

Dewey entered the new frequency, keyed the mic, then said, "My name is Dewey Andreas. I need you to do a phone patch immediately to FBI Washington, Jessica Tanzer. She is the deputy director for counter-terrorism."

"Hold, I'll need to speak with my supervisor."

"Do what you need to do. But make it quick."

Dewey waited for more than a minute. Then he heard a click in his headset.

"It's Jessica. What's going on?"

"I'm in the air, headed for New York City. I have the terrorist, Karim, in the back of the plane."

"My God, what—"

"I need you to set up a pharma team in New York," said Dewey. "Teterboro is the closest airport to the city. If that doesn't work, use Newark."

"Both airports are closed. There's a snowstorm up and down the East Coast. Whiteout conditions, the works."

"Just get a team there. You have to have one in the city, right? If not, ask CIA who they'd use if they had a situation in the area. Worst case put a team in a truck from D.C. We're going to be in the air for several hours."

"I'll get a team there," said Jessica. "Can you ask him some questions before we get him into U.S. airspace?"

"Believe me, I'd love to," said Dewey, looking to the back of the cabin. "Me interrogating him won't do any good. He tried to swallow a cyanide pill he had jammed in a tooth; he's not going to respond, in my opinion, to pain. I'll end up killing him, which is exactly what he wants."

"Got it. Let me go to work. Keep the headset on."

"I also need you to clear us through customs, FAA, et cetera."

"I'll handle that," said Jessica. "I'll clear you through to Teterboro. I'll head up there too. Tell your pilot the weather is horrible. Teterboro, JFK, Newark, and La Guardia are all shut down because of the blizzard."

"Right," said Dewey, glancing over at the pilot, whose forehead ran with sweat. He looked back at Dewey, fear in his eyes. "Better get them to plow the runway."

"I'll make sure they're ready to plow when you're close."

"What about Indiana?" Dewey asked.

"They found something in a locker. Belongs to a worker named Mahmoud. Probably your Mahmoud. He's been at Notre Dame for almost six years. Maintenance guy. I'll know more in a little while."

"Got it disarmed yet?"

"No."

Dewey stared out the window. The sky was beginning to lighten. The ocean was a dark black carpet for as far as he could see. Far, far off in the distance, he could see the beginning edge of coastline. It would be the first time he'd been inside the United States since he left more than a decade ago. He felt a tightness in his stomach—and then the warm rush of adrenaline he needed.

44

NOTRE DAME STADIUM
SOUTH BEND, INDIANA

The small team of bomb experts had gathered just outside the large, basement-level suite of rooms that served as the maintenance facility for Notre Dame Stadium. John Banker, head of the FBI munitions team, the "Bomb Squad," as it was called, had been rushed to South Bend. Banker and one of his deputies, Stella Galloway, had just begun to carefully disassemble Mahmoud's locker.

Banker faced several tough decisions. They could detonate the bomb remotely. They also could bring in one of the FBI's bomb "robots" and attempt to defuse the bomb by remote control, from a safe distance. But Banker was old-school. He knew the greatest chance of successfully defusing the bomb, given the amount of time, was to do it himself, even though the stakes were considerably higher. Besides, based on what they saw at Long Beach, detonating the bomb remotely was not an option. There was no such thing as a "remote" detonation when the result would mean the destruction of one of the country's most famous athletic facilities and Lord knows how much of the university itself.

Banker ordered the other munitions experts who had arrived on scene, many of whom he'd never met before, to leave the facility. To a

man, they all refused to leave. Even John Garvey, the head of maintenance for the stadium, refused to leave the building.

Banker and Galloway didn't bother putting on protective gear; it
wouldn't have mattered.

As the gathered group watched, only Banker knew the true import
of the situation. Jessica had briefed him on his way to South Bend. Dewey
Andreas had tortured the information out of Mahmoud just a few hours
ago, but time was passing quickly. If there was any sort of set check-in
time between Mahmoud and his bosses, and Mahmoud didn't make
contact, the bomb could be set off remotely.

Banker now noticed a faint gasoline aroma wafting up from the removed floor of the locker, a smell most casual observers would never
have noticed.

Beneath the floor plate of the locker, Banker shined a light on what
looked like a spongy, clear pillow of material. It was mashed down and
completely filled the two-by-four-foot space.

On one side of it sat what looked like two stainless steel tubes within
a glass cylinder, a pair of small red wires sticking up into the air.

"Bingo," Banker said quietly, handing the light to Galloway. He
reached down and pulled the cellular trigger from the octanitrocubane.

45

Sergeant Greer Osborne from the Reno Sheriff's Office climbed out of the van. In his left hand, he held a letter-sized FedEx envelope. K-9 was painted on the back door of the vehicle, and Osborne glanced quickly at it. He opened the back door to the van.

"Okay, Maude, come on, honey."

A large, black and brown German shepherd jumped out of the back of the van, then sat and looked up at Osborne. He clipped the leather leash to the dog's collar. As the dog sat obediently looking up at Osborne, he pulled a small Ziploc bag from the FedEx envelope. Inside the Ziploc bag, Osborne withdrew a small swatch of cloth. He held it up in front of the dog's snout for a few seconds, then put it back in the bag.

"Let's find us some . . . octo . . . oh, hell, whatever the fuck it's called, some explosives, huh, sugar?"

Osborne put the FedEx envelope back in the front of the van, then walked with Maude toward the front door of the facility.

The Reno UPS Distribution Center was a massive warehouse that bordered the Reno Airport. Nearly six million packages shipped through the center every day, packages that came in lots from all over the country, then were broken down for shipment to locations in Nevada, California, Arizona, Oregon, Washington, and Hawaii. Hundreds of flatbed trailers were lined up in the parking lot that ran for as far as the eye could see.

Osborne entered through the front door and was met by the center's general manager, Sally McDonald.

"Hi, Greer," she said as he walked in the door, shaking his hand. "And who's this?"

"This is Maude," said Osborne.

"May I pet her?" asked McDonald.

"'Course you can."

McDonald led Osborne through the small lobby and into the enormous warehouse. The scene was chaotic. Thousands of pallets loaded with packages were stacked everywhere, netting wrapped around them. Osborne counted more than twenty forklifts moving in seemingly random directions, lifting pallets and moving them toward the docking doors at the side of the building.

"What are you guys looking for?" asked McDonald. But her expression told Osborne that—like most Americans these days—she had little problem imagining the worst possible threats popping up in the least likely places.

"Needle in a haystack," said Osborne.

"Right." McDonald nodded nervously. "Will I be down for a while?"

"Hopefully not. Maybe an hour."

McDonald nodded again, then moved to the wall. She reached above a set of light switches to a large, yellow button. She pressed the button. Immediately, the warehouse was bathed in orange light. The traffic of forklifts suddenly ceased. Workers looked back toward the door where McDonald stood. Next to the yellow button, she pressed an intercom button.

"Take a break, everyone," McDonald said, her voice booming over the warehouse intercom. "See you in one hour."

Osborne led Maude down the wide aisle nearest the wall of the facility. On both sides of the aisle, pallets of cardboard packages wrapped in red netting were stacked neatly, reaching to nearly the ceiling.

The UPS distribution center was the third facility they had visited that day, the others being the FedEx facility down on the far side of the airport and a U.S. Postal Service distribution center also near the airport. Those visits had turned up nothing, but this time, as they reached the midpoint of the first aisle, Maude began to act fidgety, pulling at the leash. When Osborne tried to calm the dog, she suddenly started barking. She pulled him toward the next aisle, past pallets of boxes, barking. He let her lead him. Soon, the dog seemed frenzied. They moved quickly toward the next aisle. He unclipped her leash and the dog dashed until she came to one of the pallets, stacked, like the others, in boxes that were wrapped in red plastic netting. Suddenly Maude stopped, but she continued barking.

Sergeant Osborne caught up to the dog.

"*Control*," he ordered. Maude immediately stopped barking. Osborne reached down and gave the German shepherd a quick pat on her shoulders. "Good girl," he said.

Osborne took his radio from his belt.

"Reno five, this is Osborne."

"Go ahead, Greer," came the male voice on the radio.

"I'm at UPS," he said, moving slowly toward the stack of cardboard boxes. "I think I might have something."

The early snowflakes from the front edge of the approaching snowstorm had just begun to fall on the city. Jessica stood by her window, staring out at the city. The slowly falling snow made the city seem peaceful and hushed. She sipped her coffee cup.

Suddenly, the intercom on her phone chimed. She stepped to her desk, hit the button.

"Yeah," she said.

"It's T. J. You've got me, Barnett, Tony, and Tom."

"Go."

"We got something."

"What?"

"Octanitrocubane. In a box at a UPS DC in Reno. Bomb dog sniffed it out."

"Good work," said Jessica. "Where's the package from?"

"Jordan. It's going to a P.O. box in Brunswick, Maine."

"Let Portland regional—"

"Already done. The P.O. box is rented by a guy who pays in cash. They're going to set up a sting. Unfortunately, there's no contact info on the guy."

"Okay," said Jessica. "We should do a sketch anyway."

"Yeah, we'll try. Nobody can remember exactly what the person looks like. There are more than five hundred boxes at the place."

"What about the package?"

"We need your authorization to open it up. I assume it's okay."

"No, don't assume that. These guys are hitting randomly. What if their target is the DC itself? Probably not. But I am uncomfortable giving you that authorization. Make sure there's no trigger."

"You're right," said Barnett Williams, the FBI's West Coast field director.

"Nearest bomb squad is in Las Vegas," said Jessica. "They should be able to get over there within the hour."

"Okay, let me run that," said Williams.

"Hold on," said Jessica. "Who's running Maine?"

"Shelly."

"Patch her in," said Jessica. She began to pack her briefcase. Her phone clicked several times. Then a voice.

"Shelly Martini."

"Shelly, it's Jessica along with the working group."

"Hi, Jess, guys."

"Where are you?" asked Jessica.

"I'm at the store in Brunswick. Good news and bad news."

"What's the bad news?" asked Jessica.

"He pays in cash. No name, no contact information."

"And the good news?"

"We have some prints. On the box. I'm scanning them to Quantico as we speak."

"Okay. I want to run hard at end target prevention here," said Jessica. "I want every dog that's been trained from Boston north up there

ASAP. Triage starting geographically, Portland, Freeport, Brunswick, Bath. Hit all industrial facilities and other key landmarks. Is there a refinery up there somewhere? Let's look at fuel depots and major manufacturers. Also, universities and colleges, and L.L. Bean, while we're at it. Oh, and Bath Iron Works. You get the idea. Scour the area, especially the coast. I'd look as far south as Portland and up to—"

"I understand," said Martini.

"How many people do you have up there?" asked Jessica.

"Four at the storefront," said Martini. "I'm keeping it thin. I don't want to scare them away. Another dozen in the field, waiting for my orders."

"Good. Get them moving. I want Boston to redirect some people up there as well. Who's got that?"

"I do," said T. J. Chatterjee.

"Let's win one here for the good guys," said Jessica. "And send me the name and number of that cop in Reno—I'm going to have Lou give him a call to thank him."

46

FORTUNA'S APARTMENT

Fortuna leaned against the bathroom door. He rubbed the space between his eyes in silence. Finally, he smacked a fist into his palm.

I should have gone.

Karim had gone incommunicado, something that would only have happened if he were taken, or dead. What if Cuban authorities had caught them? What if Andreas had killed Mahmoud, his partner, and Karim in Cuba? He had to think—and quickly.

He paced back and forth across the carpet in front of a window that overlooked Central Park. Finally, he went to the fireplace. Beneath a large painting of two naked women, done by Caravaggio, sat a long rectangular ivory box. Of course, he should've done it sooner. Fortuna opened the box and stared for a few moments at the detonator. He picked it up, pressed in the code for Notre Dame Stadium, Mahmoud's cell.

He walked down the hallway to his office. Once inside, he closed the doors and flipped a switch on the wall that created a low-frequency background noise that rendered any conversation he might have inaudible to any electronic eavesdroppers.

He dialed, heard a series of clicks, then punched in a ten-digit number. After a few moments, the phone rang again.

"Buck."

"It's me."

"Did you send someone to Castroville?"

"Yes. There's a problem."

"A problem?"

"Yes. We haven't heard from them. It's been nearly eight hours."

"That's not good," said Buck. "What do you want from me?"

"Information."

"I'll do what I can and call you back. But I want something. A promise."

"What? You want me to release you?"

"Yes. They're getting closer. The noose is tightening."

"I'll consider it."

"Well, when you're done considering, let me know. And if the answer is yes, I'll get you the information you want."

"Fine. Get the information, then go."

Fortuna's throat tightened for a moment; he felt fear. He went to his room and changed into his running gear, then hit the gym. He ran a relaxed five miles with Fox News on the large flat screen on the wall. He waited for the news from Notre Dame. How long could it take for the national networks to pick it up? When he finished, he returned to his room, took a shower, and got dressed. His cell phone rang.

"What?"

"It's me. Your men are dead. Some farmer found them in a tobacco field. One was tortured."

"How many?"

"Two. Both young Arabs."

He breathed a slight sigh of relief, knowing that it meant Karim was still alive. Still, the thought of a highly trained operative like Mahmoud being eliminated said much about their quarry.

"Alex?"

"I heard you."

"Andreas just made hamburger out of your men, so you gotta figure he's really pissed now, as well as informed."

"Don't tell me what I already know," said Fortuna. "Tell me how you're going to kill him."

356

"Look," said Buck. "It wouldn't surprise me in the least if I got arrested here. I'm going to get the hell out of Dodge—real soon—and you'd better too. You know why? They just sent a small army out to Notre Dame. Was that your next target?"

Fortuna's silence confirmed it.

"Well, they stopped it. They found the material, the detonator, everything."

Fortuna stared out the window, still silent. He thought about Karim.

"You're getting perilously close to fucking this whole thing up," added Buck. "If I were you I would do what I am about to do. Disappear. How many billions do you have salted away, after all?"

"I'm not going to run," said Fortuna. "Notre Dame was a single cell. Obviously Andreas broke my man in Cuba. But that is where the trail ends."

"If they know Notre Dame was a target they'll rapidly ID your guys there. Whatever alias he was using, they'll find him. It will take a trained FBI screener less than half an hour to pinpoint the employee. Within an hour, they will have ransacked the guy's apartment, house, whatever. Then all bets are off. You better hope your protocols hold up; however you designed the cash flows, the communications, everything, if it wasn't segmented perfectly they'll be onto you by morning."

"What about Andreas? What's his status? Can you get him?"

"Like I said, I'm cut off. I have no idea. He's running free, as far as I know. You should too, while you still can. Forget about Andreas. Get out."

"Spoken like a true American. I don't have that luxury."

"Whatever. But if that remaining eighty-five million dollars isn't in my Prominvest account by noon, remember: I might accidentally e-mail your name to someone at the FBI."

The phone clicked as Buck hung up. Fortuna stood at the window for what seemed like an eternity. There were dark storm clouds over the city, and snow fell in thick blankets across Central Park, which he could barely see even though he was only a block away.

Fortuna dialed Karim again. No answer.

47

TETERBORO AIRPORT
TETERBORO, NEW JERSEY

The Gulfstream began its approach into the New York metropolitan area. Dewey stared at the weather radar map on the console, seeing nothing but a bright yellow blob across the entire sky. Above the clouds, at 41,000 feet, sunlight reflected off the jet. Soon, he knew, they would need to descend into the hell that was the weather below.

The FAA had assigned a team out of New York regional to assist the pilot, Manuel, in getting the plane through the weather and down on the ground. The group included two experienced flight engineers from Gulfstream, who gave Manuel a quick tutorial on the jet's sophisticated navigation system. He would need that to land the plane in what was zero-visibility conditions on the ground at Teterboro.

Dewey had explained to Manuel the fact that he worked with the government and that the man in back was a terrorist. Dewey had thought the knowledge of the FBI being behind his actions might calm Manuel down, knowing that he was not going to harm him once they landed. But the knowledge seemed to have the opposite effect; Manuel's level of stress seemed to grow with every passing minute.

Dewey had checked on Karim twice. His mangled knee was clearly beyond repair. If the government allowed him to live, he would never walk normally again, Dewey guessed. He'd changed the terrorist's tourniquet twice. But he didn't put a bandage on it, or give him pain-killers, even though the plane had a decent first-aid kit. Dewey wanted Karim to survive long enough to make it to the coming interrogation; he didn't care about much else, though. For his part, Karim kept relatively quiet for the amount of pain he was suffering. A few moans when Dewey changed the tourniquet, but that was it. It was obvious to Dewey that Karim had been well trained in pain attenuation.

As they came within a hundred miles of Teterboro, Dewey checked once again on Karim. He'd never seen eyes more black and angry in his life. The wound appeared to be going septic, so he poured some peroxide into the open gash, which caused Karim to kick weakly.

When Dewey returned to the cockpit, the Gulfstream suddenly began its approach, and he had to grab the door jamb to keep from falling over. As he climbed back into his seat, he noticed the dank smell of perspiration. Manuel was completely soaked through his shirt, and sweat poured from his forehead and face. He had a look of terror on his face as he spoke to FAA on the mic. Dewey put his headset back on and listened in.

"But how?" Manuel asked, fear in his voice. "If it is falling like that—"

"Manuel," said the voice, a woman from the FAA named Margaret Giessen, "you need to calm down. The runway is plowed, sanded, and ready for you to bring the plane down."

"But the accumulation's so quick. Eight inches an hour—"

"Is a lot of snow," agreed Margaret. "But you will make it through fine."

Dewey reached out, grabbed Manuel's headset and yanked it from his head.

"Listen to me," said Dewey. "You're going to land this plane fine. Stop whining and think about flying, got it?"

"I didn't ask for this," pleaded Manuel. "I fly tourists around Cuba."

"Tough shit. You don't have another option. If we don't make it, at least go down like a fucking hero."

Suddenly, the Gulfstream was inside the thick white of the snow and the windows went blank, the tinkling sound of ice against the window like a wind chime in a hurricane. Even Dewey had to grip the side of the chair to remain calm.

Still, he reached out and patted Manuel on the shoulder. "What's your favorite food, Manuel?"

"Lobster."

"Good. I'm from Maine. I know lobster. I'll tell you what. After we land, I'll make sure someone takes you to the best seafood place in New York City. How's that?"

Manuel forced a grin. "Okay, okay. Let me land it now, huh?"

"Attaboy."

"Approach, I have intercepted the localizer course," said Manuel, visibly calmer, headset back on. "I need you to confirm my altitude. I know what it is but I have no concept of whether it's correct or not."

"The system will tell you," said a male voice, one of the Gulfstream engineers. "It has the approach programmed in."

"I know, I know. I just would also like the added confirm."

"Roger," said Margaret. "You're at two thousand, descending at three-hundred feet per minute."

The plane's front window was completely white. Wet snow roiled the glass. The feeling was like being underwater. All they could see was white pounding at the window ferociously.

"On course," said Margaret. "Below glidescope."

Manuel pulled back the control column.

"Manuel, on course, below glidescope," said Margaret. "Now. I need you to pull that nose up. Okay, that's it. One mile touchdown."

Dewey shut his eyes, preferring the blackness to the white blindness of the snow. Then, suddenly, the wheels touched down, a violent bounce, another touchdown, then a wild skid until finally the Gulfstream was halted somewhere on the snow-covered tarmac.

"Nice landing," Dewey said to Manuel as he stood. "Stay here, they'll send someone to get you."

Dewey popped the stairs and a uniformed team of FBI agents climbed aboard. They placed Karim on a stretcher, secured his arms and legs with nylon straps, then carried him down the steps of the Gulfstream. One of the agents looked down at the eviscerated knee of the terrorist, then glanced up at Dewey. Dewey did not acknowledge the look. Another agent handed Dewey a phone.

"Andreas," he said.

"It's me," said Jessica. "I've given the team commander up there orders to give you access to everything."

"Where are you?"

"I'm leaving my office. I need to run by my house, then I have a chopper set to take me to New York, depending on the weather."

Dewey followed the team carrying Karim, walking through the driving snow. He climbed into the back of the ambulance. They moved quickly down the snow-covered tarmac to the terminal.

"I want to be part of the team that moves on Karim's information."

"I'm not sure I can do that. You might be fully capable but the problem, as you know, is that you will invariably have different protocols, movement commands, et cetera. I don't want someone getting shot."

"We're in this position because of my actions," said Dewey. "I'm going with the team. It's that simple."

At the terminal, a line of FBI agents stood outside the door, automatic weapons—HK UMPs—out and prepared to fire. Four black Suburbans and three long vans idled, loaded with teams of tactical assault specialists, waiting for information that would hopefully come from the terrorist.

Karim was carried down the line to the glass doors of the terminal.

"I'll think about it," said Jessica. "I know we're here because of you. Have they started the pharma sequence?"

Inside, the terminal was empty, except for an area to the left, against a far wall. It looked like an operating room. Klieg lights, four in all, were on steel stanchions that stood twenty feet high at an outer perimeter, cranked on, creating a canopy of bright white light. They illuminated a large, rectangular stainless steel operating room table. Next to the table, another table held a variety of bottles, syringes, and instruments. Two

IV bags were hanging on racks next to the operating table. A pair of monitors sat on wheeled racks. Two video cameras were on tripods next to the foot of the steel O.R. table. Two nurses in blue uniforms stood next to the operating table, between them, a short, gaunt man.

"We just walked in," said Dewey. "I see Dr. Kevorkian though."

"Bismarck," said Jessica.

Dewey shut the phone and walked to the interrogation frame. He joined a small line of agents and a few suited FBI men, who stood to the right of the area, observing in silence.

The agents lifted Karim from the gurney, placed him on the steel table, strapped him down. Bismarck looked quickly at the terrorist, moving both eyelids back as the nurses ripped off the shirt and strapped monitoring probes onto his chest, then an IV into his left arm. In the bright lights, the sight of Karim's extensive blood loss was obvious. His face appeared gray and wet with perspiration. One of the nurses looked briefly at the leg wound, but did nothing. She did a fingerprint set, then handed them to an agent, who left the area.

Bismarck took a scalpel from the side table, severed the strip of green shirt cloth Dewey had tied around his mouth. Karim stretched his jaw, then suddenly spit squarely in Bismarck's face.

"You're all going to die!" screamed Karim, his voice hoarse. "I will not talk!"

Bismarck turned calmly to the table and picked up a small white towel, wiped his face. He nodded to an agent next to Dewey, who moved to the table. Karim continued to scream.

"Three seconds," Bismarck said, holding up three fingers.

The agent pulled a Taser from his belt, then moved it against the terrorist's neck and pulled the trigger. He held it for a three count. Karim screamed the entire time, even managing to spit again, this time hitting the agent. The agent sent another round of voltage through Karim. When the agent stopped after the second three count, Karim again began screaming.

"Fuckers! Kill me! You think I haven't felt this before!" He spat again at the agent, hitting him this time in the chest. The agent moved but Bismarck turned and held up his hand, stepped to the terrorist's side.

Like a knife blade, he stabbed a needle into his neck, then pushed it in. Suddenly, Karim stopped screaming. His eyes moved back into his head, and his chest and head convulsed in spasms that rocked the steel table. After a pregnant second, he screamed at a decibel level Dewey thought might crack the terminal windows.

Bismarck moved to one of the monitors and looked at it for a few moments as Karim continued to wail in pain. Finally, when the screaming stopped, Bismarck moved to the prisoner. He stood next to Karim's head.

"We're going to get along a lot better if you don't do that," said Bismarck.

Karim panted, trying to catch his breath. He looked up for several seconds, then spat again, hitting Bismarck in the face. Again Bismarck emptied a syringe into his neck, and again Karim's eyes moved back in his head, followed by screams that shook the terminal.

Dewey stepped forward. "You're going to kill him," he barked at Bismarck. "We need him alive."

An agent stepped in front of Dewey.

Bismarck turned.

"Andreas? Is that right? Let me do my job and keep quiet or I'll ask these gentlemen to escort you out."

Bismarck checked the monitors again. He whispered something to one of the nurses, who injected a syringe into the IV at Karim's forearm.

Bismarck moved to the table again. He picked up a small, thin syringe.

"This will make you feel better," said Bismarck to Karim. "This is something called Tocinare. It's a psychotropic. It will not cause you pain. I don't want to hurt you. We just want some answers. You understand?"

"I won't talk," said Karim, strangely serene this time. "I was trained at Crimea. I have received this drug before. You waste your time."

"Trust me, you haven't tried this one."

Bismarck inserted the needle into the IV line, at the forearm. Suddenly, Karim's eyes shut. They remained shut for more than a minute.

His body relaxed, limp on the table. Bismarck moved to the monitor, checked it. After what seemed like an eternity, the terrorist's eyes opened.

"Feel good?" asked Bismarck. "I thought you'd like that."

"It feels good," said Karim. He shut his eyes again, this time for more than two minutes. Finally, Bismarck stepped from the monitors. He took hold of one of Karim's ears, shook it. Karim opened his eyes.

"You might have received Pentothal," said Bismarck. "Trust me, you haven't received what I just injected in your arm."

"Okay. It feels warm. Is it snowing?"

"Yes, it is. Do you like the snow?"

"No. I don't."

"What's your name?"

"Karim."

"Where are you from, Karim?"

"Saudi Arabia. Al-Khobar, near Dhahran."

"Family?"

"A sister, mother. My father died in the war against Russia."

"Afghanistan?"

"Yes."

"Did he work Ghawar?"

"Yes. He was a petroleum engineer."

"Karim, did you help to destroy Capitana?"

Karim remained silent. His arm twitched and he suddenly shut his eyes.

"Karim, can you answer me? Did you help to destroy the oil rig?"

"Yes."

"What about the dam? Savage Island?"

"Yes, that too."

"Long Beach?"

Karim shut his eyes again.

"Long Beach?" asked Bismarck, a hint of urgency in his voice.

Karim remained silent.

"Karim, I'm wondering about Long Beach. Can you help me on that one, my friend? Did you have something to do with it? Did you plan it?"

Karim opened his eyes. He looked alert. His lips quivered ever so slightly, but no words came out.

"I'm going to give you a different drug, if you don't talk. It will make the feeling from the first drug go away. Do you understand? It will hurt. It will hurt more than the drug before, the one that hurt. It will hurt a lot more than that."

"Don't make it go away," said Karim.

"Answer me."

"Yes, Long Beach."

Bismarck put his hand on the small needle, still dangling out of the IV at the terrorist's forearm. He pressed it in, then removed it. Karim's eyes shut, this time for several minutes. Bismarck again checked the monitors. He took another needle from the table behind him, returned, then shook Karim's ear again, as if to wake him.

"Feel good?"

"Yes."

"Can you help me with some other questions? Just basic information?"

"Yes, I will try."

"Where do you live now?"

"Manhattan. An apartment."

"Are there other attacks planned?"

"Yes, yes, of course."

"Many?"

"Yes. Many."

"How many?"

"Forty-one."

"All at once? One at a time?"

"All at once."

"Detonator? Suicide?"

"Both. Remote detonator unless we are in danger, then we set them off. We all know how."

"Where is the detonator?"

Karim's eyes grew alert. His lips quivered again, but no sound.

"Where is it, Karim?"

"No. I cannot say."

"Where is it?"

"You can't stop it now. We're not trying to kill people. Infrastructure."

"Yes, we figured that out, Karim. I need to know where the detonator is."

"Which one?"

"How many are there?"

Karim's chest suddenly convulsed. He squinted his eyes shut. "No," he whispered.

"How many?"

"Two."

"Are you the leader?"

Again, no answer.

"What is the name of your leader?"

Karim remained silent. Bismarck held the new needle up in front of Karim's eyes.

"Here comes that different drug now. You've left me no choice, Karim. It's going to make the warm feeling from the first drug go away."

"Please, no. I will tell you."

"Who is your leader?"

Karim's lips moved again, no words. He shut his eyes. Tears ran down his cheeks.

Bismarck stuck the small needle in the IV at the forearm. Suddenly, Karim began to convulse wildly, foaming at the mouth. He pushed his head up, against his restraints, banging his skull back down on the steel of the table. He repeated this several times, screaming in agony. Veins bulged at his forehead. He continued screaming and thrashing about for more than a minute. Bismarck watched the monitors. After nearly two minutes, Karim tired but still convulsed. Bismarck moved back, took another needle, stuck it into the IV. Suddenly, Karim's eyes returned to the back of his head, then closed. Bismarck gave him less than thirty seconds before he shook him by the ear.

"Most people are under the belief that a reliable truth serum exists," said Bismarck, looking down into Karim's now-tranquil eyes. "In point of fact, it's not true. What I've always found to be more, shall we say . . . reliable, is the effective interchange of pain and pleasure; in this case a synthetic mixture of oxytocin and heroin, which is what you seem to be enjoying at the moment, and xylene, something most commonly found in lawn fertilizer. Clearly you don't enjoy that one very much, Karim."

Karim stared up at Bismarck, completely helpless. Tears streamed down his cheeks. His eyelids drooped, then shut. Bismarck shook the Arab by the ear again.

"Tell me, Karim, how long have you lived in the United States?"

"Nearly twenty years."

"And has anyone ever tried to kill you?"

"No."

"Nobody?"

"No."

"So do you think it's very kind of you to hurt our country?"

"No."

"Do you know how many people you killed yesterday at Long Beach."

"Yes, I do. Two thousand, one hundred, and something."

"Two thousand, seven hundred, and seventy-one people."

"Yes."

"How many detonators are there?"

"Two."

"Where are they?"

"The apartment. The beach house."

"Where in the apartment? Desk? Kitchen?"

"In an ivory box, above the fireplace."

"Where's the apartment?"

"In Manhattan."

"SoHo? Upper East Side? Harlem?"

"Please kill me. I won't harm anyone anymore."

"What is the address?" Bismarck asked, anger in his voice. "*Where is the detonator?*"

"No," Karim whispered.

"Who is your leader?"

Karim shut his eyes. He kept them closed, even as Bismarck shook his ear.

"You've left me without a choice," said Bismarck calmly, nodding at one of the nurses, who handed him another syringe. "I'm going to make the warmth go away again, Karim. This will hurt. I don't have to do it, though. It's your choice. Will you tell me now? What is the address?"

Karim started sobbing uncontrollably, like a child, tears streaming down his cheeks. Bismarck thrust the needle into the IV at his forearm. Again the convulsions began. Karim's head slammed into the steel, up and down, slamming hard. Soon, blood appeared under his head and started a slow drip from the stainless steel onto the terminal floor. His chest arched upward. And the screams came again, terrifying screams, hoarse and savage. Bismarck moved to the monitor while he let the terrorist convulse on the table in pain.

Dewey, from the side of the frame, stood watching, mesmerized, sickened. He felt like he was watching a young boy with a housefly, slowly ripping its wings off. But this was no housefly, he reminded himself. Inside this man's head lay the key to stopping untold damage, the key to saving countless lives. If they had to rip his wings off to prevent the deaths of more Americans, so be it. He glanced at the other agents; they too looked stunned.

Bismarck allowed the terrorist to scream for another minute, then stuck another needle into his arm, which calmed him. His fast-paced breathing continued. Bismarck pushed the needle in. Karim's head fell silently to the side. Blood continued to pour from the steel O.R. table. One of the nurses lifted the supine head, placed a towel beneath the skull to catch the blood. His skull moved now like the head of a doll, seemingly almost detached from the body. Bismarck checked the monitor. Then he returned to Karim's side. He tugged at his ear. There was no response. He tugged again.

"You're losing him!" shouted Dewey. "He's all we have. Don't kill him."

"I told you to keep quiet," said Bismarck between clenched teeth, not even looking up.

Bismarck turned, pulled Karim's ear again. Slowly, his eyelids opened.

"There we are," said Bismarck. "Are you ready to answer some questions now?"

Karim's skin appeared almost blue under the light. His eyes were opened less than a quarter way. His face was covered in sweat and tears.

"Just one question, that's all. Who's the leader? What's his name?"

Karim's eyes fluttered.

"Goodbye," he whispered.

The monitor sounded a high-pitched monotone; flatline, as Karim's heart ceased functioning.

Dewey moved forward. When the agent to his right attempted to stop him, placing his leg out in front of him, then reaching for him with his hands, Dewey pushed him out of the way.

"You killed him," growled Dewey as he reached the steel table and began pounding Karim's chest, desperately trying to revive the terrorist. Two agents quickly grabbed him from either side, pulled him back.

"You fucking butcher," said Dewey, struggling to free himself from the agents, who held him at the biceps. "He was all we had."

"He was trained," said Bismarck. "There is no drug that will work if someone wants to die."

Dewey turned. The agents' grips loosened. He looked around the room, at the nurses and other agents. No one said anything.

What would've happened had Dewey done the interrogation himself, *his* way? He would never know. He walked toward the terminal door and out into the blinding snow.

48

Hector Calibrisi sat staring at the computer screen, mesmerized. On the screen, the picture showed a sidewalk running in front of a simple but pretty white Colonial. Calibrisi was watching the video for the ninth time in a row. Suddenly, on the screen, a man emerged from the front door of the house. He walked down the steps of the house, then toward the camera. The camera was out of view, the size of a gumdrop, attached to the telephone pole. The man walked down the brick walkway, then took a left and went out of camera range.

After the man disappeared, Calibrisi turned to the woman whose computer it was. "Play it again, will you?"

"Sure," said Ashley Bean, rolling her eyes.

She clicked the icon on the screen, rewinding the short clip. When the video was at the point just before the man left the house, she played it again.

"Is that Buck?" Bean asked.

"Yes," said Calibrisi. "Our mole."

"Are you sure?"

"No, of course I'm not sure," said Calibrisi. "But he's all we've got at the moment."

"Why do you keep watching the same clip over and over?"

"I don't know. There's something about it. It's just bothering me. Play yesterday's clip again."

Bean clicked an icon in the corner of the screen, displaying precisely the same scene, of Buck walking down the brick walk in front of his house. Other than the color of his suit, which today was gray, and the day before dark blue, it was hard to see a difference between the two sequences.

"Play today's one more time," said Calibrisi. "Humor me."

Bean again clicked the video from that morning. Calibrisi watched it for the eleventh time.

"I don't know why, but there's something wrong today," said Calibrisi. "One more time, Ash."

Jessica handed the cabbie a twenty-dollar bill, then climbed out of the cab. She had completely lost track of time, so consumed by the crisis, stuck at FBI headquarters for so many days on end. The cold air felt good against her legs. She walked up Wisconsin Avenue for two blocks, then took a right. She had not been home for two days. She did not own any pets, so she didn't actually need to go home. Still, she wanted to take a shower in her own shower, water her own plants, and get her own mail. She also wanted to grab a few changes of clothing; who knows when she would be back.

The sky in Georgetown was overcast. Big brass streetlights lit up the brick sidewalks, storefronts, and town houses. A rare Washington snowstorm was on its way. The winds had begun to pick up. She turned onto Twenty-fourth Street, passing Standard Bakery. The smell of fresh-baked bread wafted out. In the morning, when she was home, Jessica would roll out of bed and walk down and buy a coffee and raspberry muffin. She didn't have time right now.

Jessica lived in a brick, three-story town house in a quiet neighborhood of Georgetown, just off Wisconsin Avenue. The house was built in 1864, and still had its original floorboards, windows, and overall character. As she walked down Twenty-fourth Street, she smiled. She loved Georgetown, loved her neighborhood and street. Its familiarity—brass lanterns, brick fronts, black doors—let her escape the events of the past few days: Long Beach, Capitana, Savage Island. They dominated her thoughts almost constantly. For a few brief seconds, she thought about her neighborhood, the ordered line of town houses, the simple beauty of the thin, cobblestone street. She let herself drift away, if only for a few stolen moments.

She came to the front of her house, #88. She inserted the big silver key into the front door, turned the lock, then pushed the big, black-painted wooden door in. There, on the ground, was a pile of catalogues, envelopes, and mail. She stepped inside, shut the door behind her. She didn't have much time, one hour, before she had to catch the helicopter to New York City.

Vic Buck stared at the photograph on the wall, transfixed. The black-and-white photo showed a sailboat tipped nearly perpendicular. A fierce wind filled the large sail and pushed the sloop nearly horizontal. Perched out over the water, strapped into harnesses, two teenage girls leaned back. Behind the boat, the ocean was a choppy black, interrupted by white-caps. The girls smiled as they tore through the water.

Buck did not show any emotion as he stared at the photograph. In fact, Buck no longer saw the photograph. After a full minute of staring at it, he had stopped seeing sailboat, ocean, and teenage girls. What he saw, instead, was a beach, and an image of himself on that beach. It was the image that had been etched into his mind for ten long years now. It was the picture of himself in the future, after this whole ugly business was done and over. It was getting closer now, he felt it. He could almost taste it. But he also felt it slipping away.

Suddenly, he was awakened from his silent contemplation by the sound of a key in a lock. It came from downstairs. He continued to stare at the photograph for another few seconds. His focus returned to the image in front of his eyes. The girl on the left, he had no idea who she was, long blond hair, heavyset. But the girl on the right, the one with the smile, that one was obvious; short, auburn hair, tanned, face covered in freckles, adorable. He stared at the girl for another second or two.

He reached down, pulled the leather glove on his left hand tighter, then did the same with his right. He reached up, pulled the ski mask down from his forehead so that it now covered his face, except for the two eye-holes.

Finally, he reached to his left armpit, pulled the Glock 36 from the nylon shoulder holster. Calmly, he reached for the black steel silencer in the right pocket of his down coat. Without looking, as he continued to stare at the black-and-white photograph of Jessica Tanzer, sailing one summer day long ago, he screwed the silencer onto the muzzle of his semiautomatic weapon.

When he heard the door shut, he turned. He moved past the railing at the top of the stairs into her bedroom. He settled back, behind the door. It was nearly pitch-black, but she would be coming up the stairs, and when she did she would flip the light switch on. He didn't want to be seen when that happened.

He heard a low whistle. It was Jessica, whistling a Christmas carol, "We Wish You a Merry Christmas." He smiled, raised the weapon, cocked to fire. The sound of the whistle grew louder as she walked to the bottom of the stairs.

Calibrisi now sat alone in front of the computer terminal. He had told Ashley Bean to take a break. He finished watching the clip of Vic Buck walking down the brick walkway for what was the twenty-eighth time in a row.

Then, he saw it. He knew he would see it, and he did. He paused the video. He marked a square around Buck's hands, then zoomed the image out and in. Then, in a split screen, he quickly replayed the video from the day before. He performed the same exercise, squaring off the hands, then zooming in. He studied only the hands. The gloves. Yesterday, big, thick, ski gloves. Winter gloves. Today, the gloves were different. And this is what had eaten at him since the first time he'd seen the clip. To-day, Vic Buck's gloves were not winter gloves. No, he knew what they were because he himself had owned several pairs of these gloves. They were standard-issue CIA gloves. They were the gloves every agent was given, the gloves that were worthless in any sort of weather. They had but one purpose. Today, Vic Buck had set out to take someone's life.

Calibrisi lurched for the phone, dialed Jessica's office.

"Deputy Director Tanzer's office," said Rosemary, her assistant.

"Is she there?" asked Calibrisi, panic in his voice. "It's Hector."

"She went home, Hector. Then she's headed to New York. Call her cell."

Calibrisi hung up, then dialed Jessica's cell phone and waited for the ring.

49

The sharp, fishy aroma of clams hung on David's fingertips. He sniffed them, almost unconsciously, as he drove to work, the soft drone of Rush Limbaugh in the background. It was Friday, just before shift change. As he drove the pickup truck across the Winnegance Bridge, he took another whiff. He couldn't explain exactly why, but he loved the smell of clams.

"Why do you keep smelling your hands?" asked Dickie. Dickie Roman worked with David. They lived on the same street in Phippsburg, in a row of neat, double-wide trailers just off the main road near Sebasco.

"Clams," said David, smiling. "I went clamming again today."

"You're fucking crazy," said Dickie, shaking his head and lighting a Winston Light. "It was practically zero today."

"I love them," said David. "I love the feeling when you hit a big one just under the mud. They squirt saltwater at you. It's a game. And the taste. I just love it."

Dickie exhaled, shaking his head. "Yeah, well, I guess where you towelheads come from they don't have clams, do they?"

"No," said David. "God saved the clams for the saltwater hillbillies up in Maine, saved you from starvation."

An odd pair to say the least, a fifty-five-year-old, chain-smoking high school dropout from Maine and a twenty-eight-year-old, clean-cut, light-skinned Jordanian, they shared a laugh at their own expense. Dickie was David's only friend in Maine. Dickie was a hideous creature. They bonded over a steady diet of racist jokes, cigarettes, cheap beer, and, of course, work. Always the work. They had worked together now for more than three years. David and Dickie were part of the day crew at Bath Iron Works, two of the 1,300 men who worked, in two shifts, around the clock to build and assemble the engine works on the *Aegis*, America's most elite warship. The *Aegis* was a nimble, fast ship that nevertheless carried a complex array of highly sophisticated, advanced weaponry. There were more than 800 Aegis destroyers that patrolled the seas under the American flag, from the coast of Taiwan to the Persian Gulf.

David pulled the silver Ford F-150 into a parking lot, next to the massive green warehouse and drydock facility of Bath Iron Works, Maine's largest employer, the most important manufacturer of warships in the United States, a division of General Dynamics, one of the U.S. defense industry's giants.

They walked inside and punched their cards into the clock next to the door. They walked down the long, covered hallway to the men's locker room. David opened his locker and put on a worn pair of overalls. The locker room was crowded. It always was. He'd learned that fact long ago.

David reported to his shift and picked up where the night shift had left off. He and his nighttime counterpart were responsible for forging a custom piece of one of the large steel rods that would, in a few months time, constitute the warship's drive shaft. He inspected the work of his counterpart, Tim. He knew Tim. Tim did excellent work; David felt an obligation to work his hardest, to produce quality craftsmanship, for Tim mainly, but also for Bath Iron Works, his employer; he felt obligated to match Tim's excellent work, to live up to his end of the bargain. He ran his hands along the six-foot section of steel and nodded to himself. "Today," he thought to himself, "I will finish grinding the six shank. It's almost done. Tim will be surprised."

After an hour and forty-five minutes grinding the toaster-sized sander against the metal rod, David let the switch go. He turned the sander off and took off his mask and helmet, then his gloves. He nodded to Mark Jonas, the foreman. He had to hit the head.

David walked through the pit to the bathroom. It was located in the middle of the warehouse. He peered casually down at the ground. The stalls were empty. He went to the fourth stall. Once inside, he shut the door and unhitched the clasps on his coveralls. He let them fall to the ground. Then, he let his underwear fall on top of the overalls. To anyone looking from the outside, from the sinks or the urinals, it looked as if he was sitting down on the toilet.

But David was looking up. *There you are*, he thought. It had taken him almost a year to find a good place, a place no one would discover, ever, under any circumstance. He'd been trained to use his locker, but that wouldn't work here. He knew it the day he'd walked in. So he'd had to improvise.

Standing on the john, he reached up and pushed the square ceiling tile up, until it sat freely on his hands above the thin aluminum ceiling frame. As he'd done at least once a week for more than two years, he slowly rotated the ceiling tile so that it flipped over. He lowered it down and then sat down. He then reached down, felt the large lump taped to the underside of his scrotum and pulled it quickly from the tape. It was a small hunk of soft material, grayish, with small hard objects peppered throughout, like pieces of orange glass. He knew what it was. He'd learned how to use it. How to set the detonator. He saw the movie that showed the explosion, the film they showed all of them, of the explosion in the laboratory. Octanitrocubane. He stared at it for a moment, then added it to the pile that now resembled a small pillow. Finally, he checked the detonator. It was still in place; two stainless-steel tubes within a glass cylinder, a pair of small red wires sticking up into the air; the two wires that would receive a cellular transmission from somewhere and blow all of Bath Iron Works, and half of the small city of Bath, into oblivion. He'd set the detonator up on a weekend shift over three separate trips to the bathroom. He smiled at the sight of the device.

Suddenly, the door opened. He heard footsteps. He peered down and saw two running shoes. He didn't recognize them.

377

He looked up at the empty rectangle in the ceiling. Could the stranger see the missing square? Probably. This wasn't the first time. Unless it was the maintenance man, Joseph, nobody would care. Even Joseph probably wouldn't care. Still, the empty rectangle, the black abyss of the missing rectangle, sent shivers down his spine.

He waited as the man took a pee. If someone were to come in and have to take a crap, he would have a problem. So far, in two years, that hadn't happened.

The toilet flushed. The man walked out without washing his hands.

David stood. He raised the ceiling tile up to the ceiling and gently moved it into place.

"Soon," he whispered out loud. He smelled his fingertips once more, the odor of the clams. "Soon."

50

88 TWENTY-FOURTH STREET, N.W.
GEORGETOWN

Jessica's whistling grew louder as she reached the landing halfway up the stairs.

Buck listened, hidden behind her bedroom door. He had always liked the song. Why do some people like certain songs and not others, he asked himself. For example, he hated "Silent Night." But "We Wish You a Merry Christmas," which she now whistled, now *that* was a classic. He grinned as he considered this. Such a significant moment in the life of one person—her last moment on earth, in fact—and here he is, thinking of something so utterly trivial as which Christmas carols he preferred. Well, it made him smile, at least.

In his right hand, down at his side, the silenced Glock 36. He felt his heart rate pick up, ever so slightly. He'd killed so many people, in so many places, that it had become routine. But this one was slightly unusual, and on some level he knew that. He'd terminated people he'd known before, even liked. But never before had he killed someone who represented such a grave threat to his own personal well-being. If his heart raced, he realized as his breathing quickened, it was because he wanted it now; wanted to be on that beach, to be away from it all, to have his money. He was so close now. He would leave the country soon, perhaps tonight. And he'd insist Fortuna pay him the rest, *now*. And if Fortuna wouldn't, then Buck would turn him in and make do with what money he had. He at least had received the other $5 million now. Survival on only $15 million. He smiled again. But first he had to get away. And in order to buy the time to get away, he had one piece of unfinished business.

Jessica's footsteps grew louder on the wooden stairwell, the soft, perfect pitch of her whistle grew louder too. Suddenly, her phone beeped, a sharp, insistent ring that stopped her whistling. He heard the phone flip open. Her footsteps drew closer. The hall light flipped on. Her shadow drifted into the frame of the room, her outline suddenly appearing on the green oriental carpet directly in front of the door, which Buck stood silently behind. He watched from the crack near the hinges.

"*Tanzer,*" she said.

Calibrisi held the phone to his head. He squeezed the plastic handset so hard he thought he might break it. Finally, the cell signal picked up and Jessica's phone began to ring.

"Thank God," he said aloud, to no one.

The phone rang half a dozen times, no answer.

"Pick up the phone, Jess," he pleaded out loud. "Pick up the fucking phone."

Then, the slightly Irish inflection of Jessica's voice came on.

"*This is Jessica Tanzer and you've reached my voice mail. If this is an emergency, please call. . . .*"

"Yes, Lou," Buck heard Jessica say as she entered her bedroom, flipped the light switch.

Buck remained behind the door, motionless, silent.

"I leave in ten minutes," she said. "It will have to wait. We have two separate leads in New York City and I'm heading up after I take a quick shower."

Buck watched through the crack at the end of the door. He steadied the Glock against his right leg, but held. He could not terminate her while she was on the phone with anyone, much less the director of the FBI. Jessica moved through the bedroom into the bathroom. He suddenly couldn't see her. But he heard the sound of the shower come on.

"The target is mid-coast; Portland, Freeport, somewhere in the vicinity. The team is all over it. I don't know what the target is; tell the senator she'll be the first to know."

She returned to the bedroom. Buck watched as she cradled the cell phone between her shoulder and ear. She took a black blazer off, unbuttoned her white blouse, removed it, then took her bra off. Then, she unzipped her black pants, let them drop in a pile at her ankles. She now stood in front of Buck in only a pair of pretty red panties. She removed those too, leaving them on top of the pants, then turned and walked toward the bathroom door, where the shower was blasting away.

"That's incorrect," she said as she walked through the bathroom door. "You need to explain to the attorney general that there *are* precedents."

Calibrisi redialed three times, typing away at his computer screen as he did so, looking up Jessica's home number, which he then tried. No answer.

Then, calmly, he thought, *Could I be wrong?*

He'd known Buck for a long time. Would he commit treason? Could he betray his country?

Could he, God forbid, kill Jessica?

Over the years, Calibrisi had learned to trust no one. To trust nothing. There was only one thing he trusted. Only one thing he could always trust and rely on. It was his gut, his instinct, his frank assessment, above all else, of people.

Buck had almost surely cut Jessica's home phone line. Calibrisi tried her cell again, then again, and still a third time. He slammed the phone down. He stepped out of his office, looked at his assistant, Petra.

"Call Bill Baker at Georgetown PD. Tell them to get as many men as they can to 88 Twenty-fourth Street, N.W. Tell him it's an emergency. *Now.*"

Calibrisi grabbed his coat and sprinted down the hallway. He didn't need to grab a weapon; the only time his Glock wasn't strapped to his shoulder was when he was sleeping or taking a shower.

They'd come into the agency at the same time. But Buck had risen quicker and higher. There were a lot of reasons for that, Calibrisi knew, but the main one was that he was a good agent. An athlete; political, smart, strategic, multi-talented. And the truth is, he was one of the best wet-work killers the CIA had ever had, and that didn't just mean he was a good trigger man. He designed bold operations. As a leader, he inspired loyalty; backed up his men when they made mistakes; gave credit when credit was due. He was tough. He never asked anyone to do something he wasn't willing to do himself.

Yes, he'd learned a lot from Buck. He knew he wouldn't be half the agent he was were it not for what Buck had taught him over the years. But Calibrisi also knew he was about to kill Jessica Tanzer—if he hadn't done so already.

In the basement garage, Calibrisi flagged a motor pool car, gave the agent Jessica's address.

"Put the bluebird on," said Calibrisi. "*And* drive like a fucking maniac, you hear?"

The car peeled out and bumped onto Pennsylvania, went right.

Calibrisi tried both of Jessica's numbers again. Still nothing.

"*Fuck!*" he yelled.

Think, Hector. Think.

He stared down at his cell phone. Buck had saved his life once. He shook his head at the memory. He'd been sent to London with Buck and two others on a kill team. The target was a German, a man named Stauffer, an executive at a large German electronics manufacturer. Stauffer had been selling nuclear weapons parts—trigger components specifically—to Pakistan. The agency had decided to simply get rid of Stauffer, rather than make big deal of it. Calibrisi didn't know why, didn't ask, it wasn't his job. His job was to kill Stauffer.

It had been around midnight. An apartment in Mayfair, high floor. Infiltration had occurred two days prior to Stauffer's arrival. The team was a floor above the German, in an apartment directly overhead, owned by a Saudi prince who was away, and who didn't know they were coming, nor afterward that they'd ever even been there. A Buck touch. He called them "short-term rentals," technically against agency standard operating practices but seamless, invisible, the way he liked it.

Calibrisi had gone down to Stauffer's floor via the fire stairs at the appointed time. Entered by picking the lock, shut the door behind him. It would've been Calibrisi's fourth termination. He had moved through Stauffer's dark apartment, silenced Smith & Wesson .357 Magnum out in front of him, leather gloves, sweat pouring down his head beneath the ski mask. He'd gotten to the bedroom door.

A floor above, at that very moment, through the pinhole nightscope the team had drilled into Stauffer's bedroom ceiling, they'd seen Stauffer, weapon out, waiting next to his bed, ready to kill Calibrisi when he entered.

Calibrisi had felt the slight vibration in his pocket just as he reached his gloved hand toward the brass doorknob. Those were the days before comm buds in your ear. He'd stopped in his tracks, in the darkness, looked down, seen the two words that were Buck's signal to abort.

The apartment, the pinhole, everything; it had all been Buck's planning, his ideas. Even the two words. The two words Buck was known for, which every agent who'd worked with Buck knew meant. The two words that, more than a quarter century ago, saved a young agent's life.

Calibrisi picked up his phone.

Buck calmly pushed Jessica's bedroom door open. The sound of the shower, of water pouring down, created a soft din through the bedroom.

He glanced down at her clothing on the ground, on the bed, as he walked. He stepped slowly toward the bathroom. He felt his heart again, quickening now, calm but quickening. His mouth opened, his nostrils flared slightly. He crossed the soft, beautiful carpet, his eyes on the white bathroom door, now ajar. The steam from the shower clouded the edge of the bedroom.

The sound of the shower, so soft.

He reached the door, stopped, paused, then lifted his left hand. He placed it against the door. The leather of his fingertips left a pair of dots in the steamed dew on the wood, dots that would be impossible to dust or even to pick up chemical trace from, as the gloves were designed above all else to prevent this. He began to push the door in.

Then he felt the vibration.

He reached down. He flipped the cell open. As he read the two words on the small screen, the shock of the message struck his central nervous system like a live wire, nearly dropping him to his knees.

POWER DOWN.

51

Igor Karlove stared at the computer screen, bleary-eyed. He had left his office twice in eighteen hours, both times to go to the bathroom.

Suddenly, the scrolling letters came to a halt and the computer beeped. He leaned forward.

"There we go," he said. He hit the print button, waited for the paper to spit out, then walked with the readout out of his office, down the hall into the trading floor.

"What do we have?" asked Essinger, who was seated at the center table, feet up.

"I have a list," replied Karlove, holding out the piece of paper. "What this list represents are the one hundred most active traders within the energy complex, per your specs. I won't bore you with the details of how I built the force-rank algorithm but suffice it to say it's pretty fucking brilliant; activity was spread out across a massive number of entities in virtually every country on earth."

Essinger grabbed it, started reading, eyes intent on the paper.

"So what are we supposed to do with this?" asked Essinger. "Top ten are all well-known firms. I can't imagine—"

"Right, so here's what I did next," interrupted Karlove. "I went through all hundred of these, got rid of the ones I knew well, figuring obviously established managers like Paulson, Baupost, et cetera, aren't going to be involved in something like this. That took it down to about thirty firms. Then I looked for patterns. Same buildings. Law firms. Dates of establishment. That sort of thing. The pattern that was most interesting was legal. I am guessing whoever did this probably isn't using Cravath, right? I looked at who was using firms out of weird places, Mauritius, Cayman, that sort of thing. There was one firm, PBX, out of Hong Kong, that used a firm out of Guernsey Island, off the UK. PBX was, by the way, ninety-ninth on the list of top one hundred traders. But when I ran the Guernsey domicile back against the entire data set, that's when something interesting occurred. All of the sudden, it captured a ton of smaller stuff, in different accounts, that were variants on PBX. PBX alone had more than forty different legal entities they ran trades through. In aggregate, PBX's trading activity would've made it the sixth most active trader in the time period leading up to the attacks. I found two other managers with legal out of Guernsey. In fact, all three used the same law firm, Debenshire McGreeley."

"Who the fuck is Debenshire McGreeley?" asked Essinger.

"Doesn't matter. The point is, that became an organizing principle. Once we had them in the picture, it was relatively easy. I was able to find the biggest traders by, in effect, building up around who used Debenshire McGreeley. Here's what we have."

Karlove handed another piece of paper to Essinger.

"PBX, Passwood-Regent, Kallivar," said Karlove. "Those funds all had by far the most extensive financial activity within the energy complex. In fact, virtually all of their trades occurred on the same day, just a couple of days before Capitana and Savage."

"Where are they?"

"PBX, Hong Kong. Passwood-Regent, London. Kallivar, Wall Street."

"Who prime-brokered these guys?"

"Spread out."

"Can we find out information about these firms?"

"Already did. All three are shuttered. As of two days ago."

"Holy shit," said Essinger. "I was actually kidding when I said this might work."

"It gets better," said Karlove, sitting down next to Essinger. "I hacked into the law firm's server."

"You what?" asked Essinger, incredulous. "Igor, that's serious shit. If they caught you—"

"Chill, Josh. I was invisible. Besides, I thought we were hunting terrorists."

"I didn't say break the law."

"Well, too late. Do you want to hear what I found or should I just go turn myself in?"

"Yes, of course."

"It was easy. Like taking candy from a baby. I was inside their servers in about half an hour."

"The world is waiting, Igor."

"All three funds have one fiduciary. Guess where he's based?"

"Igor—"

"New York City. Guess who it is?"

"You've heard of him?"

"So have you. You went to Wharton with him."

"My God," said Essinger. "It's Doug Berber, isn't it? No, wait. Kramer Colasito. I always knew—"

"Stick to your day job, Josh," interrupted Karlove. "It's Alexander Fortuna."

52

Jessica finished rinsing her hair, stepped from the shower, and wrapped herself in the big towel. She heard sirens coming from somewhere close by but didn't give it a second thought until, as she stepped into her bedroom, the front door crashed open downstairs and the sound of shouting echoed up the stairs.

"Police!"

Still wrapped in her towel, she hurried out of her bedroom and looked down from the top of the stairs as uniformed Georgetown police officers stormed into the house, weapons out.

"What the hell is going on?" she said.

The policemen moved into Jessica's town house. A tall officer stepped across the threshold, looked up.

"Jessica, Bill Baker, Georgetown Police. Hector Calibrisi sent us here."

She heard her phone beeping. Turned, moved to the bedroom, then the bathroom. She flipped it open.

"What—"

"Oh, thank God," said Calibrisi.

Within half an hour, an FBI forensics team had scoured Jessica's town house. They found a cut phone line, but nothing else.

Calibrisi and Jessica rode back to FBI headquarters together. Despite having explained his suspicions, based on the images of Buck wearing the leather gloves, he couldn't stop apologizing. He escorted her to the roof of the FBI building, where a Black Hawk VH-60N was waiting to fly her to New York City.

"Please, Hector," Jessica said loudly, above the growing din of the chopper getting ready to take off. "There's nothing to be sorry for. Better safe than sorry, right?"

"Yeah," Calibrisi said, smiling, although he knew he'd been right. He stared at Jessica as she climbed into the helicopter and sat down. Snow had started to fall.

Suddenly, inside the chopper, Jessica's phone beeped.

"Tanzer."

"Director, this is CENCOM. Can you hold please for Joshua Essinger from KKB."

"Go ahead."

"Hi, Jessica?" said Essinger. "This is Joshua Essinger. I work with Ted—"

"Do you have something?" she asked.

"Yes. We may have found the terrorist."

Buck had run now for more than a mile. He'd disposed of his gloves in two separate trash cans along the way. At the front entrance to Georgetown University, he stopped. He looked around, saw no one. He went to a blue VW Jetta, slammed the butt of his Glock into the glass, shattering it. He opened the door, then started the car. He sped down M Street. He needed to move, and move quickly. The game was over. His neck was now hours away from the gallows.

Calibrisi. He must be the one running the mole hunt, Buck realized.

He had to think. He had to outthink.

He hit the green button on his cell. The phone started to ring.

"Calibrisi," said the voice.

"Hi, Hector," said Buck. "Mind telling me what that was all about?" Buck waited. The phone was silent.

"Hi, Vic," he said. "I thought you might call."

"You did?" said Buck. He took Key Bridge at more than seventy miles per hour, despite the snow that had begun to fall. "We both know what those words mean. Exactly what mission should I abort?"

"I know, Vic," said Calibrisi.

"You know what exactly?"

"There's nobody else," said Calibrisi. "Nobody it could be."

Buck saw the entrance to the Jefferson Davis Highway. He took the Jetta into the passing lane, got on the Jefferson Davis, pushed the accelerator to the ground. He would be in Alexandria in a matter of minutes, then his house. Five minutes inside was all he needed, and then he would be gone forever.

"Tell me what exactly you're accusing me of, Hector."

"Madradora."

Buck paused. He saw an Alexandria trooper ahead. He slowed down, passed the trooper. After another quarter mile, he sped up.

"Madradora?" said Buck. "Okay. Forgive me. It takes me a while to catch up to you sometimes. It always did."

"Cut the shit."

"You cut the shit, asshole," said Buck, indignant. "You're accusing me of being a fucking spy? Me? I have given my life to this country. You are a goddamn son of a bitch if you think I would betray this country. Look at my bank account. How dare you."

Calibrisi was silent. Buck felt it, that familiar feeling. When you are someone's boss, you always own them somehow. He felt Calibrisi's doubt, coming over the line, expressing itself by the silence.

"It's Andreas," continued Buck, driving the point home. "You're an idiot if you don't understand the fact that Andreas killed those Deltas. He's involved. Something happened on that rig. Something went down.

He's involved with these people somehow, some way. And now that guy is playing us."

Buck took a right on Glebe, nearly sliding into the guardrail. His home was just a block away now.

"I'm sending a team out to get you," said Calibrisi.

"You don't need to," said Buck. He saw the familiar sign, Kentucky Avenue, swung the car right. "I'm downtown. I'll come by. You can polygraph me. You can run a pharma package on me."

Left on Old Dominion. Ahead, he saw the green shutters of his house. He pulled the Jetta around the block, parked on a side street. He turned the car off, then climbed out, began a fast walk down the sidewalk now dusted in snow.

"And then when you're done," continued Buck, coming to his front door, "and I'm cleared, and the president knows what kind of circus you've been running, I'll have your job, Hector. And Jessica Tanzer's too."

53

BATH IRON WORKS
BATH, MAINE

Shelly Martini, head of the FBI Portland Regional Field Office, sat in the driver's seat of the van as it drove, sirens on. They were accompanied by two Bath police cruisers. They exited Route 1, then barreled down the underpass until they reached Washington Street, then went right. In the distance, a massive red and white crane hovered over the shipyard. Lights twinkled in the afternoon gray. A Christmas tree stood atop the crane's red and white boom, lit up for the holidays.

They had just come from Freeport. L.L. Bean was clean. They had spent the better part of the morning searching through the company's retail outlet as well as the massive distribution center down the street. They had also looked at surrounding retailers in the area. Nothing.

They parked in a line next to the main entrance to Bath Iron Works, the Kennebec River in the background. They were met by yet more squad cars. The head of BIW security, Jim Brueggelman, met the arriving convoy.

"Hi, Shelly." Brueggelman, an obese man with a big, bushy mustache, walked to Martini, shook her hand. "Is this related to Long Beach?"

"Yes," Martini said. "We found the same explosive used at Long Beach in a UPS package in Reno. It was being sent to a P.O. box in Brunswick."

"Okay. Where do you want to start?"

"What's the most important part of the facility?"

"It's all important, Shelly."

"Well, then, where are the most employees?"

"Let's start with the engine works," said Brueggelman, pointing to a huge green building down the street that towered over the street. "There's an Aegis there right now. If I was one of these terrorists, that's what I'd try to hit. Then we'll get over to the dry dock."

"Sounds good," said Martini. "How much trouble would it be to shut things down for an hour or two?"

"Shut things down?" asked Brueggelman, momentarily taken aback. "Major pain in the ass. But if you want it, you got it."

"Do it," said Martini.

Brueggelman nodded. "Okay. Give me a few minutes."

David stood atop the steel scaffold. He pressed the sander hard against the steel shank, moving to smooth out a ridge that was still too rough. Suddenly, the bright overhead lights of the massive warehouse flashed red. He knew what it meant. He'd participated in the exercises. *Evacuation.*

For a full minute, he remained atop the scaffold, taking his time to disengage from the equipment. A line of workers began to pour toward the door. Was it routine, just an exercise? Or did they know?

"Hey, Davie." It was Dickie Roman, walking from the engine works toward the line of men exiting the building. "What do you think's up?"

David looked at him from the scaffold, said nothing. In the distance, he saw the sign for the restrooms.

"Jesus, lookie there," said Roman, pointing to the far end of the building behind David.

David turned. Against the wall, a line of uniformed officers suddenly entered the warehouse. A large, black German shepherd was led by the officer in front; David knew what it meant. Long Beach. They knew. They had to know. He glanced back at Dickie. To the right, he saw Mark Jonas, his supervisor, pointing toward the line.

393

He thought back to his training.

If they suspect you, you must become a martyr.

"Hurry it up, David," Jonas said.

David started to climb down from the scaffold. At the bottom step, he stepped toward the line of departing workers, then suddenly lurched away from the line. He sprinted wildly toward the restroom. Mark Jonas began to yell, then gave chase, as did several other men. The team of FBI agents took notice, and the large German shepherd, now halfway across the facility floor, began barking furiously, then was let go and galloped toward the fleeing David.

David sprinted down the corridor, his arms pumping in a frenzy, looking back every few steps over his shoulder as the angry dog, followed by the crowd, gave chase. He burst into the empty restroom, dashing to the fourth stall. He climbed on top of the toilet. The angry barking of the dog echoed down the corridor, closing in, along with shouting. He pushed the ceiling tile aside and reached up, feeling around the mass of explosive material, searching desperately for the detonator.

The door to the restroom burst open. The animal's angry, rabid barking sent a chill down David's spine. He continued feeling through the thick wad of octanitrocubane, searching for the buried object. The German shepherd was now inside the restroom, his barking feral, crazed. Suddenly, the door to the stall burst open and the large, ferocious animal leapt toward him, saliva dripping from his mouth, yellowish teeth bared to bite. David's hands suddenly found the object, and he pulled the two end cap wires out from the material, just as the sharp fangs punctured his leg, ripping his flesh in a horrendously painful final moment.

The dog ripped mercilessly into David's leg just as he touched the ends of the wires together.

54

BATH IRON WORKS

Across the street from Bath Iron Works, the Cabin was hopping. The restaurant, a dark and cozy pizza place, was a popular hangout for the employees of BIW, their families and friends. In the summer, it would fill up early with vacationers. In winter, it was the Bath community, especially the workers from BIW, who kept the place afloat.

On this afternoon, the Cabin was packed with BIW workers who now had an hour or two to kill while the FBI searched the facility. Beer flowed freely as waitresses shuttled pitchers to the different tables. In one room, the sound of a guitar could be heard, a fast, folksy tune, the high, pretty voice of a woman covering a Joni Mitchell tune.

BIW's massive green warehouse sat directly across the street from the restaurant, completely blocking any view of the Kennebec River the place might have had. When BIW built the six-story-tall facility in the early 1970s, the couple that owned the small house that the Cabin now occupied became angry at losing their beautiful view of the river. They sold the place to Joe and Betty Wilson for $8,000 and felt fortunate to get out of the whole deal with anything at all. But Joe Wilson saw an opportunity. He turned the downstairs of the place into a restaurant and opened the Cabin. It soon became a staple in the lives of the community, a gathering place, a neighborhood pub, a place for good pizza, laughter, a place to relax.

Had anyone survived the explosion, they could have described the moment that it occurred. It was a moment in the middle of the young female singer's performance of "Big Yellow Taxi." The guitarist had stopped unexpectedly, at the same time the young woman paused mid-lyric. At this particular moment, at each table, conversation was abruptly interrupted. In the kitchen, both cooks looked up from their pizza doughs. Several of the waitresses stopped walking and looked toward the door. They all could have described that moment, had any of them survived.

But none of them did. For seconds before, two small metal wires were suddenly connected together, the combination of the wires sending a precise charge down through the stainless-steel tubing of the detonator and into the large chunk of octanitrocubane, hidden above a ceiling tile in one of the twenty-four bathrooms inside the BIW Aegis manufacturing facility.

The ion spark from the detonator illuminated the mass of material in a flash moment and after that all else was void.

From the bathroom ceiling, the infinite heat moved like a thousand lightning bolts in all directions; it was like being at the very genesis of the lightning bolt itself, and it moved with such force and power that soon the large area surrounding the bathroom, the manufacturing zone for the Aegis engine works, was a wild, hazy inferno of heat and fierce wind that toppled everything, including the massive engine blocks.

So fast was the pace of the explosion that none of the departing workers in the immediate area of the blast, nor the FBI agents who'd just arrived, had even a moment of recognition before they were pulverized into vapor.

From there, the explosion tore down through the warehouse, washing away hundreds of workers without warning. At the far end of the massive facility, workers had mere seconds, but they were enough, moments filled with awe as the south side of the warehouse, where the explosion emanated from, lit up white and silver and ripped their way. Those seconds were soon meaningless, for the force of the explosion soon reached them, killing them all.

As the heat spread, the massive corrugated steel walls of the facility buckled at their joints and soon toppled over, bringing with them the roof overhead, all within seconds, their massive height and weight acting like tissue paper trying to stop a forest fire.

And when the walls went, the fire, heat, and wind pulsed into the Bath air, exploding outward. Thundering across the small road, it moved into the neighborhoods surrounding the facility.

And all of this happened in less than two seconds.

At the Cabin, it was the noise that caused the moment. None of them knew that. All they knew is that there was a moment, and they all shared that moment, the moment less than a second after David had touched the wires together, and less than a second before two-thousand-degree heat leveled the small neighborhood restaurant as the inferno moved furiously through the snow-filled air.

Soon, the southern part of the small coastal city was aflame. Nearly two square miles of land, the epicenter of which was BIW, settled into a raging series of fires in a concentric circle around the crater.

55

17 OLD DOMINION
ALEXANDRIA, VIRGINIA

Marks and Savoy climbed into the back of a black Toyota Land Cruiser idling on the tarmac of the private terminal at Reagan National Airport. Spinale drove, tearing out of the terminal, headed toward Alexandria. For several minutes, no one said a word.

The car radio was tuned to the news, more reports on Long Beach. They listened for several minutes as Spinale hauled quickly toward Alexandria. Finally, Marks leaned forward from the backseat.

"Turn the radio off," he said.

On the seat next to him, he opened a leather briefcase. He pulled out the Wilson Combat CQB, the silencer still in place. He pushed a clip into the gun and continued to stare silently out the side window.

"You sure you don't want me and Paul to handle this?" asked Savoy from the front passenger seat. Marks returned his question with silence; Savoy knew to not ask that question a second time.

"I'm going to ask this one more time just to make sure we're thinking clearly," said Savoy. "Should we tell Jessica Tanzer and let them deal with this?"

Marks said nothing for several moments. Finally, he stopped staring out the window.

"I could sit here and think up plenty of reasons why we shouldn't tell the FBI," said Marks. "They might fuck up the case. Some government prosecutor would probably get flambéed by the kind of lawyer this guy would hire. That's if they even bring him to trial. They'd probably cut a deal with him long before that. He'd end up in some white-collar country club prison for a few years, or else witness protection, live out his days on a golf course in Arizona. I could probably think of a few more reasons why we shouldn't tell the FBI."

"But—" said Savoy.

"But the real reason we're not going to tell Jessica Tanzer is simple," continued Marks, anger rising in his voice. "There are certain human beings who deserve to die."

Buck entered through the side door of the white Colonial. Green shutters, a pair of Japanese maples in the front yard, between which ran a stone walkway.

The neighborhood was called Beverley Hills, a residential neighborhood just a few miles from downtown Alexandria. The residents were upper middle class; lawyers, doctors, finance types, a few dual income government couples. People knew their neighbors. Kids could play in the street without fear.

The house was empty, his wife, Debbie, a fifth-grade teacher, still at school.

Upstairs, Buck pulled out the small leather Coach weekend bag and frantically placed a few items in it, toiletries, a change of clothing. He went into the walk-in closet off the master bedroom. He pulled a chair from against the wall and stood under the overhead light. He jimmied the metal sides of the light fixture, creating enough room for his fingertips. He pulled the light fixture down. He reached his fingertips up blindly. Stuffed in the space above the metal casing, he felt two small objects. He pulled them out then pushed the light housing back into place. He stepped down and replaced the chair against the wall.

Looking down, he studied the two passports. Both showed the same photo, Buck, slightly younger, slightly more hair. One was Canadian, with the name John Smith. The other was a U.S. passport, same name. For the head of the CIA national clandestine service, a man who could order up a virtually unlimited supply of fake passports, these were unusual. They were off the main CIA and Interpol databases. There was no way for the CIA to track him.

He placed the U.S. passport in the duffel bag and stuffed the Canadian one in the pocket of his coat. From his sock drawer, he removed a silenced handgun, a SIG M26. He checked the clip. Then he went back downstairs.

The Land Cruiser moved rapidly up Tennessee, winding its way through the chilly afternoon air, now filled with light snow.

When they saw Old Dominion, Spinale took a left, then slowed the vehicle to a crawl. He pulled across the street, then down to the end of the block. Marks and Savoy climbed out.

"Keep your eyes open," said Savoy to Spinale. "We'll be right out."

Buck walked to the kitchen and grabbed a bottle of water from the refrigerator, then walked to the front door. As he reached to open the door, he noticed something, the kind of thing perhaps only a career CIA operative would notice. At the end of the stone walkway, his eye cast right. Snow was falling heavily, but he still noticed it. Across the street, down several houses, the dark steel outline of a black SUV, steam quietly rising from the tailpipe into the cold air.

Buck grabbed the SIG M26 semiautomatic handgun from the bag, then stepped through the kitchen, opened the back door, and sprinted across the lawn to the back fence, then along the back of the fence to the neighbor's yard, ducking behind a boxwood hedge.

From behind the hedge, Buck marked two men, moving quickly between his neighbor's house and the house two doors down from him. Their dark outlines were shrouded in snow as they moved.

He raised his weapon, cocked to fire, but held.

He remained silent, still, waiting and watching as the men passed behind his neighbor's house. He had a clear shot at the men. But he didn't shoot. He knew that killing them would not help him, not right now anyway. He needed time, not the possibility of a screaming neighbor. He watched as the two large men moved stealthily along the back wall of his home.

Savoy moved to the corner of the house, where he looked into the window. Signaling to Marks, they got down on their knees and crawled beneath the window, to a door that led to a dimly lit room, which they saw was the kitchen.

The door was unlocked and Savoy slipped quickly inside the kitchen, followed by Marks. Weapons out, they moved quietly through the room. At the stairs, Marks signaled that he would go upstairs, while Savoy moved to the television room.

Upstairs, Marks moved rapidly, room by room, searching for Buck. In the master bedroom, he looked quickly at the photographs of Buck and his wife, sitting on the shelf of a bureau. On the desk, Marks noticed that the light was on, but the lamp shade was askew. He walked to the desk and opened the top drawer. It was empty. To the side of the desk, a silver frame lay on its side. He picked it up, but the photo had been removed.

In the master closet, the shelves were neatly stacked with clothing, except for one, which looked as if someone had ransacked through it.

Marks walked back downstairs. When he saw Savoy, he shook his head, indicating Buck wasn't there.

After watching the men enter his house through the kitchen door, Buck moved in the opposite direction, through yard after yard, running to Halcyon. He emerged at the side of a brown ranch and came to the sidewalk.

Buck thought of the millions in his bank account and smiled to himself in anticipation. Sure, it would have been easier to just slip away, but far less memorable.

At the sidewalk, he took a left, stooping slightly and stepping at a casual pace down past the turnoff of Old Dominion, across the street. He crossed in front of darkened homes toward the back of the black Land Cruiser, now less than five houses away. He moved casually, just a man out for a late afternoon stroll. If he was lucky, there would be nobody in the vehicle. If there was someone in the vehicle, he hoped they wouldn't be looking out the back window. Worst-case scenario, there would be someone, and he would look out the back window. In that case, he hoped they would believe it was just an older gentleman out for a stroll.

He came upon the Land Cruiser, steam billowing from the tailpipe. He made out an outline of a person, seated in the front seat, looking toward his house, waiting.

Moving alongside the car, Buck removed his SIG M26. Dropping the leather bag on the ground, he placed his hand on the driver's-side door. He waited a moment, then quickly pulled the door latch. He yanked the door open, thrust the silenced weapon into the SUV, and in a precise, trained move sent a bullet into the head of the young driver before he had any idea what was happening.

Marks descended the stairs and nodded to Savoy. They moved to the kitchen.

"He's not here," whispered Marks.

"Basement?"

Marks nodded.

Suddenly, both men looked up, noticing something down the street. The lights of the Land Cruiser had turned on. The car suddenly lurched forward.

They moved quickly through the kitchen, out into the backyard, where they retraced their steps. Emerging through the side yard next to the brick house, they came upon Spinale's body, contorted on the ground, a large chunk of his skull missing. A wet pool of dark blood was gathering on the snow-covered tar.

"My God," said Marks.

Less than an hour later, Reagan National Airport and BWI Airport in Baltimore were swarming. All flights out of both airports had been temporarily grounded while authorities searched for the fugitive.

But forty miles to the east, on the small tarmac of a private airstrip in Dunkirk, Maryland, Buck flipped the switch on the King Air C90. The twin propellers came to life. He moved the plane down to the end of the snow-dusted runway, then turned, pushing the throttles all the way forward as he steered the plane down the runway. Just fifty feet from the trees, the plane bumped lightly up, its wings lofting the craft into the darkening sky.

Buck allowed a smile to cross his lips as he felt the plane settle into flight. "Wastin' away again in Margaritaville," he hummed aloud as the twinkling lights of the coastal towns disappeared beneath him and the plane soared out over the dark waters of Chesapeake Bay.

56

NEWARK INTERNATIONAL AIRPORT

The FBI Black Hawk VH-60N made it as far north as Newark, before being forced to land on the tarmac at Newark International Airport, the blinding white of the blizzard making it impossible to fly any farther. After landing, Jessica moved into the cockpit and placed a set of earphones on her head.

"I need a live patch to CENCOM," she instructed. "Secure channel."

Frustrated, Jessica stared out the front window of the chopper as snow blanketed the skies outside. A pair of clicks on the headset.

"Hold for CENCOM Commander Fowler," came the female voice. Another click.

"Jess, it's Bo."

"What do we have on Fortuna?"

"We have a hard location," said Fowler. "Upper East Side, 1040 Fifth Avenue. What do you want to do?"

"Patch in Maguire."

A few seconds later, another voice.

"Maguire."

"Mel, tell me you're good to go," said Jessica.

"I have four teams ready to move," said Melvin Maguire, FBI's commanding agent at Teterboro. "I can have them running right now."

"I want a hard cordon," said Jessica. "One block out. Don't let anything in or out. And get NYPD backup."

"Already done," said Maguire. "They've got at least fifty men holding on my command."

"Good," said Jessica.

"How many you want on the assault team?"

Jessica paused, glanced at the Black Hawk's pilot, thinking.

"There's a detonator and we need to hit quietly," said Jessica. "I want a tight team; your two best men. Tell him the target, Bo."

"1040 Fifth Avenue."

"They go in fast, quiet, and they shoot to kill," said Jessica.

"Got it," said Maguire. "I'll get them moving. I assume you want the hard cordon in place before you send in the team."

"No," said Jessica. "This is real time. Get them going, let the cordon follow. Fortuna has a detonator and there are forty-one more targets. I want the team moving right now. And one other thing."

"What?" asked Maguire.

"I want one other person on the assault."

"You can't be serious—"

"Dead serious," said Jessica, cutting him off. "Get him whatever weapons he wants. I want Dewey Andreas on the kill team."

Fortuna stared at the computer screen, watching the oil futures market as it spiraled wildly out of control. The U.S. government accusing the Saudis of the attack on Capitana had been an unexpected bonus. Most analysts assumed the Saudis and their greed would drive them to a deal. Fortuna agreed, knowing from personal experience that there existed no more powerful emotion on the Arabian Peninsula, in the Fahd house, than avarice. It would win out in the end. But for the moment, another Saudi trait, pride, had widened a rift between the two allies that had caused more damage—and made him more money—than he'd ever dreamed of.

Numbers, money, had long ago lost its power to impress or excite Fortuna, so used to it he'd grown, to having it, to making it. But even he could not help but shake his head in momentary awe at the wealth he'd created.

A day ago, his $10 billion gambit was worth more than $27 billion. Now, it was nearing $32 billion. But the ride was over, at least for now. After several hours of work, Fortuna had completed moving the funds out of the positions he had established through Kallivar, PBX, and Passwood-Regent. Those entities were now shut down, the money placed in an entirely new set of foreign legal entities unrelated to the energy industry and to America.

Finally, he stood up and tried to reach Karim yet again. No answer. He felt tightness in his chest, but pushed it away. *Karim is dead.* He knew that now.

Setting off the detonator would be the final act. But he would need to do it only after he was airborne. The country would descend into utter chaos the moment he began setting off the remaining bombs. Every airport in the United States would immediately shut down. Yes, he would need to be airborne before he struck.

He called Jean.

"Jean—"

"Yes, Alex."

"Bring the car around. I'll be down in two minutes. Then call Pacific Aviation. We'll need to charter a jet; Karim is still not back. Get the biggest Gulfstream they have available at La Guardia, capable of going to Europe."

"La Guardia is closed. The storm—"

"Tell them we want to fly out as soon as they reopen the airport."

"Where should I tell them we're going?"

"Tell them Paris. But we're going to Beirut. They don't need to know that until we're over the Atlantic."

Fortuna hung up. He walked to his bedroom. From beneath his bed, he pulled out a large duffel bag, prepacked. In it, some clothing, a laptop with any information he would need, passports. Everything else—photographs, diplomas, anything that might remind him of his life in America—he left behind. Once again, the cord would be cut, only this time it would be he who did the cutting.

He glanced around his room for the last time.

Ten minutes after leaving Teterboro, the black Suburban pulled up in front of Fortuna's apartment building. In silver block letters above a pair of large French doors that marked the entrance to an elegant granite prewar apartment building: 1040.

Snow was falling heavily. The scene looked eerily peaceful. The doorman was a small man, young, and he watched the thick snowflakes as they dropped downward from the sky. He stood just outside the door. The lobby behind him was deep red, lit by a crystal chandelier that hung down.

Dewey and two SWAT-clad FBI agents jumped out, ran toward the building entrance, weapons out. The FBI agents both held HK MP7 automatic machine guns out in front of them, handguns holstered at the waist. Dewey held his Colt M1911 .45 caliber semiautomatic handgun. Dewey also brought a Colt M203 carbine combat assault rifle, grenade launcher attached to it. He kept the powerful rifle slung over his shoulder, a full magazine of 5.56mm cartridges as well as two grenades ready to go, if necessary.

"Can I help you?" asked the doorman.

One of the agents held up an ID.

"FBI. Step out of the way. We're securing the building."

"What—"

"What floor is Alexander Fortuna on?" asked Dewey.

The doorman struggled to speak.

"What floor?" Dewey barked.

"Penthouse," the doorman croaked.

"Key," said Dewey. "And you might want to leave."

The doorman, nearly paralyzed by fear, handed Dewey a small gray card. He and the two agents walked quickly back to the middle of the floor where the elevators were.

Dewey could feel it now, the proximity to the mission's target.

407

Whatever fatigue, whatever worry he had in Cuba, it was all gone now, replaced by a warmth suffusing his entire body and a salty taste in his mouth, the flavor of adrenaline. His heart raced as he waved the card before the small black sensor next to the elevator then stepped inside. He swept the card across the red light and pressed the PH button.

The elevator climbed up through the twenty-eight floors of the building. Quickly, Dewey checked the clip on his gun. His forehead, armpits, and chest dripped with sweat. He looked in silence at the two agents.

"We drop anything that moves," said one of the agents.

"We find the detonator," said Dewey.

"Yeah, that too," said the other agent.

Fortuna walked down the hallway, into the living room. Above the fireplace, he opened the ivory box, removed the detonator, placed it in the duffel bag. He walked to the elevator, dropping the duffel bag on the ground. He walked past the elevator, to the kitchen. There, he opened the Sub-Zero, reached in, pulled out a carton of orange juice, removed the cap, then started guzzling. He'd been at the computer more than two straight hours. He was ravenous, thirsty.

Suddenly, he heard the elevator door bell chime, announcing someone's arrival.

Fortuna let the orange juice fall to the ground. He sprinted back down the corridor, toward the duffel bag. All he cared about now was the detonator. The elevator was thirty feet away. He galloped down the dimly lit hallway. But then, suddenly, the small green light above the door lit up; the elevator chimed again, and he stopped dead in his tracks; he wouldn't make it. He turned, ran back to the kitchen, ducking inside just as the elevator doors opened.

Dewey watched the lights climb through the numbered buttons on the elevator wall. He thought of Capitana, of his men. He thought of the remaining targets, along with countless civilians, waiting to be destroyed.

He swallowed, his teeth dry, his eyes focused. As the elevator came to its stop at the penthouse, Dewey raised the Colt.

The door opened and the FBI agents stepped quietly into the entrance of the apartment. Dewey followed. Before them, a brilliant cherry sideboard sat against the opposite wall. A large painting of an American flag hung above it. Next to it was a massive mirror. Dewey looked for a moment at himself. He was a disheveled mess. His short hair looked patchy due to the hasty cut back in the mall bathroom in Cali. His pants were stained with blood and sweat. He thought of the irony; an impartial observer would have thought *he* was the enemy.

He smiled for a mad instant; he hadn't felt this alive in more than a decade. This was a feeling he'd subsisted on as a soldier; the feeling of mattering, of risking it all for a higher purpose. He was alone in so many ways now, but he felt the warmth of a hundred thousand brothers beside him, American brothers, veterans, men, boys who fought before him, or fought alongside, who died for this country trying to protect it.

Beneath the painting, a duffel bag lay on the ground. Dewey stepped toward it, unzipped it. Inside, he found a laptop, several passports. And the detonator. He held it up, showed it to the agents, then slipped it into the pocket of his leather coat.

One of the agents signaled to Dewey with his hand. They moved right, Dewey left.

In the kitchen, Fortuna searched quietly but frantically for a weapon. He thought he'd placed a Glock 21 somewhere in the room, in a drawer or cabinet, but he couldn't find it. Was his mind playing tricks on him? He needed to stay calm.

He peeked his head outside the door frame. He saw two SWAT-clad agents, machine guns out, moving slowly, cautiously down the hallway toward the kitchen. He pulled his head back inside the kitchen.

From the knife drawer, he had his choices. There were more than a dozen long, sharp blades, but instead Fortuna pulled out a razor-sharp William Henry steak knife. He gripped the knife in his right hand, blade tip down.

Dewey couldn't believe the size, the sheer scope, and opulence of the apartment. It opened up into a massive room whose glass wall ran the length of the building and framed an incredible tableau of New York City, the dark patch of Central Park, then lights to the east and south, snow falling in whiteness everywhere. The room was filled with stunning antiques and furniture, with yellow walls and with art everywhere.

He walked down the hallway and entered a bedroom. On the walls were photos of a good-looking man, an American, with dark brown hair. On the dresser were photos of the man, playing lacrosse, in a graduation gown. On the wall, he saw a degree. It was from Princeton. Alexander Blodgett Fortuna, class of 1999.

A cold chill climbed in a vector, up from Dewey's knees, through his stomach, into his mouth. This was the terrorist's, Fortuna's, inner sanctum. He knew it, felt it. He searched through drawers, finding expensive clothing, even a large vial of cocaine.

He walked past the large bed and opened the door. Inside was an office. Dewey looked through the drawers of Fortuna's desk. In the top drawer, he saw a file with the word "Marks" on it. Inside of it were documents, articles, and photos of Ted Marks.

More files; Savage Island, then Capitana. He pulled out the file and found diagrams of the facility.

Then, he saw words that caused him to stare in stunned silence: "Andreas, Dewey." He picked up the file and flipped through it. Photos of him going back years, articles on his trial, photos of his wife, Holly, and Robbie.

Fortuna moved calmly into the windowless pantry off the kitchen. On a large shelf, chest-high, he moved several cartons of pasta to the side, then climbed up onto the shelf, eye level to the door. Gently, he pushed the pantry door closed.

Fortuna waited a painstaking minute. He heard no footsteps, nothing, only silence. Another minute passed. Then it came, as he knew it would. Suddenly, a crack of white light appeared as the pantry door opened.

The black silhouette of the machine gun's barrel appeared first, followed by the large frame of the gunner, stepping silently into the pantry. Fortuna heard the faint brush of the agent's hand on the wall, searching for the light switch, just inches from his head.

Fortuna swung the razor-sharp tip of the knife in a vicious strike at the agent's neck. He slashed the blade sideways, directly into the nape of the neck. The blade carved through skin, muscle, and cartilage, the force of Fortuna's slash so strong that the blade severed all the way through to the agent's spine. Just as quickly, Fortuna pulled the blade back out. A gurgled cough was all that came from the man as he dropped to the ground.

Fortuna knew the second agent would be right behind the first, and he quickly climbed down from the pantry shelf, stepping over the rapidly growing pool of blood on the marble floor. He pulled the machine gun from the dead man's arms, then stepped back into the kitchen, crouching, hugging the cabinets, weapon trained at the door.

The other agent stepped into the kitchen. His eyes looked right, away from Fortuna, searching. Fortuna pulsed the MP7 just once. The low serial thud of automatic-weapon fire interrupted the silence. A pair of rounds shattered the agent's skull, splattering blood and bone on the white door, dropping him to the ground in a contorted pile.

Fortuna moved, MP7 out in front of him, toward the hallway and the elevator that would deliver him to his escape.

Dewey heard something. Barely discernible, a grunt from somewhere in another part of the enormous apartment. He turned from the terrorist's files and moved, Colt out.

Dewey crouched and moved out of the bedroom, weapon drawn, finger on the steel of the trigger. He exited the bedroom, moving quickly toward the entrance foyer. He hugged the wall as he moved, Colt cocked to fire. Down the hallway, he saw the elevator, then heard a low chime and watched as the doors opened.

He ran now, weapon out, finger on trigger. A figure suddenly appeared from the other side of the bank, black hair: Fortuna. Dewey raised the weapon and began to fire as Fortuna turned, the barrel of a machine gun aimed at him. Fortuna started firing and a furious wash of lead ripped the air. Dewey dived to the ground, rolled, came up firing. Fortuna anticipated it, stepped back. Dewey's shots missed, but they forced Fortuna away from the elevator, preventing his escape. The doors of the elevator shut.

Again, the barrel of the machine gun emerged, another spray of bullets. But Dewey had already crawled through a doorway off the hall.

Inside the dimly lit living room, Dewey quickly holstered the Colt at his back, then swung the M203 off his shoulder. From the belt pack, he took a .40mm antipersonnel round, quickly inserted it into the M203 chamber. He slid his hand to the forward trigger.

Dewey moved along the wall of the living room, closer to the elevator. He looked through a crack between another door and the wall, spied Fortuna's black hair at the opposite end of the elevator atrium, looking for him. Suddenly, Fortuna fired again, auto hail, sweeping the MP7 across the wall at thigh level, and Dewey had to dive to the ground as the line of lead pocked the wall, tearing through the plaster just inches above his head. After the line of bullets crossed immediately above him, Dewey crawled forward, put the tip of the M203 in the door frame and fired the grenade launcher.

The grenade whistled as it traveled across the elevator atrium, striking the wall across from the elevator, then exploding. The floor shook as the explosion destroyed everything in its vicinity, ripping the ceiling down, furniture, art, walls, and scorching the floor. Several small fires sparked immediately. Dewey moved the fire selector to auto hail, and pulsed the carbine trigger, sending 5.56mm cartridges in a furious spray across the wall of the hallway.

Receiving no counterfire, Dewey stood and moved through the door, through the burnt-out elevator atrium, M203 in front of him. The debris from the grenade was choking, blinding. He looked on the ground for the corpse of the dead terrorist, but found nothing. On the ground, the MP7 Fortuna had been using lay, the magazine spent.

Past the demolished atrium, he moved down the long corridor to the kitchen. At the kitchen entrance, he saw the first SWAT-clad agent slumped on the ground, head gone, blood everywhere. The second agent he saw a second later, lying in a large pool of blood, neck gashed. But no Fortuna.

In the back of the kitchen, Dewey saw an open door. A crimson shoe print on the marble floor. A stairwell leading upstairs. He moved to the stairwell, carefully. It was a tight space, and he harnessed the M203 back over his shoulder, took out the Colt, inserted a new clip, then began his ascent.

At the top of the steps, another door, also open. Cold air blew into the stairwell. Dewey moved through the door, inch by inch, expecting the terrorist to attack, but nothing came, and he stepped onto the snow-covered roof. Fresh tracks led across the roof, to the Fifth Avenue side of the building. Then the tracks disappeared over the side of the roof.

Dewey ran to the ledge, looking down. More than halfway down the building, almost invisible due to the falling snow, Fortuna dangled from a rope, desperately descending along the side of the building. Dewey found the rope, reached for his ankle sheath, pulled the Gerber blade out. Reaching forward, he cut the thick nylon rope. Suddenly, the taut line popped and went limp. Fortuna suddenly dropped and disappeared into the blinding snow.

Fortuna's hands quickly grew bloody and raw as he climbed down the face of the building, toward the street. He descended quickly, moving two floors at a time, trying not to look up or down, bouncing his feet against window frame after window frame as he descended. He let rope through his hands in increments, ignoring the pain as the nylon sliced through the skin on his hands, each length of rope tearing away at his palms.

Suddenly, he felt a tug on the rope, then it went limp. A sense of airlessness bloomed in his spine, then turned into panic as gravity pulled him helplessly toward the cement at least ten stories below.

Fortuna clawed for a window ledge as he dropped away, legs kicking the air. His fingers grabbed the closest ledge, but the granite was slippery, and he kept falling. He tried to grab the next ledge, again his fingers could not hold, then another ledge, again unsuccessfully, his rate of descent accelerating uncontrollably.

A small terrace came rapidly up at him then, and he saw it as it grew larger in the fraction of a second it took him to fall, and instinctively, in that half second, he braced himself, landed on the hard granite of the terrace with a painful crash, then rolled. He ignored the pain, looking for a dazed moment at his hands, which were now raw and bleeding profusely.

Fortuna kicked in the French door that led to the terrace, entered the apartment, ran limping past an elderly woman, who started screaming. Through the apartment door, he found the stairs and took the final five flights to the building's basement as blood dripped from his torn-up hands. He exited through the building's delivery entrance onto sixty-ninth Street. He walked calmly, limping, down sixty-ninth Street to the corner of Fifth Avenue.

On Fifth Avenue, he looked uptown and saw two police cars pulling up to the front of the building, then a pair of black Suburbans. He walked casually to the Mercedes parked a block south on Fifth, climbed in back.

Dewey took the twenty-eight flights from the roof recklessly, jumping from landing to landing, each floor going by in a matter of seconds. He sprinted through the empty lobby, through the front door, past a flock of NYPD officers arriving on the scene. Outside, he looked around frantically. He searched the spot where Fortuna would have fallen, finding nothing but pristine, untouched snow.

On Fifth Avenue, Dewey looked south as a black Mercedes lurched from the sidewalk onto a snow-coated Fifth Avenue. He pulled the M203 off the shoulder harness. From the belt pack, he took the other .40mm antipersonnel round, quickly inserted it into the grenade chamber as he ran toward the fleeing sedan.

At the corner, he stopped, aimed carefully, then pulsed the trigger just once. The grenade screamed from the chute, sailed in a hard line down Fifth Avenue toward the Mercedes. Suddenly, the car lurched left. The grenade whistled by; two seconds later it struck a yellow taxi, incinerating the vehicle in mortar and fire.

Fortuna leaped into the back of the black sedan.

"Drive, Jean!" he screamed. "Fast. East Hampton. Move it."

Jean hit the accelerator and the S600 peeled out. He flipped it into all-wheel drive and the tires gripped the pavement, barely registering the snow that had accumulated, more than six inches in an hour and a half.

"What happened?" asked Jean, anxiety in his voice.

"Drive," Fortuna said from the backseat. "Just drive the fucking car."

Dewey saw a cab in front of the building, stopped at the light. He ran to the front door and opened it, pulling the cab driver from the car and hurling him to the ground. Looking in back, he saw a young, wealthy blond-haired woman and her daughter, dressed up, petrified.

"Get out," he barked. "Now."

Dewey peeled out, down Fifth Avenue, into its heavy rush hour traffic, in pursuit of Fortuna. He turned left where the Mercedes had just turned, but couldn't mark the car. He took a right on Park. After a few blocks, running red lights, swerving in and out of traffic, which was now slowing down because of the snow, Dewey saw the black sedan three blocks ahead of him. He sped ahead and tried to catch up with the speeding vehicle.

He flipped open the cell phone and pressed the button for Jessica.

"They set off another bomb," was the first thing Jessica said. "Bath Iron Works in Maine. It's pandemonium. I've got a mess on my hands."

Dewey remembered going there as a teenager with his grandfather, to see the launch of the USS *Samuel Roberts*. He quickly put the thought from his mind. He needed every ounce of focus he could muster.

"I have one of the detonators," Dewey said. "He's running for the other one. He killed the two agents. I'm behind him in a stolen taxicab. Have you run his other properties?"

"I'm in the back of a chopper on the tarmac at Newark. The largest shipbuilder in America and a large chunk of the surrounding town was just leveled by a bomb and there are hundreds of people dead, maybe thousands. I can't even get through to CENCOM. No, I haven't run it. I can't get *through*!"

"Keep cool," he said, weaving through traffic.

"You need to stop him before he gets wherever he's going," she said, encouraging Dewey in return. "Shoot to kill. Run his car off the road. Do whatever you have to do."

"I will. Call me when you have the location."

The snow was starting to accumulate in large piles on the streets. The Mercedes glided along quickly, but was not out of control. The cab was one of many that filled the street behind it. But the Mercedes moved quickly. Dewey was having a hard time catching up for a clean shot.

At Thirty-sixth Street, the Mercedes turned left and entered heavy traffic queued up for the Queens Midtown Tunnel. Dewey was a dozen cars behind. He slid the cab out to the left, rolling down the window. He picked up the Colt. He moved up alongside the row of cars, into the breakdown lane barely wide enough to fit the cab. The front bumper bounced against the guardrail several times as horns blared at him. He moved toward Fortuna's dark sedan.

Fortuna's sedan was queued up in the fast-moving express lane. Dewey rolled down the window. He prepared to fire.

Fortuna turned and looked out the back window. Several cars back, he saw the cab, trying to move up the breakdown lane. His view was partially obstructed by a snowplow. He couldn't see the face of the driver.

"There's somebody behind us," said Fortuna, looking at the rear-view mirror. "In a cab."

"I see them," said Jean. "What do you want me to do?"

"Keep moving," barked Fortuna. "Get through the fucking tolls."

"We're almost there."

"Where are the weapons?"

"In the trunk. Open the center hatch. You can reach the case from there."

"Gloves. Do you have any gloves up there?"

Jean turned, saw for the first time Fortuna's mangled hands. He said nothing, reached for the glove compartment and pulled out a pair of leather gloves.

Swallowing the pain, Fortuna pulled the leather gloves onto his hands, blood oozing from the sides of the gloves as he did so. He pulled the leather cushion in the middle of the seat to the side. He pressed a latch on the console beneath the leather and the center section folded neatly down. He reached into the trunk and felt for the metal case, finding it and pulling it into the backseat. He opened the case. Inside, two HK UMP compact machine guns lay, along with four Glock 32s.

He selected a pistol and positioned himself to fire at the approaching cab.

Suddenly, a snowplow, just behind Fortuna's sedan, turned in front of Dewey. It cut him off completely. Dewey could only watch as the terrorist's sedan made it to the express lane gate and slipped out of Manhattan, the snow shrouding the back of the car.

Dewey had to back up a few feet to get around the snowplow. It took him nearly a minute to push his way back into the toll line.

The phone chimed. It was Jessica. "Where are you?"

"Queens Midtown Tunnel. I just missed him. He may have seen me."

"We still don't know where he's heading," said Jessica. "Don't lose him."

"I'm having trouble keeping up," said Dewey. "He's driving a Mercedes with four-wheel drive and I'm in an old cab."

"In case he's headed toward Long Island, I have LIPD setting up roadblocks."

After the tunnel, Fortuna's sedan climbed onto the Long Island

Expressway and quickly sped up. Dewey lost sight of the Mercedes as he waited for what seemed like an eternity at the tollbooth.

"You still there?" he asked.

"I'm here. The president is declaring a state of emergency. Bath, Maine, is on fire. This is insane."

"You got that right."

"Did you get a look at his plates?" she asked.

"No. And now I've lost them. I'll call you back when I catch up."

Dewey flipped the phone closed.

"Fuck!" he yelled. He slammed his fist down on the steering wheel in frustration.

The roads were a mess, and getting worse. Cars were pulled off to the sides of the road, while those brave enough to keep driving in the thick snow were going so slow they were in the way of Dewey's being able to pursue the fleeing terrorist.

But if there was one benefit of growing up in Maine, it was that he had learned to drive in the snow. He had lost track of the car. For nearly twenty minutes he drove as fast as he could, barely keeping the cab from flying off the road or into another car. He searched for Fortuna's sedan, but saw nothing.

His phone rang.

"Jess?"

"Yeah," she said. "We think he's heading for the Hamptons. We're trying to get the exact address."

"Roadblock," Dewey grunted, straining his vision ahead for a glimpse of Fortuna's car.

"We have the county sheriff setting up a roadblock on the LIE at the exit for Route One-Eleven."

"Where is that?"

"Manorville. Exit Seventy."

"I'm getting close. What if he already got off?"

"Then we're fucked," she said. "We're taking off right now. Or trying. It's going to be hairy. I'll call you in a few . . . I hope."

The Mercedes roared down the Long Island Expressway, its thick snow tires and all-wheel drive making the piles of snow barely noticeable. If there was a challenge, it was the cars alongside them, parked on the sides of the highway or even occasionally in the middle of the road, strewn about by drivers unprepared for the wintry conditions, not helped at all by snowplow crews who were unable to keep up with the conditions.

"If there was someone, we lost them," said Fortuna.

"Good, boss."

"Go to the estate. I don't have the detonator."

"The plane—"

"Just drive, Jean. And turn on the radio."

Jean pressed the button for the radio. Some French music came on.

"Turn that shit off," said Fortuna.

"What do you want? Classical?"

"The news, you dumb fuck. Ten ten."

Jean maneuvered the big sedan through what was an obstacle course of cars as he moved the dial for the radio.

On 1010 WINS, a woman was describing the chaotic scene in Bath, Maine, where Bath Iron Works had just been destroyed by a bomb.

Jean looked back.

"Was that one of ours, Alexander?"

"Yes, Jean," said Fortuna. He felt a slight smile cross his face. But it vanished just as quickly, for Fortuna knew that the government had to have been closing in for the bomb to be set off. Fortuna tried to remember the name of the cell; he pictured the boy's face, but he could not remember his name. He closed his eyes for a moment, chided himself for his bad memory, then prayed for the young bomber. He opened his eyes, slammed his fist down on his knee, came back to the task at hand.

"Make this car go faster. We're running out of time."

At the Route 111 exit off the Long Island Expressway, a long traffic line was now backed up nearly a mile. Eight New York State troopers were running a roadblock stop-and-search, looking for the black Mercedes sedan they knew might be coming their way. The line of snow-covered

419

vehicles was being waved through as quickly as possible. At the front of the line, four officers stood, two with automatic machine guns. The snow had continued unabated, making the lines move slowly. Two false alarms, one a Mercedes S600 driven by a seventy-eight-year-old woman on her way to her home in East Hampton, and another driven by a chauffeur for a couple from Quogue, caused a further delay.

Jean sped the Mercedes along the highway and came upon the slow-moving line for the exit.

"We have a problem," he said, turning the radio down.

Fortuna leaned forward from the backseat. They could make out the glow of blue flashing lights from the police cars.

"A welcoming committee," he said. "Can we get off before the exit?"

"This *is* the exit, Alexander. The last exit was more than five miles back."

"Shit!" Fortuna yelled. He slammed his fist down on the seat. Then he looked behind him, searching for anything suspicious.

"What should I do?" asked Jean.

"Get in the side lane and move up to the front."

Fortuna unlatched the seat compartment that led back into the trunk. He pulled out both of the UMPs.

"There are half a dozen troopers up there, Alex! They're running a fucking checkpoint. They're looking for us!"

"I'm less worried about them than about what's coming behind us." Fortuna ducked his head and began to crawl from the backseat into the trunk of the Mercedes.

"There's nobody behind us."

"Not yet there isn't. Now get up to the front of the fucking line and stop jabbering. Don't panic when they pull you to the side. Be polite. They will be looking for a black Mercedes. When they ask you to pop the trunk, do it."

Fortuna pulled the seat latch from his position now in the trunk, closing off the compartment. He lay down inside the trunk, looking up in the dark, weapons trained back at the trunk latch, waiting.

In the taxi, Dewey continued along the highway. Twice the cab spun out only to be saved from tumbling down a side hill by the guardrail. After another ten minutes, his phone rang again.

"Hi, Dewey." Jessica's voice was nearly drowned out by the sound of the chopper behind her. "Where are you?"

"Still on the LIE. I lost him."

"I just got off with the deputy running the Manorville checkpoint. You should hit the line soon."

"Do they have their weapons locked and loaded? He'll know what they're looking for—if he hasn't already gotten off the highway."

"Yes, of course."

"Where are you?"

"Over Long Island, coming your way."

"Do we have the location of his house? Anything turn up at his office?"

"Nothing. We're talking with local police in East Hampton and Southampton. We should have a location within five, ten minutes tops. When we do, if my pilot can get through this mess, we should be able to get there quickly. Just keep following him. Hopefully they'll stop him at the checkpoint. I'm sure he won't go down easily. If you come on him before then, take him."

Suddenly, Dewey heard a short burst of beeping noises from his cell phone. He looked down.

"Shit," he said. "I'm losing the battery on this phone."

"Let's get off," said Jessica. "Call me when you get to the checkpoint."

Dewey powered off the cell phone. Ahead, he saw the brake lights of a van shine red through the falling snow. He came upon the line of traffic, winding ahead through the falling snow. Dewey accelerated toward the breakdown lane, sliding lightly into the guardrail, then pushing up alongside the traffic line. Far in the distance, he saw the blue flashing lights of the police cars.

The Mercedes made its way to the front of the police line, where it was immediately flagged. Not less than five deputies and two state troopers came quickly to the side of the vehicle, two of them brandishing M60s.

Jean opened the window as he slowly inched forward.

"Can I help you, officers?" he asked politely. He handed them his license before they could ask for it.

"Out of the car," said the policeman holding the machine gun, training it on Jean's head.

"Yes, sir," he said, opening the door and stepping out into the snow, arms above his head.

"Where are you going?" one of the uniformed troopers said, shining a flashlight on the license, then into the sedan. Another officer opened the passenger-side back door, revealing an empty car.

"Southampton," said Jean. "I'm a chauffeur for Mark Bluntman. Do you know him?"

The officers didn't respond to the question. Two officers searched the sedan while a third patted down Jean. The officers moved around behind the car.

"Pop the trunk," barked one of the troopers from behind the car.

Inside the trunk, Fortuna heard the trooper's words. He felt sweat on his forehead. His heart pounded.

Jean leaned into the car and pressed the trunk button.

Fortuna heard the latch click just in front of him. As if in slow motion, the dark steel above him moved upward. Light entered the space and he felt blinded for a moment. When the trunk was just a few inches ajar, Fortuna suddenly kicked up with his right foot as he pulled back on the triggers of both weapons. Before the officers knew what was happening, bullets splattered across their chests, sending blood in a patchwork behind them, across the front windshield of a minivan, the dark-haired woman inside screaming as she watched the troopers get slaughtered in cold blood.

Standing up quickly, Fortuna turned in the trunk and kept firing, aiming his weapons at the troopers in front of the sedan. One was able to get a round off, but it struck the steel of the trunk in front of the terrorist. Fortuna leveled him with several bullets to the skull.

Jean had already ducked back into the vehicle.

"Drive!" Fortuna yelled. Suddenly, the explosion of a gun behind him echoed, followed almost simultaneously by the clang of a bullet striking the trunk next to him. Fortuna wheeled to face the new threat.

Dewey maneuvered up the breakdown lane until he was just a few hundred feet from the flashing blue lights of the police checkpoint. The line had stopped. Several police officers were gathered around a car; it was a black sedan. All four policemen had their weapons drawn as a stocky Arab with a ski hat climbed out of the front of what Dewey now saw was the Mercedes. The Arab with the ski hat wasn't Fortuna, but Dewey knew it was the car, that the man was involved. Had Fortuna gotten out? Perhaps he'd pulled what, in Delta, they called a "dog leg"; jumping out of the car a mile back and tracking alongside the highway to avoid the checkpoint. He pushed the taxi toward the front. After being frisked, the driver of the Mercedes leaned into the front seat as four of the troopers moved behind the car.

Suddenly, the staccato burst of automatic weapons rang out. *Fortuna.* Dewey opened the door and ran toward the scene as he saw Fortuna stand up in the back of the Mercedes trunk, a machine gun in each hand. He mowed down the police behind the vehicle, then turned. Standing in the trunk, using the open trunk as a shield, he turned toward the remaining officers in front of the car and sprayed them through with lead, killing them all.

Dewey raised the Colt as he ran, struggling to keep his footing in the thick, wet snow and underlying ice; he slipped but kept moving. He fired the first shot, which rang loudly as it hit the steel of the trunk, missing the terrorist. Fortuna turned in time to see Dewey, and he arced the machine gun in his right arm across his chest, starting to fire. But Dewey's second shot struck Fortuna in the stomach, dropping him down into the trunk. At the same time, the Mercedes lurched forward, shutting the trunk with its sudden momentum. Dewey's final shot struck the steel of the trunk once more as the car peeled away.

All around, Dewey could hear screams coming from inside the cars near the grisly scene. Several cars attempted to screech away from the horrible carnage.

Running to the nearest police car, which was idling next to the scene, Dewey jumped into the front seat. He stomped on the gas pedal and sped forward, chasing the black Mercedes which was now a quarter mile away, still visible. This was a far better ride than the taxi had been, but the snow was getting even thicker. Still, Dewey kept the accelerator to the ground, his body humming with the knowledge that he'd wounded his prey.

He picked up the police radio.

"I need somebody," he said.

"Dispatch. Who is this?"

"My name is Dewey Andreas. You have at least eight dead officers at the Manorville checkpoint. I'm working with the FBI and in pursuit of the killer. I need to be patched into FBI CENCOM immediately. Jessica Tanzer. This is an emergency."

Fortuna punched the compartment latch in and squeezed into the backseat, his face contorting in pain. Jean looked in the rearview mirror.

"Alexander," he said. "Are you okay?"

Fortuna was silent, except for a labored panting.

"Alexander," he repeated, knowing his boss had been injured.

Jean craned his neck and looked around at Fortuna. Fortuna held his hand against his stomach, but dark blood oozed out over the gloved fingertips.

"Get to the house," he said, his voice barely above a whisper. He closed his eyes.

"Aw, shit," Jean said. "You're hurt. Oh, man. You can't die, Alexander."

"Don't be a fucking woman," whispered Fortuna. "I'm not going to die."

The Mercedes soon entered the town of Bridgehampton, which was silent in the middle of the winter night. They passed through the town, whose snow-covered main street was deserted in the winter storm. In the rearview mirror, Jean could see the headlights of a police car, gaining on them, less than a quarter mile away.

"Someone's following us," said Jean. "Police car."

"It's Andreas," said Fortuna in a pained grunt.

"Who's Andreas?" asked Jean.

"Where are we?"

"Bridgehampton."

"Throw me your hat," Fortuna said.

Jean tossed it back to Fortuna.

Intense pain stabbed at Fortuna's gut. He had to stop the bleeding. He wedged the wool cap into the entry hole on the left side of his stomach. He seemed to have no exit wound, but the internal damage was obviously substantial. He balled up his body in the fetal position, seeking to slow the bleeding and ease the extreme pain he felt from the porous material in the wound.

It wasn't working.

Unfolding his body, then removing and using his belt, Fortuna managed to cinch the cap more tightly about, and inside, the wound. The pain worsened, but for the time being, the bleeding stopped.

"How long?" he asked Jean.

"Five minutes."

"Dewey, it's Jessica."

"Where are you? They just killed the entire police crew."

"I'm in the air, we're over Southampton."

"Do we have a house? Where's he headed?"

"Nothing. They're back-matching legal entities but it's taking time."

"I'm behind him, in a police cruiser, less than a quarter mile. I shot him. He's wounded."

"Keep the line open."

Dewey pressed the pedal to the floor and careened through the deserted, snow-swept streets of Southampton, then Bridgehampton. The cruiser had incredible power, as well as snow tires. But the Mercedes kept moving forward at a torrid pace.

In East Hampton, the Mercedes took a fast right beyond the small town, Egypt Lane. Dewey struggled to follow, the snow not having been touched yet and more than a foot of powder on the ground. They passed massive houses, brick, or shingle-style homes that towered in the distance, surrounded by fences, gates, security. A left followed, Further Lane. The Mercedes actually increased speed in the terrible conditions. On the tight lanes, Dewey pressed the pedal and came close to hitting a tree. He had to get closer, but was losing him. Down Further Lane, Dewey moved in closer as the Mercedes barreled down the thin, tree-lined road, branches sagging down under the weight of the thick snow. Around a set of sharp corners, Dewey maneuvered the police car, nearly losing control.

As Dewey came flying around a corner, just before a large, over-hanging elm tree, the Mercedes stood at the side of the road, next to the man from the checkpoint, in a white sleeveless T-shirt, despite the snow. By him stood Fortuna. Both had machine guns. Dewey saw the red blot of fresh blood at Fortuna's midsection as both men opened fire on his car as he came out of the turn. The bullets shattered the windshield as Dewey ducked, then swerved, out of control, sliding sideways, blindly from beneath the steering wheel, trying to get past the Mercedes. A patch of black ice appeared beneath the snow; suddenly the front of the cruiser slid uncontrollably to the left, through the slippery snow, and he felt it then, in his spine at first, the center of gravity shifting, the car beginning to leave its axis, its positioning, and traction on the ground, and with eighty miles per hour of g-force, the combination sending the car rising. Only a fraction of a second, yet it felt like an eternity. The car left the ground and began a series of flips and rolls down the road.

As the car rolled, Dewey struggled to keep his grip on the wheel and foot on the gas pedal. His momentum would not take the cruiser past the Mercedes and if the police cruiser landed on its roof, he was dead. They would still be in front of him, waiting, firing. If he landed wheel side up, though, he might just survive.

One roll, two, three, four, until finally the last one seemed to last longer. The car came to rest on its side, then slowly settled onto its wheels with the momentum of the run. This was it: Dewey gunned the engine, which roared and hurtled the destroyed cruiser forward, keeping him a moving target, a threat even, to the gunmen, until he lost control and shot into the woods and down an embankment. Down the side of a snow-covered hill it plunged until it made an abrupt stop against an old stone wall at least a hundred feet below the road.

Dewey had struck his head hard against the steering wheel. His nose bled profusely and his ears rang. But he could not give up. He looked to his right for the cell phone. Gone. Same with the Colt.

Seize the opportunity, he thought.

He tried to unbuckle his seat belt, but it was stuck beneath a heap of wedged-in metal from the door, which had been pushed in during the tumble. He felt for his Gerber knife, strapped to his left calf. It was hard to reach but he just was able to grip the hilt, as suddenly bullets began to shower the cruiser, Fortuna's driver giving chase down the hill. Dewey smelled gasoline then. He took the serrated upper edge of the blade and used it to rip away at the nylon seat belt. More bullets from the terrorist's machine gun pelted the metal of the cruiser, and the aroma of gasoline became stronger and more immediate. He finally cut the seat belt. He climbed desperately out of the wrecked door, moving as quickly as he could away from the police car, sidling into the forest before the killer could see him.

Dewey ran along the stone wall. He turned back and for a quick second saw a flash of light as the Mercedes' lights illuminated the icy hillside. He could see the police car halfway down the hill, and the terrorist descending the hill to kill him. The terrorist held the gun at mid-waist and sent volleys off every few seconds until one of the bullets struck the leaking gas and the police car ignited into bright orange flames, illuminating the stocky Arab. Above, the Mercedes pushed away.

Dewey moved up the icy hill as quickly as he could. By climbing along the remains of an old stone wall, he made little noise. He felt pain throughout his body now, pain to compete with his shoulder wound. Fatigue compounded the sharp bolts of trauma in his stomach, ribs, in the right side of his head above his ear. His nose poured blood into the snow as he walked.

Then the warmth came. He began to taste it, the warm dose of adrenaline he'd come to rely on again and again since the attack on Capitana, fueling the final yards of his ascent.

Dewey watched from the hillside above as the terrorist got down on his knees, trying to get a good look in the burning car to confirm Dewey's demise; finally, resigned, probably assuming the job had been done, he turned to hike back up the hill.

Dewey waited. He tasted a snowflake on his lip, others melting against his warm cheek. His breathing grew slower as he anticipated the next move. The killer climbed quickly up the hillside. The flames from the burning police cruiser began to dissipate into dark smoke as the terrorist climbed. The terrorist started to whistle as he neared the road, a dissonant tune that Dewey didn't recognize. The compact HK UMP hung from a strap around his neck. By the time he was near the top of the hill, he was winded, and Dewey could hear him breathing heavily.

Dewey waited with his knife out. As the killer approached Dewey's tree and stepped onto the snow-covered road, Dewey stepped calmly from behind the tree. He clutched the man's forehead and pulled his blade across his throat, once, twice, then stabbed him through his ribs and into his heart. The man crumpled to the ground. Dewey grabbed the weapon, ran down the road now, following the tire tracks left by the Mercedes in the snow, praying that he'd catch Fortuna before the terrorist reached the detonator, dawning a terrible new day God knew where. Down Further Lane he ran, navigating through the snow and ice until in the distance he saw a set of stone and iron gates, the tire prints running up the lane.

He sprinted down a long driveway, covered in snow, that seemed without end. His lungs burned as the cold air bit at them and at his throat, along with years' worth of cigarettes and Jack Daniel's. But he didn't slow, even when he crested a hill, heard ocean, saw lights. The snow seemed to be lightening. Windows twinkled far in the distance. He had a downhill pitch now and he kicked even harder toward the house. As he came closer, the largest home he'd ever seen came into view, a stunning mansion that stretched left to right in a vista around a large circular driveway. There must have been a hundred windows on the three-floor expanse. Shingle and dark shutters as far as he could see, painted with snow.

There in the driveway, behind a fountain that sat in the middle of the circle, sat the dark outline of the Mercedes, still running, door ajar.

Dewey ran to the Mercedes with the machine gun extended in front of him. A trail of blood from the open door intermingled with tracks through the snow. He sprinted to the front door of the house, which was wide open, following the path of blood on the ground. He continued in through a large dining room, then a dimly lit hallway.

He felt pain in his head, but ignored it as he moved toward the target.

He had only himself now, and whatever he could bring.

Throughout the house, he could hear ocean pounding angrily against the shore.

At last, he came to the light. In a large room at the far end of the mansion, dark green walls, a blazing fireplace. Then the terrorist, Fortuna, his back to him.

Ignoring the blood that coursed down his lips from his nose and ears, and his hands still sticky with the other terrorist's blood, Dewey kicked in the French doors and stepped into the large, warm room. He aimed the HK UMP at Fortuna. Fortuna turned in the chair. In his hand, a shiny silver object that looked like a television remote. *Detonator.* He held it up.

Had he pushed one already? More? All of them? Dewey wondered. *Or is he bargaining for his life?*

Fortuna appeared ashen, almost white under a sheen of perspiration. He panted in short bursts. Still, under it all, Dewey could see the face of the man he was; the sharp outline of his nose, hair slightly long, brushed back. Even near death, there was a charisma, composed in part by his looks, and by eyes that penetrated Dewey from half a room away. Looking down at the tan carpet, a large pool of blood surrounded the area beneath the chair. From his waist down, Dewey could see that the terrorist's pants were drenched in crimson. He stared back at Dewey, holding the detonator in his hand.

From this close, Dewey could see that Fortuna's gloved index, middle, and ring fingers were poised above three of the buttons near the detonator's bottom.

"This button sets off a bomb at Staples Center in Los Angeles," said

429

Fortuna, barely above a whisper, obviously in extreme pain. "This one will trigger a massive bomb that's in a locker at O'Hare."

"The third?" Dewey asked.

"The third. That one wasn't easy." He paused, struggling to take in air. "There's a bomb in a closet at the Supreme Court in Washington. We needed a woman to do that. Karina."

Dewey kept the machine gun trained on Fortuna. He stepped forward into the room.

"Put the weapon down," said Fortuna. "And don't move."

Dewey walked forward, ignoring Fortuna's demand, finger on the trigger and gun aimed squarely at Fortuna's head.

"Put the detonator down," said Dewey.

Fortuna grimaced at a spasm of pain. "I'm just the beginning," he said. "The tip of the spear. You can't stop it. My father, my brother. They will come behind me. They won't stop."

"I have brothers too," said Dewey. "A hundred thousand brothers. This is nothing new to us. We've dealt with your type before."

Fortuna's eyes moved from Dewey to the detonator to the flow of blood in his lap. He was minutes away from bleeding out, and they both knew it.

"Is it medical attention you want?" Dewey said.

Fortuna opened his mouth, then shut it. Shook his head.

"Not very convincing," said Dewey, "or you'd push those buttons, kill a few thousand more people, before I empty this HK into your head."

"It was never about the people," said Fortuna.

"Right," said Dewey, anger in his voice. "Yet you killed my men. You've killed thousands already."

"When you come to our countries, what do you do?" asked Fortuna, eyes meeting Dewey's. He paused to let another wave of pain pass. "Vietnam? Afghanistan? Iraq? Lebanon? You are so powerful it doesn't matter that in the plain light of day, when you take away the names of the countries, what you are doing is no different. Except that you are an entire government. Thousands of men, pouring in, with permission, permission because *you yourselves make the rules!* And you destroy lives. You destroy whole towns."

"I don't speak for my government." Dewey tried to anticipate where Fortuna's mind was drifting. As much as he wanted to shoot him, it would almost surely result in at least one detonation. He tried to buy time. "Who do you speak for?"

Still keeping the detonator in front of him, Fortuna smiled faintly. "When I was four, my mother took me to the sea, the beaches near Costa Brava," said Fortuna. "It's the only memory I have of her. Her name was Rhianne." He inclined his head slightly toward the wall behind Dewey, where a tall oil painting hung. A stunning, dark-haired beauty standing in a white sundress, holding the hand of a small boy.

"Your soldiers patrolled that part of my country," continued Fortuna, anger seemingly fueling his strength. "That day, we walked all the way home. She bought me ice cream at the beach near Costa Brava. One of your soldiers whistled at her. She—" Fortuna stopped abruptly, then continued. "She . . . pulled my hand, quickly, toward home. They told her to stop. She was scared. There was nothing in her bag. *There was nothing in her bag!*"

Fortuna stopped. He pulled his hand up from his stomach. He stared for several moments at the thick red that coated his gloves.

"They shot her," he whispered. "Just . . . *shot* her. My mother. *Do you understand now?*"

"Yes, I understand," said Dewey calmly, eyes locked on Fortuna's. "We all have losses. I lost my boy, a woman I loved. But killing doesn't bring them back. I wish it would. I've killed a lot of people. When you see the life go out in someone's eyes, someone you just killed, maybe someone who deserves to die even, you hope the life will go out in you too. But it doesn't." Dewey paused. "Did taking down Capitana and murdering my crew, did that bring your mother home? Did killing all those people, destroying those places, did that bring her back? Is she here right now?"

Fortuna's eyes took on a glazed aspect. "It helps," he said simply. "Maybe another little boy won't lose his mother. Maybe those soldiers won't be standing there anymore. If I cripple you, you'll keep your armies here." He struggled against the pain again. "If I destroy enough, then perhaps you can worry about your own. You can stay here, worrying about your own streets, your own buildings, and maybe some little boy in a country that you have no right to be in, maybe his mother won't be gunned down in front of his eyes."

"And right now," Dewey asked, anger in his voice, "at O'Hare? What about the little boy standing in line holding *his* own mother's hand?"

Fortuna stared back in silence. Suddenly, the detonator dropped to the ground.

Dewey fingered the trigger of the UMP.

"What did I do?" asked Fortuna, looking at Dewey. His eyes fluttered. On the ground, the pool of blood had grown wider.

Dewey gripped the cold steel of UMP in both hands now. Slowly, he raised the weapon level with his sternum. Bending at his knees just slightly, Dewey unloaded the UMP into the terrorist.

"I'll tell you what you did," said Dewey. "You picked the wrong country to fuck with."

57

THE WHITE HOUSE
THREE DAYS LATER

The small mahogany door cracked open and Cecily Vincent, the president's assistant, leaned into the Oval Office. "They're here, Mr. President."

The president, who was sitting with his boots up on his desk, leaned back and said nothing. He was reading the first draft of the State of the Union speech he would give later in the week.

"When you finish, *Marine One*'s ready to leave."

"Are they all here?"

"Yes, Mr. President."

It was Saturday afternoon in early January, a rare snow falling on Washington. He wore blue jeans and a Navy blue chamois shirt that his father had bought him at L.L. Bean's when he was in college, a senior at Columbia, more than forty years ago. It had numerous patches sewn onto it. It was in terrible shape and the Salvation Army probably wouldn't have taken it. But it was his favorite shirt.

"Send in Chiles and Putnam. I want to get this over with. Tell the young lady to wait."

The president took his boots from on top of the desk and sat up. He stood behind the large cherry desk as the door opened.

Louis Chiles, the director of the FBI, and Roger Putnam, the secretary of state, walked in. Putnam was dressed in tan, wide-wale corduroys and a heavy sweater. He looked like someone's grandfather, dignified and professorial. Chiles wore a suit, looking more like a corporate executive than the nation's top law enforcement officer.

The two men had been here many, many times before. Today, Putnam looked mildly inconvenienced. Normally, a Saturday in January would find him at his ski house in Jackson Hole, but he'd canceled all his winter trips the day he returned from Saudi Arabia. Chiles had the demeanor of a Boy Scout at his first camp out: excited, surprised, elated, still blown away by the experience of actually being allowed to come into the Oval Office.

"Good afternoon, Mr. President," said Chiles as he walked in. Putnam simply nodded when he made eye contact with the president. The president said nothing, and didn't return Putnam's gesture. He watched as the two men sat down.

The two men sat down across from each other on the two large Chesterfield sofas in the middle of the Oval Office. The president remained standing behind his desk.

Putnam knew what was coming. He probably could've written the words the president was about to say.

Chiles was about to be blindsided.

"Mr. President, I have a complete debrief on 'the Fortuna affair,' as the press has dubbed it," said Chiles.

"I'll keep this short," said the president, pointedly ignoring Chiles. "Because I *have* to keep it short. Because I have to get on a goddamn plane and fly for seven and a half hours so I can go and kiss King Fahd's ass for a day and a half and clean up the fucking mess you two made."

"But, Mr. President—" said Chiles.

"Shut the hell up, Lou," interrupted Putnam quietly.

But Chiles forged ahead. "Mistakes were certainly made, but it was the FBI that ultimately broke the plot."

"The FBI?" said the president incredulously. "The same FBI that failed to foresee the destruction of Capitana, Savage Island, Long Beach, Bath Iron Works? The attempted assassination of Teddy Marks? The

434

FBI that jumped to incorrect conclusions and helped drive this man"—he nodded toward the secretary of state—"to make accusations against a staunch American ally, accusations that created what is now a full-blown energy crisis?"

Chiles somehow continued to maintain his positive glow, smiling and nodding his head as the president spoke. "I understand, Mr. President, and I want you to know it won't happen again. We've all learned—I've learned—some very valuable lessons. Already, we've convened an interagency group—"

"You're fired," interrupted the president.

"But . . . I've got four and a half years left in my term—" said Chiles.

"You'll resign today. I want a resignation letter signed before you leave the White House."

Chiles was silent. For the first time, his smile dissipated and a look of shock overtook his face. He sat back. He reached up and loosened his tie. He rubbed his eyes.

"You worked hard," said the president. "Resign and go out, if not a winner, at least with dignity. I won't say a bad thing about you and I'll do everything in my power to prevent an investigation of your conduct as FBI chief. I'll help you land somewhere, some professorship somewhere, private equity, a law firm, whatever."

Chiles continued to rub his eyes. Milton Academy, Harvard College, Harvard Law School, Debevoise & Plimpton, the District Attorney's office for the Southern District of Manhattan, the U.S. Attorney General's office, Assistant Director of the FBI, Director of the FBI. He stood face-to-face with his first failure, a big failure, a failure for the ages.

"I understand, Mr. President," he whispered, looking up. He stood up and walked to the president's desk. "It's been a pleasure and an honor to serve you, sir." Chiles extended his hand. The president reached out and shook his hand.

"Thank you, Lou."

Chiles walked to the door and left.

Putnam leaned back in the couch. He reached his arm up and stretched it across the back of the big Chesterfield, toward the president. "Well . . ."

The president continued standing.

He'd known Roger Putnam for more than two decades now. The first time the president ran for governor of California, the time he lost, Putnam had been the junior senator from the state. Putnam had endorsed him, despite the fact that the president was only thirty-four years old and had no political experience.

"You know," said the president, "I only wanted you here in case Lou went psycho on me."

The two old friends laughed. The president walked to the sofa and sat across from Putnam. He reached out and poured a cup of coffee for himself. The laughter quickly ended and the silence came again.

"I wasn't aware you were going to Saudi Arabia," said Putnam.

"Do I need your permission?" asked the president.

"No, of course not. That's not my point. Mr. President, I'm an old man. We've known each other a while now. You don't need to ask me for anything, and you don't have to explain a thing to me."

"I know I don't. You can't resign yet, Roger. But this spring, after we clean up this Saudi mess, you'll retire. You fucked up. You fucked up not just because you threw that coffee cup against the wall and got pissed. You didn't listen to me. You disobeyed a direct order. And worst of all, you were wrong."

Putnam smiled. "I agree with you. Every word. I'm sorry."

"Before you leave, I want you to help me find your replacement. I don't want it to end this way, not between you and me."

Putnam stood up. His eyes were red. He smiled. "You can count on it. Good luck over there."

"I'll call you on the way home. Will you be in Jackson Hole?"

"No. Call the switchboard. I'm heading to Venezuela to see if we can't get some oil from those crazy bastards in Caracas."

"Good luck."

The secretary of state walked toward the door of the Oval Office.

"Do me a favor," said the president. "Tell Cecily to send in the young lady waiting in the Cabinet Room."

"Yes, sir."

The president walked back to his desk and began packing his briefcase.

After a few minutes, the door opened.

"Mr. President?" asked a young, freckled, pretty, auburn-haired woman as she stepped into the Oval Office.

"Jessica," said the president. "Come in."

"Thank you, sir," she said. She walked toward the president and stood in front of his desk. He looked at her, stepped to the side of the desk, and walked toward her. He reached his hand out and shook her hand. She looked around the Oval Office.

"Is this your first time here?"

"Yes," she said. "I've been to the White House several times, of course. Just never in here, sir."

"Well, get used to it. I'd like you to be my national security advisor."

"Myron Kratovil—"

"FBI. Lou's out."

Jessica was silent. After a few moments, moments in which she stood silently in shock and disbelief, she smiled. "I'm honored. But I'm not qualified. That is, there are people a lot more qualified than me."

"I agree," said the president. "There are a few people who, on paper, are more qualified than you. But I don't care. We need creativity, courage, intuition, guts, the ability to keep asking the hard questions. We need some luck, some faith even. We've been through the worst attack on U.S. soil in our history, but you prevented it from escalating into something much worse. There are plenty of resumés in this town. I want them working for you, not the other way around."

"I'm honored, Mr. President. I wholeheartedly accept. When do you want me to start? I can start tomorrow. I have an appointment this afternoon."

The president smiled and closed his briefcase. "I want you to take a vacation. Go away."

"Victor Buck hasn't been caught, sir. I'm not going to go on vacation until he's apprehended."

"That can wait. If you're not willing to take a vacation, the offer is rescinded."

"I understand," said Jessica. "Thank you. I'll do that."

"I have to go," said the president. He picked up his briefcase and walked toward the door. "By the way, how is Dewey Andreas?"

"He's at Bethesda," said Jessica. "He suffered some bruising on the brain. His shoulder was badly infected. He was in tough shape. But he'll be okay. He's strong."

"So are we, thanks to him. The Supreme Court. California Aqueduct. The largest paper mill in North America. Half a dozen refineries, universities. O'Hare, Sears Tower, Notre Dame Stadium. The list goes on. We have much to thank Dewey for."

"Yes, I agree."

"You seem to know him a bit," said the president. "What do you think he'll do now?"

"I don't know, sir."

"Maybe you can pass something along to him, Jess, next time you see him?" asked the president.

"Sure. Anything, sir."

"This morning, I asked Senator Bowman, from his home state of Maine, to nominate him for the Congressional Gold Medal," said the president. "She was happy to do it. I'm also going to nominate Dewey for the Presidential Medal of Freedom. When he's better, we'll have a big to-do at the White House."

"I'm sure he'll be happy to hear that, Mr. President."

The president glanced at his watch.

"You know what, I have a few minutes," the president said. "Let's tell him together."

Room 717 at Bethesda Naval Hospital was austere and small. The one special feature was the spectacular view, which took in the Washington skyline in the distance, including the Capitol Building and the Washington Monument.

A knock came at the door.

"Dewey?" asked Jessica from outside. There was no response.

Jessica went to the door and slowly opened it. She was followed by the president. Two Secret Service agents waited outside the door.

Inside the room, the bed was empty.

"Maybe he's in here," said the president.

He knocked at the bathroom door. No answer.

Jessica went to the bed and pressed the nurse call button. A few moments later, the door opened and a nurse stepped into the room. The nurse, a thin, short woman with gray hair and glasses, did a double take when she saw the president.

"Do you know where Dewey is?" asked Jessica.

"He left an hour ago," said the nurse. "He checked himself out. Dr. Bartholomew tried to get him to stay for a few more days. Brain injuries, you know? He's far from fully recovered. But he refused."

"Did he say where he was going?" asked Jessica, incredulous.

"No," the nurse said. "I'm sorry, he didn't."

Jessica turned to the president. "Let me get a few agents—"

"No," interrupted the president, smiling calmly. He looked at the empty hospital bed, then turned back to Jessica, reached his hand out, and patted her softly on the shoulder. "Let him go."

58

THE SANDPIPER HOTEL
BARBADOS
FIVE WEEKS LATER

More than 1,500 miles to the south, in a luxurious suite at the Sandpiper Hotel in Barbados, midnight approached.

Dewey sat up in bed. He felt burning in his shoulder. It was a pain that would probably never go away, a piece of shrapnel so small two surgeries had been unable to find it. But he could feel it. He slowly removed the sheets from his legs and stood up.

He dressed quietly in the living room of the large hotel suite. It was a clear night. He glanced for a moment out the window. The moon created a shelf of reflected silver light on top of the black Caribbean water. He walked to the dresser. In the top drawer of the dresser, he reached in and took out a black, light-duty tactical wet suit. He felt for the handgun he'd placed inside the drawer, a Colt M1911 .45-caliber semiautomatic. Quickly, he placed it in the watertight pocket on the right calf of the wet suit. He tied a small ankle sheath to his right leg that held a long, black combat knife, Gerber, double serrated, fixed blade, the word "Gauntlet" engraved on the side. Sharp as a razor, small traces of dried blood still caked into the teeth.

He walked down the deserted beach a half mile to the docks, also empty. He saw a boat berthed at a mooring, about a quarter mile from the dock, a dark blue Mako he'd noted earlier that day. He dove in the water, swam to the boat, climbed aboard. He pulled the plastic casing off the starter unit. He pulled two wires from the ignition block and tied them together, then touched them to the jack. The pair of Evinrude 250 horsepower engines rumbled to life. He untied the boat from the slip and backed it out from the dock, guided only by the light of the full moon. Glancing about, he saw no one.

Within a few minutes, he had the Mako at full throttle and was firing across the calm waters at more than sixty knots. He would be in Mustique in a little more than an hour.

Mustique, the most exclusive island in the Caribbean, perhaps the world, had its own charter of government, tax laws, and justice system, largely unnecessary since the only residents were wealthy Europeans and Americans. The only natives were hired hands: chefs; housecleaners; laborers; garden and landscaping crews; workers at the small hotel on the island, the Cotton House; or at Basal's, the island's sole restaurant. There was no unemployment; if you were fired, they escorted you from the island back to Barbados, where most of the workers came from.

Beyond the wealthy businesspeople, descendants of royalty, trusta-farians, were the celebrities who liked the remoteness of the place. David Bowie and Mick Jagger both had homes on the island.

Then there were the sketchier types, the ones with lots of money but some question as to how they'd gone about getting it.

Dewey pushed the speedboat through the warm, cloudless night.

He circled the small island twice, letting the moonlight illuminate the jungle-covered hills. The houses along the shore were beautiful, appearing every mile or so, large and private. The houses higher up on Mustique's hills appeared like mountainside castles, sprouting up suddenly against the monotonous backdrop of trees and bush, illuminated by lights their owners' egos drove them to keep on at night, others by the crystal white of the moon, so bright tonight.

From the northwest shore of the island, at a place with little beach and no homes visible at water's edge, he saw the house. Barely visible from the water because it seemed to form out of the natural topography, it was the highest point on the island, a small mountain on top of which sat the place, and the man, he'd come to visit.

Dewey put the boat in at the deserted shoreline. He tied the boat to a coconut tree at sand's edge and climbed out. Leaping from the bow of the Mako, he hit sand and jogged to the tree line that bordered the sliver of sand, looking for a path. Near a large calabash tree fifty feet down, he saw a rope and darkened lantern. There was the path. He could feel the rush of warmth in his head and body as the adrenaline began to kick in. He walked slowly up the dirt pathway that he knew would lead him to the villa.

The path led up a winding course. It went up the steep hill for at least half a mile until suddenly the deep bush and low, thick tree cover opened up to the well-manicured yard of the villa. The moon was bright. It lit up the yard clearly, creating an eerie glow. In the middle of the yard was a long swimming pool surrounded by chairs.

It was nearly three in the morning. He had to move quickly. The wet suit helped to conceal him against the dark trees. The sweat poured down Dewey's face.

Silently, he walked along the edge of the grass, looking for signs of life. There would likely be a guard or two, if he knew his man.

Past the swimming pool was a large pool house. He walked across the lawn to the side of the structure.

Dewey reached down to his ankle and removed the dagger from its sheath. He held its grip between his teeth as he inched along the edge of the wooden structure.

Peeking his head out from behind the pool house, Dewey had a clear and unobstructed view of the mansion. It was a rambling, modern place. From left to right, glass windows spread in a moonlike arc. In front of them, a massive slate deck. The house looked like a series of glass cubes, dropped on the mountaintop and then connected by breezeways.

A dim light illuminated the arc of glass from outside. Within, the home was dark, except for a lone light in the far left end of the place.

He watched the scene for several minutes, looking for guards. He saw no movement, except for tree leaves swaying gently in an occasional breeze.

He waited several minutes and finally saw movement. A lone guard walked from a pathway at the left of the house and crossed the terrace, armed with an AEK-919K Kashtan submachine gun, held professionally before him.

Dewey crawled across the wet grass to a hedge across from the pool house. He picked up a stone and tossed it toward the pool, where it made a dull splash. He left the handgun sealed in the pocket of his wet suit. He stood and took the knife from his teeth as he waited for the man to approach.

From behind the hedge he could see nothing, but he heard the steps coming across the slate. The footsteps were quick, but not panicked. He wanted the guard to come, but not to call for backup.

The sweat now poured unabated down Dewey's tanned face. The moment was coming again, the one he'd learned to understand, the moment in which he conquered the fears of any man, in which he used all of his physical attributes, his energy, his desire, in the one thing he'd been trained so long ago to do.

Kill.

The guard emerged from the hedge and Dewey moved. Quickly, he slashed the combat blade in a ferocious line across the mercenary's neck, so forceful that he nearly cut the man's head off. His eyes rolled back up into his head as he dropped to the ground, blood gurgling uninterrupted from his neck.

Dewey took up the guard's weapon and moved quickly up the path to the big terrace and stepped slowly along the glass, trying to get a view inside the massive spread. He stood in the middle of the wide, sweeping arc of glass that created what was, during daytime, one of the most glorious views of the blue ocean known to man. He waited. He would wait as long as he had to.

He stared at the bright moon reflected in the glass. Suddenly, a light went on. He saw movement. A bald man climbed out of bed, naked.

Dewey felt nothing now. No nerves or emotion at all. He moved the AEK's fire control selector to full auto. Suddenly, he pulled the trigger back, fired the machine gun low, the long, black barrel across the glass, swept it quickly as he stepped forward, washing the glass in a furious spray. The sound of thick glass shattering in the humid night air filled the sky.

The man inside ducked as bullets tore through windows. Dewey completed the horizontal zag across the entire back of the house, sparing the man inside but destroying everything else. He suddenly stopped firing and stepped forward, kicking aside a still-standing piece of glass as he tracked the man who now cowered in the corner.

Dewey dropped the submachine gun to the ground. He pulled his Colt M1911 from the pocket of the wet suit. Slowly, he raised the weapon. He stepped forward, over the transom of shattered glass. He aimed the .45 caliber handgun at the traitor's head.

Dewey's thick brown hair was wet with sweat now. Droplets poured down his tanned face. He took the last few steps toward the traitor. He stood above the man for several moments, the Colt's muzzle just inches from his head. He waited, long enough for the man to finally turn his bloodshot, fear-filled eyes up at him.

"Hi, Vic," Dewey said. "Bye, Vic."

EPILOGUE

SEMBLER STATION
COOKTOWN, AUSTRALIA
SIX MONTHS LATER

The afternoon sun blazed down onto the dry country road. The road was a thin, black, raggedy-edged lace strung across countless miles of empty ranch land. The temperature, just before noon, had already climbed above a hundred degrees. A line of peeling white cattle fence ran to the horizon. A driveway, cut in dirt and stone, branched off the road. A large steel sign bridged the driveway: SEMBLER STATION in rusted lettering.

Few people on earth had ever been down this lonely road before. It sat in the proverbial middle of nowhere, somewhere in the northeast provinces of Australia, a region called Queensland, near the coast. After a time, a pickup truck puttered along at a slow pace. The old pickup was light green, its paint faded, a little rust, a Ford. The low sputter of the engine interrupted the silence. It came slowly to the crest in the small hill, stopped in front of the driveway. The passenger door opened. The man climbed out.

"Thank you," he said, then closed the door behind him.

He wore jeans, an old, faded blue Lacoste shirt with a small tear at the midriff. He had long brown hair that fell down unkempt below his ears, a beard, and mustache. He was dark brown from the sun. His eyes stood out, blue eyes that you could see from across a room. He was good-looking, but with an edge; there was a meanness there, a distance.

But what stood out the most was not his eyes. On the man's left arm, a strip of crimson ran south from the shoulder blade, out from under the shirt; a scar that looked like a wide ribbon, jagged, as stark, as severe as the violence it implied. But he didn't care what people thought. Not of the scar, not of him.

He walked under the steel sign, down the driveway, backpack over his shoulder. Low hills were covered in brown grass, stub wheat, and cypress bush. Empty vistas of blue covered the sky. Untouched ranch land spread out in every direction. The white wood of the cattle fence ran in a straight line as far as you could see. He followed the driveway a full mile. Sweat poured from his forehead and chest as he walked, soaking the blue shirt. His boots were soon covered in dust.

At the driveway's end, a large, beautiful farmhouse, yellow clapboard with white trim and black shutters, surrounded by gardens. In the distance, a series of barns and outbuildings spread out like a campus. Beyond, cattle dotted the hills for as far as you could see.

In front of the farmhouse, a tall man with longish, silver hair was talking with a pair of ranch hands. He stopped talking as the stranger approached.

"Afternoon," said the man. "I'm looking for Joe Sembler."

"I'm Joe Sembler."

"They said you might be hiring."

"You looking for work?"

"Yes, sir."

"You been a hand before?"

"No. My father owned a farm. But no."

Joe Sembler looked at the stranger in silence, scanning his muscled body with his eyes. He slowly started to nod.

"You handle a horse?"

"Yes."

Sembler paused. He stared for a moment at the scar on Dewey's arm.

"What happened to your arm?" he asked.

The man stared back at Sembler. He remained silent.

"We could use another rider," said Sembler finally. "These guys'll get you set up." He pointed his thumb at the two men he'd been talking with.

"Thank you," said the stranger.

"What's your name?" asked Sembler. "Where you from?"

The stranger paused for a moment. His hesitation didn't take long enough for Sembler to notice. Two, maybe three seconds in all. He smiled, stepped toward Sembler, extended his hand to shake the rancher's hand.

"I'm American," he said, shaking Sembler's hand. "My name's Dewey Andreas."

A thousand miles away, the warm morning breeze funneled scents of lilacs from the gardens next to a blue stone terrace. The seasonal winds came from the Mediterranean Sea, easterly currents that met the low plains along the coast of Lebanon, then dispersed through canyon after canyon, finally climbing up into the hills above Beirut. Today they provided a welcome coolness to the man and woman on the blue stone terrace of a massive villa on Patula Hill, in the small town of Broumana.

"Are they gathered?" asked the tall man, an older man, whose face still showed, despite its seventy-three years, the good looks that were once legend. Atop the man's head, a block of gray hair was combed elegantly back, longish, parted down the middle. He sat next to the gunite swimming pool, shirt off, his long, tan legs dangling in the cool blue water.

"Yes, Aswan," said Candela, the twenty-two-year-old Saudi beauty who acted as Aswan Fortuna's personal assistant. She was cutting flowers from a rosebush next to the swimming pool. "They are inside."

Fortuna stared for a moment at Candela. She smiled at him. He did not smile back. She stopped cutting flowers, then walked across the terrace to Fortuna. She sat down next to him.

"You worry me sometimes, Aswan," she said. "Please smile for me. I know you're sad. But there is much to be thankful for."

"I'm thankful for you," he said, placing his right hand against the girl's cheek. "Will I always have you?"

447

"Always and forever."

Candela brushed her long black hair back, shook her head back and forth, and smiled at Fortuna.

He stood up and walked to the edge of the slate terrace, looking down across the Broumana hills, in the distance Beirut. The black sea behind the city's edge shimmered in the sun. Surrounding the perimeter of the mountainside chalet, he counted half a dozen men, machine guns in hand.

"Always and forever," he whispered to himself.

Fortuna walked around the pool and inside the house. Four men sat at the kitchen table. They looked up at him.

"The envelope arrived," said one of the men, holding a large manila envelope up in the air. "It is very grainy. But it should be good enough."

Fortuna reached for the envelope and ripped it open. He stuck his hand inside, pulled out a black-and-white photograph. He stared for several minutes at the photo, his eyes wide, the flesh of his face flushing red. He stared for more than a minute in silence.

"Let us see," said Nebuchar Fortuna.

He reached for the photo, but as he did so, Aswan Fortuna swung his hand through the air, slapping Nebuchar across the face with the back of his hand.

"Where did we get this?" Aswan demanded.

"An intermediary," said one of the men. "London. Borchardt, the weapons dealer. We needed the cleric to pressure him."

"What's his name?" he barked angrily.

"We don't know yet," said one of the men.

"It cost us more than four million dollars—" Nebuchar said.

"I don't care about the money!" shouted Aswan Fortuna, interrupting his son.

He threw the photo onto the table. It was grainy but showed a soldier: good-looking, young, American. He wore a military uniform. In his right hand, he held an M-60, pointed up at the sky. Black war paint ran in thick stripes beneath his eyes. He had short-cropped brown hair, a sharp nose. He stared straight ahead, a hint of danger in his menacing pose.

Fortuna calmed. He pointed at the photo. His anger transformed into steel resolution.

"I don't care what it costs," he said slowly, hatred and fury pooling like molten metal in his voice. He turned to Nebuchar. "Or how long it takes. I don't care how many people we have to kill, or how many of our own must die. This is the man who *killed my son*. We will go to the ends of the earth to hunt him down. Do you hear me? Wherever he is, we must find him. We *will* find him."